Praise for *The Marriage Slip*

"In her third novel, *The Marriage Slip*, Barrow explores the intersection of expectations and reality through suburban mom Audrey's struggle with her marriage, career, friendships, and motherhood. Readers will groan, cry, and cheer on Audrey as she navigates an inexplicable yet precious gift from the universe—a second chance. Have tissues handy because this novel will grab readers by the heart and not let go until the last page."

— Kristin Kisska, Agatha Award–nominated author of *The Hint of Light*

"In her delightfully engaging third novel, Laura Barrow explores what might happen when a crumbling relationship gets an unexpected do-over. I was instantly drawn in by the relatable characters and intriguing time travel, but *The Marriage Slip* also packs a tremendous amount of truth, with insights about motherhood, equal partnership, and how to find the magic in our ordinary lives. I loved this book!"

— Hadley Leggett, author of *All They Ask Is Everything*

THE MARRIAGE SLIP

OTHER BOOKS BY LAURA BARROW

Call the Canaries Home

If We Ever Get There

THE MARRIAGE SLIP

A NOVEL

LAURA BARROW

This is a work of fiction. Names, characters, organizations, places, events, and incidents are either products of the author's imagination or are used fictitiously. Otherwise, any resemblance to actual persons, living or dead, is purely coincidental.

Published by Lake Union Publishing, Seattle

www.apub.com

EU product safety contact:
Amazon Media EU S. à r.l.
38, avenue John F. Kennedy, L-1855 Luxembourg
amazonpublishing-gpsr@amazon.com

ISBN-13: 9781662529139 (paperback)
ISBN-13: 9781662529146 (digital)

Cover design by Kimberly Glyder
Cover image: © Hatcha, © Lana Brow / Shutterstock

Printed in the United States of America

For my family.
My heart. My home.

The wound is the place where the light enters you.

—Rumi

CHAPTER 1

June 2023

Memory is a fickle notion. Over the years, my mind has played hide-and-seek with some of the most pivotal moments of my life, while the random and mundane have become indelible, forever melded into the meandering code of my genetic makeup. One time, when I was filling out forms at the pediatrician's office, I forgot Ruby's middle name for a solid thirty seconds. It's Beatrice, by the way, after Travis's grandmother. Not my favorite choice, but a concession I was willing to make in lieu of christening our second-born Ruby Prince Perkins for no other reason than because Travis considered *Purple Rain* an iconic masterpiece. The memory lapse was short lived but terrifying. How could a fact so fundamental just evaporate into the ether, while the theme song of *Daniel Tiger's Neighborhood* seems destined to live rent-free inside my brain forever?

I work my key into the lock of our traditional two-story with cream siding, another gift from Grandma Beatrice. Sort of. After Eadie was born, we practically burst out of our one-bedroom apartment. It seemed like kismet that Beatrice wanted to relocate to a retirement community just when I was toying with the idea of converting my car into an extra bedroom. When she offered to sell to us at two-thirds the market value, we couldn't exactly turn her down. Of course, back then, we didn't know about the attic mold or the tree roots encroaching on the pipes.

What's more, we stupidly decided against a routine inspection, since Grandma Beatrice assured us the home was solid. Since then, we've spent so much time and money addressing the bones of the house, we've barely touched the cosmetic updates this place so desperately needs.

Its peeling navy shutters appear black in the darkness, but there's a faint light emanating from the kitchen window. I hope Travis has fed the girls dinner, at least. I left a chicken-and-rice casserole in the oven before popping out for a last-minute property showing—a client who insisted on a sunset appointment. Of course, I obliged, even though evenings are hardly the most convenient time to escape from my family. Leaning my weight against the door, I heave it open and am immediately greeted by the strumming of a familiar chord progression. Travis has been composing a song for his band to record. He's spent weeks plucking out the chorus, only changing a note or two with each repetition. I hope the practice session means he's buttoned up dinner and finished bedtime routines with the girls, though history doesn't give me a lot of confidence.

But when I hang my purse on the coatrack, I catch a glimpse of our galley kitchen, and my jaw tightens. Puddles of rice are splattered across the dinner table like confetti, as if the girls were actively avoiding their plates. The half-consumed casserole sits atop the oven, uncovered—an invitation for flies. I take a measured breath and steel myself for the task of de-ricing the entire house. It's irritating but expected. "I'm home," I call out, forcing my feet past the mess into the living room.

"Hi, Mommy!" Ruby sings from her perch on the sofa, where Travis continues picking out notes, only lifting his head for a beat to acknowledge my presence.

"Hi, baby." I bend down to run my fingers through her nearly white hair. My smile turns to a grimace when I snag on a tangle, landing on something wet and sticky. I don't have to pull my hand out to know it's rice.

"What have you guys been up to?" I ask, though I already know the answer. Absolutely nothing. Debris is strewn about the floor—backpacks and shoes and dirty socks, not to mention a pencil sharpener that appears to have exploded on the white wool rug. What's more, no one is wearing pajamas. No one appears to have taken a bath. And no one seems remotely concerned that I am dangerously close to lighting this house and all its contents on fire. Still, my smile remains intact, a feat I feel is worthy of some kind of medal. The girls are certainly old enough to help out with chores, but I don't want to be the bad guy, yet again, and interrupt their fun. Besides, my anger isn't directed at them.

"Just stuff," Eadie says with an indifferent shrug. Lying on her tummy, she doodles in her sketchbook, her wheat-colored braid snaking over her shoulder. For a fleeting moment, the three of them seem so idyllic, lazing about without a care in the world, like a picture in a holiday ad. I can almost appreciate the scene. But resentment is a far more active emotion than nostalgia, and someone has to keep this house from turning into an episode of *Hoarders*.

"Well, I see everyone had dinner," I note, hoping Travis will interpret my icy undertone and the message I'm really communicating.

But Travis only stills his strumming and looks up at me long enough to say "Yep. All ready for bed."

It's a lie, but I swallow hard and retreat to Grandma Beatrice's weathered kitchen, my hands balled into fists. Once again, I push down the burning desire to rip off the vintage floral wallpaper that's curling up at the edges. As someone who studies real estate design trends, it seems a cruel irony that my house is so painfully outdated. The cream Formica counters are chipped at the edges, and the vinyl linoleum floor makes me feel as if I've just stepped into *The Wonder Years*. Pulling in a centering breath, I remind myself that this is the house we could afford at the time and I should be grateful to live here. No one gets everything they want in life. At least not all at once.

The scent of baked chicken hangs thick in the air as I wipe the remnants of dinner from the table, then sweep the floor, gritting my teeth when rice sticks to the broom like stubborn slugs. I shake it into the trash can as best I can manage, then move on to the dishes teetering precariously atop the counter. Travis has been kind enough to stack the plates but couldn't possibly be bothered to do the actual work of washing, drying, and storing them in the correct locations. I send him telepathic messages, hoping an eye roll or a slammed pantry door will alert him to my disappointment, but Travis only strums louder, hypnotizing the girls with his mellifluous tenor voice like a postgrunge pied piper.

I pick up the casserole dish and briefly consider throwing it at his head. But if there's one skill I've honed over the past few years, it's masking my true emotions in front of our children. A thin layer of rice has fused to the bottom, not enough to salvage, though Travis would disagree. If it were up to him, our refrigerator would be packed with week-old barbecue and expired take-out condiments. Even so, he's always reminding me to discard starchy foods in the trash can instead of the disposal. I've never really understood the reason for this inane rule. I often wonder if he invented it only to make my life more difficult. Discreetly, I peek around the wall dividing the living room from the kitchen, simultaneously reassured and annoyed to find him still serenading the girls. A rebellious ember catches fire in my chest. The trash can is so far away, and the idea of trekking across the kitchen to reach it might very well be the ill-fated Jenga piece that sends me toppling to the ground. A forbidden thought tiptoes its way into my fingers, tugging at my common sense. And then, ever so gently, I tilt the dish, scoop the rest of its contents into the sink, and watch with something like satisfaction as the sticky bits of white circle the drain.

Maybe it's petty, but these days, petty seems to be our preferred love language. Unfortunately, this time I've overplayed my hand, because a flurry of rice stubbornly floats to the top of the rising water. My face flushes with panic.

With nimble fingers, I flip on the switch to my left and wait for the loud gargle that will suck everything into the pipes—to where, I have no idea. But instead, an ominous hum fills my ears, a sure sign something is stuck in the mysterious darkness of the garbage disposal.

And I know exactly what that something is. *Damn these ancient pipes!* I flip off the switch and perform a quick sweep of the blade to no avail, then dig out the plunger from beneath the sink. Throwing my weight into it, I pump the wooden handle like a flustered EMT, telling myself it isn't my fault, that maybe it's a plastic fork or a straw or another one of Ruby's doll teacups that got swept into the drain. But in my panic, the only feat I've accomplished is to turn the water a sickening shade of milky white, and in my gut, I know I'm screwed. Which means there is no way I'll be telling Travis about this. As he rarely does the dishes, chances are high he won't notice. Stowing the plunger, I decide to call a plumber first thing in the morning, then rummage around in the drawer for a dish towel.

The time on the microwave flickers 7:39, reminding me that bedtime is closing in. I wonder if Travis will notice on his own. As I begin drying plates, I finally hear him yawn from the living room, which I find a little perplexing. In the past seven minutes, I've transformed the kitchen into a spotless culinary utopia, while Travis has only managed to add another layer of wear to the divot in the sofa. "Time for bed, girls," he finally groans, rising from his perch and stretching his wiry legs. "Go brush your teeth."

For reasons I've never been able to understand, Ruby and Eadie obey their father the first time he asks them to do something. I, on the other hand, must deal in various negotiation tactics, like holding toys and electronics hostage, until my very reasonable demands are met. Their feet patter up the stairs. A door slams, followed by an incessant pounding. "I was here first!" Ruby wails from the hallway.

Travis joins me in the kitchen and picks up a dish towel under the guise of helping. But since the bulk of the work is finished, I know it's more for show. I bite my lip, hoping he won't notice the glaring problem I've strategically attempted to shield with my body.

As if hearing my thoughts, he casts his gaze behind me. "Why is there water in the sink?"

My stomach flips. "The garbage disposal is on the fritz again," I reply, trying to make it sound like a minor issue. But the crease in his brow proves he's not convinced, and he moves around my blockade like a man on a mission.

"Did you try plunging it?"

"Of course I did. But something's stuck down there. Between the girls, there's no telling what it could be," I lie, knowing full well I should have included myself in that equation. "I'll call someone in the morning."

Predictably, Travis rolls his eyes. "I can fix it. Just give me a sec to grab my tools."

With that, Travis storms to the garage, where he rifles through coffee cans like a disgruntled bear. There's an earsplitting clatter, accompanied by a string of curse words that does not bolster my confidence in his ability to get the job done. Moments later, he returns with an assortment of wrenches in his fist and a headlamp strapped to his skull. Then he lumbers beneath the sink. I hold my breath while he tinkers around, grateful he can't see the guilt written all over my face.

Finally, he declares, "Well, I found the problem." His voice sounds as if it's coming from deep within a cave.

"Really?" I work my teeth over a thumbnail.

"Did you put rice down the drain again?"

A knot churns in my gut, but I'm prepared for this. "No," I lie, and not particularly well. My cheeks are on fire.

"Someone did."

"Well, I didn't," I say more forcefully. Lexy is always telling me that when you make a mistake, you have to react the way a man would—double down. Deny and deflect. And at this point, I am 100 percent committed to this mistake. I will die on this rice hill.

"Hold on a sec," Travis mumbles. "I think I've—" There's a loud popping sound, followed by damning silence. A silence so dangerously heavy, I can practically feel him cursing me out in his mind. Before I can work up the courage to say something, Travis slowly emerges, his russet, close-shaven beard bearing the unmistakable evidence of my lie. It's covered in squishy white granules and other unidentifiable particles I'm too afraid to decipher. Inwardly, I cringe, but don't give myself away. The Audrey from a few years ago would have apologized. Back then, I would have offered Travis a clean towel and begged for forgiveness, promised to change my food-flushing ways. But as soon as that rice came shooting out of the pipes, something snapped inside me, too, and the dam bridling every resentment, every quip, every dirty dish burst into a million jagged pieces.

"Fine!" I confess. "I did it. You win. You always win. But do you know why I put rice in the garbage disposal, Travis?" Pulse racing, I supply the answer before he can respond. "Because I bought the rice, I cooked the rice, I cleaned up the trail of rice the girls left on the table, and in a few minutes, I will drag Ruby to the bathtub to wash rice out of her hair." With each indictment, my voice grows louder. "So, when it was time to do the dishes, I lacked the desire—nay, the physical energy—to walk the two and a half feet to the trash can. Which, by the way, is filled to the brim, thanks to you. And maybe I, possibly, in a moment of sheer exhaustion, discarded rice in the garbage disposal because"—I lift a finger to drive home the point—"and here is the thing that makes zero sense to me: It's a garbage disposal!" I leave out the part about being petty, for obvious reasons.

As he wipes a chunk of masticated food from his chin, Travis seems unimpressed by my emotional breakdown, even mildly annoyed. "I've told you a million times to stop doing that. You'd think you'd learn your lesson after the potato-peel disaster."

My eyes flutter like baby-bird wings, because I can't fathom that, after everything I've just shared, this is his takeaway. "Do you even hear me? I'm trying to tell you something. I'm trying to be honest with you for once." I pinch the bridge of my nose and siphon off an exhale. "I can't do this anymore, Travis. I can't have this same conversation with you."

I'm not sure what I expect him to say, but my words clearly don't stick the landing. He only shakes his head as he pulls himself up to his full six-three height, towering over me. "I don't understand the problem. I fixed the disposal. I think the words you're looking for are *thank you*," he adds, with all the grace of a martyr.

"This is not about the disposal! This is about the fact that you're never around to help when I need you. Instead, you conveniently show up after everything is already done so you can point out how I could have done it better. And I'm tired. I'm so tired." My voice cracks on the last phrase, because it just might be the truest thing I have ever said. And that's when the words that have been testing the fences of my mind finally make their way into my throat.

"Maybe we should . . . take a break," I hear myself say, so low that at first, I'm not sure he heard me.

"OK, you're right," he concedes, seeming more inconvenienced than destroyed. "I'm going to take a shower while you cool off. We can talk about it in the morning."

"No," I call out before he can walk away. My restless hands dig around inside my back pockets. "I mean a break from me and you. Like a . . . trial separation." I fill my lungs and steady my voice so I won't have to say this again, because it's taking every molecule of my physical and emotional strength. "I think some time apart from each other will help us decide if this is really what we want."

The silence that follows gnaws at my conscience, and I pray he'll say something, anything, to soften the blow I've just dealt.

When his gaze finally meets mine, his cheeks have lost color, the bowed lips that both girls inherited have petrified into a thin line. "Are you serious?"

And though it nearly steals my breath to admit, I nod, too ashamed to repeat myself. I'm not the sort of person who throws in the towel when things get difficult. But I am officially out of ideas.

"Why are you doing this, Audrey?" he asks softly, his clear-blue eyes so full of hurt. Though they're trained on the wrench in his hands, they are branding a reprimand into my soul.

All the gravity in the room gathers atop my chest, pressing down like thick concrete, but I can't take it back any more than I can take back the past few years. The toothpaste is out of the tube, and there is no way to force it back in. "I'm sorry. I just . . . I can't anymore."

Shaking his head, he scoffs, and I brace myself for another shouting match. "How can you say that to me? After everything we've been through," he utters, but his words don't have any fight. His voice trembles, and it takes me aback. I expected him to be angry, maybe call my bluff. But tears seem a bit melodramatic. We both knew this was the next logical step. It's been weeks since he touched me, longer since we've kissed. A million years since we've had sex. Where exactly did he think this relationship was headed? Even so, I am breaking my husband's heart in real time, and I hate myself for it.

"Look, no one wants this marriage to work more than me. I'm just as disappointed as you are." This is not untrue. After all, I was the one to suggest the counseling sessions Travis didn't want to pay for out of pocket. And I was the one to create a spreadsheet of our biggest recurring arguments, along with a list of potential compromises, but Travis dismissed it as just further evidence of my control freak personality. Maybe he was right, but who doesn't want to be in control of their life? At least I was trying, which is more than I can say for him.

"You're not disappointed. You're not even crying," he points out. "God, how can you be so emotionless? You're like . . . you're like an ice queen!"

"Like Elsa?" Ruby says, materializing at the edge of the kitchen. There is a deep crinkle in her baby forehead that immediately melts my frustration. She's almost five, but she still has those same pudgy legs and puckered tummy that make me swoon to hold her, to feel the weight of her childhood in my arms before it slips away forever.

"That's not what he means," Eadie chimes in, nudging her with a sharp elbow. "He means she isn't fun to be around."

The accusation lands with a thud, and I wonder how much they heard. How many times have I told them they couldn't download whatever social app their friends were on because they might see something inappropriate? But in the past thirty seconds, I've managed to steal years from their childhoods. What's worse, I know Eadie is right, because I am a drag on this family, a black hole sucking in all the light surrounding it. But I wasn't always like this. Travis made me this way.

I try to speak, but my throat is clogged, and the damage is already done. I wish I could take back the last few moments, say it better. But after so many years fielding the same soul-depleting arguments, I think I am more than justified to be a tad overemotional.

The time on the microwave flashes 7:45 p.m., the boxy numbers sealing the exact time of our marriage's death. And I know I'll remember this moment forever. But like I said, memory is fickle. It only includes the parts we agree with. History, on the other hand, is sticky, like the rice clogging my garbage disposal, slowly coalescing into a tight little ball until, one day, it's destined to explode when you least expect it.

CHAPTER 2

Three Months Later

Early-afternoon sunshine filters through the bay windows of the freshly painted kitchen, a lovely sage, magnifying flecks of dust that I hope potential buyers don't notice. As I admire the way a beam of light dances across the glittering marble countertops, I feel a slight tingling atop my head and burrow a finger in my hair to scratch it. I'm sure it's just nerves. This renovated mid-century has been empty for close to four months, but I'm hopeful I can clinch this. My last two deals went belly-up in the option period, and I'm not sure how much longer I can count on Travis's income. This Sunday will mark the end of our three-month trial separation, and we've scheduled a meetup at a pub to discuss where to go from here. Since he rarely responds to my texts with more than two words, I'm assuming he won't want to reconcile. Honestly, I'm not sure if I want to either. It's been lonely on my own, but in many ways easier. At least I don't have to worry about whether he remembered to mow the yard or take out the recycling on Thursday mornings. As with everything else in my life, it's less hassle to just do it myself. There's also less laundry.

Thankfully, Mr. and Mrs. McCloud appear entirely enamored by the floor-to-ceiling cabinetry framing the farmhouse sink, where an array of freshly planted pothos trail directly above, just low enough to kiss the windowsill. As the young couple shares a smile of approval, I silently congratulate the seller for adding the plants. While my own house boasts one plastic fig tree and two wilted ferns on life support, I know it's the tiny details that can turn a house into a home.

"What about the roof?" Mr. McCloud ventures, his voice a little deeper now. I can tell he's trying his best to add a few more rings of life onto his twenty-something years. It's kind of adorable and reminds me of the way Travis and I sounded when we first went car shopping—like a couple of kids pretending to be grown-ups. A dry lump forms at the base of my throat, and I shake away the memory, fixing an expression I hope looks unfazed. Sweat beads sprout along my brow, and I feel another tiny prick somewhere behind my ear. Discreetly, I graze it with the tip of a fingernail. "It's a little worse for wear," I reply honestly, "but the other agent assured me it's good for another five years at least."

With a slow nod, Mr. McCloud chews on this information, like he isn't certain whether this is a satisfactory answer or not. Sensing a sag in his excitement, I comb through my mental drawers in search of something to offset his uneasiness. "You haven't seen the backyard yet," I point out, feigning excitement, then lead the two of them toward a pair of French doors that overlook a swath of emerald grass flanked by two giant oaks. "It's a corner lot, backs right up to the floral gardens of the art museum. Plenty of space for a pet to run around." The words wilt as they leave my mouth. Willow's memory sneaks up on me at the most inconvenient times, her black fur and chocolate eyes so full of trust. Not a day goes by that I don't think of her, but I need to keep my emotions in check until this showing is over. I stow away the mental picture and clear my throat.

"It would be a paradise for children," I say, redirecting my thoughts to Ruby and Eadie. For the first time, I'm struck by the realization that maybe I should consider getting us a new place of our own. If Travis and I can't reconcile, maybe a blank canvas is exactly what I need to stop seeing old ghosts in every room. Since he moved out, the house doesn't feel like mine. Despite the fresh coat of paint in the living room, it still feels haunted by nine years of promises—promises to remodel the kitchen and repair the broken tread on the top step and retile the master bath. And Willow. But a new home would mean a new school for the girls, new teachers, new friends. And right now, what they need most is stability. Considering the past few months, we owe them that much at least.

As she follows me into the sunlit yard, Mrs. McCloud rests a hand atop her swollen belly and arches her back. Save for the tiny basketball protruding from her middle, she's slim, one of those women who wears pregnancy well, like a mere inconvenience rather than the agonizing nine months of swollen ankles and raging acne I endured. The wistful expression blooming on Mrs. McCloud's flawless bronze face tells me I was right to save this part of the tour for the end because she's obviously envisioning a gaggle of mini McClouds scaling the low, gnarled tree branches. "I love it," she declares, turning to her husband with a look I've come to recognize as *smitten*. Her seal of approval dispels any lingering worries about a leaky roof, because he looks at me with eager eyes and asks, "How soon can we start the process?"

My chest lightens, but I manage to keep my expression neutral. "Once the two of you agree on a number, I'll draw up the paperwork and give the seller a call," I say, trying not to sound too excited. Then checking my color-coded calendar on my phone, I mentally run through the rest of my day. It's Ruby's birthday, and Travis and I agreed on a family celebration with cake and ice cream before he takes them for the weekend. After that, I'm expected to go out with Lexy on what she assures me is *not* a double date with a guy from her CrossFit class. But she's made this promise one too many times for me to believe her.

"Come on," she said at lunch, where we picked over a jellyfish salad at that new Chinese restaurant in the city she's been eyeing. The thing about being friends with an unapologetic extrovert is that she pushes me—more like throws me—outside my comfort zone. And I have to commend her, because my comfort zone is about the size of an eco-cabin. If it weren't for Lex, I never would have gotten my Realtor's license. I'd probably still be refolding graphic tees on the display table at H&M. "Don't you think you should at least give yourself permission to feel things again?"

"I feel lots of things," I said, sidestepping the question.

"I'm not talking about drowning your sorrows in cheap takeout, Audrey." She lowered her voice and leaned forward slightly, her cornflower eyes seeing right through me. "I meant below the equator."

I feigned offense. "I'll have you know I'm only ordering top-shelf guacamole." But I knew what she meant. And she wasn't wrong. Before he left, it had been months since I'd been in the mood for anything physical with Travis. And now that he's gone, I find myself staring a little too longingly at that shirtless guy in the Old Spice commercials.

"Not the point." She shook her head. "You know I love Travis, but you've given him all the time he needs to realize what an idiot he is. This is not the part of the movie where he comes running back with some grand gesture. This is the part where you realize you're better than him and have an epic glow-up, get a manicure and a blowout that makes him go wild."

"Highlights are not going to make me feel better about my marriage ending."

"That's because you haven't been to my girl," she said, feathering platinum waves that reach just below her dainty chin. She's been after me for months to switch to a middle part. But while it makes her look like a sophisticated celebrity, it makes me look like Alfalfa. "Besides, it's like Dolly once said." She tossed her hair. "Sometimes great hair is the best revenge." But I don't want revenge. I just want to get back to when our roles seemed so easy and defined, when I didn't resent my husband for not picking up the slack because the line was pulled taut and there was only one fish on the end of it. Now there are two, and the pole has been dragged so deep underwater, I can't even see it anymore.

My head tingles again, but this time it feels like something is stabbing me with a needle. How many times have I scratched my head since we arrived almost an hour ago? Twice? Five times? I try to recall the correct answer when something sharp pricks the base of my neck, and genuine terror settles into my bones. "Can you excuse me for a moment?" I say, then retreat inside and make a beeline for the kitchen.

Once alone, I abandon all subtlety and scrub my head like a maniac. What I wouldn't give for a tiny rake to drag over my scalp, but the kitchen is inconveniently devoid of any gardening tools. I fling open an island drawer and miraculously locate a freshly sharpened No. 2 pencil, then begin drawing angry circles along my cranium. Lead poisoning be damned! At this point, I'll graciously accept bubonic plague if it means I can keep my fingernails away from my skull for longer than three point two seconds.

Releasing a sigh of relief, I mine my brain for an explanation. Dandruff, maybe? But a dry scalp makes no sense. I haven't changed shampoos, and I carry around a water bottle big enough to hydrate a camel. It is at this precise moment that a sickening revelation occurs to me, fully formed. My fingers buzzing, I scramble to unlock my phone. As my eyes hungrily trail down my inbox, I mutter a desperate prayer beneath my breath, hoping that my suspicion won't be confirmed. Pressed to close a sale by the end of September, I've fallen behind on correspondence from the girls' teachers. If this is what I think it is, there's no way I'm going to make it to my 2:00 p.m. showing, much less my "casual get-together" this evening. Hidden beneath a week's worth of science fair, ballet, and softball emails, there it is. The subject line of the email from Eadie's teacher stares back at me like a guilty verdict, except I can't fathom what I've done to deserve this punishment. Lice Outbreak Confirmed.

Oh God. Not again. How can three little words wield so much power over my weekend? This is the second time since the beginning of the school year. And if one of the girls has lice, the other most certainly does too. Reflecting on my head of thick blond hair, which both Ruby and Eadie have inherited, I realize my afternoon hours are now accounted for. They will be spent shampooing heads, laundering sheets, and mining three trillion strands of hair for eggs so tiny, I'll need a magnifying glass and Travis's headlamp to locate them. Sure, it's his weekend, but there's no way he'll take on the task of eradicating bloodsucking parasites from our offspring—not just because he won't want to, but because he won't do it right. He'd probably only scan for any visible bugs before declaring them cured.

Closing my eyes, I take a deep breath and recalibrate. As much as I want to blame Travis, he isn't the one who gave us lice. But I have a pretty good idea who did. My thoughts circle around Sonia Gill, my health-conscious neighbor who once brought homemade Goldfish with flaxseed to a class party. She's likely the reason we're all in this mess again—only three weeks later. The crackers had been annoyingly delicious, but obviously a desperate ploy for approval. Unlike me, Sonia is the sort of mother who refuses to put chemicals in little Penelope's hair, insisting that mayonnaise works just as well as lab-tested, scientifically proven formulas. Before Ruby came along, I used to care about that sort of thing, too, scrutinizing every label before tossing an item into my grocery cart. But these days, I don't have time to be picky. Having a second kid was like going from a leisurely drive on a quiet country road straight into rush hour traffic on the expressway. Most days, I'm just relieved to have survived another day. Also, I'd like to point out that neither of my children has grown a third eye.

As I stand here doodling on my scalp, I zero in on two solutions. I can either check the girls out of school, rush them home, and debug all of us—God willing—in time to get this offer to the sellers before birthday cake. Or. I can pretend I didn't see the email and send them to Travis's with insects nesting in their hair. Let him deal with the fallout. Maybe then he'll finally begin to understand the kind of pressure I've been under all these years.

Ashamed, I shake the thought away. Of course I can't do that. From the beginning of the separation, we promised not to make the girls pawns in our battle. It was the *only* thing we agreed upon.

Chewing the inside of my lip, I decide I'm going to have to rush this appointment along with the McClouds. They are expecting the baby in two months, so time is of the essence, but at the moment, time is a commodity I can't afford to spare. I smooth my slacks, then speedwalk to the backyard, where I find the couple sparring in measured tones. But I don't have time for dillydallying. As they split hairs over dollars and cents, actual lice are multiplying in my hair, building thriving communities to sustain generations of baby lice! What is the singular of *lice*? *Lie*? *Louse*? Maybe it's like *fish* and the singular is also the plural. I fan myself with one hand. The itching must be affecting my ability to grammarize properly! All the more reason to scramble to the school ASAP, before the overeager parents jam the pickup lane. They'll block my escape to the parking lot, and I'll never be able to salvage the evening.

Impatience gets the better of me. "How about you two come up with a number that feels right to you and give me a call," I interject, hoping I don't sound as desperate as I feel. "I'm so sorry, but I have to pick up my kids. There's been an . . . incident." An understatement, to say the least. More like a catastrophe. As a rule, I don't bring up my personal problems with clients, but in this case, it feels justifiable.

"I hope everything is OK," Mrs. McCloud says, appearing genuinely worried. I resist the urge to tell her that no, everything is not OK. In fact, it is taking every ounce of mental energy to refrain from tearing my hair out by the fistful.

"Oh, everything's fine," I lie. "We'll touch base later this afternoon, once I get a better idea of your lice point—I mean price point!" That draws a strange look from Mr. McCloud, who seems like he is second-guessing my ability to get the job done.

I force a smile, but I'm not sure I can prove him wrong.

CHAPTER 3

Practically flying, I rush through yellow lights and roll through stop signs until I land in the parking lot of Bonnet Hill Elementary School. Once I shut off the engine, I tug down my mirror and inspect my hair, hoping the bugs will remain tucked away for the duration of this interaction. I do not want to be *that* mother. The one who didn't read the email last week. The one responsible for reinfecting half the student body. No matter that Travis was on the email chain, too, because no one will raise an eyebrow that he simply missed the memo. Which he always does. I was the one who let it slip through the cracks.

When I stumble into the office, Megan, the attendance clerk, welcomes me with a thousand-watt smile. "Mrs. Perkins, it's so good to see you again. How are you?"

Her innocent greeting hits me with an unexpected weight. It's Travis's last name, and if this separation goes the way I think it's going, I'm not sure how much longer it will be mine. I give her a smile that I hope doesn't look suspicious. "Fabulous," I lie, as something skitters around behind my ear. Keeping a safe distance from the reception desk, I pray that whatever is happening on my head feels worse than it looks. I ball my hands into fists until my fingernails nearly puncture the flesh of my palms. "I need to check out my girls," I say as normally as I can manage.

"No problem," Megan replies cheerfully, her smile cracking just a sliver. When she swivels to reach for the phone behind her, I allow myself one frantic scratching session, then glue my hands firmly at my side. After Megan hangs up, she levels her gaze at me. "They should be down soon," she says, her eyes trailing over my burning cheeks. I feel certain she can sense something is amiss, but if she suspects anything, she doesn't say it. "So glad that Ruby locked in one of our pre-K spots," she notes brightly, perhaps picking up on my nervous energy. "It must be nice to have the girls in the same school."

"Definitely," I say, remembering the mind-bending logistics of last year. It was nearly impossible to get Ruby to the partially subsidized day care across town in time for Eadie to beat the tardy bell. Travis's teaching position didn't allow for much flexibility in the mornings, so this was one of the many tasks unofficially assigned to me. Under normal circumstances, I would take this opportunity to chitchat further, but right now I lack the ability to put on that kind of show.

Behind me, the door opens, carrying with it the scent of something spicy and a touch intoxicating. I risk a glance and clock Julian Mitchell wearing dark jeans, a white T-shirt, and an open blazer. He breezes toward the welcome desk in a pair of black Vans that give off the sort of laid-back vibe I both envy and admire. Julian is the rare unicorn of a man who manages to appear simultaneously casual and professional, not to mention insanely good looking. I imagine that exotic smell that follows him around is money, but since I faithfully hoard Paulo's Pizza points like rare coins, I could be wrong. It occurs to me that Travis still has unfettered access to our pizza points, not to mention Chipotle, and I worry he'll waste them on his financially stunted bandmates before I can change the password to my accounts. These are things you don't think about before you decide to take a break from your marriage. Julian probably doesn't care about his pizza points or even know they exist. He probably only eats gourmet flatbreads with fig and prosciutto or some other premium ingredients I can't pronounce. In any case, how should I know? My limited knowledge of Julian comes from what I've overheard through the parent grapevine. By all accounts, he's divorced, ridiculously wealthy, and single-handedly responsible for revitalizing Bonnet Hill's town square by investing in new developments.

With the faintest flecks of gray in coffee-colored hair set against a rich, dark complexion, Julian looks distinguished and confident, the sort of man who knows what he wants and always gets it. They say looks don't buy happiness, but from where I'm standing, they sure as hell can't hurt. And Julian Mitchell seems objectively happy. I would be, too, if my name were on the plaque of the school's outdoor classroom, a project funded by a major donation after the opening of his latest restaurant. This action alone made him a saint and a stud in the eyes of the staff and PTA moms. And some of the dads. He's certainly wealthy enough to afford private school for his two sons, but lucky for our provincial elementary school, none exist in Bonnet Hill.

Leaning his weight against the counter, Julian removes his expensive-looking sunglasses. "Aren't you the picture of perfection today," he says to Megan with a wink.

She bats him away, but her voice goes high and giggly. "Oh Mr. Mitchell, you're too kind."

"No really. Did you do something with your hair?" He gestures toward the sleek waves cascading over her shoulder. "It's very Blake Lively."

"Just a few highlights," she admits, tucking back a strand of blond. She's full-on blushing, and I can't blame her. Julian possesses the sort of magnetic charm that manages to prick even my cold, jaded heart. Watching him smile is like watching the fallout of a traffic accident. I know it's rude to stare, but I can't bear to look away. "What can I do for you today?" Megan asks, eager for whatever the task may be. I'm certain that if he asked her to polish his shoes, she would cheerfully oblige.

"I need to check out Malachi." He purses his lips. "Dentist appointment. Apparently, he has two cavities."

"Oh no," Megan chirps.

A tiny stab of jealousy gives me pause. I try to remember a time when Travis took the girls to the dentist or any scheduled medical appointment but come up short. I wonder if Julian was always the sort of father to manage dentist visits or if being divorced forced him to step up. If that's the case, maybe this separation could be just the thing to shake Travis into reality, force him to actively participate in his children's hygiene for the first time in nine years. But would it be enough? Even if he does surprise me Sunday with newfound resolution to be an equal partner, I haven't decided yet whether I'll let him back into my heart. Travis isn't the first person to let me down, and I don't know if I'm brave enough to wait around for another disappointment.

"Guess that's what happens when you consider Sour Patch candy a legitimate food group," Julian says, pulling me from my thoughts. "If you ask me, he deserves ten more."

I stifle a laugh. Ruby subscribes to the same philosophy, but by the grace of God, she inherited Travis's impeccable dental genes. Julian must have heard me, because he turns, his liquid eyes questioning.

"Audrey, right?" He gestures toward me with an open palm.

"Right," I supply, my cheeks flushing red. I didn't expect him to notice me, much less remember my name. We've only crossed paths on a couple of occasions and always at school events. Of all the times I would have loved to chat with Julian, now is definitely not that time. Not when my head is a hotbed of insect activity. Still, I say, "Good to see you again," and awkwardly accept his extended hand.

"You guys have an appointment too?"

"Sort of," I say, my optimistic facade cracking. With my washing machine and a bottle of pesticide. But he doesn't need those details, so I say, "It's Ruby's birthday. She's my youngest."

"Well, that's as good an excuse as any to ditch school in my book." He smiles again, and I feel my heart rate tick up a notch. There's another prickle at the nape of my neck, but I can't tell if it's lice or my nerve endings on alert. "How old?"

"Five," I say, overcome by the reality of that statement. How is it possible that I ever lived in a world where Ruby and her two hundred personalities didn't exist? Five years seemed to fly by in a blink, taking with them her babyhood, which I'm wholly unprepared to lose.

"Big year," Julian notes, shaking his head. "Malachi is ten going on nineteen this month. I miss the days when he wasn't embarrassed to be related to me."

I have a hard time believing this but offer a sympathetic look anyway. I can completely relate. Eadie hasn't even hit double digits yet, and she looks at me like I'm an obnoxious stranger who stalks her games and performances. Ever since the night I upended our lives, she's been nursing a pretty pernicious grudge against me. Before Travis moved out, we sat the girls down and explained the situation in the simplest terms. "Mommy and Daddy are having trouble getting along and need to take a time-out from each other for a little while, but you did nothing wrong. This is not your fault," I reiterated over and over. A sentiment Ruby seemed to grasp. Her biggest concern was where Travis was going to live. She'd worried he might have to camp out in the backyard like a vagrant. She seemed relieved when we told her he would be sleeping only a few miles away and would still be there for all her soccer games. But Eadie was old enough to understand the implications of a "time-out" and cried fat, angry tears. "I know it's not our fault," she said, sidling up to Travis, as if picking sides. "It's yours. You're never happy anymore. I'd want to move away too." In case I somehow miss her clipped tone and cold shoulder, she taped a handwritten sign on her door that read **NO ICE QUEENS ALLOWED!**

When I realize Julian is waiting for me to reply, I shake myself free of the memory. "I totally understand," I say. "My oldest is nine."

"So, you know then," he says, with a discerning look. "Last week, Malachi missed the bus. He made me drop him off at the 7-Eleven across the street. The whole thing felt like a drug deal or something." He shudders. "They get a few hormones, and suddenly I turn into the shady guy in sunglasses who promises to avoid eye contact in public."

I concur with a smile, though my heart contracts at the memory of Eadie ignoring me at her softball game last weekend, slipping into

Travis's truck without even saying goodbye. And I know she saw me, because I cheered her on louder than any other parent, as if somehow this would convince her of my love. "You and me both."

"You guys have birthday plans?"

Thinking of Travis and our evening, I feel a twinge of sadness. Birthdays in our house are never going to be quite the same. Last year, for Eadie's eighth, we hosted a glow dance in our living room. Travis DJed while I painted faces. "Just . . . family stuff," I say, avoiding any mention of our messy arrangement.

His wide brown eyes light up like an idea has just occurred to him. "Listen, you should stop by my restaurant this weekend." He pats down his blazer, searching for something, then reaches into a pocket and pulls out a business card. He plucks a pen from Megan's desk and scribbles something on the back, then passes it to me with two fingers. "They make a birthday lava cake there that Ruby would go crazy for. All the kids do. Just tell them I sent you and dinner is on me."

For the briefest of moments, our fingers brush, and the action is slow enough to make me wonder if it's intentional. "Thank you so much," I manage. "I'm sure the girls will love it." But unless Julian's restaurant serves boxed macaroni and cheese, I'm fairly certain they'll hate it. Still, the gesture is nice, and the way Julian's eyes linger on mine a beat too long makes my cheeks redden. Being a married mother of two has never been a magnet for the male gaze, but I finally feel good in my skin again. Lately, I've managed to get in a few workouts a week at FlexCore, and I'm catching glimpses of the woman I used to be before my abdomen grew two humans. It helps that Travis no longer lives with me, always sneaking candy and cakes into the pantry to derail all the progress I'm making. Sure, I can use some help in the fashion department, but I'm not a total lost cause. On the rare occasion a man throws me a compliment, I smile and flash my wedding ring. Though I haven't taken it off, I'm technically unattached now. Does that mean I still have to reject a kind gesture on the off chance it might be flirting?

Anyway, it probably isn't, because Julian Mitchell is so far out of my league, he's practically playing another sport altogether.

A heavy door swings open, snapping me out of my reverie, and Malachi emerges, hauling a giant cardboard box. It looks like it might be a science project.

"There's my guy," Julian says, wrapping an arm around his slight son and tousling his too-long hair with a fist. "You ready to go?"

Malachi nods reluctantly, then offers the box to his father and heaves his backpack over a slouched shoulder.

"I mean it, Audrey," Julian says, throwing me a finger gun. "I'd love to see you there."

"We'll try," I promise. "Thanks again." It does not escape my attention that he said *you* instead of Ruby, a fact that even Megan seems to note with a hint of side-eye. I'm not sure what to make of it, but truth be told, the idea of crossing paths with Julian outside the sticky, ammonia-laced halls of the elementary school makes my skin tingle. Maybe Lexy was onto something.

Ruby comes tearing through the door a few minutes later, and I can't help but smile. With her rainbow-sequined lunch box dangling from one hand and a giant matching backpack, she looks like a turtle wearing an oversize shell. When she catches sight of me, her pudgy face comes alive, and a slow grin reveals an adorable gap where a front tooth should be. It hadn't been quite ready to come out, but she was determined to be the first kid in pre-K to lose an incisor. I was impressed when she pulled it herself but disappointed she'd done it at Travis's place, where the tooth fairy had left a punch card for a tenth free Slurpee beneath her pillow. Not exactly a reasonable substitution for the glittery silver dollars I'd bedazzled for this very purpose. Travis insisted he hadn't been prepared with cash and that Ruby had loved the gesture. I was livid but not surprised. It was exactly the sort of thing I expect from him, but then again, we hadn't discussed the going rate of currency in our children's illusions before everything came crashing down.

"Mommy!" Ruby shrieks, wrapping her chubby arms around my waist.

"There's my birthday girl," I say, bending slightly to slip a hand around her frame. "How was your day?"

"We played 'Everybody's It' in PE, and I got the most people out!" She beams, her ash-white hair brushing the tops of her shoulders. It looks clean, but I'm certain it's harboring bugs. Discreetly, I part it with a finger to inspect, but I'm quickly distracted by the door opening again.

Eadie appears, holding her recorder case in one hand and a short stack of chapter books in the other. Unlike her sister, she does not look excited to see me. Carefully, she tiptoes her way around a hairline crack in the polished concrete floor, and I once again find myself wondering why. She never used to do that.

"Some notice would have been nice," she says when she reaches me. "I was in the middle of a test." Her reaction is expected but not as harsh as anticipated. For better or worse, our firstborn is a planner to her core and a serial overachiever. She does not accept less than a hundred percent from herself or anyone else, and surprises like this tend to ruffle her feathers. The way she looks at me, I feel like she's sizing up my ability to parent and deeming me unfit, like maybe she could do a better job. And maybe she could. Wouldn't a good mother just buck up and find a way to make it work with the father of her children, stick it out until the bitter end? It's not like Travis was abusive or manipulative or unkind. He just wasn't . . . enough. Had wanting more from Travis resulted in less of him for the kids? These are the questions that keep me awake at night.

Before I can defend myself, Ruby looks up at me with her father's enormous blue eyes and scrunches her nose. "Do I get to go home early because it's my birthday?"

"Yes, honey," I say, aware that Megan's eyes are on me too. "I wanted to spend some extra time with you two before you go to Daddy's house tonight."

"Yay!" Ruby sings, her voice soaring along with her hands.

But Eadie seems unconvinced. "You didn't do that for my birthday." Like mine, her shoulder-length hair is slightly darker than her sister's, more honey than white. Also like me, she can sniff out a lie a mile away. But because she's a good big sister, she has the decency not to ruin the moment for Ruby, who has already begun listing off all the things she wants to do as soon as we get home. "And Dad lives in a smelly apartment," Eadie clarifies with an eye roll, "not a house."

Briefly, I consider tucking a few air fresheners in their luggage but quickly banish the thought. It's been hard, but I'm getting better at relinquishing control when the girls are out of my care. Besides, I have too many fires of my own to put out, starting with a thorough insect extermination.

CHAPTER 4

"It's not fair!" Ruby says for the third time, wrinkling her brow. Her hair is twisted into a wet knot atop her head, and she's perched on the rim of the bathtub, her feet dangling and kicking against the porcelain. "You said we were going to do something fun for my birthday." Lately, Ruby has taken to slipping into a low, demonic voice when she's angry, and it grates on my already frazzled nerves. "And this is *not* fun." Tucking her chin into her chest, she crosses her arms and shoots dagger stares at me.

I can't disagree. My own wet hair is piled atop my head like a sad ice cream cone, and the medicated shampoo trickling over my scalp makes me want to scratch worse than before. "It is kind of fun if you think about it," I say. "It's kind of like a spa day." But the scowl on Ruby's face tells me she isn't buying it, so I cave. "I'm sorry," I admit. "I needed to get you both shampooed before your dad gets here, but I promise we are still going to eat cake and open presents."

"Then why didn't you just tell us that?" Ruby asks, throwing out her hands. "You lied!" My preschooler is way too smart for her own good. Normally, I appreciate this quality, but right now it is incredibly annoying.

Ignoring her, I continue working the solution through Eadie's hair while she sits at my bathroom vanity. She blinks a few times before clapping a hand to her eye. "You got it in my eye, Mom!"

"I'm so sorry, honey! Here—let me just—stay there." I reach for a hand towel and run it under the faucet, then dab it across Eadie's left eye, which is now sealed shut.

"You're making it worse!" She snatches the towel and darts for the sink, where she frantically splashes water over her face. When she's finally calmed down, I finish lathering her scalp with my fingers. Eadie has always been tender headed, so much so that the slightest contact with her head sends her into screaming fits. She yells for me to stop, but I'm being as gentle as I can, and time is of the essence. Travis should be here any minute. *Should* being the key word. He's notoriously late.

"You're hurting me!"

"I'm not trying to hurt you, Eadie. But I have to be thorough."

"You're doing it too hard!"

I'm about to apologize again when there's a knock at the front door. My stomach lurches. It's unlike Travis to be early—or on time, for that matter—and I'm not expecting a package. In any case, I'm not exactly prepared to entertain guests. Annoyed, I dry my hands, then weave through the living room toward the source of the rapping with Ruby on my heels. Whoever it is has just knocked a second time. I dig out my phone and click on the security video feed. Travis didn't think it a prudent investment, but I welcome the ability to screen visitors.

When a clear picture of my porch materializes on my phone, I zero in on the unfairly tall and curvaceous frame of Sonia and her mini me, Penelope, from across the street. If possible, Sonia's inky curls are even shinier than usual, her full petal lips a glossy shade of coral. As I envy the way her thick eyebrows arch in just the right place, I wonder, not for the first time, how a woman with a kid, a PTA position, and what appears to be a full-time job as a social media influencer has time to put herself together like that. Every day. I lack both the budget and time for buying new clothes, which Lexy tells me is a travesty given my new physique. But it's hard enough just making our kids presentable. Granted, I've never met anyone else with 122,000 followers, but the real-life Sonia seems every bit the persona she has crafted online. Her daily content is a vacuous stream of cleanses and detoxes and serums sprinkled with the occasional vegan foodie post. If that weren't enough, she also snaps photos of herself each morning wearing whatever impractical ensemble she's selected for the day. I don't think I've ever seen her in a pair of joggers, but if I ever do, I somehow know I will loathe her even more.

Every time Sonia comes over—usually unannounced—I'm reminded that I'm losing a battle that has been rigged against me, one that I never volunteered to fight. Nearly a foot shorter than her, with skin the tone of cauliflower, I'm far too busy to stay atop fashion trends and school gossip. And because I've yet to embrace the whole crop top movement, preferring my fitted button-downs, I apparently suffer from what Lexy refers to as *basic-white-girl syndrome*. But there's nothing wrong with being basic. The word implies that I've covered all the essentials.

"Audrey?" Sonia chirps, tilting her ear toward the door. "Are you home?" She's wearing kitten heels and a snug turquoise dress perfectly tailored for her Barbie dimensions, bearing a casserole dish topped in aluminum foil. At her side, little Penelope dangles a pink gift bag. Eyeing the food on my screen, I consider my options. I haven't made anything for dinner yet, and the last time she brought garlic naan that was to die for. In the absence of a suitable alternative, I open my Paulo's app to check my pizza points and am horrified that they've been decimated to nearly nothing. Travis beat me to the punch. *That sadist!* He doesn't even like Paulo's, which means he only squandered my hard-earned emergency pizzas to punish me. It's working, because now I have no plan for dinner. Except Sonia. I'm tempted to open the door to see what she's brought, but that seems ill advised given my current hair situation.

"Who's at the door?" Ruby asks loudly in her ringmaster voice.

I whip around to face her. "No one," I whisper. "Just a salesman."

"It sounded like Penelope's mom," Ruby prods. "Maybe she brought me a present!"

Sonia must have heard us because she calls out my name again, and I know it will be impossible to continue ignoring her with Ruby watching. "Is that Ruby in there? We wanted to drop off her favorite dinner and a gift. Just a little something for the birthday girl." I roll my eyes, because Ruby's favorite dinner is plain noodles with butter, but my children like to try on alternate personalities when they dine in other people's homes.

"She did! She did bring me a present," Ruby practically sings, racing for the door. "I'm coming, Penelope!" But before she can reach it, I catch her in a bear hug, because there is no way Sonia Gill is going to see me and the girls this way, three heads all donning chemical treatments and swirled into the hairstyle of shame. One whiff and she'll know we have lice. At first, she'll be empathetic, her warm-brown eyes studying us with pity. She'll insist on bringing over some of her homemade mayonnaise solution, which decidedly will not work. Then Sonia Gill will do what she does best. She will text everyone she knows that Audrey Perkins and her girls have lice. Again. And while I know I should share this information myself with the school to avoid further spread, I'd rather do it by email, like the coward I am.

"Sorry, sweetie, but we wouldn't want to give them lice, would we?" I point out gently. Her face falls, but she nods. I release her and stand up, still wondering what to say to this woman. Lying has never been my strong suit, so I'm surprised at how easily I'm able to feign a cough and creak out a greeting, hoping that Ruby will not sabotage me again. "So sorry," I groan. "I can't open the door. We're all sick with fever. Might be Covid," I add, hoping this will convince her to go. But maybe leave the food.

Ruby cuts me a confused look, but she doesn't refute my lie.

"It's all right," Sonia replies brightly. "I had it a few weeks ago."

"Or flu," I add a little too loudly. "Probably flu."

"I'm not really worried about my immune system, Audrey. I consume enough beta-carotene to power a ship," she says with a slight laugh that needles me in just the wrong way.

"I'd really rather not risk it. I'd feel horrible if we infected you," I say, though I don't mean it. For some reason, the idea of Sonia surrounded by a mountain of snotty tissues would make my evening about 90 percent more enjoyable.

She taps the toe of her heel a few times, blowing a stray curl out of her eyes before finally lowering the dish and bag to the doormat. "All right," she relents. "I'll just . . . leave it here." She runs her teeth over her bottom lip, as if rethinking this move, then presses an ear to the door. "Are you sure you're OK in there?"

"One hundred percent." I add a hacking cough for good measure. "Thank you so much for coming by." When I turn around and see Ruby staring me down, guilt coils around my gut.

"But you're not sick," she says, as if she's just caught me committing a felony.

"I know that." I take a deep breath and release it calmly, because I am the adult in this conversation. "But it wasn't a good time for visitors." I should know this answer will not suffice for Ruby. She looks up at me, her sky blue eyes seeing right past the obfuscation, such a stark contrast with her white hair. If I'm being honest, it creeps me out a little when she stares at me like this, like I'm in a *Children of the Corn* sequel and this kid is devising plans for me.

"But you lied. Again," she declares, dragging out the word like an indictment, pointing an accusing finger directly at my chest.

"Yes, I guess I did technically lie," I admit, "but you know, sometimes it's not really a lie if the lie helps someone. And in this case, we'd be helping our friends, because they won't come inside and get lice." A simple courtesy Sonia did not extend to me, which really makes me the hero in this situation. I wait for Ruby to grasp my meaning while silently congratulating myself for coming up with something so apropos on the fly. Crossing my arms, I hold my ground. She's right. I lied. But given the circumstances, who could blame me? At least, this is what I tell myself. The truth is, the last few months have put a strain on my usually pleasant demeanor, and I'm not emotionally stable enough right now to entertain Sonia's perky meddling. The woman must have an app alerting her to my elevated stress levels, because she always seems to come over at the exact wrong time. Even Travis had trouble escaping her. "The point is, sometimes Mommy needs a break from people."

Her face sags, and all the fire has left her voice when she says, "Like you needed a break from Daddy."

My breath lulls in my chest. I'm not sure how to respond. Things with Travis were so much more complicated than that. A flash of memory surfaces, stealing my smile. The first year we were married, when Iris had forgotten to call or send a card on my birthday, Travis noticed my sour mood. When he finally pried the truth out of me in the middle of a Dave & Buster's, I cried, and he held me and stroked my hair. "You can't help the family you're born to, Audrey, but you can choose the one you die with. And I plan to be there for every birthday from now until you get sick of me. I'll be like this chewing gum." He plucked a wad of spearmint from his mouth before popping it back in and gulping it down. "You're stuck with me forever now."

I looked up at him through tears, confused. "Did you just swallow that?"

"It was meant to be an object lesson." He shrugged. "It worked on my students."

"Well, I hope you told them that's a myth," I pointed out, slightly disgusted but touched at the same time. "Your body will pass it in a couple of days."

Undeterred, he floundered for another example. "Then I'll be like the glitter on this gross carpet." He gestured to the matted floor that harbored the remnants of a million birthday celebrations and dirty shoes. And maybe even a few pieces of chewed gum. "Impossible to get rid of." He squeezed me tighter, and I let myself believe him. Because wasn't that what it meant to be in love? Dependability. Someone to laugh with through the good, the bad, the boring. At least that's what every sitcom had taught me growing up. True to his word, Travis stayed. Until I told him I didn't want him to. It took time to learn there's a difference between being physically present and actually showing up for someone. But there's no way to explain all this to Ruby, so I just sigh and motion her toward me. I squat to face her and scoop her into my arms. "No. That was different, sweetie. But you know I will never need a break from you, right?" I say. She draws a hand to her cheek, swiping away a stray tear. I want to cry alongside her, but being a parent means doing a lot of pretending.

Tucking her into my chest, I hold my breath to stave off the chemical smell in her wet hair. "You know Daddy and I both love you and your sister. And you're going to have so much fun at his place tonight, right?" I say, pulling away. As if she heard her name, Eadie emerges from the bathroom like a hungry deer, looking wary but intrigued. I'm convinced she wants to join our hug, but the massive chip on her shoulder won't allow it. I haven't suffered long enough yet to earn back her trust, and I'm starting to worry I never will.

When I nudge Ruby's shoulder, a tiny smile creeps across her lips, and my chest feels a little lighter. I knew the separation would be hard on the girls, but each day feels like new terrain, and I'm never certain if I'm saying the right things. I reason that if there is a God, surely he must give out points for trying, right? And no one could say I haven't earnestly tried to make things work with Travis. I think back to his birthday last December, when I scrounged up two floor tickets to see Salvage Sound, his favorite band. I'd scored them from a grateful client at a huge discount. When he opened the envelope, Travis was surprised, maybe even stunned. I stupidly assumed we'd go together, even though mosh pits are hardly my scene. But he decided to take Marcus to the concert. His bass guitarist.

Planting my hands on my knees, I invoke a lighter tone. "Now, you don't look a gift horse in the mouth, do you?"

Ruby eyes me dubiously. "What does that mean?"

I jerk my head toward the door, hoping Sonia isn't lingering on the porch. "It means don't look so glum," I say with an encouraging grin. "You're having your favorite meal for dinner."

CHAPTER 5

I must admit that Sonia's vegan red-lentil curry is better than anything I could have rustled up. A few more meals like this one, and I may be persuaded to sing a different tune about her. Ruby and Eadie, on the other hand, pick at their food, confirming the only spice they can stomach is salt. As the three of us cluster around the kitchen table, I gently pry for details about their days, which Ruby is all too happy to provide. Eadie, on the other hand, can't be bothered to respond with more than a one-word answer. To grease the wheels, I initiate our family game, Two Truths and a Lie. It's something Travis invented when Eadie was just a toddler and the sole reason we learned about the bully who had been defacing her artwork with poop scribbles. To his credit, Travis has always been better at connecting with the girls, getting them to open up when I couldn't, but on days like this when Eadie is a closed book, I don't care to debate who gets which family traditions.

"So today I saw a deer on my way to work," I begin. "I ate a jellyfish for lunch. Annnnd . . . I met a kind stranger who gave me a gift." The challenge hangs in the air as I study their faces for a tell. Ruby purses her lips in thought, but Eadie is like a stone, not bothering to look up from her plate. She used to love this game.

"No way you ate a jellyfish!" Ruby says, confident she's figured me out.

"I absolutely did."

"You didn't." Without looking up, Eadie chimes in, her voice as gray as a heavy storm cloud. "It would sting your mouth like it stung me at the beach that time."

My eyes go misty at the memory of Travis pulling a terrified Eadie out of the clear-blue waves, carrying her to safety on the sand, where I doused her leg in vinegar. As much as I want to forget the difficult times and move forward, Travis is woven into the fabric of our lives. Even if I could untangle the threads, I wouldn't want to. We were happy once. Back then, it felt like we were a team, two people breezing through parenthood because we had only one child, and that child was so much better than every other kid we knew. Eadie didn't throw tantrums in public, didn't beg for treats in the grocery store. She loved going to preschool and learned to read faster than all the other students in her class. Maybe because she was surrounded by Travis's bandmates all the time instead of peers, she adopted such a wide vocabulary that her teacher used words like *precocious* and *bright* and *articulate* to describe her. When other parents lamented over the challenges of marriage and family, we nodded along and pretended to understand the struggle. But we didn't. Because Eadie was like this tiny adult who loved Travis's music as much as she loved reading fantasy chapter books with me. We'd hit the kid jackpot.

And then Ruby was born.

And all those gold stars we'd given ourselves became a not-so-hilarious joke. It turned out, we knew nothing about sleep training or separation anxiety or sibling jealousy. We weren't emotionally evolved or genetically superior or even lucky. We were just stupid.

Finally, I say, "Is that your final answer?"

Ruby nods, and I pause for dramatic effect. "You're . . . wrong! Lexy and I went to a Chinese restaurant for lunch, and we totally had jellyfish."

Ruby scrunches her nose in disgust. "What did it taste like?"

"Exactly what you'd think. Like a blob of mushy goo. I hated it."

There is a flicker of interest in Eadie's eyes, but not enough to win her over. She tucks a strand of blond behind her ear and returns to boring a hole into her plate with her gaze.

"Then I don't believe the last one," Ruby decides. "You didn't get a gift from a stranger. That's the lie!"

Technically, Julian is not a stranger. But it's perfectly fine to smudge the facts in the name of family bonding. "Wrong again," I say with a waggle of my eyebrows. "A very nice man heard it was your birthday, and he invited us to eat at his restaurant."

Ruby considers this, not especially impressed. "Do they have macaroni and cheese?"

"I'm sure we'll be able to find something you like there," I reassure her, although I'm doubtful whether this will be true. Julian's restaurant is a high-end seafood place. The one time I tested shrimp linguine, Eadie called it squishy, while Ruby feigned illness and refused to try it at all.

"My turn. My turn!" Ruby says, unable to contain herself any longer. She's perched on her knees, bursting with ideas. "I got to be the door holder today, so Henry got sad and cried so loud Ms. Martin had to call his mom. Then Jonah peed his pants and the whole class had to evacuumate so it could get mopped up." I stifle a smile at the word she unwittingly invented, knowing that soon she'll abandon this habit, just as Eadie had. Until age five, Eadie referred to potatoes as *buttatoes*, an adorable habit we still tease her about. Ruby pauses in contemplative thought before finally landing on her last statement. "And we found a cat at recess, but Loki brought it inside and he was allergic and then we all had to go to the bathroom to wash our hands. And Ms. Martin was even madder than when Henry was crying." I decide that if even one of those things is true, it confirms that preschool teachers are severely underpaid.

"Well," I say, steepling my fingers. "I'm going to go with door number three." I'm dubious that a horde of four-year-olds could smuggle a cat into school under the nose of Ms. Martin, who once sent home a strongly worded letter chastising me for not teaching Ruby to tie her own shoes. The woman has been managing preschoolers longer than I've been alive. She runs a tight ship.

"Wrong!" Ruby shouts. "We did find a cat and he was orange and white and we named him Mr. Buggles and he licked my hand. We fed him a Fruit Roll-Up. But I don't think cats should eat Fruit Roll-Ups. Do you, Mommy? Maybe we made him sick." Ruby's face is stricken with worry creases, and my heart melts at her thoughtfulness, delayed but sincere nonetheless.

"I'm sure Mr. Buggles is fine," I say. "But in the future, let's not feed our furry friends unless Ms. Martin says it's OK," I add, winking. Knowing that even Ms. Martin doesn't have all her ducks in a row makes me feel a little better about this whole repeat-lice situation—which I'm slightly terrified to inform her about. It also provides a tiny bit of vindication for the shoelace letter. "So . . ." I tap a finger to my chin. "Which one's the lie?"

"It was Jonah!" Ruby reveals before I can take another stab. She's practically beaming, totally enjoying the fact that she's deceived me. "He *did* pee his pants, but that was yesterday so it doesn't count. It's Eadie's turn now," she says, shifting her gaze to her big sister.

"I don't want to play," Eadie says. But I can tell she's trying hard not to comment on the Fruit Roll-Up debacle, as she considers herself an expert on anything that creeps, crawls, or flies. For Halloween last year, she dressed up as a veterinarian (which Ruby repeatedly mispronounced as *vegetarian*), made all the more precious by the fact that Ruby was dressed as a bandaged kitten. But I can't let Eadie stonewall me. Not when she's about to leave me for an entire weekend.

"You guys excited to go to Dad's tonight?" I try between bites.

Eadie picks at her food. "No. I hate having to share a bed there," she mumbles. "Ruby sleeps like an octopus."

"Yes, but a very cute one," I point out, throwing a wink at the octopus in question.

"I wonder what an octopus tastes like," Ruby asks.

"And she talks in her sleep," Eadie adds, unamused.

"Well, you fart in your sleep!"

"Do not!"

"Do too!"

"Why are you always such a brat?" Eadie yells.

"You can't call me that! Mom said you can't call me that. Mom!" Ruby looks to me, her eyes pleading for backup.

Rubbing my temples, I try to prepare myself for the turn this conversation is about to take. The girls are in their prime argument era, and since Travis moved out, relations between them have only deteriorated. Heaven forbid I chastise one of them, or the other pounces like a cheetah lying in wait, piling on more abuse. This morning, I scolded Ruby for making us late to school again, and Eadie called her "slower than continental drift," which was both mean and scathingly accurate. It's almost as if seeing Travis and I separate has convinced them that they shouldn't have to live together either. "Eadie, please apologize to your sister."

"Why do you always take her side?" she shoots back.

"I'm not on anyone's side," I say, trying to keep my cool. "I'm on the side of peace. I'm Switzerland."

This elicits a death glare from Eadie, followed by a heavy pause. "Now," I say, in a way that means I'm serious.

"Fine." Leveling her shoulders, Eadie fixes her sights on Ruby and offers a sardonic smile. "I'm sorry . . . that you are being such a brat."

I shoot her a warning look, and she rolls her eyes.

"OK," she mumbles, her shoulders deflating. "I'm sorry."

The apology seems to satisfy Ruby for now, but the scuffle has sapped all the energy from the conversation, and I don't want to end dinner on a negative note. Gathering my resolve, I clear my throat. "So . . . what do you think you guys will do at Dad's?"

"Nothing," Eadie says, pushing a pile of rice around her plate. "Jamie will probably come over again."

"Who's Jamie?" I ask, my interest piqued, heart thudding apace with slight alarm. I know both of Travis's bandmates and most of his coworkers, and I've never heard him mention a Jamie before. The name is gender neutral, and my sudden desperation for clarity unnerves me.

"Dad's friend," Ruby says brightly. "She plays guitar, too, and sometimes she sings to us at bedtime."

"Oh," I say, feeling a tad faint. Dinner congeals inside my stomach, and suddenly I regret having two helpings of curry. *She.* The floorboards of my heart give way as that one little word sinks in. We never drew up the fine print of our separation, but I just assumed that neither of us would date until the three months were up. Did Travis just decide to move on without telling me? I make a mental note to broach this when the girls aren't around, but I'm not sure how to do it without sounding like the jealous ex. Especially when I'm the one who suggested this break in the first place.

"So, you like Jamie?" I ask, fishing for more information.

"Yeah." Eadie shrugs. "She's nice to us." And though I know she hasn't come right out and called me an ice queen, I'm self-aware enough to understand the subtext.

CHAPTER 6

Eadie sits on my bed, brooding over her iPad. As I give her hair a final once-over, I broach the idea of a playdate, hoping that some quality time with her BFF will make her hate me a little less. "Maybe Payton can come over next week after school," I suggest brightly. "You guys haven't gotten to play together in a while."

"I don't want to," she says, my optimistic mood bouncing off her. "And anyway, we're too old to play."

Nine is hardly the age to abandon tea parties and dress up, both of which I know Eadie secretly still enjoys. No, she is smart enough to gather that her playdates with Payton have always served two purposes. While the kids run wild upstairs, Lexy and I are able to get in some adult time that feels almost unreachable these days. Eadie is punishing me. And I can't say I don't deserve it. Still, I try to chip away at the ice between us.

"Well, maybe you don't have to play. Maybe I could take the two of you out for Froyo instead? Would you like that?"

There's a trace of hesitation in her response, and for a moment, I think I've finally piqued her interest. But then she shrugs and reaffirms her stony expression, her freckled cheeks turned down at the corners. "Whatever." Her go-to answer for everything these days. I'd actually prefer a vehement no or a whiny *Gosh, Mom, that's so lame.* Anything but resignation. Every time Eadie diverts her eyes from me, the way she does now, a tiny dagger scrapes at my chest.

"I want Froyo!" Ruby shouts, plopping onto the bed stomach first.

"You only want it because Mom said I could have it."

"No, I don't! I wanted it before. Hey, guess my favorite animal."

Eadie rolls her eyes at the ceiling. "I don't know. A panda."

"That was my favorite animal yesterday. What's my favorite one today?"

"I don't care."

"It starts with a *B*."

"Why are you so annoying?"

"You can't say that! It's my birthday! Mom!" Ruby's eyes implore me for help, but I'm too exhausted to curate a measured response. Instead, I lock myself in the bathroom where I've stashed a pile of miniature REESE'S cups behind a box of tampons. I rifle through the bag and peel three pieces, then plant myself on the toilet and nibble away the outer layer of chocolate. The temporary rush of sweetness mutes their fighting, and for one fleeting moment, all is right in the world.

~

By the time Travis shows up—sixteen minutes late—the girls are washed and dried, their bags packed, and their stomachs full. Before I can answer the knock at the door, Ruby is already careening toward it like a rogue missile. She flings it open and barrels into Travis's waist, her fist clutching Noodle, the pink stuffed elephant Travis bought her the day she was born. "Daddy!" she exclaims.

"Happy birthday, Bumble Bee." He squats down to pull her into his chest, and I catch the way he closes his eyes when he breathes in her hair, like holding his little girl is the highlight of his week. No one can deny he's a good father, just not the greatest partner.

Standing in their shadow, I swallow hard and rub my elbows to keep from melting. Travis never had any trouble expressing love to his kids, making them feel as if they were the only people in his universe. I envy them a little, remembering the way he used to get bored during movies, his gaze always drifting over to me as if I was more interesting than whatever was happening on the screen. I know how mesmerizing it felt when I was the center of his world, like the heroine in a romantic comedy. That's the thing about movies, though. They take two diametrically opposed people and force them together until one of them makes some grand gesture and they magically fall in love. Cue the sweeping orchestral ballad, roll the credits, and voilà—happily ever after! But what happens after the last note plays and the screen fades to black? Maybe Mr. Darcy became a serial napper and left his wet stockings on the bed and never remembered to refill the toilet paper, and then one day Elizabeth decides she would prefer to live alone and escapes to a nunnery to knit scarves for the homeless. Something tells me that this is a far more likely ending than the one I've watched so many times, but no one wants to see that story. No one wants to think about what happens when the love of your life becomes part of your past instead of your future.

Glaring at Travis, I resist the temptation to pummel him with questions. Questions like "What time should we meet Sunday to discuss the future of this marriage?" and "Who the hell is Jamie?" and, most importantly, "What kind of morally bankrupt person steals all the jointly owned pizza points?!" But it's our baby's birthday, and after so much disappointment in her short life, I won't be the one to spoil her special day with an interrogation. So, I swallow my pride and remain silent.

"I'm a whole hand," Ruby says, proudly wiggling all five fingers.

"Are you sure?" He gives her a Popeye glare. "You don't look a day over four to me."

His teasing brings a spark to her eyes I haven't seen in days. Whenever her father is around, the magic is obvious. Ruby blooms like a sunflower, and Travis is the sun. I feel guilty that these moments must now be planned, carved out on the calendar like a doctor's appointment. "We have something to tell you." More serious now, Ruby looks up at him through thick lashes, takes a deep breath, and purses her sweetheart lips as if she is about to deliver bad news. "We got the bugs again."

A crooked smile takes shape on Travis's face, and he looks to me. "What's she talking about?"

"Lice," I say, folding my arms. "It's going around again. The school sent an email," I add, letting this information hang in the air, wondering if he'll pick up on what I really mean. *Why am I always the one to field communication where it concerns the girls?*

"Oh no!" He tousles her hair. "No fun to spend your birthday with little vampires on your head. I vant to suck your vlood!" he says, lurching for her as he wiggles his fingers. Ruby dissolves into a fit of giggles. From behind me, Eadie inches forward, hesitant to seem too invested in the conversation. She's working hard to keep her frown, but when Travis waves her over, she's a goner. A smile creeps across her face, and both girls wrap their arms around his neck as if he is their long-awaited savior. Leave it to Travis to bring the fun into a miserable situation. *Don't mind me. I'm just the one to keep them alive and free of parasites.*

"I took care of it," I say, though he didn't ask me to elaborate. "You probably don't have it, but you'll want to wash the bedding at your place just in case." Lucky for Travis—in this situation—he's lost a lot of ground in the hair department over the last few years. Like his father, who went bald before middle age, at thirty-five, Travis is on track to join the Hair Club for Men before forty. Despite this, I have to admit he's still attractive in an all-American-boy kind of way, with a strong jawline and kind blue eyes that can coax a smile from almost anyone, even my blowhard boss. Sometimes I find myself missing the way his self-deprecating humor could always break the ice at our company Christmas parties. Because he is tall with a brawny chest, this trait often takes people by surprise. He could always make me laugh. It's one of the things I miss most about him. But a marriage needs more than pithy one-liners and tired dad jokes to stand the test of time.

When he rises slowly from his haunches, I notice he looks tired, and he's lost weight. Travis has always been husky, but with each visit, the pudgy strain on his jeans has steadily deflated, his black Nirvana T-shirt now hanging with a couple of inches of give. My eyes trail over his biceps. They look firmer than I remember, and I catch myself wondering if he's been working out. In the nine years we were together, he never so much as lifted a dumbbell. My thoughts fly to this Jamie person who strums guitar alongside my husband and sings my children to sleep like some Disney princess. The idea of Travis falling in love with a woman who isn't me makes my heart twist in a way I didn't know was possible. But how can I blame him? I'm the one who asked him to move out. Maybe the writing is already on the wall and I should put more effort into my outing with Lexy's friend tonight. Maybe I shouldn't have felt guilty about my interaction with Julian. When Travis locks eyes with me, his smile dies. He isn't here to see me. Though we're standing two feet away, we're a galaxy apart. Clearing my throat, I motion him inside, and he steps over the threshold, acknowledging me with an obligatory nod.

Eadie follows, wrapping her arms around his waist while Ruby tugs on an arm, dragging him toward the kitchen, where her birthday cake waits on the table. Following behind, I feel like an outsider in my own home. Mothering has never come easy for me. Maybe it's because Travis sort of resembles a big kid himself, but he has an unmistakable aura that makes him a magnet for children, including ours. He won middle school teacher of the year at the district level last year, surprising no one.

I dig around the junk drawer for candles and a lighter, then grab a serrated knife while Travis sweeps Ruby up and plants her atop his shoulders. "Are you ready to party tonight like it's 1999?" he sings in falsetto. If there's ever a chance to insert a lyric reference, Travis seizes the opportunity. He asked me to marry him via the Bruno Mars song "Marry You" and his bass guitar outside my apartment one night. Even my crotchety elderly neighbor, who complained about my long showers disrupting his sleep cycle, told me to say yes. But I didn't need any encouragement. I'd known I wanted to marry Travis long before he pointed up at me from the courtyard, like he was choosing me to be on his dodgeball team. It was the having-a-baby part that worried me. The memory sends an acute ache to my chest. But since the separation began, those two twentysomethings have seemed to me like a couple of naive strangers.

"What are we going to do?" Ruby asks, wrapping her arms around his neck. She's nearly choking him in a headlock, so Travis peels off her fingers, loosening her grasp. "Well, first I thought we could go to the batting cages, and you can show me that moon shot you been working on," he says as I stick five green candles atop the cake. Since Ruby is all about panda bears these days, I ordered the cake weeks ago from a bakery downtown that specializes in animal designs. It's a three-dimensional jungle-scape with fondant bamboo sticks adorning the edges, something I never could have created myself and far more expensive than Travis would approve of. I'm sure he's wondering how much it cost, but to his credit, he doesn't ask.

"Can we go to a movie?" Eadie asks, her sour attitude all but eclipsed now by her father's larger-than-life presence.

Travis sets Ruby down in front of her cake and takes a seat in between the girls. "Sure. If Bumble Bee wants to go, I'm game." He gives an easy shrug.

I shouldn't be annoyed, but I hate that my time with the girls today has been whittled away by parenting responsibilities, while Travis gets to take them out for fun and games. And I hate that I resent the flicker of excitement on Eadie's face. She never looks at me that way anymore.

"Don't stay out too late," I say, sitting down across from him. "Eadie has a ballet performance Saturday evening. I packed her costume, but you'll need to put her hair in a bun and apply some light makeup. Think you can do that?" I say, imagining our nine-year-old showing up to the recital looking like a Kardashian or Bozo the Clown. I'm not trying to provoke him, but as soon as I say this, I can hear how pedantic it sounds out loud.

Per usual, he takes my seriousness as an opportunity to make a joke at my expense. "Me not sure," he grunts, knocking his fists against his chest like a gorilla. "Big dumb dad no understand how to operate brush." Though he says this to the girls, there's no doubt it's intended for me. Gripping the edge of the table, I suck in my lips to keep my emotions in check. After nine years of marriage, Travis knows exactly how to push my buttons. He throws a wink at Ruby, who is laughing, thoroughly entertained by his caveman impersonation. Even Eadie stifles a smile. Fixing his gaze on her, he scrunches his face in concern. "Hey, Speedy Eadie," he says. "What happened to your eye? It's all red."

She rubs it with her fist. "Mom got the shampoo in it." Her tone is coated with irritation that seems a bit melodramatic, in my opinion.

"It was an accident," I point out, in case this isn't obvious. "I was pressed for time." Because I'm always pressed for time.

"*And* we didn't get to do anything fun for my special day," Ruby complains. I conclude that the three of them are now in cahoots against me.

Travis touches a finger to Eadie's cheek and grimaces. "Yikes. Did you flush it with water?"

"Yes," I answer on her behalf, annoyed that he wouldn't assume as much. "It's fine. It should clear up soon if she stops messing with it."

"Until it does," Travis says, waggling his forehead, "maybe we can get you an eye patch and be pirates. Savvy?" he asks, adopting a Jack Sparrow accent.

"Aye aye, matey!" Ruby salutes him.

"Oh, that reminds me!" He snaps his fingers and turns to Eadie again. "I heard a great joke from one of my students yesterday. What did the left eye say to the right eye?"

Eadie seems to mull this over until finally she shrugs and makes a face. "I don't know."

"Between you and me, something smells," Travis deadpans, and then a self-satisfied smile unravels across his lips. Even though Eadie rolls her eyes, the corners of her mouth betray her as she shakes her head. "Dad, that was really bad."

"Then why did you smile?" he says, pointing a finger at her, his face 100 percent serious now.

"I didn't!"

"You did."

"I did not!" she says, but what was once a grin has spread into a full-blown belly laugh, and I'm forced to admit that Travis has a way with them I'm not sure I'll ever be able to replicate.

"We should sing to the birthday girl now," I suggest brightly, moving to light the candles.

"Presents first!" Ruby shouts, eyeing the giant box resting on the coffee table. It's wrapped in bright-purple paper with a matching bow nestled atop the center. From across the table, Travis cuts me a look. I know he's silently checking if I purchased the life-size panda bear Ruby had requested weeks ago. I confirm with a subtle nod. While I'm normally the more practical minded between us, I can't deny our youngest her one birthday wish when we've taken so much from her this year. As it was absurdly expensive, Travis and I agreed to purchase the one large gift together and forgo any other presents.

We move to the couch, trailing after Ruby as she makes a beeline for the box. When she presses her hands together and flashes her puppy dog eyes at me, I nod my approval, and she promptly begins ripping the paper. Travis produces a pocketknife from the back of his jeans to slice the packing tape, and the rest of us watch in exaggerated awe as Ruby plucks out a giant furry panda. With wide eyes, she beams at us, her face a mixture of surprise and delight, and I have zero regrets. They say money can't buy happiness, but for $122, we have purchased a moment of sheer joy for our baby girl. "I love it!" she shouts. "Can I take it to my room?"

"Sure," I say.

With Eadie tucked between us on the couch, Travis and I accidentally lock eyes for a beat, sharing a moment of mutual adoration for these amazing creatures we made. I wonder if it makes him as emotional as it makes me. Breaking his gaze, he clears his throat and motions Ruby over.

"Actually, before you do that, Bumble Bee, I've got one more present for you."

The nostalgia of the moment has passed, and I glare at him. "But we said we were only doing the one gift." I'm smiling when I say this, but my tone is dripping with venom.

"We said were only *buying* the one gift," he points out, shielding the words from Ruby with the back of his hand. There's a subtle smile on his lips that irritates me, and I know immediately that I'm beaten. "You know Daddy would never miss the chance to serenade his girl. Eadie, bring me your ukulele," he says, and Eadie dutifully darts upstairs. My mood sours. Even if I'd known about the create-a-gift loophole, I could never match one of Travis's musical creations. Nothing makes the girls feel more special than hearing their daddy meld lyrics and melody, especially when they are his muses.

After Eadie returns bearing the bright-pink ukulele Travis picked out for Christmas last year, he begins tuning up the strings. While it has served as more of a decoration in Eadie's room than an instrument, in less than a minute, Travis is strumming out clear, tinny chords like the virtuoso he is. When he starts singing, I recognize the tune of Little Richard's "Tutti Frutti," but Travis has changed the words to "Ruby, Ruby."

Ruby, Ruby. What a cutie!
Ruby, Ruby. She's groovy!
Ruby, Ruby. Shake your booty!
Ruby, Ruby. Sing it to me!

Ruby obeys, wiggling and moving around, her face lighting up each time Travis repeats another silly line. Eadie jumps off the couch and joins her sister, the two of them nodding in time to the lyrics like bobbleheads. For a moment, I let myself imagine that Willow is nestled in the midst of us, at the center of it all, reveling in the everydayness of our lives, perfectly content to be an observer. But even after five years, it still hurts to sit with the dream for too long, so I banish the thought and force down the lump in my throat.

Even though Travis has once again managed to show me up, I can't help but smile. Because even if it's fleeting, the girls are happy and no one is fighting, and we are laughing. I want to box this feeling up, throw in some silica gel packets, and store it in my closet. I want to save it for when I'm alone again, for when my favorite people in the whole world are with their favorite person in the whole world. I can't blame them for being so in love with him. After all, he used to be my favorite person too.

CHAPTER 7

After they leave, I hover near our fireplace mantel, where our wedding photos are still displayed in brushed-nickel frames. Since Travis left, I've added a mosaic vase filled with silk peonies and painted the dingy blue walls an unremarkable shade of white called Ivory Wool. Lexy helped me do it a few weeks ago. We knocked it out in a day, which only proves how easy it would have been for Travis to help me paint after I mentioned it about a million times. He hates the new color, though he never said as much. I could tell by the way his eyes trawled over the place with visible contempt tonight.

I trail a finger over the images of myself draped in white chiffon. Our wedding day unfolded in such a blur, so quickly that the only proof I have of our nuptials are these amateur photographs taken by Travis's cousin, who used the wrong exposure and had an inexplicable obsession with the zoom button. I've always hated them. Just as I hated my off-the-rack maternity dress and the homemade invitations we slapped together on short notice. We hadn't been ready for a wedding, much less a baby, but when those two pink lines appeared, Travis seemed almost giddy at the idea of becoming a family. I, on the other hand, was terrified. We were like a scientist and a Neanderthal watching a solar eclipse. One of us thought it was a majestic thing of beauty, while the other feared it signaled imminent destruction. Even so, I tried to match his excitement because I loved him. And seeing him happy had been enough to patch over the ever-present potholes of worry, the fear that, deep down inside,

I was no better than my mother, that bad parenting was genetic and maybe none of us are evolved enough to outrun our DNA.

Despite everything, there's something about this particular photo that pricks at my heart—Travis's hands cradling my blossoming belly. I wonder if we would have sealed the deal if we hadn't gotten pregnant with Eadie. We were so different before the girls, so starry eyed and gloriously unconcerned with lists and potty training and meal planning. Sometimes, I miss the people we used to be. Even so, I wouldn't trade the sleepy snuggles and infectious giggles and *I love you, Mommys* for all the leisure time in the world. The girls are my everything.

But no good will come of dwelling on a past I can't change, so I stow away the memory and decide to vacuum the entire house from top to bottom. It takes longer than I'd like to suction every nook and cranny, but I'll be damned if even one of those little suckers survives to upend another day of my life. I'm wrapping the cord around the machine when my phone rings. I dig it out of my back pocket, wondering if the McClouds have decided on a price point yet. I shouldn't have left them before securing a commitment, and I fear I may have lost them to first-time-buyer nerves. Instead, I see Lexy's platinum-blond hair and sky blue eyes lighting up the screen.

Before I put her on speaker, she's already barking at me. "What the hell? Why haven't you returned any of my texts?"

That's when I notice seven missed messages, all from her. "Sorry," I say, scrolling through. The subject of each text seems to revolve around plans for tonight.

We're meeting at Sunny's at 8.

Wear the red dress!

Do you want to borrow my new heels?

Under no circumstances will you wear a blazer.

His name is Dirk, but you can't judge a man by his name, because he's totally gorge.

Hello?

Are you avoiding me??!

Dirk? I chew over the name, rethinking this entire idea. It's the sort of name Travis would have ribbed me about. In a past life.

"Did you hear what I said?" Lexy asks.

"Yeah," I lie. "Don't worry, I'll be ready." This is a fallacy of epic proportions. Checking my watch, I note that I have less than an hour to complete the impossible task of dressing myself.

"Be honest with me, Audrey. Are you planning to wear a button-down shirt?"

"What is so wrong with a nice blouse?"

"First of all, no one under seventy uses the word *blouse*. Second, it's a cry for help!"

"Fine. No buttons," I say, resigned.

"Want me to come over, and we can get ready together?" Lexy continues, oblivious to the series of crises in my life today.

"No," I reply. Even knowing about Jamie, I don't want to make tonight any more than what it is—a casual get-together and most assuredly *not* a date. "Sorry, it's been a stressful day. I'm trying to close this deal at work, and then the girls got lice, which means I got lice, which means I'm panic cleaning. Plus, it's Ruby's birthday and Sonia dropped over for a visit—"

"You didn't let her inside, did you?" Lexy asks. I'm annoyed but not surprised that she has completely sidestepped my whole bloodsucking-parasite saga in lieu of her nemesis.

"Of course not," I reassure her. "I'm not an idiot."

"Good, because that woman is the last person who needs to know about your . . . situation," she says with just the slightest hint of disgust.

According to Lex, Sonia began the rumor that my girls were the source of the first outbreak, which wasn't true. At least I don't think so. "And I'm sorry," she adds, her tone a little softer now. "That sucks. You know I'd help you, but I'm trying the get Payton squared away before the sitter gets here. Sterling is on a business trip, and I'm barely functioning on my own as it is." I want to empathize with her, but Lex only has one child and a perfect husband who cooks dinner three nights a week. A few days on her own won't kill her.

Even though Lexy is a few years younger than me, and maybe a little more prone to drama, we have a vibe that works. She's the communications chair on the PTA and keeps me informed about all the relevant—and totally irrelevant, but much more interesting—events and gossip. What's more, we worked together at Harlow Realty until Lexy obtained her broker's license and branched out on her own into commercial real estate. "I can't believe she was elected treasurer," she says, still stuck on Sonia. "Melissa only suggested it to be nice, and now she comes to every meeting and complains about the most minute things. The slides are too tall for her precious Penelope, the teachers don't assign enough homework, the cafeteria serves garbage that her kid will never eat. Did you know that Penelope brought vegan sushi yesterday? Sushi for a four-year-old, Audrey! Who does that?"

"I don't know," I say, guiltily thinking of the lentil curry I consumed mere hours ago. "Maybe she really means it. I mean, I'm not exactly the most health-conscious parent. It's nice that someone is asking for some accountability."

"She's asking for attention," Lexy says without missing a beat. "Her Instagram page is basically a shrine to herself. She live streamed her Brazilian! I will never be able to scrub those images from my brain. And have you forgotten about the whole trying-to-steal-your-husband thing?"

"She wasn't trying to steal Travis," I say. Honestly, I'm not really sure if I believe this, but since Lexy tends to deal in hyperbole, one of us has to rein her in when she goes too far. "Not that it matters anymore,"

I say, remembering the way Travis barely met my eyes when he said goodbye this evening. "Besides, Sonia's married."

"Like that would stop her. She was making a move on him. You think it's a coincidence she happens to take out her garbage at the exact time he does, five minutes before the truck comes."

She has a point. Admittedly, I've always been a little suspicious of Sonia, as she seems to find any excuse to talk to my husband. What's more, every year she invites us to her annual barbecue, which isn't so much a barbecue as an opportunity for her to show off her picturesque yard and spacious gazebo. It amazes me that after five years of rejection, she still bothers to ask.

"I'm just saying," Lexy continues, "it's probably better if she knows as little about your personal life as possible. You don't want her to know that you have lice." She pauses for a beat, then adds softly, "Or that Travis left."

I can't disagree with her. I don't really want to talk about the separation with anyone right now, much less my nosy neighbor, who can't possibly understand what it feels like to have marital problems. By all appearances, Sonia's husband, Amir, is entirely smitten with her, as is the rest of the male population. It wouldn't surprise me if Travis thought of her in *that way*, but the few times I've broached the subject, he firmly denied any interest and seemed entirely unruffled by Sonia's ambushes.

I drag the vacuum to the hall closet and shove it inside, then scale the staircase to tackle the girls' bedrooms, my foot catching on the top step where the tread has come loose. I've asked Travis to fix it a dozen times, but it looks like I'm going to have to do it myself. Sometimes I think this house resents us for replacing Grandma Beatrice and is trying to kill us. "I have to finish up a few more things here. But I'll see you tonight," I promise, nearly out of breath.

"All right, but don't be late. You are no longer running on TST." Travis Standard Time could be anything between a fifteen-minute delay or a total no-show. The reminder conjures a dull ache in my heart that gives me pause.

Forging past the feeling, I end the call and throw open the door to Eadie's bedroom. Her lemon-colored comforter is neatly tucked around the mattress. The floating shelves above harbor a systematically arranged display of achievement—softball and ballet trophies arranged chronologically by year, and a Student of the Month plaque perched at the end. Over in the far right corner, her desk is tidy, with art supplies in various bins and baskets, and the American Girl dolls she pretends to be too grown up for carefully tucked into their double bunk bed. When Lexy complains that Payton is like a vacuum cleaner set to reverse, I feel a little guilty that my nine-year-old is so responsible. Since she was old enough to reach the crisper drawers, she's packed her own lunches. Sometimes, it feels as if I gave birth to myself.

In many ways, I wish Eadie could be a little more carefree, a little less worried about results, a little more like her baby sister. Since the separation, I've noticed how she's begun to count her steps. Literally. Her feet carefully avoid cracks and imperfections in the sidewalk like land mines. If she makes a mistake, she backtracks and starts again, as if somehow she'll be able to protect herself from whatever calamity waits in her path. Of course, I can't let on that I've noticed these odd little quirks or ask her to open up about them—because I'm the enemy. Given all she's been through, it isn't hard to understand why. In her mind, our family was the picture of happiness. But that's because she never heard the hushed arguments that bubbled up after she went to bed. She didn't read the passive-aggressive texts exchanged every time Travis missed a pickup or parent meeting. She wasn't there to hear the exasperation in my voice during my sob fests on Lexy's couch. Eadie only saw what we allowed her to see, and for that, I suppose I am grateful. Ruby, on the other hand, is more forgiving. Maybe it's by virtue of her tender age, but she doesn't seem to remember the way her parents fell apart that night. She only remembers the way I held her as she polished off the ice cream sandwich I gave her after the dust of our argument had settled.

Despite all this, I don't regret asking for space. For better or worse, these last few months have shown me I'm capable of existing without Travis. Although that was never really in question. The real question is whether I want to. And the jury is still out on that one.

I gather up Eadie's sheets, then haul the bedding next door and start in on Ruby's room, where I do my best to ignore the empty chip bags and leftover Easter-candy wrappers that peek out from beneath her bed. I've told her a million times not to eat upstairs, but she seems to have taken this rule as a challenge, always finding novel places to conceal the sticky evidence of her crimes. Though I realize I'm only enabling her bad habits, I can't help tidying up her room. I sweep the trash into a pile and gather cups half filled with water, then toss a few naked Barbies into a basket.

Satisfied, I scoop up the linens, combine them with Eadie's, and head for the hall. It's hard to see anything beyond the mountain of laundry obscuring my view, and I stub my toe on the accent table that hugs the wall. I curse under my breath and take a moment to collect myself, wondering if Travis is going to take the same measures tonight at his place. Probably not. At this very moment, the three of them are probably donning eye patches and having a crazy pirate dance party. I start down the staircase and breathe a sigh of relief as I make it past the loose step, making a note to deal with it later. Craning my neck, I do my best to lift the bedding above my head so I can see where I'm going, but it's hard to make out much of anything, and my hands are too full to grip the railing.

Carefully, I dip a toe ahead of me, rooting around for a safehold, but am met with a terrifying emptiness.

And that's when I realize my mistake.

I am weightless for a fraction of a second, floating like a hang glider, my feet tangled amid the sheets, until gravity wins. A sickening crack thuds in time with each collision as I hurdle down, down, down.

And I think to myself, as I tumble into oblivion, *This is how people die.*

CHAPTER 8

Waves of searing pain reverberate against my skull, and the low murmur of voices thrums around me like white noise. I strain to make out the words, but my ears feel as if they're underwater. Cracking an eye open, I examine my surroundings through a hazy sliver and clock an IV protruding from the back of my hand. *That's odd.* My sluggish gaze trails along the plastic tubing attached to a bag of clear fluids perched to my right. Next to it is a monitor bearing a thin line that seems to oscillate between peaks and valleys. I tilt my head to decipher its meaning, but from somewhere above, a fluorescent light blinds me. I'm in a hospital. Of this, I'm fairly certain, but I have no recollection of how I got here.

Before I can come up with a reasonable explanation, a nurse appears at my bedside. She's short and very smiley, with pale, freckle-dusted skin. Her auburn fringe bangs tug at the corners of my memory, but my brain can't place her yet. As the cloying scent of chemical detergent wafts into my nostrils, a strange familiarity settles over me, but déjà vu doesn't feel like the right word. "Glad you're back," the nurse says. "You seemed so peaceful, I let you doze for a minute."

She touches a warm hand to my arm, and all at once, I'm struck by a montage of memory—the interrupted appointment with the McClouds, the incessant itching, Eadie's swollen eye, the half-eaten birthday cake, the tangled bedsheets. As I massage my temples, the final piece of the puzzle snaps into place, and I remember. The fall. The way my stomach lurched when I lost my footing and tumbled down the stairs like a wounded paratrooper.

A ticker-tape parade of questions rolls through my mind, but my mouth doesn't seem to be working. How long was I out? Who called 911? Most importantly, where are the girls?

"It's about time to check you again," the nurse continues, moving to the foot of the bed.

Though I have no idea what *check you* means, I concur that this is probably a good idea, as I'm experiencing what can only be described as a severe case of mental fog. Sliding my back against a pillow, I attempt to push myself up by the heels of my hands, but something heavy weighs down my midsection, pushing forcefully on my bladder like a boulder. When my eyes locate the source of the pressure, my breath hitches. One of two things must be true. Either my stomach has grown a massive tumor the size of a watermelon, or I'm pregnant. The latter is impossible, as I haven't had sex in months, since well before Travis moved out. And even if we had conceived, there's no way I would be this enormous!

Despite these two indisputable facts, I close my eyes and attempt to count back nine months to discern the fertilization date of this impossible baby. But I finally realize the exercise is futile because—and this is the most important part—I do not remember being pregnant! At least not recently. And that would be a pretty huge thing to forget, as both my babies weighed in at a staggering nine pounds. (Thanks for that, Travis.) After Ruby was born, I swore on my grandmother's grave that my uterus was indefinitely closed for business, and Lexy and I celebrated my IUD with giant mimosas.

Yet at this very moment, a nurse is slipping a gloved hand inside me, causing me to tense every muscle in my body. I grip the bedsheets with gnarled fingers. While my first instinct is to kick her away, a part of me wonders if perhaps I've damaged my reproductive organs in the fall. As I lie frozen, my limbs go numb. But maybe this is all standard procedure?

Even so, I can't help commenting on this development, and loudly. "What the hell is happening right now?" I demand, unsure who I'm shouting at. I have no memory of a double date last night, but maybe Dirk roofied me and lured me into bed, and now I am . . . what, having his baby? I don't think I ever actually met Dirk, and the timeline is impossible, but there is no other explanation for what's happening. Or is it happening at all? With the exception of one puff of marijuana in college, I've never done drugs, but I imagine this is what it must feel like to be on a bad acid trip.

"I'd think after the first kid, you'd have a pretty good idea by now," Travis says with a touch of sarcasm. I recognize his tenor voice immediately, and a strange dread settles over me, sticking to my skin like a heavy fog.

"Travis?" I whisper. Though I know the voice belongs to him, I don't trust my eyes as they trail up the familiar softness of his chest. He's standing at the side of my bed, staring down at me as he fiddles with a candy wrapper. His disheveled hair is browner and fuller than I remember, creeping low down his forehead in twisting tendrils, the gray flecks barely noticeable. But most baffling, his hairline has somehow been restored to its former glory.

"Did you . . . get plugs?" I hear myself ask. It is the least of my concerns, as I'm in stirrups with my bare bottom exposed. But it's the only question I can manage. The nurse stifles a chuckle, and I'm reminded of her presence.

Travis cocks a bushy eyebrow. "No?" Then he tentatively touches his forehead and seems to rethink this answer. "Why, do you think I should?"

Ignoring the question, I squeeze my eyelids closed, confident that when I open them again, he'll be gone. But this doesn't happen, and I'm only more irritated to see him still hovering above me. "What are you doing here?" I finally ask, disturbed by the sound of my voice. I know it's mine, but it sounds desperate and afraid and far more out of control than normal Audrey.

"Seriously?" He shoots me a disbelieving look, then checks behind him. "You just yelled at me for going to get a TWIX, and now you're upset I'm here? Make up your mind, Audrey."

A flicker of remembrance ignites something inside me, but my mental engine is still in park. I'm certain this conversation has happened before. But the last time it wasn't a TWIX. It was a SNICKERS, and he abandoned me for a full thirty minutes while he broke into the vending machine, only to bemoan that he'd bruised his knuckles in the process.

"This has happened before," I finally say, still dazed, "but that was . . . God, that was when I was pregnant with . . . Ruby." Considering the fact that our youngest child celebrated her fifth birthday hours ago, I'm not sure what to do with this information.

Staring into his cerulean eyes, I decide that my brain is broken. I am in a coma. Or dead. Maybe in hell. It makes perfect sense, because childbirth was the most painful thing I've experienced to date, including that time I stumbled upon a wasp's nest in the girls' playhouse. I lock eyes with Travis and somehow know what he is going to say next.

"Stupid machine wouldn't take my dollar." Flexing his fingers, he grimaces. "But I showed it." He seems pleased with himself as he snaps a TWIX in half and takes a bite. "Want anything?" God, he looks . . . better. Younger. Maybe even . . . happier? If a little heavier than earlier this evening. The bags beneath his eyes are practically gone, the ridges of his jaw less pronounced, softer and rounder. His stomach swells in a dome beneath his green polo, and I know, without seeing, that it is carpeted in thick black hair.

"Did you . . . gain weight?" I hear myself ask.

"All done," the nurse says, patting my leg. I think maybe she's trying to escape the awkwardness of the situation, because she busies herself with a clipboard.

Travis seems offended, his shoulders shrinking. "Shit, Audrey, it's just one candy bar," he grumbles, chewing a little slower. "I'm going to forgive you for that one since you're about to give birth to our child," he adds, holding up a finger. But I can tell my words have grazed him. "I thought you liked my stocky build. You said I was like a sexy teddy bear."

I hear him clearly, but my brain has seized upon the *give birth* part, my synapses scrambling to rearrange his sentence into a pattern that makes sense. "I did say that . . . didn't I?" I admit under my breath. The only problem is, I can't remember when. His words churn around in my head like a dust devil in the desert. "I . . . I fell down the stairs," I say, in case somehow everyone has failed to notice.

"What?" Travis is incredulous. "You did? When? Is the baby OK?" He locks eyes with the nurse, who is studying him with new interest.

"Baby seems fine," she says, glancing at the vitals on the monitor. "Audrey, when did you fall?" There is a seriousness to her tone now that makes me second-guess myself. I did fall. Didn't I?

The answer is clogged in my brain and slow to come out of my mouth. "Just a little while ago," I say, touching a hand to my forehead.

She tilts her head. "How did it happen?"

Perhaps sensing an accusatory tone, Travis widens his eyes, his focus darting from me to the nurse. "Wait a minute. I didn't push her, if that's what you're thinking. I didn't push you, Audrey. Tell her."

"No one said you did, Mr. Perkins. I'm simply trying to assess the situation. Audrey"—she fixes her eyes on me from her perch at the foot of the bed—"tell me what happened so we can figure out the best way to help you and baby."

"What *baby*?" I demand. But when I study their faces for an answer, they exchange a look that makes me feel like the odd one out.

"Babe, you're in labor," Travis says slowly, like maybe reading his lips will help me process the outlandish sentence he has just spoken.

"I can't be!" I point out. "I was just doing the laundry five minutes ago. And I fell down the stairs because of the lice."

Travis raises an eyebrow. "Who has lice?"

"I do!" My face is burning with humiliation, but I'm not the one who should be embarrassed. Why should I be interrogated when they are clearly the ones clueless about the facts here.

He places a hand on my arm and leans in so close that his breath grazes my cheek. "Audrey, I need you to listen to me very carefully, OK?" There is a warmth in his expression I haven't seen in months, and I think he may actually be concerned about my health. "You didn't fall down the stairs. You do not have lice. And I'm not fat," he adds, more slowly. "You aren't thinking clearly, but it would make total sense if you weren't feeling . . . yourself. You are having a baby, after all."

There he goes about that baby again! One of us must be drunk. And then I remember the house showing this afternoon, and the memory slowly downloads into my cerebrum. Mrs. McCloud is pregnant, which caused me to reminisce about delivering my babies. That must have provided the fuel for this crazy fantasy. Admittedly, I've never experienced a dream this lucid, but this explanation soothes my nerves long enough for me to regulate my breathing. "I have to go back to sleep," I announce, because it's the only logical solution. Maybe when I wake up, I'll have a bump on my head and a cast on my leg, but my soon-to-be ex-husband will be in his own apartment, where he belongs, and I will not be pregnant with a baby I've already delivered.

"Sorry, hon. That won't be possible," the nurse says with a chuckle as she squeezes my calf. I don't like the way she dismisses the idea so readily, and I let her know this by throwing her the stink eye. It's a free country. Just let her try to stop me. But as I sink into my pillow and close my eyes, a sharp pain shoots through my abdomen, growing more intense as the line on the monitor peaks. She calmly reassures me the pain will pass soon, but it feels as if someone is wringing out my uterus, and I am 100 percent certain I'm going to black out. Actually, I would much prefer that. "This isn't happening!" I moan.

"I'm afraid it is," says the nurse. I'm not sure how it's possible to hate someone as much as I hate her in this moment, but I want to throw darts at the constellation of freckles on her cheeks. "Sure you don't want that epidural?"

"Of course I want it!" I snap, because if none of this is real, it doesn't matter if I follow my five-step birthing plan or not. "While you're at it, why don't you just shoot me up with some heroin." I laugh a bit maniacally, drawing a concerned look from Nurse Freckles. Even so, she removes her gloves and says, "I'll alert the anesthesiologist."

"Wow," Travis says, his eyes widening. "I'm surprised you changed your mind. You were dead set on going natural again."

For once, he's right, and this irritates me. Much to his bewilderment, I decided to shun the advancements of modern medicine to ensure the girls were born as healthy as possible. But since I already made good on that promise five years ago, it seems a moot point. If I'm going to deliver this child again, I'm damned sure going to do it with drugs.

~

"You can do this, Audrey. Just a few more pushes, and she'll be out." By now, Dr. Reddy has joined Nurse Freckles, his gray-stubbled chin obscured by a face mask. "When this next wave of pressure comes, I want you to bear down as hard as you can." Through thick lashes, his kind inky eyes scan the monitor again. Angry and confused as I am at this turn of events, it's impossible to dislike the man. The corkboard behind Dr. Reddy's office desk is a shrine to his patients, every square inch covered with pictures of chubby babies and toddlers and awkward teenagers, even a few adults in wedding attire. His grandfatherly hands delivered both our babies with such gentle efficiency that, even now, I mail him perfectly curated Christmas cards of our family of four. Between contractions, it occurs to me that this year, there will only be three. And for just a moment, my heart deflates. When he meets my gaze again, he gives an encouraging nod, and I know this baby is going to come out whether I'm on board or not. Dr. Reddy's familiar voice is a balm to my confused and racing heart. Gripping the bed railing, I lock in on his steady eyes and decide to give him my best effort. I lean into the pain and channel everything I have and bear down.

Travis creeps behind him and, half grimacing, ventures a peek beneath the sheets.

The color drains from his cheeks, and his lips go gray. I assume Ruby is crowning, because Travis looks as if he's going to pass out on my elderly doctor, leaving me to deliver this child alone. "I don't know how you're doing this, babe," he mutters, his voice dazed.

"That makes two of us," I say, and I mean it. "Would be a lot more manageable if I could hold someone's hand," I eke out through gritted teeth. Though *hold* is not the right word, because I plan to maul Travis's fingers until they resemble limp noodles.

Picking up on my tone, he tears his eyes away from the gruesome scene and scurries to my side. "How are you doing?" A deep crinkle forms between his eyebrows when he offers me his hand. He's uneasy, but I suspect this is mostly due to the fact that Travis cannot abide blood or bodily fluids in any form. When Eadie got sick on the way back from an amusement park two summers ago, he pulled over and excused himself, leaving me to deal with the red-Slurpee throw-up splattered across the back seat. It looked like a crime scene.

"OK," I grunt, because no word in the English language can adequately describe what I'm feeling right now. When another wave of pressure sweeps through me, I squeeze his fingers so tightly, a few of his knuckles crack. But Travis doesn't protest. He lifts the back of my hand to meet his lips and plants a soft kiss, a half grin forming on his scruffy face when he pulls away. Then he winks at me, and my heart stutters. It's been months, maybe longer, since he's winked at me like that. For a moment, I forget we're separated, and I revel in the familiar warmth of his smile, the way his left incisor sticks out just slightly. A heavy dose of memory winds through me, and I feel just a tiny bit braver, which is good because the pressure in my midsection returns with a fury. As the contraction swells to a climax, Travis reaches for my chin and tilts it toward him.

"Hey, look at me. You can do this, babe." He says it so confidently, I believe him. "You're the strongest person I know."

The warmth of his fingers on my skin reassures me, so I pull in another deep breath, then tuck my chin into my chest. And I push.

I push down five years of petulant arguments about the money, five years of angry tears and endless nights pretending to be asleep as he lay breathing beside me in bed, five years of birthdays and loose teeth and first days of school. Five years of joy and love and pain slip away as Ruby finally slips out of me, new and perfect and crying.

When Dr. Reddy places our daughter atop my chest, the tears come spilling out, and I am broken. I lock eyes with the man I fell in love with and see that Travis's cheeks are wet too. He clasps a hand atop Ruby's pink, wrinkled back, his eyes glistening just as they had the first two times we did this together. And as I look at him looking at us, I can't help but want the life we used to have—two happily married idiots who have no idea what the next five years will hold.

CHAPTER 9

If I'd known how amazing an epidural could be, I would have gotten one the first time I delivered Ruby. And with Eadie too. Besides, knowing the baby I'm holding in my arms will survive on butter noodles and hot dogs, it seems I may have needlessly tortured myself. As I cradle Ruby to my breast, grazing her feathery white head with the tips of my fingers, I feel as if I'm trapped inside the photo that graces the cover of her baby book. Strands of sweaty hair hang loose from my bedraggled ponytail as I take her in, entirely in love. All over again. If this is a dream, it is the sweetest one I will ever have, so I savor the moment, inhale the intoxicating newness of her scalp—because all too soon, she's going to grow into the sassy little girl who, just today, accused me of being a liar.

Did that really happen?

Of course it did. While this moment is amazing, it's not where I belong. I can't lose myself to the delusion, however real it seems.

It's strange how some memories live inside your bones. When I reposition Ruby, my arms remember the precise weight of her body. All nine pounds, two ounces, and twenty-one inches of her feel exactly as they did five years ago. Like her sister, she is undoubtedly big for a baby. Big, but so, so small. Her limbs quiver as they stretch and unfurl, her tiny hands balled into angry fists. She makes a pinched face, and I can sense she's about to cry, so I tuck her beneath my chin, where she relaxes, nuzzling her warm cheek against my collarbone. As I run my lips over her forehead fuzz, I can hear the shallow whistle of her breath, and I am lost in the miracle of this moment that I have somehow managed to experience twice.

My brain is at war with itself. While part of me is basking in this euphoric glow, another part realizes this is impossible. Preposterous. Entirely at odds with the laws of nature. I have quite possibly gone insane. But Ruby's mottled skin is velvety soft, and holding her makes me feel a tiny bit tipsy, drunk on the nostalgic scent of Johnson & Johnson shampoo mingled with fresh baby wipes.

Aside from the epidural, so far the evening is playing out largely as it did the first time. Travis has gone to buy me a cheeseburger from Shady's, my favorite patio bar and grill. If my memory is to be trusted, he'll have Eadie in tow to welcome her little sister. She'll bring Noodle, a stuffed elephant with a pink bow around its neck that Travis will buy in the hospital gift shop, though he'll complain that it is ridiculously overpriced. I place my palm on my forehead to stem the tide of information rushing to my brain. The past and present flow parallel in a river of muddled memory; it's hard to separate the strands. Even so, I'm excited to see little Eadie again. There was a silliness about her I haven't seen since well before the separation, since Travis and I were happy, really.

Still numb from the anesthesia, I am blissfully unaware of pain, which makes it easier to focus on the question at hand. How the hell is this happening? Travis has this theory that God is just a master gamer and we're all trapped inside a simulated reality. I always hated the idea that someone is up there just pulling the strings to see what will happen, that none of us has any control over our destinies. If that's the case, then what's the point of it all? But now, I wonder if maybe Travis is onto something. Maybe whoever is in charge got drunk and accidentally sent me back to a level I've already completed. I suppose there are worse places to end up. They could have sent me back to when I started my period in seventh grade pre-algebra—with absolutely zero preparation, courtesy of my mother. Considering her history, I should have been the most prepared, but Iris was far too busy with her own social life to notice any telltale changes in me.

Aside from the labor pains and extreme confusion, so far this hallucination has been nothing short of incredible. How often have I wished I could freeze my children exactly as they are? To have the universe bend time and space for me?

As if to prove this point, the door swings open, and Eadie bounds into the room. Except that it isn't Eadie. It's a version of her I've committed to memory, alongside every other version—pixie-cut Eadie, after we visited the hair salon for the first time; gap-toothed Eadie, when she lost her first tooth; vegetarian Eadie, when she learned that chicken nuggets were, in fact, made of chickens. That version only lasted a week, but she cried when she gave in to a corn dog at the fair. Today, she's silly Eadie, her chipmunk cheeks flushing red, the way they used to whenever she couldn't contain her excitement. Before her family turned upside down. Before she started hating me.

As I expected, she's wearing a pink Strawberry Shortcake shirt and a red polka-dot skirt, clutching Noodle with two chubby hands. My heart skips a beat when she meanders toward me, her guarded expression giving way to wonder when she sees the baby in my arms. Her eyes are wide, her pink bowed lips parted in awe. A hurricane of emotion swirls behind my eyes because I am staring into the past, and for the second time today, I'm crying. Eadie climbs onto the bed, and I scoot over to make room. With one arm still cradling Ruby's back, I tug Eadie into the opposite side of my body and wrap an arm around her tiny shoulders. Unable to help myself, I drift closer, then press my nose to her hair and breathe in. She smells like syrup and sour milk and watermelon shampoo.

"Sorry, she took off ahead of me," Travis says, trailing into the room, out of breath.

"It's OK," I reply, honestly because right now, I need to hold this child more than I need oxygen. I can't tear my eyes from her. Our family photos haven't done her justice. She's even more cherubic than

I remember. Her baby teeth have been restored in all their adorable glory; her gangly limbs and edges replaced by soft rolls. She is radiant and perfect and so, so happy. I miss this version of my little girl, even as I miss the serious nine-year-old she will become. Of course, I always knew she would eventually outgrow her lisp the way she outgrew each new pair of shoes. I just didn't think she'd outgrow me, at least not so soon. Then again, I never thought I'd outgrow my marriage, so maybe I'm the last person to judge. Maybe future Eadie deserves to be angry with me as long as she needs to be.

"I want to hold her," Eadie says, and the soft tinkle of her voice startles me because it has changed so much. Five years in a child's life might as well be a hundred.

I brush away a tear and somehow manage to find my voice. "Sure. Hold out your arms like this." I demonstrate how to cradle the baby's head, then carefully lower Ruby into her sister's waiting arms. A giggle escapes Eadie's smile as she presses her cheek against the baby's.

"I want her to sleep in my bed," she insists, then plants a kiss atop Ruby's forehead.

Travis meets my gaze and flashes a grin I'm unable to ignore. I return it with a sad smile, thinking of a sleeping octopus and her warm, heavy limbs. In a few short years, Eadie will angrily scrawl the words *no little sisters* in bright-red marker on her bedroom door, and I will help her scrub it away with a Magic Eraser, calmly telling her that little sisters are supposed to drive you crazy, lamenting that I never had a sister to annoy.

"I see you gave her your present," Travis says, catching sight of Eadie smooshing Noodle into Ruby's chest. "Hope she likes it. Thirty-two dollars for a rip-off of Dumbo is criminal."

I'm supposed to reply with an eye roll and call attention to his cheapskate tendencies, but all I can do is marvel. Because my baby is holding my baby. And it occurs to me that maybe this isn't hell after all. Maybe it's heaven.

CHAPTER 10

I'm waiting in a wheelchair just outside the hospital entrance, with Ruby strapped in her infant car seat on my lap. I tried to convince Dr. Reddy I wasn't fully healed yet, but he insisted there was no medical reason to keep me longer than two days. Not that he could help me anyway. My problems go way beyond anything he can treat. Also, I'm afraid telling him about my time slip will only result in a psych eval, and that wouldn't be good for any of us. But going home means accepting that everything is totally fine. That waking up five years in the past is completely normal. And I worry that the longer I stay here, the harder it'll be to get my old life back. If this is all just a dream, future Audrey is totally screwed. I close my eyes and speak to her directly now, wherever she is. *Wake up! Wake up!!!*

Our old red Honda inches beneath the awning, and Travis emerges from the driver's side. I traded it in last year for my Prius, and the sight of its flaking paint and dented hood makes me feel a bit cheated. Gently, Travis lifts the car seat from my lap and secures Ruby adjacent to Eadie in her booster, then fiddles with the straps until they're snug. Then he takes me by the arm and guides me to the other side of the car, opens my door, and buckles me in too.

When his arm grazes my breast, my heart skips. I forgot how attentive he was after the girls were born. When we brought Eadie home, he was so careful with us both, driving fifteen miles under the speed limit. A police officer even stopped him for going too slow. The determined expression on his face now is not unlike the one he wears when maneuvering the treacherous winding roads of *Mario Kart*, riddled with malicious turtle shells and banana peels. Today there's only the occasional roadkill and an inordinate number of red lights, which make the silence that much more deafening.

It's Travis who finally speaks first. "So, how are you feeling?"

Considering that I'm wearing a pad the size of Texas and my breasts have mutated into rocks, I'm not sure how to answer. I'm rooting around for an acceptable response when Eadie interrupts. "Mommy, guess what."

"What, honey?" I ask, still trying to acclimate to the reedy sound of her voice. But I know exactly what she is going to say. I remember this conversation as clearly as if it happened yesterday.

She smirks like she has a secret. Except I already know what the secret is because I was angry about it. Livid, actually. "I smoked today!"

"No, you didn't," Travis says with a widening smile. Then, to me, he adds, "She picked up a cigarette butt at the park, and I knocked it out of her hand. Now she thinks she smoked, and she's been telling everyone about it, including Mrs. Murray, who I'm pretty sure is going to report us to CPS. It's embarrassing as hell, but one day it will make for a good story. Am I right?"

He was right. It *did* make for a good story, one I told at Eadie's birthday parties year after year. But at first, I was legitimately terrified, worried she'd contracted hepatitis or meningitis or some other horrifying *-itis* I had yet to discover on WebMD.

The rest of the trip is largely quiet. It's the first time I've been alone with Travis in three months, and I find myself at a loss for suitable discussion topics. What do I say to the man who called me an ice queen before storming out with gummy rice in his hair and three packed suitcases? The rice had been my fault, but it wasn't the only reason we fell apart. There were so many, too many to count. Still, my mind sifts through a Rolodex of recurring arguments—most of which boiled down to time and money, the two natural resources that seemed to decline in direct proportion to the number of children we created. Before Ruby was born, I didn't care if Travis was a few minutes late or forgot to put the wet clothes in the dryer. But after, those seemingly tiny mistakes could shift our little family's solar system entirely out of orbit. When it was "purple day" at preschool and Travis forgot to switch out the laundry, Ruby dissolved in a meltdown and refused to leave the house wearing green, which made me late for my 9:00 a.m. showing, which meant I lost a client, which resurfaced that bitter, age-old argument about who had the more flexible schedule. Spoiler alert—it has always been me.

Rubbing my elbows, I roll back my internal clock by five years, trying to remember which parts of our lives have actually taken place. The band is a safe enough bet, as he's been playing alongside his buddies, Marcus and Dane, since college. Travis had composed a few original pieces, but they mostly performed old covers, running the gamut from Pink Floyd to the Clash. They'd gone through a litany of potential names but had never landed on one that stuck.

"So . . . how's the band going?" I try, not sure how much I actually care. The conversation is merely a distraction from my dissociative state.

"Seriously?" He cuts me a disbelieving look.

Did I ask the wrong question? Aside from the girls, music is Travis's passion. "Of course," I say honestly.

"Yeah. I mean it's . . . good. It's just that . . ." He looks over at me, massaging his chin as if he isn't quite sure what to make of me. "Well, you never ask about the band anymore."

"Yes I do," I reply, a touch too defensive.

"No." He shakes his head, impassive. "Actually . . . you don't."

I feel the heat seeping into my cheeks as a familiar indignation grips my resolve. "Travis, don't be ridiculous. Of course I have."

He shrugs. "Whatever you say."

The phrase needles me, dredging up a barrel of conversations he's tapped out of using the words *whatever you say* because it is so much easier than unpacking the complexities of a disagreement. I want to call him on it, but now isn't the time to pick a fight, so I focus on the houses lining our street, taking note of subtle details that comfort me—the way Mrs. Murray has planted chrysanthemums, just as she has every Labor Day since we moved in. The way the elderly couple down the street displays a pride flag for their grandson. Even Sonia's Garden of Eden that somehow manages to thrive effortlessly despite water restrictions. It all calms my racing heart. Though our house could use a facelift, I've always loved this neighborhood. It isn't one of those cookie-cutter planned communities that sprawls across the Dallas suburbs but rather a hodgepodge of mid-century architecture, no two exteriors quite the same.

I steal a glance at Eadie in the back seat as she fishes Froot Loops from a cup and wonder what else she's been subsisting on in my absence, but it doesn't feel like the right time to ask Travis. Considering the mood, he'll only see it as an attack on his parenting abilities. Eadie's face is sticky with the remnants of strawberry milk, and her hair is matted on one side, which comes as no surprise. She's always considered hair brushing an act of torture. And despite how many times I've tried to teach him, Travis has never garnered interest in learning how to braid or even effect a basic ponytail. Hair is strictly my domain for no other reason than I have more of it than he does—arbitrary, in my opinion. By that logic, he should take on the brunt of the cooking because he eats more than the rest of us, but the only meal he can manage is frozen corn dogs and boxed macaroni and cheese.

To be fair, I have nothing against junk food in moderation, but if it weren't for me, no one in this house would be able to pick out a vegetable from a lineup. Wellness appointments with our pediatrician always feel like an inquisition. *Do they drink sugary sodas? Are they eating enough dairy? What about fiber?* The correct answers are always *occasionally*, *definitely not*, and *I have absolutely no mothertrucking idea*. Tracking the frequency of my family's bowel movements is perhaps the least illustrious thing on my to-do list. But Travis never goes to those appointments, so why should he care about nutrition?

Trying to distract my thoughts, I tug down the mirror to inspect my appearance. It's something I've been avoiding, worried I might not recognize myself, that I'll realize how much the past five years have aged me. The first thing I notice is my cheeks. They're fuller, softer. The melasma marks that have recently cropped up along my jawline are missing, and the pinprick scar above my left eye is gone. I earned it two years ago during the infamous wasp attack of 2021, when I tried, unsuccessfully, to exterminate a nest living in the girls' playhouse.

As if reading my thoughts, Travis says, "You look amazing, hon. Seriously, you can't even tell you just pushed a person out of your body."

But I can tell. The entire region beneath my waist feels like a grenade has gone off. I attempt a smile because I know he's trying to be sweet, and a mist of nostalgia taps on the door of my memory. I'm almost certain he made the same remark the first time we drove Ruby home, but it's becoming more difficult to separate history from imagination. It feels as if I'm trapped inside a movie I've seen before but can't quite remember all the lines.

The compliment churns up emotions I haven't felt in months, and I swallow the dry lump in my throat. I try to remember the last time Travis told me I was beautiful but come up short. It must have been ages before the rice fiasco. After that, he could hardly bear the sight of me. I couldn't blame him. I didn't like me much either.

~

When we pull into the garage, the reality of my situation cascades over me, and my heart freezes. At some point, I'll have to get out of this car and go inside our house. The place where Travis taught Eadie to ride her bike, and where the girls took their first steps, and where I planted my first vegetable garden in the backyard. It had failed miserably. But still. It was all part of the adventure. Tears spring to my eyes. This house is a memory box. But it's also where our marriage died, and I'm not ready to return to the scene of the crime yet.

When Travis circles around to free Eadie from her booster, I stay frozen solid, my back ramrod straight as sweat beads sprout along my hairline. I hear him release the lock of Ruby's car seat, but I can't seem to make my legs work. My door swings open, and our eyes meet, but still, I can't muster the energy to pull my body out of this car and into my past. Our past. Just when I was finally beginning to imagine a future without Travis, I'm right where I began.

"Everything OK?" he asks, and I think he truly means it. There's a crinkle in his brow, and he's examining my face like he's worried about me.

"Fine," I lie. "I just need a minute." Actually, I need so much more than that. Five years, to be exact. I close my eyes, wishing Travis would stop staring like I'm an invalid and take the girls inside already so I can steal this car and get back to the hospital, tell Dr. Reddy I've left something essential behind and it just so happens to be my mind.

"All right, but hurry up. Willow's already chomping at the bit to see you. She's been pacing by your side of the bed since you've been gone."

My heart catches. It feels as if someone has gripped me by the base of the neck. So much has happened since my fall, I haven't had time to digest the ripples of this time slip. How could I have forgotten? Hot tears spring to my eyes, and that's all it takes to will my feet out of this car. Pushing past Travis, I hear Willow's short, high-pitched barks before I see her. When I burst through the door, breathless, there she is, her tail wagging so fiercely it bobs her head from side to side. And as she saunters toward me, her nails tapping an animated dance across the linoleum, a sob wells from deep within me. It's a primal, gut-wrenching sound that makes my entire body shake. My knees give out, and somehow I'm on the ground, and Willow is bathing me in kisses.

"Seems a bit melodramatic." Travis follows behind with the girls in tow and cuts me a strange look. "You were only gone a couple days."

But I barely hear him with my ear pressed against Willow's neck, tears drenching her fur. "I missed you so much," I whisper. I pull away to look at her and stroke her face. The warmth of her breath grazes my palm in steady streams, proof that her lungs are working. A voice in my head is shouting that none of this is real, that it's all too good to be true, but I shut it out because my eyes and ears and heart can't all be wrong. Willow is here and whole. And for the first time in five years, I am whole too.

From behind me, I can hear Travis sigh, his voice weighted with confusion. "You and that dog. I swear, sometimes I think you love her more than me." He might be right.

I've never put much stock in ghosts, but now I'm forced to rethink every belief I've ever had. Because I'm clutching Willow to my chest, the same dog I held while Dr. Chang injected her with a lethal poison that slowly stole her warmth, taking with it a piece of my heart. As I nuzzle my face against her soft black fur, I ask myself the question I've been asking for the past forty-eight hours. *How can this be happening?*

I remember the crisp October morning when I plucked a little black Lab from a litter at the corner of Turner and Sixth; she practically leaped from the box into my arms. I remember that day just as clearly as I remember the very end, when her body was broken, her tiny whimpers begging me for answers I didn't have. I'll never forget the empathy in Dr. Chang's eyes as she helped me choose an urn for her ashes. "She was so lucky to have you, Audrey. Try to hold on to the good moments." But her words didn't soften the loss, and over time my sadness turned to resentment toward the one person who could have saved her. The person who never loved her the way I did.

There's a paw print set in clay that rests atop our mantel, a bittersweet reminder that my love for Willow was real and meaningful. But it's only a remnant. It could never fill the Willow-size hole that pierced my heart the day she drifted away. Now, by some miracle or a glitch in the matrix, she is resurrected—perfect and warm and just as happy as she lives in my memory. Her black fur with faint slivers of caramel glistens in the sunlight streaming through the windows, and her brown eyes dance as her bottom wiggles back and forth. True to her breed, Willow loved everyone in our family and warmed to each of the girls after they came along. But I was her person. Judging from the way her tongue sweeps over my cheeks, it seems I still am.

Maybe this isn't a dream or a parallel universe where I'm destined to relive every heartache and wrong turn. Maybe the five years I've spent arguing with Travis about the mortgage and the garbage disposal were never meant to happen. Maybe *this* is reality. In any case, now that I'm here, staring into the ever-trusting eyes of my best friend, I can't help but think this isn't some kind of punishment for mistakes I've made in a past life. It's a gift. For the first time since waking up in the hospital, I know what I am supposed to do.

Ruby's birthday was two days ago. September seventh. I do the mental math and realize the implications. In one week and four days, Willow is going to die.

Except, this time, she won't. Because I'm going to save her.

CHAPTER 11

It's been six hours since Willow returned to me. Or maybe I returned to her. In any case, now that we're together again, impossible as it seems, all is right in the world—even as it is so very wrong. Most of the time, she dutifully stands vigil as we lie on the bed, snuggling the girls, as if she knows something dangerous is lurking. Little does she know it's me who is going to protect her.

It's a little after 6:00 p.m., and Travis has conveniently escaped to "pick up dinner," even though Mrs. Murray has brought over enough meat pies to sustain us for weeks. At least one of us has managed a jailbreak. While he's gone, I bounce a fussy Ruby around the living room while Eadie watches *Paw Patrol* on her tablet. I forgot about colic. The first six weeks of Ruby's life were a battle of wills, transforming our once peaceful home into a pressure cooker every evening. She cries, which makes me cry, which makes Travis try to comfort her, which only makes her cry harder. When I inevitably accuse him of holding her wrong, or patting her back with too much force, he leaves, feigning some unoriginal excuse. And I can't blame him. It's as if Ruby is angry at us for bringing her into the world, punishing us with cries that make me question my life choices. I could have been a travel blogger or a flight attendant or one of those professional wine tasters who vacations in idyllic vineyards in the South of France. Or a nun. I can't decide which I'd prefer, but anything is better than torture by ear damage. It's amazing how quickly a person can oscillate between warm fuzzies and existential despair, but this is all part of the magic of having an infant.

Luckily, Mrs. Murray stopped by about two seconds before I self-destructed and asked if there was anything she could do to help. She was kind enough to hold Ruby while I took an overdue shower, but when she told me to "enjoy these moments, dear, because they pass all too quickly." I rolled my eyes. What a huge load of crap. For all I know, these moments may last forever. Maybe I'll be trapped on this merry-go-round of giving birth and shushing a screaming infant and arguing with Travis in perpetuity. *No.* I will not make the same mistakes again. I will not be the same person I was before my fall, angry and resentful. I'll communicate this time, tell him when I'm upset instead of letting it fester. At least then I can truly say I left everything on the field.

As I wander the house with Ruby wriggling against my chest, I can't help but notice all the subtle changes—or, rather, the lack of them. Above the fireplace mantel, a collage of wedding pictures are framed in the exact same diamond configuration where I hung them years ago, but the wall is all wrong. I close my eyes to clear the fuzz in my brain. The new paint color is supposed to be Ivory Wool, but a stubborn blue envelops me in a mist of regret. Everything is exactly as I remember it, not a thread out of place. The only thing that's changed is me, because I'm not the girl in that picture anymore, carefree and hopelessly in love. I'm wiser now. Wise enough to understand that Travis and I weren't ready to jump into marriage just because we got pregnant. There is so much more we should have discussed besides the cost of a ring or the amount of sea bass to order or the color of my bouquet. Plans we should have made to accommodate our shifting lives. Maybe if we had, we could have made good on our vows. Maybe he would have been there to help with the lice, and I wouldn't have fallen down the stairs into a rerun, and we would be happy. If only.

I shuffle through the rest of the house, humming "You Are My Sunshine" softly in Ruby's ear, but it only seems to irritate her. She's worked herself into such a fit that her face has gone brick red, and her nose is stuffed. Instinctively, I know I should suction it with the bulb syringe, and I suspect it's in the nursery upstairs. Slowly, we make our way toward the staircase, and I chew my lip. I haven't scaled it since the lice catastrophe. I have no desire to repeat my almost fatal mistake, especially while holding my newborn, but Ruby's cries are enough to inch my feet toward the bottom step. Cradling her with one arm, I clutch the railing with my free hand, determined to make it to her bedroom unscathed. Willow encourages me with a nod, as if to say *It's OK. I'm right here.* Her vote of confidence makes me braver, and with slow, measured breaths, I climb, reminding myself that I've performed this task successfully thousands of times.

When we make it to the landing, the tightness in my sternum dissipates, and I pad down the hall to the nursery with Willow on my heels. The door creaks open, and I'm greeted by soft yellows and whites. A crib is nestled in the center of the room, veiled by the ladybug mobile my mother sent. It didn't match the color scheme, as it wasn't even on the registry. But Iris never cared about honoring my wishes. A rocking chair is perched in an adjacent corner, and a soft-white dresser is set off to my left.

Gently, I tug open the top drawer and find a stack of neatly folded onesies. I remember these. Some were gifts from the baby shower, and some were Eadie's. I pluck out the green one with yellow ducks and press it to my nose, inhaling the scent of my past. It smells the same: clean, like baby powder and a hint of fabric softener. But Ruby still fusses against my chest, so I shuffle to the changing table and rifle through the drawers until my fingers locate the bulb. Carefully, I lay Ruby atop the padding and begin suctioning her nose, plugging the opposite nostril just as I have a thousand times before. It's amazing how familiar this feels, the intimate business of caring for another person's every need. But Ruby is not appreciative and commences her crying with even more gusto than before.

I attempt swaddling her like a burrito—that always worked on Eadie—then move to the rocking chair, where we teeter back and forth to no avail. I try nursing her again, but she's too angry to eat, so I press her against my chest until finally we both break into sobs. What did I do to deserve a colicky baby again? How did I ever manage to do this the first time around? What lesson is the universe trying to teach me? Willow nestles herself at my feet and whines helplessly.

Maybe I should ask Mrs. Murray to take her for a little while before I completely lose my shit. I'm not emotionally stable enough right now to care for an infant, and I haven't so much as glanced in Eadie's direction today. What kind of mother doesn't know how to comfort her child? What's more, I have five years of perspective, so this should be easier. But it's not, and that only makes me feel more defeated.

I sing a lullaby again, this time trying "Rock-a-Bye Baby," but it doesn't comfort her. And as I pay attention to the words, I realize how morose they are. Travis has never been a fan of traditional nursery rhymes, always opting for contemporary tunes instead. Thinking of his birthday performance just a couple of days ago, I wonder if maybe he was onto something, not that it would help me now. My voice is terrible—a fact that many people have pointed out, including Travis, who once asked me if I had a hearing problem when I tried to sing along to Bon Jovi with him at Friday-night karaoke. That was years ago, before the kids. But desperation shreds whatever dignity I have left, and I allow the words to gather slowly beneath my breath until I manage to eke out something resembling a melody.

Ruby, Ruby. What a cutie.
Ruby, Ruby. She's groovy.

She doesn't seem to mind that I'm out of key, and a soft gurgle replaces her screams. Afraid to spoil the moment, I sing a little louder, careful not to jostle her. She peeks up at me, as if waiting for more, but I can't remember the rest of the song and the silence frustrates her. When she breaks into another cry, I frantically comb the corners of my memory for the rest of the lyrics. I picture Travis strumming the pink ukulele on our sofa until, finally, the words come to me.

Ruby, Ruby. Shake your booty.
Ruby, Ruby. Sing it to me.

As my shaky voice filters through the room, something incredible happens. Ruby settles, her little eyes fluttering, as if she knows the song and is trying to place it in her baby brain. I sing it again from the top, and her rigid limbs give way as she sinks against my breast. It's too early for her to smile, but that is exactly what she does, her little lips tugging up at the corners. And just like that, I'm a goner, entirely smitten with this creature who has just screamed at me for an hour. The moment is so sublime, I can't even remember being angry.

"Sing it again!" Eadie shouts, bounding into the room. She's already shaking her little hips around, and I can't help but comply. Her enthusiasm melts my inhibitions, and I sing even louder, reveling in her smile. I haven't seen her this happy in ages. Like a flash of lightning, I catch a glimpse of her at the glow party we threw for her eighth, streaks of neon pink and green splashed across her freckled cheeks, every inch of her dusted in pure joy. The image almost makes me forget the words of the song, and I struggle to stay in the moment. When Eadie grows bored, she demands that I rhyme her name, but it's harder to come up with anything that works, so I improvise.

Eadie, Eadie. She's a sweetie.
Eadie, Eadie. Lamborghini.

That line makes her practically giddy. We're caught in a fit of laughter when Travis appears with a quizzical look in his eyes. "Everything . . . OK up here?" I didn't hear the garage open, and he's caught me off guard.

"We're fine," I say, still smiling as I tuck a strand of hair behind my ear. "Just . . . singing some tunes." I flash Eadie a secretive wink.

"So I hear. And how come nobody invited me to the party?" he asks, lurching for Eadie, a smile spreading across his face. Willow darts around in frenzied circles, and Eadie squeals so loud it startles Ruby in my arms. He snatches Eadie up in a bear hug and blows a raspberry on her tummy. Lost in their laughter, I steal a glance down at our baby, who is drifting off to sleep again. I can't imagine a more perfect moment.

This is exactly how I'd hoped our lives would stay forever, but somewhere along the way, this happy family of four—five—was stolen from me. Or maybe I was the one who lost it. My chest aches with regret. How did we veer so far from this place?

And how in the world can I enjoy this moment in all its perfection, knowing what's coming?

CHAPTER 12

Once the girls are finally asleep, I dig around my top drawer for pajamas. I'm over the moon to discover my pineapple-print muumuu, which I'm 99 percent certain Travis gifted to the Salvation Army last year, though he would never admit it. Pressing the flannel to my nose, I inhale the scent of Gain mingled with my past and remember all those hours of British period pieces I watched while nursing my babies in the wee hours of the morning. It's the least sexy thing I've ever owned, but it's soft and roomy and, most importantly, a giant flashing stop sign. When this sucker goes on, any visions of canoodling fly right out the window—undoubtedly why Travis gave it away.

"Message received," Travis says, taking note of the folded tent in my hands. He tugs off his sweatpants, balls them up, and tosses them in the laundry basket. He's standing next to our bed wearing nothing but a pair of black boxers stamped with little red chili peppers, an image that triggers my hibernating libido. My cheeks flush hot as I remember that Travis prefers to sleep in his underwear so his body can "breathe." I think of how his hands used to roam over my curves during the night and wonder how the hell I'm supposed to sleep beside him. I must be staring, because he adds, "Unless, of course, you want to fool around first." He winks and flashes a little half smile that snaps me out of my daze.

I pull the muumuu to my chest, as if this will dispel whatever kinky scenario he's cooking up. "Absolutely not!" I say, in the same tone I imagine a nun might use if she'd just been propositioned.

"Geez. You don't have to dismiss it so quickly," he says, seeming offended.

I didn't mean to hurt his feelings, but one of us has to stay firmly rooted in reality, and it clearly won't be him. "I'm not—I just . . . had a baby, and you know it will be a while before we can . . . be intimate again," I say in the kindest voice I can muster. "Six weeks at least." For the first time since fate threw me back on that delivery table, I'm a little grateful for the circumstances. I have the perfect excuse to avoid sex for a couple of months at least. Hopefully, I won't be here long enough to follow through on that timeline. After everything we've been through, I'm far too bitter to fake a good time. Besides, sex with Travis would only complicate things when I finally wake up from this dream, however lucid it may be. But what if I'm still here? What if I'm stranded in limbo forever and there's no returning to the way things were? What's more, who's to say I won't slip through time again, like a record that keeps skipping backward? I can't imagine being transported to my life before the girls. That would break me.

"Yeah, I know," Travis says, inching closer. "That doesn't mean we can't do . . . other stuff." He eyes me up and down, then tugs me toward his hairy chest with one arm and presses me against him. For some reason, I avert my eyes. I've seen him naked thousands of times, but it's weird to feel the heat of his skin seeping through my shirt after being separated for three months. Weird, but also comforting. I let myself sink into the soft ripples of his chest, confused by my body's response. Apparently, nine years of marriage is a lot harder to write off when it's staring you in the face, and a part of me misses this—the easy closeness we used to have. Travis tilts my chin toward his and studies my lips. "You know I'm amazed by you, right?" The compliment, coupled with his embrace, throws me for a loop. I draw a hand to my neck. I'm sweating. It's been months since Travis touched me, and even then I'm pretty sure he was just dusting a mosquito off my arm. This sudden intimacy unbalances me. As I zero in on the little cleft in his chin, I almost forget about my spreadsheet of disagreements. There is no denying my husband is attractive, and he's only sexier when he says things like that.

"Why?" I ask, trying to place the memory. If it happened five years ago, I can't remember it, but I'm certain I would have safely sealed it away.

"Because you made the two people I love more than anything in the world," he says, locking his fingers behind the small of my back. "Except you, of course. Well, Ruby is growing on me," he admits, "but she'll be a lot more fun when she stops upsetting the neighbors. Think I'll call her Bumble Bee. She's tiny but painful."

Slowly, he leans down and plants a soft kiss on my lips. And though there are a million reasons why I should push him away, I let him. When his mouth meets mine, so familiar and warm, I see our lives unfurl like a film, and I am lost in the story of us. Audrey and Travis. How could I have forgotten? We were good together once. Maybe even perfect for one another. But that was before he let me down in the worst ways, and I'm not sure if I'll ever be able to really trust him again.

Blinking out of his spell, I pull away and clear my throat. "I should probably get changed. Ruby will be up soon. I should get some sleep while I can."

"Sure thing," he says, releasing me, but the way his smile cracks makes me feel guilty.

There's an awkward lull as I wait for him to make his way to his side of the bed. When he finally lies down and pulls the comforter over his almost naked body, I head for the bathroom, clutching my muumuu in a death grip. It's ridiculous to feel self-conscious in front of Travis, but I did just have a baby. Besides, we are separated, after all. Even if he isn't aware of this fact, I'm unable to scrub the past five years from my brain. I will not be taking off my clothes in front of him, no matter how good of a kisser he is.

And God, he's a great kisser.

When I'm alone, I undress in front of the vanity and inspect my postpregnancy body, pinching the loose skin around my middle. Ruby really did a number on me. It's going to take a ridiculous amount of Pilates to get my old body back. Future Audrey is leaner and more toned than current Audrey could ever have imagined, but that's because she no longer has to operate on interrupted sleep and vats of nipple cream. It also helps that she can finally afford a quality fitness regimen at the downtown studio near her office, a blessed fifty-minute escape from the never-ending hamster wheel of real estate and motherhood. Every Monday, Wednesday, and Friday after I drop the girls at school, I head to FlexCore and torture my abdominal muscles into submission. Luckily, I have so many mental lists to compile that I can distract my prefrontal cortex from the pain. My workouts at FlexCore are where I hammer out the details of my overscheduled days and weeks—birthday parties and dentist appointments and potential listings and about a hundred volunteer sign-up sheets. All the things Travis thinks just magically happen. On reflection, I don't think Travis has ever offered to bring a snack to softball practice or head up a costume fitting for ballet or collect gift cards for a teacher on maternity leave. If I don't specifically ask him to do something, he won't do it. Sometimes not even then.

Dragging my hands down my face, I note the bags under my eyes and steel myself for the impossible task of getting into bed next to my husband, an act that should be as natural as putting on pants. But so much has changed since we last lay together, our bodies brushing against one another in the tangled dance of sleep. Despite my constant shoving, Travis never was able to stay on his side of the bed.

Briefly, I consider checking myself into a hotel, but who would nurse Ruby when she wakes in two hours? Also, past Audrey has not yet made a name for herself at Harlow Realty, and I doubt our joint checking account could accommodate a luxury like that. As of now, I've only just begun at the company, since Lexy brought me on almost nine months ago, right before I found out I was pregnant again. Ever since meeting her at Eadie's day care Christmas party two years ago, she'd been after me to quit my temp job and become her mentee, hailing the benefits of working on commission. She wasn't wrong. Real estate is going to be a game changer for my financial situation. But right now, I'm still a relative newbie at work. In other words, we're broke. I can't afford a hotel. I can't even afford a latte—though God knows I could use the caffeine.

Once I've pulled on my nightgown, I brush my teeth and take my time flossing. When I'm finished, I meticulously inspect my pores in the mirror, then alternate slapping my cheeks. It's worth it every so often to rule out the possibility that I've accidentally ingested psychedelic mushrooms. Once I've convinced myself for the seven hundredth time that this is my reality, I take a cleansing breath and head to the bedroom, where I find Travis reclining against a stack of pillows, his face flickering in the low light of the television. Most notably, a slice of chocolate cheesecake rests in his lap.

"What are you doing?" I ask, eyeing him as I slip beneath the covers, careful not to let our bodies come within a foot. Hopefully, if I leave a respectable gap between us, he'll get the idea.

"What does it look like?" He cuts me a confused look and shovels a forkful into his mouth. "I'm eating."

"I realize that. But why are you eating in my—I mean, our bed?" Crumbs in the sheets were number seven on my list of disagreements, right between leaving dirty clothes on the floor and pretending to listen when I share important information that directly pertains to his schedule. I once caught him polishing off an entire plate of spaghetti on my side of the bed. He'd used my sleep mask as a coaster.

Still chewing, he crinkles his brow. "Because I'm feeling peckish," he says in a playful tone that's meant to make me smile. It doesn't.

"Beds are for sleeping," I point out. "Not for eating."

"They're also for having sex, and since that's not happening anytime soon, I'll take the next best thing." He flashes me a wink and swallows another bite. A tiny glob of chocolate has gathered in the corner of his mouth, but I resist the urge to tell him. "There's nothing wrong with having a little snack in bed."

"There is when you aren't hospitalized or a nursing home resident," I mutter.

He narrows his eyes. "I know what this is," he says, pointing his fork at me as if he's onto something. "They have a name for this. You're food shaming me. You know I may have gained a few sympathy pounds over the past nine months," he says, placing a hand to his slight belly, "but don't forget who made all those late-night runs for fried pickles."

He isn't wrong about my pregnancy cravings, but that's neither here nor there. Leave it to Travis to turn a very valid observation around on me. "This is not about food. It's about hygiene," I say pragmatically.

"Well, what about her?" He jerks his head at Willow, who is innocently nestled at my feet, minding her own business.

"What *about* her?"

"Do you think she craps rainbows? I mean, who knows what kind of parasites she may have picked up, sniffing piss all day. And yet you never hear me complaining about all the fur in the sheets." He levels his gaze at me in a challenge. "If the cheesecake goes, so does she." He clutches the plate to his chest, then defiantly brings the fork to his mouth. Slowly. At this rate, it will reach his mouth by tomorrow.

My jaw goes rigid, but I'm not surprised. When we first started dating, Travis seemed to take to Willow easily. Most of our dates ended in a walk around my old apartment complex, with Willow's wagging tail leading the way. But after we married, it didn't take long for Travis to start noting all the little ways his life had changed as a dog owner. It seemed three was a crowd. He complained when I bought the more expensive brand of dog food because Willow's gut couldn't handle the generic version and made snide comments about the astronomical emergency vet bill when she had a bowel obstruction. Never mind that it was his fault for leaving his boxers on the floor. And he never even apologized for causing the whole debacle in the first place. It was easier to blame Willow because she couldn't defend herself.

I fluff my pillows with a fist and reposition myself. I don't have the energy for another ridiculous debate. Besides, given the future I know is coming, it won't make a difference anyway. Our marriage is probably toast. "Fine," I relent. "Knock yourself out." I tug on my sleep mask, wishing for earplugs instead. As I lie there trying to tune out his chewing and the canned TV laughter, I try to remember where I used to store the handheld vacuum cleaner. I'll need to run it over the sheets in the morning.

As if reading my thoughts, Travis finally says, "You could have some, too, ya know."

I sigh. A typical Travis move. If I can't beat him, he'd prefer for me to join in his madness. But it irritates me more than usual this time. I sit up and tear off my mask. "Travis, do you realize how hard it's going to be for me to lose this baby weight? Even though I will sweat and plank and lunge like a maniac, I still won't be able to look at another donut without gaining three pounds? And you—" I'm too annoyed to finish my sentence.

"Come on," he says, teasing me with a forkful of graham cracker crust. He's waving it around airplane style, the way we used to do to get the girls to eat their pureed peas. "You only live once." He waggles his eyebrows.

But he's wrong. Sometimes you live twice. Sometimes the life you thought you already lived comes back to bite you in the rear, and you have to rehash tired conversations with your ex about things you thought you already put to rest. And if that's the case for my foreseeable future, why the hell do I care about a few crumbs in the bed or a few extra pounds in my trunk? Let future Audrey worry about that.

"Give me that," I finally say, reaching for his plate. I sink my teeth into the creamy, chocolaty goodness, and let out a dizzy moan. It feels irresponsible to let myself enjoy this moment, because there are so many real problems to worry about, so many wrongs I should be trying to set right. But maybe enjoying this slice of cheesecake is doing exactly that. I think of the rustic sign that hangs in Travis's mother's kitchen. **Live, Laugh, Love. EAT.** It's too kitschy for my taste, but maybe Lillian is onto something. After all, I can't deny the sheer happiness coursing through my veins, so against my better judgment, I let the flavor seep into my tastebuds and linger, because it's impossible not to.

It tastes like heaven.

~

I switch off the lamp, fluff my pillow, and roll onto my side. Even before any thoughts of divorce, I was never a snuggler. Iris hadn't been one to linger in my bedroom past a simple good night. And although I knew she loved me, it was less in a physical-touch kind of way, more of the gift-giving way. Once, when I reprimanded her for neglecting to pay the rent on time, she apologized with a new pair of Doc Martens and a gift certificate to Sam Goody, both of which proved to be unhelpful when we had to find another place to live. Travis, on the other hand, comes from a large family of three brothers and one sister, who even now greet one another with full-body embraces, followed by hard, resounding pats on the back. Like a good-natured football team. At night, he seems to thrive on stealing my scant body warmth.

When the darkness sets in and the stillness envelops us, it's as if he's grown extra limbs, all of them grasping at me like vines. The weight of his extremities is suffocating. I politely peel them off and cling to the edge of the mattress, but he creeps across the invisible line dividing my side of the bed from his. I can feel his breath on my neck as he curls a hand around my waist and tugs me into him. He rests his chin against my back. And because I'm too tired to resist, I let my eyes fall heavy.

Maybe it's the hormones or the cheesecake or the pineapple muumuu I thought was lost forever, but I decide to swallow my pride and let him hold me. Just for tonight.

CHAPTER 13

When sunlight pours in through our bedroom window, I muster every ounce of my willpower to lift my head a meager inch. It feels like it's been replaced by a bowling ball. I'd forgotten that Travis snores, and I was up three times last night with Ruby. The house is eerily silent. I strain to confirm there isn't a baby crying or a preschooler whining or a noisy husband milling about. As far as I can tell, I'm alone.

For a fleeting moment, I wonder if I'm finally back to my old life. If this is the case, I'm not sure how to feel about it. Of course, I would miss my babies, but there's a reason birds push their fledglings out of the nest. If I hadn't already survived these years of sleep deprivation, I would now seriously be considering the odds of death by parenthood.

Don't get me wrong. I love being a mother, but the early stages were never my favorite. Life got so much easier once the girls could communicate their needs clearly and, more importantly, reach the snacks by themselves. Before my fall, Ruby and Eadie were practically self-sufficient, entirely capable of surviving for days on their own if something tragic were to happen to me. Sure, they'd exist on Nutella sandwiches, buttered noodles, Popsicles, and whatever mind-numbing sitcom they could find on Netflix. They still needed me, of course, but not in the same way. Ruby needed me to kiss her scrapes and wash her favorite pair of tie-dye leggings and play a million games of Pie Face. But Eadie is a tougher nut to crack. And since the separation, she's become even more determined to refuse my help. The same little girl who used to beg me for five extra minutes of stories before bed would rather miss every question on her math homework than ask me about long division. I wonder what those little girls are doing now in some parallel universe.

The nostalgia doesn't last long, because as I clock the old chevron drapes, my heart sinks. They are supposed to be sheer. Travis's side of the bed is empty, and the sheets are rumpled where his shape once lay. But most notably, there's a furry black lump at the edge of the mattress, warming my feet. Every time I see Willow, my heart leaps in gratitude.

I reach for my phone on the nightstand, disappointed by the ancient model, not to mention the giant crack defacing the screen. It runs right through the center of a photo of Travis and me cuddling Eadie on the pumpkin-patch hayride at a goat farm. That was the day she discovered candy apples and made herself sick eating a whole one. I smile at the memory and swipe the screen. There's a message from Travis.

> Thought you could use some extra sleep. Took Eadie out for breakfast.

Lately, my brain has been a pinball machine of memories, bouncing my lived moments around so quickly I can't place them. But this time, the picture lands clearly in my hippocampus. Eadie is going to return later this morning wearing her yellow galoshes and a paper waffle hat, and Travis will stuff a half-eaten omelet in the back of the refrigerator that I'll throw out later this week when he's running errands. I remember this day because it will cause a huge argument, during which Travis will call me a "food fascist," whatever that means, and I will wisely instate the three-day rule wherein leftovers shall be eliminated if they are uneaten after the aforementioned length of time. I'm a little mystified and impressed by my prophetic abilities, but they don't make me feel any better about being stuck in this time loop, because I've already muddled through all these petty arguments. And won.

Normally, Travis is too cheap to entertain eating out, but kids dine free on Mondays at Waffle Queen. Still, it was a thoughtful gesture, and the least he could do, considering I spent my night feeding Ruby and massaging a clogged mammary duct. Speaking of my breasts, they feel as if they have tripled in size since yesterday, and I appear to be leaking. I reach down to find two giant splotches on my shirt, which make me wonder about the time. Ruby's been feeding every three hours, so I suspect she's due for another nursing session, but she must be asleep still. The temporary bassinet in the corner is blissfully quiet. I want to wake her to relieve the pressure, but I'm not ready to sacrifice this rare moment of quiet. I've forgotten how much I enjoy having ownership over my body, the freedom to wear whatever top I want and lose track of time without inconvenient reminders like this. The idea of being attached to Ruby for another six months is one I'm not willing to entertain right now. It's one of many routines I thought I'd left in the past, to say nothing of potty training. That's a fresh hell I have no desire to revisit, so I push away the thought. I'll cross that bridge when or if I meet it.

For now, I drink in the silence, grateful for the chance to catch my breath. Lord knows I could use a beat to recalibrate and figure out some sort of plan to get my life back on track, though I have no idea how to do this. Briefly, I toy with the idea of orchestrating another fall down the stairs, but it makes me uncomfortable. The way I see it, the odds are fifty-fifty. I'll either slip through time or break my neck, and I don't want to tempt fate. The last time I fell, I ended up pushing a baby out of my vagina. Besides, I don't want to make any big moves until after September twentieth, when Willow is officially safe. After that, I might be able to think a little further into the future.

As if hearing my thoughts, Willow inches closer, and I cup my palm over her ears. She responds by nuzzling against it, then cranes her neck to lick my cheek. The warmth of her doggy breath carries a rush of tangled emotions to my eyes, and I let the tears fall freely. I press my forehead against hers for as long as she lets me, afraid the moment will slip away and I'll lose her again. I don't think I could bear it twice. Even before the girls were born, I was never one of those people who treated my dog like a child or an accessory. I never dressed her in a Halloween costume or bought her a raincoat or trotted her around in those ridiculous rubber booties the shih tzu down the street wore on walks. Willow was far too practical for shoes of any kind. The only article of clothing she needed was the yellow bandanna gracing her neck. I'm not proud of it, but on our daily outings, we would silently judge the perky single women pushing their bow tie–wearing Pomeranians in strollers. If I'd tried to put Willow in a stroller, I'm pretty sure she would have rolled her eyes at me. We were equals. We *are* equals, in every way that matters.

Through some magic I've never understood, she's always seemed to know when I need her most. If Travis and I had a fight, she cowered in her kennel until he left the house, then silently crept onto the couch and rested her head in my lap. If Eadie cried bloody murder that I'd given her the wrong brand of fruit snack, Willow would patiently wait out her tantrum before snuggling up next to me in bed, nudging her wet nose into my side, as if to say *Can you believe these people?* I was her person. And she was my everything.

When I was little, my mother said we couldn't have a dog because she was allergic, which wasn't true. I didn't know this until I was nine and our neighbor, Mrs. O'Grady, asked if I could feed her Chihuahua while she was in the Cayman Islands visiting her son for two weeks. Taco was seventeen, blind, and incontinent, but I was so starved for the opportunity to test my dog-owning skills that I jumped at the chance. Unfortunately, Taco didn't offer much in the way of entertainment. His rituals included growling at nonexistent entities and peeing on the carpet every time I tried to pet his stiff fur. Suffice it to say he wasn't going to win any congeniality contests. After my first few visits to Mrs. O'Grady's house, I couldn't bear the thought of leaving poor Taco on his own, wandering around aimlessly and bumping into walls. So I made the ill-advised decision to hide him in my backpack and smuggle him home. We made it four days before he blew our cover, barking like a maniac when he escaped from my bedroom and discovered my mother's boyfriend lighting up a joint on our couch. I think it must have been the smell that set him on alert. And honestly, I was a little proud of him for finding his way without my help. Needless to say, my mother was not impressed. "I already have too much to take care of around here. The last thing we need is another thing that eats," she said. By *thing*, I knew she meant me. But after the whole debacle, the one piece of information I took away was this: my "allergic" mother had seemed perfectly healthy the past four days. Not one sniffle.

A therapist would probably tell me that this is why I fell so hard for Willow when I first met her in that street vendor's playpen. I'm pretty sure it's irresponsible and possibly illegal to buy dogs on the street from strangers. But once I was out of college, having a dog of my own seemed a long-overdue rite of passage. Fresh off a breakup from my first grown-up relationship, I'd been wandering the storefronts downtown, drowning my sorrows in an ice cream cone I couldn't afford, wondering what the hell I was supposed to do with my newly minted business degree. And that's when I stumbled upon the old man peddling puppies out of the back of his van. Willow's littermates were white and chestnut or some combination of the two. But Willow was the only black Lab. A few streaks of copper ran down her slick back, shining lighter beneath the sun's rays.

I peeked into the back of the van—a poor decision, upon reflection—and bent over the lot of them, watching the puppies wrestle and chew on tails and ears. But my attention always returned to Willow who seemed to have no interest in puppy things. When our eyes locked, she pushed her way through the chaos and perched on her hind legs, pressing a paw into the mesh netting of the playpen. Travis thinks I'm embellishing the next part of the story, but he wasn't there, and the moment is stamped onto my brain so clearly, I couldn't forget it if I tried. As I stooped down to greet her, Willow looked up at me with those watery brown eyes and whimpered. And then, apropos of nothing, she reached out her other paw and waved. It was a tiny motion, so subtle that another person might not have noticed it. But I did.

Call it fate, but after that, I knew there was no way I could leave that van without this dog. I also knew that the sign in front of the playpen read **$200**, which I didn't have. My manager job at an H&M was not exactly a career plan, and payday was still three days away. But sunlight was waning, and I had a hunch the man might be willing to come down on price. "Any chance you'd be willing to negotiate on this little guy?" I asked brightly.

"It's a girl," he pointed out, then pursed his lips. "I'll let her go for half. The black Labs are always harder to adopt anyway," he added. My heart lurched. It was all I needed to seal my dedication to this creature who already had my heart in her paw. And with that, I handed over my last hundred dollars with no idea what we were going to eat or how I was going to pay the pet deposit to my landlord. But when the vendor plucked her out and handed her to me, Willow licked my hand and nuzzled her nose beneath my chin, where she fit perfectly, as if she was meant to be there all along.

This is the history Travis has never truly understood. In our early days together, he knew I was a twenty-three-year-old business graduate working retail in the city. He knew I kept a color-coded planner where I marked all our dates in highlighter yellow (statistically, the easiest color to see). He knew that Tuesday was laundry day and that I preferred chocolate to flowers because the former lasts longer. He knew my father was absent and my mother might as well be.

And he knew I had a dog.

But he didn't know that Willow wasn't just a dog to me. I'd never bothered to accumulate many friends on two legs, and after she came along, I had even less interest in meeting new people. Willow conveniently occupied every role that a human might—comforter, confidant, therapist, snuggle buddy, exercise partner. She filled in the gaps of my life so seamlessly that I never realized how much I truly depended on her to make me whole. Until she was gone.

Running my hand down her back, I sift through our time together, counting every breakup, every disappointment, every heartache she carried me through, including the pregnancy after Eadie, the one that didn't last. No one had offered the words I needed to hear, not even Travis. In the end, it was Willow's silent devotion, her steadfast vigil, that brought me back from the edge of despair. "I'm going to save you," I whisper to her, wondering if she understands. When I pull back, she tilts her head to examine me, and I think maybe she does. In her usual way, I think she is perhaps the only other soul who can sense that something is different, that the trajectory of both our lives is about to shift.

CHAPTER 14

When the doorbell rings, Willow calmly trails me down the stairs. I try to recall who is on the other side of the door but can't squeeze the memory loose.

By the time I've swung it open, I wish I hadn't. Wearing kitten heels and a fuchsia blazer, Sonia stands on my porch, cradling Penelope, who is wearing a matching dress and tiny shoes that seem a bit pointless for a person who cannot yet crawl. If the infant in her arms didn't have the same thick black hair as her mother, I might mistake Sonia for a Dolce&Gabbana model who has just stolen a baby. I tighten my robe, suddenly very mindful that I'm not wearing a bra.

"Sorry for just dropping in on you, but we haven't officially met yet," she says. This isn't true, but I can't expect her to remember this, as she is probably a figment of my imagination. Our daughters will go on to be playmates at school, even if their mothers won't share more than a polite hello on our walks around the neighborhood. Once my children were old enough to develop opinions, I resigned myself to the fact that they could choose their own friends. Penelope is a sweet kid, but thank God for Lexy. Her daughter, Payton, has been soul sisters with Eadie since they were in diapers, and I know how lucky we were to score the pair of them.

"I'm Sonia," she says, repositioning the baby so she can extend a hand.

Reluctantly, I shake it, noticing her fingernails match the rest of her outfit. This does not surprise me. I wonder how they hold up against dirty diapers, but I can't imagine Sonia wiping a baby's bum. Maybe she outsources that part of parenthood to a nanny or her husband. "Audrey," I supply, forcing a smile. This entire interaction feels counterfeit, since I know the two of us will hardly speak over the next few years. I suppose that's mostly my fault, but we aren't exactly cut from the same cloth. If I'm polyester, Sonia is luxury cashmere.

"We moved into the house across from Mrs. Murray a few weeks ago. She mentioned you just had a baby, so I thought I'd stop by and introduce myself, see if you need anything." She shrugs, and the shoulder pads of her blazer nearly reach her ears.

"That's so thoughtful," I say. The house in question boasts a huge backyard with a decked patio, gazebo, and full outdoor kitchen, the only one on the block. I always secretly coveted that property, if only for its ability to host large outdoor gatherings, though I realize this makes no sense. Travis and I are not the sort of people who do such things, as we lack both the energy and budget required to throw frivolous parties. Still, it was always a fun aspiration, if also a total fantasy. But it isn't Sonia's fault that she unwittingly undermined my delusions, so I smile and say, "Welcome to the neighborhood. It's so nice to meet you."

"You too," she says, seeming relieved. "Penelope here is four months old, so it seems we may have a lot in common." She coos to the baby. I seriously doubt that, but I don't let it show. Sonia, I learn, is an influencer, a "profession" that still sounds made up, even though I know she probably brings in more money than I do in any given month. Granted, right now I'm making zilch. Turns out having a baby isn't really conducive to one's financial security, especially when you work on commission. This is all the more irritating because I spent four years getting a useless business degree when, apparently, all I needed was a decent phone camera and a knack for getting people to buy overpriced vegan beauty products. I suppose I would also need to be five seven with invisible pores, so perhaps I wouldn't have had as much success as Sonia. Not that it would matter. As a person who avoids bringing my phone in the bathroom, afraid I might accidentally live stream a bowel movement, I'm more of a content consumer than creator.

"Speaking of babies," she says, craning her neck, "where's your little one?"

"Sleeping," I say. "And my husband took our oldest out for a bit so I could get some rest." Hopefully she'll catch my drift.

But she doesn't. "Travis is *such* a wonderful guy," she fawns in a singsong voice. "Amir works ridiculous hours. We hardly see him."

I want to empathize with her, but my brain has seized upon the part about my suddenly accommodating husband. Did he go over to welcome them without me? The idea makes me uneasy, but I force a smile. "How do you know Travis?"

Her face comes alive, her brown eyes wide like almonds. "Oh, he brought over a package the other day. It was delivered to your house by mistake. A papaya hair mask. I was about to lose my mind over it and contact my sponsor, but then he showed up like a knight in shining armor." This is not an accurate description of my husband. He's more of a spoon-wielding-gamer-in-pajama-pants sort of guy.

"Did he?" Travis didn't mention the visit, and his omission makes me wonder if he finds Sonia attractive. Having the benefit of foresight, I know that Sonia is about to invite herself inside, so I strategically attempt to head her off. "I was just about to eat breakfast. You know how it is with newborns. I'm pretty much running on empty these days," I explain. And I'm not lying. My head is throbbing. I haven't consumed anything since the cheesecake last night, and my body reminds me with a low gurgle. I forgot that nursing a baby carved an unsatiable hole in my stomach.

"Oh, of course," she says, still flashing those impossibly bright teeth. But as I pull the door closed, I catch the way her smile falters when she looks down at Penelope, like she is steeling herself to go home. There's a crack in her features I recognize. It's the same *What the hell do I do now* look I mastered after Eadie was born. Those first few weeks of parenthood were a whirlwind of emotions, so complex it was impossible to verbalize my feelings. The undeniable euphoria was wrapped in loneliness and mourning for the diaper-bag-free life I had just sacrificed on the altar of motherhood. Since then, whenever I saw another new mother out in the wild, I offered a nod of solidarity, wondering if her plans also included pumping and dumping last night's glass of wine, then crying in the shower. My heart stutters, and I wonder if maybe *I* was Sonia's plan for the day. A fresh wave of guilt washes over me.

"Listen," I say as she turns to leave. "If you're hungry, I could rustle up some breakfast for us . . . if you want?"

If possible, her cheekbones lift even higher. "That sounds lovely," she says, which makes me wonder if there's anything in my refrigerator that qualifies as lovely. The only thing that comes to mind is leftover cheesecake—which, come to think of it, doesn't sound so bad right now. But maybe I'll wait to finish that off until after she leaves. I decide that's a perfectly reasonable thing to do. Surely, carbs don't count in the multiverse.

~

Seated across from Sonia holding her baby at my kitchen table, I study her flawless bronze complexion with interest. She's an oddity for sure, the likes of which I tend to avoid because it makes me feel like an utter failure in the beauty department. She must be in her mid-thirties like me, but she doesn't have bags beneath her eyes or silver strands encroaching upon her espresso beach waves. They cascade over one shoulder, each curl defined with just the right amount of loose springiness. I want to pull one just to see if it will recoil back into place. Instead, I thread my fingers through my shoulder-length hair and tug when they snag on a tangle.

"This looks wonderful," Sonia notes brightly, surveying the meager spread before us. I hardly think eggs and toast count as wonderful, but they are pretty much the only edible breakfast options in our home. I hope Travis stops by the grocery store on his way back. It occurs to me now that eggs aren't vegan, and I notice Sonia foregoes my sad attempt at an omelet and reaches for a piece of dry toast instead. The butter won't do either. "Normally I juice in the mornings, but Penelope was up half the night with indigestion, so I didn't get a chance to eat. I hardly had time to get dressed."

I'm not sure what I'm supposed to do with this information. Offhand comments like this are the reason Sonia and I will never move beyond our superficial relationship. To be fair, she's trying to normalize herself by admitting that a newborn is challenging, which I can appreciate. But she makes this statement wearing a chunky gold-chained necklace and matching hoop earrings, and I don't trust people who don statement jewelry before 9:00 a.m. on a Monday. Any day, really. Especially when I am still sporting last night's muumuu and a robe that reeks of sour breast milk. When Sonia looks away, I cup a hand to my mouth and smell my breath, which doesn't inspire confidence. But I wasn't expecting company.

"So how are you feeling?" she asks, bringing her coffee mug to her coral-painted lips. Her thick eyebrows knit together in concern, making me wonder if I look worse than I feel.

"Fine." I've only just slipped through a wormhole and woken up in labor. But aside from the fact that my body feels like it's been flung against a glass window, I couldn't be better.

"Having Penelope wrecked me physically and emotionally," she goes on with a dramatic eye roll. As if agreeing with her, Penelope gurgles. "No one tells you how hard it's going to be to recover." She takes another dainty sip from her mug, then adds, "And don't get me started on the hemorrhoids."

A piece of toast lodges in my throat, and I expel a violent cough. Of all the ways I saw my morning playing out, I did not envision discussing hemorrhoids over breakfast with Sonia Gill. I reach for my drink. When I finally recover, I clutch a fist to my chest and clear my throat, which is coated in breadcrumbs. "Very true," I manage to say.

"The sleep deprivation is really doing a number on my mental health." As is my current break from reality.

Sonia leans in closer, her eyes twinkling. "You know, if you need something to replenish your energy, I just received a huge sample pack of these multivitamin gummies with grape-seed extract. I feel like a new woman. I could drop them off later, if you'd like," she offers brightly.

But unless Sonia's gummies contain cannabis, I seriously doubt they are going to help my situation. "That's OK. I just need to sleep." What I actually need is a time machine, but in the absence of one, sleep will have to suffice. Though at present, it feels equally unattainable.

"Well, if you ever need someone to help out, I'm available. Maybe I could walk your dog or—"

"No," I say a little too loudly. From her perch at my feet, Willow snaps her head to full attention like she knows we're discussing her. I didn't mean to sound combative, but I can't entrust Willow to anyone else's care, least of all a near stranger. Her death is the only thing I have any control over in this parallel universe, and I intend to make good on my promise to her. "I'm sorry," I say, shaking my head. "I didn't mean to be rude. It's just that . . . she's kind of a bolter, and loud noises can set her off. She needs *me* to walk her," I say, hoping Sonia won't pry.

Thankfully, she doesn't. "Of course," she replies warmly, touching a hand to my arm. "Well, then maybe I could watch the girls sometime. I'm happy to keep them for a bit while you rest. We mothers have to stick together, you know," she says with a kind smile. It seems genuine, if a little too perfect. Even so, I'm a thousand percent certain I will not be asking Sonia Gill to babysit.

"What about family?" she asks. "Will your parents come to help for a bit?"

It's a valid question, but not one I'm prepared to answer. My mother is not what I would call maternal. She had me when she was only sixteen, so I can't really blame her, but it seems too soon to drop a heavy fact like this into casual conversation, so I clear my throat and say, "I never met my dad, and my mother . . . she's got a lot going on right now." The truth is, I'm not really sure what she has going on right now. If I remember correctly, she's gallivanting across Utah with her live-in boyfriend, a man ten years her junior, so only six years older than me. They won't last. He'll leave her at a gas station in Vegas in a few months, and she'll call to ask for bus fare back to Dallas. She did, however, respond to Travis's birth-announcement text—a picture of Ruby's wrinkly face peeking out of a pink blanket—with a heart emoji and the message She looks just like her Mimi! Her loophole to avoid being called Grandma. "It's ludicrous! I'm only forty-six," she said after Eadie was born. "Couldn't you have waited a few more years before making me an old woman?" It was a pot-kettle moment that I chose to ignore, because Iris Faber does not respond well to criticism, especially as it relates to the inconvenient timing of my conception. As if, somehow, *I* were the one responsible for my untimely birth.

I clear my throat. "Travis's parents moved to Florida a few years ago, so we're on our own right now."

"You're lucky," Sonia says. "After Penelope was born, my parents came from India and stayed for a whole month to help with the baby and the move. We were living in a two-bedroom apartment at the time. One bathroom." She holds up a perfectly manicured finger. "I walked in on my father taking a bath with my Himalayan salts. Do you know what that does to a person?" She sighs. "Don't get me wrong—I'm grateful for the help. But I thought they'd never leave."

My mouth goes dry, and I reach for my water. My mother's absence doesn't hurt as much as it did when I was small and she missed a choir performance or forgot to pick me up from school. Iris and I were no Lorelai and Rory, and since she didn't know what to do with me, I doubted she would know what to do with a grandchild. She didn't come for Eadie's birth, so it only made sense she wouldn't come for Ruby's. Honestly, it was better this way. Easier than having to pretend we needed each other. I gave up that ruse long ago.

The only thing I need right now is my girls. They are the single consistent thread connecting me to a future that has slipped through my fingers. Are they waiting for me there, wondering where I am? Do those versions of them even exist anymore? Without question, I will love them in whatever shape they take, but I can't deny that I miss Ruby's incessant questions and sassy quips, the way her clothes smell like pencil shavings and earthy sweat when she bounds into the car after school. I miss Eadie's determination and the dusting of freckles she will earn after summer vacations at the beach. I'm surprised, but I even miss her scowling at me. I need to know what's happened to those little girls, so full of life and experiences, even as I bask in the glow of their babyhood.

No matter what happens, from this moment forth, I'm going to do everything in my power to figure this out, not just for me, but for every version of them.

It may be selfish and probably impossible, but I need all of them.

CHAPTER 15

When Sonia and Penelope finally leave, I sink into the couch and consider the facts. It is September 2018. Closing my eyes, I rewind my mental reel and do my best to orient myself. Miraculously, my unreliable memory comes through, and I construct a rough timeline. This is the year Meghan and Harry were married. Beyoncé performed at Coachella. I got the job at Harlow Realty with Lexy, and I just gave birth to Ruby, who will give Travis and me a run for our money in the sleep department. A new job and a new baby will test the limits of our sanity. But at this point in life, we are young and healthy and strong. Travis still has a respectable head of hair. Covid hasn't happened yet. *Oh my God.* Covid hasn't happened yet. My eyes jolt open, and a cold worry snakes through my veins.

Is this why I've been hurled back in time? Am I supposed to single-handedly stop a worldwide pandemic with a newborn attached to my breast and a preschooler in tow? I filter through a few possibilities, none of which seem particularly feasible, as no epidemiologist will find my Marty McFly story credible, and my scientific vocabulary is pretty much limited to what I've learned from Doc McStuffins. If this is the universe's plan, I will be the first to acknowledge that it is monumentally inefficient. At this point in my life, I still can't pee alone, so tackling global catastrophes seems a tad out of reach. In any case, we're still a year out from Covid. And right now I don't even have control of my own body. When I look down at my top, I realize I'm leaking. Again. Maybe I should wake up Ruby and feed her. *Focus, Audrey. Focus!*

I've never been the sort of person to laze around without a plan. And in the absence of a routine, I'm coming completely undone. On a whim, I try speaking the problem into the ether of the internet. "Alexa, what should I do if I fall down the stairs and wake up five years in the past?" A few seconds of silence before a clear, emotionless voice responds. "On arrival, adjust your eating and sleeping schedule to the local time as soon as possible."

Damn. If I'm going to be here for the foreseeable future, I might as well start figuring out what the old Audrey should be doing. Maybe I can capitalize on my future knowledge in other ways: invest in stocks or start-ups that will go gangbusters in a few years. At the moment, I can't think of any, and I wish I paid more attention to CNBC and less attention to marriage and relationship podcasts. A fat lot of good they did.

Picking up on my anxiety, Willow cuddles up next to me, resting her head on my knees. I give her a thorough scratch, grateful for her warmth. It almost convinces me that I'm really here, breathing in the musky scent of my best friend, a smell that is so distinctly Willow. With one hand, I cradle her head, and with the other, I dig out my cell from my robe pocket. One thing old Audrey and new Audrey have in common is unwavering trust in a well-executed calendar. Digitized, organized, colorized, and foolproof—at least for me. Travis, on the other hand, never appreciated the unseen work that went into maintaining the minutiae of our daily responsibilities, lining them up like dominoes that, if followed to a T, allowed for everyone to participate in their various activities.

Even though I cc'd him on everything, Travis dropped the ball enough times that I no longer trusted him to make a single rendezvous without a reminder text or phone call. Jogging his memory about things I streamlined long ago was exhausting, especially since I went through the trouble of enabling push notifications for us both. Honestly, I have no idea how he's managed to make it this far in his career. Or life in general. All I can figure is that he's one of those annoying people whose personality compensates for chronic lateness and a general blasé attitude about everything. He holds the maddening belief that the party won't dare start without him, while I'm usually the idiot planning the party.

As such, my calendar has always been my daily bible, and while I've neglected to take advantage of this the last few days—distracted by the minor inconvenience of having a baby—it seems as good a time as any to recalibrate my schedule. I scroll through September and find a detailed time capsule of our routine, our family life organized into tidy, familiar bullet points—pink for Eadie, green for Travis, and bright yellow for me. Mondays are green for band night. Travis plays lead guitar with Marcus and Dane, neither of whom happen to be married or have children. Which probably explains why they seem entirely perplexed why Travis can't make practices more than once a week. Wednesday evenings are pink for dance class, Thursday afternoons are after-school jazz band rehearsals for Travis. By Friday, we are usually too exhausted, not to mention broke, to do much of anything besides lie around and stream a movie.

Aside from these recurring activities, there's a yellow bullet on Sunday with the words **HOUSE SHOWING!!!** I know myself well enough to understand that this particular showing is a big freaking deal. I only use three exclamation points if something is truly deserving of extra punctuation.

And then it hits me.

Five years ago, Harlow gave me the drop on a listing in a high-end development on the outskirts of Bonnet Hill. Looking back, I'm sure this was because he had a hunch it wouldn't sell, but at the time, I was ecstatic at the chance to prove myself. He gave me three months to secure an offer on it before passing it along to a more seasoned agent. The house was fabulous—five thousand square feet—even if the rural location was a bit of a trek. To close a deal in Thornwood Estates would have catapulted my career so much sooner, making my first sale a whopping $60,000 in commission. That's nearly all of Travis's income for an entire year. Selling the home would have given me a foothold in the area, making luxury real estate a possibility for my future.

But that's not what happened.

Instead, Ruby made her debut two weeks early. Sleep-deprived and staring down the impossible task of juggling two children, I asked Lexy to show the property a few times while I was on maternity leave, and she generously agreed. But each time, she returned with the same depressing feedback. The house was too expensive and too remote to appeal to potential buyers. In the end, I hadn't gotten a single offer and Tag Finkle usurped the listing, earning the name Douche Bag Tag from Lexy. He promptly sold it, of course, which only made me feel like even more of a failure. It wasn't his fault I flubbed, but it didn't make me hate him any less.

But that was then, and this is now. Correction: That was then, and this is then. Again. I shake my head, willing my muddled brain to focus. Here is what I know. I now have five years of real estate experience under my belt, and the negotiation skills to clinch this deal. I can do this. Besides, if I don't find something else to think about, I'll only torture myself by pining for the life I had. So instead of whining about what I've lost, I'll make lemons into lemonade, give myself the life I should have had all along. More money would mean more freedom, maybe a nanny or a housekeeper to give me some breathing room. Just the idea of it makes me feel lighter. I still have a week to prepare, and this sale could change the trajectory of our lives. Maybe it can even prevent the thousand arguments Travis and I will have about money, or lack thereof.

Willow licks my hand, reminding me of my biggest priority, and I wonder if maybe I'm taking on too much. But I can't sit around waiting for the next thing to happen. I need to feel in control of my life in some small way. Besides, if I can save Willow, I can do this too. I've already changed minor details of my past, like getting the epidural and inviting Sonia inside for breakfast, and nothing bad has happened as a result. At least not yet. It seems entirely reasonable that I can make bigger ripples if I really try. And if this is a second chance, I want to make the most of it for the sake of the kids, for the sake of our future together. Didn't someone famous once say the definition of insanity is doing the same thing over and over again and expecting different results? So, I'll do something different. I'll do a lot of things different.

CHAPTER 16

When Travis returns with Eadie, I'm perched at the kitchen table, nursing Ruby. Riveted by the news of the past, I'm elbow deep in a Google rabbit hole. Clearly, I didn't pay enough attention the first time around. War and political scandals and celebrity gossip sprawl across my feed with salacious captions. I'm about to click on another unhelpful article about the royal wedding, as if Meghan's sixteen-foot-long veil holds the key to my destiny, when Travis plants a kiss on my forehead. "How you doing?"

"Fine," I say, as if it's the most natural thing in the world for my almost-ex to greet me this way. My body hums with electricity even as my mind is still trying to decide how I feel about the warmth of his lips on my skin.

"Hopefully you got some sleep," he says, moving past me.

"Yeah, I did. That was thoughtful of you to take Eadie." Hearing her name, Eadie plants a sticky kiss on my cheek. "Hi, Mommy!" She kicks off her galoshes, then makes a beeline for the television. My eyes follow her path as I clear my throat. "Sonia stopped by." I let the pronouncement hang to try to glean some meaning out of his reaction, but he only nods as he stashes his leftovers on the top shelf of the refrigerator.

"They seem like a nice couple," he says, meeting my probing gaze.

Maybe a little too nice. "They do,"' I say in agreement, still unable to read him. "Don't you think she's a little . . . I don't know . . . surface level?"

"Depends on what surface we're talking about."

"She tried to . . . hug me," I add, reflecting on the awkwardness of the exchange. Our breakfast conversation had been surprisingly pleasant. But just as I had determined not to write Sonia off entirely, she leaned forward, craning her free arm, and instinct took over. I dodged her rather ungracefully.

"Ohhhhh," Travis says, and I can hear the sarcasm in his tone. "Let me guess. You gave her the old sidestep and shoulder pat?" Travis knows better than anyone how I feel about personal space and once bought me a T-shirt with a porcupine and the words **ALLERGIC TO HUGS**. A fair assessment, I suppose, since I caused a bit of a kerfuffle at Eadie's baby shower. Travis's aunt Denise had cornered me in front of everyone and scooped me into her bosom. I indulged her for a few seconds, but when she didn't let go, my fight-or-flight response kicked in, and I nearly shoved her into the pile of gift bags. In my defense, I didn't come from a hugging family. When I left for college, Iris had rubbed my arms and mumbled something about staying grounded in the moment. But she hadn't hugged me. Besides, Aunt Denise was not a tiny woman, and in any other setting, I might have maced her.

"Excuse me if I find hugging a tad too personal. 'Hi, nice to meet you. Do you mind if I squeeze your entire body now?' I mean, in what context aside from a search and frisk is that ever OK?"

Travis sighs, unconvinced by my argument. As he is the sort of person who once hugged our Uber driver, I'm not surprised. "Well, what did she want?" he calls over his shoulder, rifling through the pantry for a breakfast dessert.

"She offered to bring me some weird energy supplements."

"The grape-seed extract gummies?" he asks, his eyes brightening.

"How did you know that?"

"She gave me her handle when I went over there. It's all totally sustainable stuff—designer clothes, bougie food, beauty products. You should check it out."

The suggestion rankles me. Does he think I need a makeover? What's more, Travis harbors zero interest in those kinds of things, which leaves only one plausible reason why he would follow a bombshell like Sonia. Maybe Lexy was onto something after all. "Why are you following a beauty blogger?"

"For the freebies," he says without flinching. "She does giveaways all the time. I wanted the pumpkin-seed protein shake," he adds. "I didn't win it, but she brought it over anyway. Like I said, nice couple."

I roll my eyes. I shouldn't be surprised. The key to Travis's heart is free stuff. I swear he goes to Costco just for those minuscule frozen food samples. Speaking of food, I'm reminded that we are glaringly short on groceries and a number of other indispensable items, including diapers.

"We need to go shopping," I note. "We're out of everything."

"All right, I'll swing by Costco later this afternoon."

But there is no way I'm staying here with the kids while Travis steals my chance to meander around the aisles of my favorite store. It is perhaps the only place that could make me feel like myself again. The old Audrey would have used this as an opportunity to rest up, but I'm finally understanding that no amount of sleep is going to cure this head trip. I have to get out of here, even if it means braving a grocery trip with quite possibly the cheapest man on the planet.

"I'm coming."

~

We've been perusing the canned-fruit aisle for approximately a thousand minutes when Eadie starts whining. "She's sitting in my spot!"

This isn't true, as Ruby's car seat is tucked responsibly in the basket surrounded by two huge packages of toilet paper—hardly the most desirable seat in the grocery cart. Travis hadn't understood why we needed so much, but if I can't solve a global pandemic, at least I can ensure our hygiene. "No she isn't," I say. "Besides, you get to ride in the front, and everyone knows that's the best place to be."

But Eadie isn't buying it. "But I want to sit there!" With an angry pout, she points at Ruby, who is sucking on a closed fist, frustrated when it produces no milk. I'll have to feed her soon.

"Too bad," Travis interjects firmly. "You're sitting here. Or you'll have to walk."

"Walk!" Eadie shouts, already trying to free herself.

I roll my eyes. Travis should have known how that would play out. The only thing worse than Eadie throwing a tantrum is Eadie throwing a tantrum unrestrained by a seat belt.

When she realizes she's trapped, Eadie cries up a storm and starts kicking her legs. She reaches for a bag of pretzels nestled to her left and hurls it behind her. Luckily, it misses Ruby's head and lands safely beside the car seat, but it's too close for comfort and my patience is wearing thin.

I bend down, level my gaze at her, and smile sweetly. "How about you stay in your seat, and when we get home, you can have ice cream."

Eadie's eyes light up, but Travis is visibly annoyed. "Why do you reward her when she's acting like that?"

"I don't reward her," I say, though now that I think about it, he's sort of right. Of course, I won't be admitting this.

"Whatever you say," he says with a sigh. *Those damned three words again.* I want to throw an uppercut to his nose. Instead, I shoot him a death glare as I reach for a box of Mott's.

Travis bends down to inspect the price tag on a jar of generic applesauce. Pursing his lips, he gives a satisfied nod and plucks one off the shelf.

"No, not that," I say as he moves to put it in the cart.

"This is twenty cents cheaper an ounce than those." He gestures to the box of pouches I'm clutching with the desperation of a wild animal who has just been cornered.

"Yes, but it's messier, which means I have more dishes to wash, so it's worth it to spare myself the headache. Besides, Eadie prefers these." I hold the box a little tighter.

"She also prefers green M&Ms over peas, but she's four and unemployed. Her opinion doesn't count."

"It does when I'm the one running her around on errands and she's begging for snacks. Am I supposed to just pass her a vat of applesauce and say, 'Bottoms up'?" My pulse quickens, but I remind myself to breathe slowly. I refuse to have another pointless public argument with Travis. Last time we were very politely asked to leave Chick-fil-A when I laid into him for attempting to reuse the same Styrofoam cup from his last visit. I will never work up the courage to show my face there again, which is incredibly annoying, as the other location is fifteen minutes out of the way.

"Look, all I'm saying is that a little inconvenience never killed anyone."

But he's wrong. Because if Travis doesn't allow me this one small luxury, I might throttle him right here in the middle of aisle nine. My fingernails are puncturing the cardboard as if this one snack is the solitary thing holding me together. I do not understand how past Audrey managed to remain composed amid a billion absurd arguments like this, but my hat goes off to her. I'm precisely one breath away from coming completely unhinged. I fix my gaze on the space between his eyes and attempt to steady my posture. "Travis, I need you to hear me when I say this. I don't care if we have to take out a second mortgage to pay for these pouches. I am not leaving this store without them. Do you understand me?" Even I'm a little scared by the gravelly timbre of my voice.

He shakes his head, irritated, but the resignation in his response tells me I've won this battle. "Ten four, captain." Then, turning to Eadie, he shields his mouth with a hand and adds, "Guess we'll just cut back on those ballet classes to afford them, honey." He's smiling, but there's just enough venom to tip me over the edge, as *I* am the one who pays the bills!

I'm just about to remind him of this when a buttery, high-pitched twang pricks at my ears. "Oh my *Gawd*, Audrey! What are you doing here? You should be in bed!"

As I swivel around, my heart soars, immediately melting my frustration. I don't think I've ever been more relieved to see a person since making my descent into crazy town a few days ago. Lexy is sporting an adorable cream jumper and clutching the black, gold-clasped Fendi bag she won at Harlow's Christmas party six years ago. Correction: one year ago. By contrast, I'm drowning in Travis's old Astros sweatshirt. To her credit, Lexy doesn't mention the fact that I've chosen to pair this fashion atrocity with flannel pajama pants and Crocs with socks. Her blond hair is pulled back into a messy bun that looks effortlessly adorable. It's a style I've tried to achieve on multiple occasions, but the effect is more like a droopy cinnamon roll. I should resent her for this, but I've never been able to fault my best friend for her natural beauty because it is equally matched by her loyalty. She's been there for me through every upset at work, every argument with Travis, every manic moment with the girls.

Lexy is perhaps the only person in my adult life that has always had my back, no questions asked, and the instant I see her slight frame, tears spring to my eyes. "Honey, are you OK?" she asks, tentatively patting a hand atop my shoulder. Lexy knows I'm not a hugger, so when I wrap my arms around her, I detect the concern in her body language. When she pulls back to study me, I catch sight of Payton perched in the shopping cart seat. Like Eadie, she is a former version of herself I almost lost in the corners of my memory, but her blond curls and thick black lashes remain unchanged. She's always been a dead ringer for her mother.

"I'm fine," I manage to mutter. But the way Lexy is sizing me up leads me to believe she is not convinced.

She ventures a nervous glance over at Travis like I might be an unreliable patient who has just escaped the hospital. "Are you sure?"

I nod my head like a maniac, but the action is negated by the fact that I'm still holding her like a lone buoy in open water. "Just happy to see you."

The worry in her eyes seeps away, and a smile takes over her elfin face. "Well, that's a relief. I didn't even know you were out of the hospital. I would have come, but no one bothered to tell—Oh my goodness! Is that her?" she asks, her gaze landing on the car seat in the shopping cart, where my cherubic infant sleeps like a perfect doll. Lexy leans over to get a better look, her eyes wide and doting. She is entirely smitten, and I can't blame her. Though Travis and I seem genetically wired to oppose one another, there is no denying we make beautiful babies. "Oh Audrey, she's perfect," she says, touching a hand to Ruby's cheek. "I still can't believe you're out running errands just days after you gave birth!" She swats me gently on the arm with her bag. "Are you crazy?"

Yes, I want to say, but how can I possibly communicate the neurons misfiring in my brain without scaring her away? And I *need* Lexy. She's the only person that listens to me, really listens, with no judgment and no ulterior motives. She gets me in the way I wish Travis could, but I suppose it's too much to ask for your husband to also be your best friend, especially when kids are involved. "I needed a break," I say truthfully.

"That makes two of us," she says, emitting a long sigh. "The office has gone off the rails since you've been gone. Tag stole another one of my clients, and you would not believe the pressure Harlow is putting on me to make a sale this month. He's driving me insane with his pointless quotas. I'm not sure how much longer I can stay there."

This is all old news, as I know Lexy is going to get her brokerage license in a few years and break out on her own into commercial real estate. Her new company is going to land some of the biggest deals Bonnet Hill has ever seen. I'm a little jealous of future Lexy's success, but she's promised to bring me on when she expands the company. Besides, before we were colleagues, we were friends, and it is so difficult to make mom friends. I'm not exactly an extrovert, so it's not like I had that many before Eadie was born. From the moment I met Lexy at the day care holiday party, she's provided the commentary to my internal thoughts, saying the things I was no doubt thinking but far too buttoned-up to mention aloud.

"I don't understand why she asked us to help if she was planning to do it all herself," Lexy whispered, referring to the room mother, who had hand stitched twenty-two little personalized stocking ornaments. "I mean, what is she trying to prove? There's no award for self-sacrifice, lady."

"I mean, it's pretty amazing she did this all by herself. It's all very . . . resourceful," I said, not wanting to throw the poor woman under the bus, especially considering I'd only signed up to bring canned frosting. But Lexy was right. The cranberry-popcorn garland and six dozen homemade snowflake cookies took the whole thing to another level. I could never manage snowflakes without losing a few of the appendages.

"So is homesteading, but you don't see me over here raising chickens." A tiny smile crept across her face. "I'm Lexy, by the way," she said, extending a hand.

"Audrey," I supplied. "It looks like our daughters are BFFs now." I pointed to Eadie, who was whispering a secret in Payton's ear. When they noticed us staring, the two of them dissolved into a fit of giggles, drawing a smile to my lips. My heart settled. I'd been so worried that my oldest child would be like I was at that age—terrified of making eye contact with anyone who might want to engage in conversation. But Eadie proved to be different. There's nothing quite like seeing my offspring succeed at a social skill that even now eludes me. Fortunately, with Lexy, I've never had to carry the conversation. It always unfolds like a spool of thread, never complicated or forced. Since that day, the four of us have been inseparable. The fact that she is standing in front of me feels like a gift, and I'm not ready to let her out of my sight.

"Speaking of work," Lexy says, tearing her gaze from Ruby, "I can't wait until you're back in the office."

"You won't have to wait much longer," I say without a second thought. "I have an open house on Sunday."

Travis cuts me a look. I can tell he is completely flabbergasted by my shift in plans. "You do? You didn't mention that to me."

"I'm mentioning it now," I say, like it is completely normal to return to work a mere week and a half after giving birth. I suppose in America, it actually is. But Travis has a point. I had arranged to be home with the baby for twelve weeks. We cobbled together a childcare plan, deciding to hold off on day care until the spring to offset my loss of income. I have no idea how we are going to handle both kids while I make this sale, but I'll figure something out.

"You can't be serious," Travis insists. "Ruby is awake at all hours of the night, and you're exhausted. Besides, I'm supposed to go back to my classroom next week. How are both of us going to manage work right now with an infant? This isn't what we planned."

None of this is what I planned, but I suppose we all have to make sacrifices for the greater good. Maybe if Travis were more supportive of my work, I could be as successful as Lexy. Her husband, Sterling, is pretty much an equal parent in every respect. For Payton's fifth birthday—a *Fancy Nancy*–themed tea party—he made almond macarons that were to die for, even if Travis shoved three of them in his mouth and complained they were dry. "There's an open house for the property in Thornwood Estates. I have to be there."

"But I've already cleared my morning for that," Lexy tries in her sweet lilt. "I was planning to show that property for you. It's no problem, hon."

Her tone is sympathetic. And while I'm grateful for her thoughtfulness, I can't let this opportunity pass me by knowing what it could mean for my commission. As long as I'm stuck here, I might as well turn a profit. If I am going insane, it might take a lot of doctors and money to fix my broken brain.

"Thanks, but I've got it. I'm actually . . . kind of excited about it."

Lexy looks uncertain, and Travis's eyes go wide and glassy. I feel a little guilty for switching gears on him without warning. But after I sell a $2 million home, Travis will come around.

And just like always, he will see that I was right.

CHAPTER 17

Sunday Morning

I wake up early in the throes of a fitful nightmare. An angry helicopter is swooping down, its propellers threatening to decapitate me as I attempt to run away, tripping over my feet. When my eyes flutter open, I clock the source of the engine. Travis is breathing at the ceiling, open mouthed. In the three short months we were separated, I grew accustomed to a noiseless sleep. I'll have to rustle up a pair of earplugs if I hope to survive another night next to him.

Silently, I slip out of bed and pluck Ruby from the bassinet in our room. We settle in the rocking chair nestled in the corner, and I nurse her, an archaic ritual I thought was behind me. Yet these are the moments when I feel the true necessity of my existence in this alternate dimension. If my hungry baby wriggling against my chest is my new reality, if there is no going back to the way things were, then I will not fail my children. I won't allow a future where the helpless bundle in my arms doesn't grow to be every bit the vivacious, fearless, and annoyingly opinionated child she is meant to become.

As I study the way Ruby pulls her tiny eyebrows together in frustration, trying to latch, a core memory crystallizes. It is the same pouty face she pulled at her first swimming lesson at the Y, when she refused to get in the water and boldly announced that she didn't need to learn to swim because she had "fwoaties." It took weeks before she dipped a toe in the pool. At the end of the summer, Travis and I were equally thrilled when she finally dared to bury her nose in the water and blow bubbles. We celebrated like idiots, clapping and hollering until the other parents looked on with quizzical expressions, their toddlers all dog-paddling in confident circles around them. Travis always said that because Ruby had come into the world early, on her own terms, she couldn't be bothered to operate on anyone else's timetable. On this one point, I happen to agree with him.

The memory makes me homesick for a life I'm not sure was ever truly mine, and hot tears prick my eyes. How is it possible to miss a person so much while I'm holding the fragile weight of her in my arms? Ruby is here, pressed against my bosom, but she is not the same ruddy-cheeked, gap-toothed girl I have to goad into the car every single morning. *Slow as continental drift.* I can almost feel my heart sighing. That version of her is lost somewhere in a future that is growing harder to hold in my imagination, the colors slowly bleaching out.

Willow must sense my tangled emotions, because she lets out a soft whine from where she lies near the foot of the rocker, pulling me out of my reverie. While Travis sleeps through nearly all our nursing sessions, Willow seems tethered to me by an invisible thread, dutifully rising when she hears me wake at all hours of the night. As soon as my feet brush the floor, I can hear the gentle rustle of her limbs shifting, like she's been summoned for a very important job that cannot be managed without her presence, and if I'm being honest, I think she is right about that. Just having her here gives me just enough fortitude to steel myself for whatever future lies ahead.

I tear my gaze from Ruby and wipe the tears away, deciding that I will not dawdle away the hours in my memory. I need to focus on what I can control, so I tug out my cracked phone and use the blessed moments of silence to brush up on the Thornwood Estates property.

Ruby emits tiny, adorable gurgling sounds that make me rethink my decision for a split second. But as I caress her sticky cheek with the back of my hand, I remind myself that I'm doing this for her and her big sister. If I can't count on this marriage to last, I need to step up and guarantee the financial security of this family. Gingerly, I lift her to my chest and cup a palm to her soft, squishy backside, taking an extra moment between pats to breathe in her glorious baby scent until it reaches the tips of me. If I'd known how much I would miss the smell of a freshly bathed infant, I would have paid good money to bottle it up. But maybe it's a good thing I forgot. The last thing Travis and I needed was another baby. Throwing a third kid into the mix most definitely would have hastened our separation. I shake the thought away as I rise from the rocker, then carefully lower Ruby into the bassinet.

"Don't worry," Travis groans as he rolls over to face me. His hair is mussed, and his rough-shaven cheek bears the imprint of the ruched throw pillow. He flashes me a crooked smile and a not-particularly-comforting thumbs-up. "I've got this, babe."

"I know." A lie. He most definitely does not. Case in point: Yesterday, I escaped to Walgreens for twenty minutes under the guise of needing nursing pads because I knew he wouldn't ask questions. What I'd really needed was a good cry in the car, but I couldn't even do that properly, because I'd only just made it out of the driveway when a frantic Travis called to ask where *we* keep the baby wipes. As if the damned Huggies aren't neatly stacked in the electric warmer on the changing table his sister gifted us. Where they always are. As if I—jealous, sleep-deprived mother that I am—might be hoarding all the wipes in a secret location because I leap at the chance to change every single dirty diaper myself. It isn't enough that I have to keep a running mental tabulation of how much milk is in the fridge; or how much longer Eadie can get by in her shoes before I need to drag her, kicking and screaming, to a Payless; or how many weeks it's been since we've changed the sheets. I must also catalog every minute piece of information that remotely affects anyone in this family *and* be ready to dispense that knowledge at any given moment.

Gathering my fortitude, I head to my closet to find an outfit that is classy but breathable—i.e., something that says *I sell mansions*. But that is also stretchy. I wrinkle my nose at the tapered pants hanging along the bottom rung and finally decide on a billowy sundress that hugs the top of my rib cage. After a quick shower, I manage to transform myself from tired, milk-stained, pineapple-muumuu mom into slightly-less-tired mom in a floral midi dress that conceals my postpregnancy belly.

But my revitalized appearance doesn't seem to reassure Travis. As we study my results in the mirror gracing the back of our door, he drops his head and lumbers out of the bed, circling around to the end, where he plants himself on the mattress. "You sure you're ready for this?" he asks, trailing a finger down my biceps. "You don't have to go back to work yet. Why the sudden rush?"

The warmth of his touch makes my skin prickle, but I resist the urge to melt against his bare chest as I have a thousand times before. I'm not falling into that trap again, the lure of those liquid blue eyes and lumberjack hands that know the precise amount of pressure to apply to my lower back. If I let him have his way, he will make my knees go all wobbly, and I'll never get out of here. Chemistry has never been the problem with me and Travis. It's biology that will do us in. While my DNA is hardwired to make lists and tick tasks and pin things to my inspiration board, Travis moves about the world with more of a *what will be will be* approach. It's that kind of recklessness that once cost me Willow, and I won't allow him to muddle my thoughts today, of all days.

"I'm ready to get back into the swing of things, and this could be a great opportunity for me . . . for us," I add, feeling slightly guilty. "If I can prove to Harlow that I can sell this house, that I can cater to a more exclusive clientele, it could open up my career."

Travis blows out his cheeks and shakes his head. He pulls a hand to the back of his neck and rubs it, unable to meet my eyes. "OK," he finally says, throwing a wistful glance at Ruby in her bassinet. "If this is what you want, I'll support you one hundred percent." He pulls a tight smile, then clicks his tongue in a way that means he is about to tell me something that will annoy me. "But this means we're going to have to circle back to that thing you said we could never talk about again."

There is a long list of topics I refuse to discuss with Travis. Whether it's acceptable to reuse dental floss, whether 1 percent milk is any less nutritious than whole, whether the song played for our first dance should have been Queen's "Somebody to Love" instead of Etta James's "At Last." But from the look on his face, I gather he isn't referring to any of these topics, so I dare to ask, "And what would that be?"

"My parents," he says with a wince. "You said we couldn't depend on them for help, but you know as well as I do that the day care won't take Ruby before six weeks, and I've got to go back to work tomorrow. I've had two substitutes quit already, and my students can only watch *The Sound of Music* so many times. Principal Phillips is breathing down my neck about lesson plans. It's easier if I'm just there." *Easier for whom?* He drops his gaze and lowers his voice. "I might have mentioned to my mother that we could use their help."

"You what?" My brain has gone fuzzy, but I'm pretty sure Travis has just admitted to inviting company into our home. Lillian and Bill live in Florida, which means they will be staying with us for an indeterminate length of time. What's worse, they will bring their tiny ill-tempered dog, a chiweenie named Alfred, who has an underbite and barks at the doorbell and viciously guards Willow's favorite toys. Though he's around the same age as Willow, Alfred has always seemed old to me, the sort of scrappy, invincible creature destined to outlive his owners and inherit a trust fund.

Here's the thing. I adore Travis's parents. Lillian is maternal in a way my mother never was, the sort of mom who still proudly displays the macaroni jewelry box her son glued together in the second grade. She makes the best chicken-fried steak and mashed potatoes I've ever tasted and sends a check for twenty dollars in the mail every year on my birthday. Where my mother was entirely unhelpful after Eadie was born, only dropping by the hospital to awkwardly deliver a stuffed giraffe, Lillian was a godsend. She and Bill swooped in and stayed for two weeks, taking nighttime shifts with the baby and whipping up soul-warming dinners. But they were still two extra people in our home—two people nesting in our living room on a lopsided air mattress. Lillian woke early every morning, greeting the crack of dawn with the tinkling of dishes and pans, while Bill operated his phone at full volume on our couch, slowly pecking out birth announcements to his ten thousand relatives, stopping every so often to yell out a question. "Lillian, how do I send one of them little picture things?"

"You mean a GIF," she hollered from the kitchen over the sound of running water.

"I mean a picture. Like that dancing squirrel you sent for my birthday."

"For heaven's sake, Bill. The baby's sleeping!" she shouted, like a person intent on waking a sleeping baby.

It was entirely too many people in our home—two too many, to be exact. When I got pregnant with Ruby, I politely declined their offer to visit, at least for a few months. We were able to stave them off until Christmas. Now, the prospect of hosting my in-laws makes my head swirl. Even so, they've always been supportive of our little family in their own chaotic way, and there is a part of me that aches at the realization that I might be divorcing them as well.

"It just . . . came out," Travis says, looking desperate. "I don't know. You said you wanted to go back to work, and it hasn't even been two weeks, and I . . . I panicked, OK?"

"So instead of talking through your concerns with your wife, you called your mother?"

"That's not fair, Audrey." The regret in his voice gives way to irritation. He runs both hands through his hair. "You sprang this on me out of nowhere, when we had a plan. Besides, my mom wants to help."

"That isn't the point," I shoot back. "You made a unilateral decision without consulting me."

A gruff laugh escapes his chest. "And you're one to talk? You just decided to go back to work without informing me. In front of Lexy, no less. And what about all your crazy rules. No eating in bed, and no shoes in the house, and you have to flush on both number ones and number twos now."

He has a point about the first part, but the latter makes my head swim. I pinch the skin between my eyes, trying to process the accusation. These are not *crazy* or *new* rules, by any stretch of the imagination. And no matter how much I strain my hearing, I cannot connect the dots.

But Travis is not deterred. "And remember when you went to that hippie mindfulness class with Lexy and just decided that we don't eat pork anymore?" He points to his chest as if he is the victim of some grave injustice. "I happen to love pork."

"That's not the same thing!" I proclaim, a little too loudly, then throw a furtive glance at Ruby, who flutters her eyes briefly before drifting off to sleep again. I inhale a long, shaky breath and draw upon my rapidly depleting reserve of patience. "Please call your mother back, and tell her we're fine," I say, more in control, even though I could not be further from fine. I can't even see fine. In fact, *fine* is a state of being I'm not sure I will ever experience again. Now I wish I enjoyed when things were fine when they actually were, instead of wishing things were great.

"For now, I just need you to keep everyone safe." But by everyone, I really mean Willow. As if on cue, she sneaks over from her perch by the rocker and noses my thigh, reminding me that she should be at the top of my priority list, and I can't lose sight of that. When she buries her face in my dress, I bend down and run my hands over her fur, finding the light stripe down her smooth back. As I do every morning, I calculate the time I have left before her accident. *Four days.* Every detail about that evening is carved into my hippocampus, forever casting a shadow over any joyful moment I might experience in the next five years. "And don't let Willow outside," I add with an edge. Four days or not, I don't want to tempt fate. "I'm serious, Travis. I'll walk her myself when I get back."

I don't mean for it to come out rude, but my thoughts pulse with snatches of her last moments—Willow's broken body crumpled in the street, the thin trail of crimson seeping from her floppy ear as it lay open on the hot asphalt, the skidding of tires, and the pathetic plea in her soft whines. I press my eyes shut to block out the sound and try to convince myself that I can prevent it all. What's more, Willow was only seven when she died, in the prime of her life. She could live well into her senior years, maybe even into her teens. She would be there when Ruby starts preschool and when Eadie learns to throw a softball. The thought sends a wave of euphoria through my heart, because in this new future, my best friend will live. Even if my marriage is still going to die.

CHAPTER 18

A tiny seed of doubt blossoms in my sternum when a stone monument bearing the words **Thornwood Estates** rolls into view. At the neighborhood entrance, I'm stopped by a portly guard who asks to see my identification. He squints at my driver's license photo, then raises a stern eyebrow and takes down my plate numbers, a subtle reminder I don't belong here. Given that it is Sunday, he must conclude I am not part of the help and seems genuinely perplexed by my presence, but he returns my license and waves me through the gate anyway, training his eyes on my dusty bumper as I roll out of sight.

Making the turn into the neighborhood, I take in the scenery, so very different from my own modest but eclectic street. On these lanes, every house tells the same story, and it is one of wealth and privilege, the kind of security that has always been out of reach for me and Travis. Here, there are no cars parked on curbs, no sticky children playing outside, no garage sale signs or advertisements for lost pets. Each manicured yard bears the evidence of an expert lawn-care team. It seems the grass really is greener in this part of Bonnet Hill. It grows in neat, even rows, and matronly trees are trimmed like carefully pruned stalks of broccoli.

When I reach the roundabout at the dead end, my listing appears on a thick carpet of vibrant emerald, the crown jewel of the neighborhood, with its sweeping turrets and window boxes overflowing with petunias and English ivy. It's stunning, even more beautiful than I remember and somehow statelier than the professionally taken photographs suggest. The previous owner is a retired player from the Dallas Cowboys who "needed" a larger garage to accommodate his growing Maserati collection. Considering that I'm still a relative newbie at Harlow Realty, I'm a bit flabbergasted that my surly boss has afforded me the opportunity to sell this place—five thousand square feet of unparalleled luxury, no doubt an anomaly for Bonnet Hill. He must know the cards are stacked against me. But if I can make some headway today with potential buyers, who knows what the future may hold for my career?

When I pull into the sage-lined driveway, I'm keenly aware that my bedraggled Honda doesn't exactly project an air of confidence or success. This morning, I discovered a sippy cup beneath the passenger seat that had been festering for days and an explosion of Froot Loops in the back seat.

With my dress blowing in the breeze, I circle the house, traversing flagstone pavers that lead to the stately wraparound porch. The listing is so new, it doesn't have a lockbox yet, but I swung by the office to pick up a key. When the door groans open, I'm greeted by soaring ceilings trimmed in thick mahogany beams and matching hand-scraped wood floors. Notes of pine and citrus follow as I make my way through the seemingly endless living space and pull up the shades on the floor-to-ceiling windows. When I reach the chef's kitchen, I rest my things on the immaculate marble counter and conclude that no one has ever cooked a meal on this eight-burner gas stove. Such a tragedy.

How often had Travis and I perused the aisles of Home Depot, daydreaming about renovating Grandma Beatrice's ancient kitchen? To put our stamp on it and make it truly ours. I conjure late-night conversations cuddled in bed as we toyed with installing an island where the girls could eat their frozen waffles in the morning and finish homework after school. There was a time when I did enjoy cuddling in bed, I suppose. Predictably, he had preferred the slightly cheaper quartz countertops, while I insisted on a light granite. But none of it mattered. Anytime we managed to save a little money, some new catastrophe would arise—squirrels in the attic, a burned-out water heater, an HVAC system that went kaput in the fiery pit of summer. It would have taken more than paint and Sheetrock and new tile to fix what had broken between Travis and me. Maybe history can be repeated, but it can't be erased.

By some miracle, I've managed to arrive early, so I meander up the stairs, through the seven bedrooms and five and a half bathrooms. I'm busily opening up closets and turning on lights when I hear the front door snap shut, and the faint echo of footsteps emerges from somewhere down below. A fresh batch of nerves awakens in my stomach, but I refuse to be intimidated. Not now. I did not go hurtling backward through time and give birth—again—not even two weeks ago only to fail now. *This is it. Pull it together, Audrey.* I draw in a calming breath and close my eyes, then head toward the noise. As I descend the staircase, I feel a bit like a Disney princess readying myself for my big moment. But my excitement quickly wilts when I spot a wiry-haired woman in a brown velvet tracksuit and running shoes nosing around the fireplace. She looks like a speed walker who's popped inside for a restroom break.

"I hope it's OK I let myself in," she says. "I saw the signs and thought what the hell. Always wanted to know if this place has a better steam shower than ours."

And just like that, my hopes are dashed. She pokes around for a few more minutes, inspecting the bathrooms and "disappointing" wine cellar before announcing that the house isn't as ostentatious as the outside led her to believe. Apparently satisfied, she slips out the door. Her departure seems to spur a trickle of activity. A few other curious neighbors drift through, also lured by the semifamous seller. I hear their whispered gossip as they float through each room, nodding along, unimpressed when I brightly offer up the facts I've memorized.

When they leave, I shore up my certainty, trying to convince myself that the perfect buyer will walk through the door, that my trip to the past has to be for a reason, and maybe that reason is to pocket a huge chunk of change that could drastically shift the course of my life. I stare out the window, certain that a sports car will materialize in the drive.

And then it does.

I blink a few times to be sure I haven't imagined it. But if my eyes are to be trusted, a yellow Porsche is rolling toward me. When the engine purrs to a stop, a young couple emerges, and it takes every ounce of energy to tamp down my smile. I don't want to scare them away.

"Welcome," I say, motioning them over the threshold with a Vanna White imitation I immediately regret. "My name is Audrey, and I'd be happy to help you with any questions about the home." My voice comes out high and syrupy, as if it's been hijacked by a teenager.

"Thanks," the man says, though he doesn't seem especially thankful. He has a lean build and wears a creaseless sports shirt and sunglasses. His topknot doesn't scream *businessman*, but the tall blonde at his side is sporting a CHANEL handbag and a glittery tennis bracelet, so I gather someone in this relationship has deep pockets. I wonder if they've made their fortune in tech, maybe created one of those apps I should have invested in five years ago. If we'd had any extra money lying around.

"Feel free to explore," I say, trailing behind as they wander the space. "Every appliance is top of the line, and there are en suite bathrooms in every bedroom. Oh, and of course, the backyard has a heated pool and spa, abounding with flora and fauna—an absolute oasis." *Abounding with flora and fauna?* I don't think I've ever used the word *abounding* before in conversation with another human, and I worry I'm beginning to sound like a virtual assistant. I'm sure these people can tell I'm entirely out of my element. Even so, I can't seem to stem the tide of words evacuating my mouth. "I'm not sure if you're aware that Thornwood Estates was voted the safest subdivision in Bonnet Hill for the third year in a row, which is a huge plus if you've got kids." *Stop. Trying. So. Hard.*

"We don't," the man replies flatly.

The words scald me, and I'm not sure how I'm supposed to respond. But I shove down my uneasiness and forge ahead, pointing out the ornate detail in the custom kitchen cabinetry and the fully automated security system.

"I mean, honestly, you can't find West Coast style like this anywhere in North Texas. There's a butler's pantry here and a climate-controlled wine cellar."

"Technically, that's a wet bar," the man says, gesturing. "You mislabeled it online. Which is unfortunate."

The observation dampens my resolve. It's not the sort of mistake Lexy would make, and even if she had, she would know what to say to reel this couple back in. But all I do is mumble something about website malfunctions.

"I was hoping for something a little more spacious," he goes on dryly. "My girlfriend and I entertain often, and this setup just isn't going to suit us." I wonder what kind of schmancy events these people are hosting as I recall the last party Travis and I threw, a casual Super Bowl gathering last February, before our relationship went completely off the rails. It was only Lexy's family and Travis's bandmates, Marcus and Dane, but the stress of feeding six people was enough to spark an argument about the jalapeño poppers I'd neglected to pick up from the store. As it had been Travis's idea to host the party in the first place, I pointed out that perhaps he should have bought his own damn poppers and suggested where he might shove them. Admittedly, it was, hands down, the dumbest argument we've ever had, and I was embarrassed for Lexy to witness the magnitude of our marital dysfunction. "I had no idea things were this bad between you guys," she whispered when we were alone in the kitchen. "Do you want me to put you in touch with a good lawyer?" she offered, eyeing me with pity. And even though I waved away her concern, for the first time, I allowed the thought of divorce to wedge a foot in the back door of my mind.

"It's cute," the woman says, pulling me back to the present, or past, or whenever this damn moment existed in the space-time continuum. "But I think we were looking for something a bit more . . . contemporary."

As this home was entirely renovated a few short months ago, I'm not sure exactly what they were expecting. I sweep my brain for facts about the property, hoping for some nugget of information that will make it appear futuristic, but at the end of the day, no matter how many bathrooms it boasts, this is just a house. And I know all too well that when a potential client looks at me the way this woman is now, there is nothing I can say to change their mind. Feeling out houses is a bit like dating. When a buyer steps into their forever home, they just . . . know.

When the couple has seen quite enough, they make a graceful, if somewhat icy, exit. "Thanks for stopping by," I call after them. When they're gone, I close the door and lean my shoulders against it, letting my head roll back in defeat. My breasts are sore, my feet are aching, and I'm no closer to making this sale than I was five years ago. I look down at my chest. Three hours have passed, and I've ended my morning the same way it began. Leaking. Ruby must be starving by now. As am I. My stomach growls with the rabid kind of hunger that only comes from nursing a ravenous baby. It feels like a tapeworm has established residency in my gut, stealing my life force and my patience.

I look outside, and the driveway is empty. It appears my prospects for the morning have all come and gone, so I trudge outside and pluck the OPEN HOUSE sign and stuff it into my trunk. I need to call Travis and tell him I'll be home shortly, but when I reach into my purse for my cell, it's not there. I've left it on the counter right next to—

A jolt of panic courses through my veins. *The key.* I left it in the kitchen. *Stupid. Stupid. Stupid.* My stomach grows queasy contemplating my short list of options. I can venture over to a neighbor's house, but I'm not sure if rich people lend cell phones to unknown persons in battered Hondas. Or I could drive back to the entrance and ask the scary security guard for help. Neither of these options appeal to me, so I circle the property, wondering if perhaps there's another way inside. Surely, people in Thornwood Estates don't lock *all* their doors.

But it turns out, they do. Because after a thorough inspection, I'm forced to admit that every possible entrance to this place is sealed.

Briefly, I contemplate scaling the balcony, but I've never been particularly limber. And with my luck, the upstairs windows are probably locked.

Just as I'm about to make my way across the street, a black Mercedes pulls into view.

I watch with curiosity as a trim man wearing dark-wash jeans and a white blazer hops out of the car.

"Are you the agent?" he calls out, approaching me. He removes his sunglasses and tucks them in his jacket, and I'm immobilized by a flurry of strange sensations. Julian Mitchell is staring back at me. The man who flirted with me just days ago. Was he flirting, or did I imagine it? His brown eyes are kind and his smile hypnotic. It makes me forget how to form words with my mouth, so I mumble some nonsensical syllables that are supposed to be *Yes, I'm Audrey* but instead come out as "Yessum oddly."

"I'm sorry, did you say your name is Oddly?"

"Audrey," I correct, way too loudly. Then, as I realize I've just shouted at him, I fold my arms across my chest to hide the milk stains.

"Perfect. Sorry I'm late, but I've had a hell of a time getting here from the city, and I'm only in town for the week. Any chance I can persuade you to stay a little longer?"

Color returns to my cheeks, only to drain again when I remember the inconvenient fact that I have no way of letting this man inside. My shoulders sink with my spirits. "I'm afraid I've locked myself out, and to make matters worse, I've also left my cell phone inside. I know that probably sounds made up, but I swear it's the truth."

"You're right. It does sound made up." He's deadpan, making me squirm in my flats. Even so, there's a playfulness about his tone and that familiar flicker of sarcasm in his eyes that eases my worry. "But you're just normal-looking enough to make me want to help you, Oddly." The corners of his lips turn up, and he flashes a suave wink. This is perhaps the least flattering compliment I have ever received, and yet it validates me in a way he cannot possibly understand. *I AM normal. I am not crazy. My brain is not broken.* He slips his phone into my palm and flashes a wide grin. "I'm Julian," he says. "I'm happy to wait for you until the cavalry arrives."

Little does Julian know, *he* is my cavalry, my knight in shining Armani shoes, who has single-handedly salvaged my morning, hopefully in more ways than one. Judging from his choice of transportation, and what I already know about him, he is just the sort of person who would thrive in a house like this one.

I thank him profusely and accept the sleek iPhone, then dial Lexy's number. When it rings a few times, a nagging worry creeps in, and I will her to pick up. Lexy's number is one of two I know by heart, and I really don't want to call Travis, as it would only affirm his opinion that I'm taking on too much, too soon. Besides, it's company policy to keep an extra key of each listing at the office for emergencies, and Lexy knows this. On the fourth ring, Lexy answers, and my chest finally loosens. "Thank God," I exhale. Then, moving out of Julian's earshot, I quickly explain that she is my only salvation and while I don't want to pressure her, a lot of money is on the line. "If this buyer slips through because of a stupid mistake like this, I will never forgive myself," I whisper.

"Relax babe," Lexy says in her easy way. "I've got you. I'll be there in twenty."

"Oh, and bring a sweater," I add, remembering my other, messier predicament. I'm grateful she doesn't question the latter, but that's Lexy. If I asked her to show up with a gallon of bleach and a shovel, she'd bring a tarp just in case.

"Look, I'm not trying to tell you how to live your life," Lexy says in a tone that tells me she is most definitely about to disprove that statement, "but maybe this is the universe telling you that you shouldn't be out selling houses right now. You should be home with your adorable baby."

I concede she may have a point. At the moment, however, I'm extremely unhappy with the universe. The universe owes me a win. When I return Julian's phone, our hands graze for the briefest moment, and a flicker of familiar excitement pulses through me. For the first time this morning, I think maybe something good is finally on the horizon.

Julian Mitchell looks like a win to me.

CHAPTER 19

I check my watch discreetly, then throw a confident smile at Julian perched beside me on the granite porch steps. We're far enough apart to avoid any awkward accidental touching, but the late-morning air is heavy with expectation. Hopefully, he doesn't view this mistake as representative of my professional abilities. I've never done something so careless, and I decide that the temporary amnesia is merely a side effect of time travel.

Julian lets out a long sigh, which I take as a cue to fill the excruciating silence. "If you don't mind my asking," I say, plucking up my courage, "what is it that brings you to Bonnet Hill?" I'm pretty sure I know the answer, but I pretend to be completely ignorant about his recent divorce.

He relaxes a little and leans back on his elbows. "I'm a property developer for a firm outside of Atlanta," he says, "but my ex grew up here, and she wants to move home to help her father out. He's getting older and was just diagnosed with Parkinson's, so I can't really fault her."

My skin prickles with curiosity. Wealthy, attractive, *and* compassionate. "So, you're moving to be closer to your kids?"

"You're very astute, aren't you?" he says, eyeing me with a hint of distrust. "Never told you I had any."

My confidence careens on a downward spiral. Hopefully he doesn't think I'm a stalker.

Before I can decide how to respond, he pulls out his phone and flashes a picture of his boys. I recognize Malachi immediately, five years younger but still every bit the adorable kid I remember. An older boy with scrawny limbs and braces wraps an arm around him in a side hug. Julian shrugs. "I don't plan to leave Atlanta anytime soon. But it would be nice to have my own place when I come to visit them. It's hard to be a dad when you only have them weekends and summers."

"I see," I say, knowing that Julian will not only decide to move to Bonnet Hill but will bring new business the likes of which our postage-stamp town has never seen. A persistent thought tugs at the fringes of my mind. It's probably an overstep, but knowing what I know, I would be a worthless Realtor not to seize the opportunity. I take a long breath. "And have you ever thought about developing any properties here in Bonnet Hill? We may be a small suburb now, but businesses are growing by leaps and bounds." This may be a tad hyperbolic, but it doesn't *have to be* an untrue statement, especially if Julian Mitchell were to invest a few of his millions. Which he will, with or without my help. Of course, I'll have to expand my certification, invest in myself to be an effective liaison, but I've got time.

He cuts me a grin that makes my heart skitter a beat. "You are quite the saleswoman." Then, running a hand through his close-shaved hair, he adds, "Actually, I have toyed with the idea, but I've got too many projects as it is. I can't manage a permanent move right now, but it certainly isn't out of the question down the road." My stomach flutters with the possibility, making me temporarily forget about my imaginary tapeworm. I can tell I've lit a spark in his mind, and for now, that's enough.

When Lexy finally pulls up in her SUV, I practically fly to meet her. "Thank you thank you thank you," I say, pressing my hands together as I close the distance between us.

"Hey, what are best friends for?" With a proud smile, she reaches into her tote and passes me a coral knit sweater, followed by a shiny silver key, the only thing standing between me and this sale. Because I know once Julian tours the house, I can sell him on it. And then, if I'm lucky, I could snag him as a client for future deals. Grateful, I pull the sweater over my head.

"So, how's it going?" she asks, clocking Julian on the steps.

I try to manage my excitement, but my smile is officially out of control. I throw a quick glance back and offer a polite wave before returning my focus to Lexy. "I don't want to get my hopes up, but this guy could be my golden goose."

"Seriously? Way to go." Nudging my shoulder, she gives him another once-over. "Cute too," she notes appreciatively. Then, redirecting her sights on me, she straightens and says, "OK, what do we say when opportunity knocks at the door?"

The answer is so familiar that the words roll right off my lips. "Network to net worth." Lexy forces me to repeat this mantra whenever I'm feeling crappy about my productivity. Usually, I begrudgingly humor her, but today, I am 100 percent drunk on the Kool-Aid.

She flashes a wink and squeezes my hand. "You got this, babe."

And with a vote of confidence from my best friend, I think maybe I actually do.

~

After we've toured the entire property from top to bottom, Julian clasps his hands. "It's a great house," he says as I lock the door. "Let me do some thinking, and I'll get back to you."

A broad smile catches fire across my face. "Wonderful. Let me just get you my information," I say, rummaging around my purse for a business card. He accepts it with a kind smile, studying the less-than-flattering photo I had Travis snap with his cell.

Finally, he leans forward conspiratorially, as if something has just occurred to him. When he looks at me, there is a flash of possibility in his eyes that sends a ripple of heat up my neck. "Tell you what. Let's discuss it over drinks. Tomorrow night?"

The undercurrent of flirtation is unmistakable. "Tomorrow?" My mouth goes dry. The prospect of being alone in a bar with an undeniably attractive, successful, and by all accounts single man makes my pulse race. If he asked me the same question five years ago, before everything with Travis went south, I would have said no. I would have thanked Julian Mitchell profusely and politely suggested a more professional setting to avoid any confusing signals. But that was then. The real Audrey, the one floating somewhere in the outer banks of the cosmos, is separated from a man who might already be dating a mysterious musical vixen named Jamie. That has to count for something. Doesn't it? Besides, I'm not planning to fall into bed with the guy, just get him to like me. Get him to trust me enough to see I could be an asset to his business interests. And if he happens to bear a slight resemblance to Taye Diggs, is that a crime?

"Sure," I say, though it occurs to me that Travis will not be thrilled about an impromptu business meeting, which is exactly what I plan to call it. Though there's absolutely no reason to tell him who the meeting is with. He has meetings all the time with his superior. Alone. Principal Phillips is happily married and old enough to be a member of Beatrice's bridge club, but that's beside the point. Aside from the fact that I don't even remember how to flirt, I *have* recently shoved a person out of my body, and I've never felt less appealing. I'm sure Julian isn't thinking of me that way.

"Great," Julian says, his eyes holding mine. There's something in his expression I can't quite decipher, and the subtle tilt of his head makes me curious. Finally, I tear away my gaze, and a flutter of anticipation surges through my middle, immediately followed by a fresh pang of guilt. Over the course of my marriage, I have been many things—a good pretender when things were bad, a meticulous worrier when things were good. But I've never been a cheater or even entertained the thought of betraying Travis. So, I steel myself. This will be a business meeting, and Julian Mitchell is a potential client. Nothing more.

CHAPTER 20

When I arrive home, I'm buzzing. If I can't get my old life back, I suppose I'll just have to start from scratch and build a better one. The way things are going, I might even prefer this version, starring a handsome property mogul who miraculously seems to have taken a shine to me. I am determined to close this deal.

When I hang my purse near the door, I note the house is unusually quiet, and a sliver of worry creeps in. I refrain from calling out in case the girls are asleep and pad softly through the entryway to the living room.

And that's when I see them.

Still wearing his Christmas tree pajama pants, Travis is splayed across the couch, hugging a throw pillow to his chest. It rises and falls with each rhythmic breath. Willow is curled on the floor, her paws dripping in neon pink. With watery eyes, she looks at me helplessly, as if to say *I'm so sorry.* And there, at Travis's feet, is Eadie, wielding an open bottle of nail polish. She bites her bottom lip adorably as she attempts to paint his toenails with unsteady strokes. But Travis twitches each time she makes contact, and the bottle jostles precariously in her tiny fist.

With a thousand-watt smile, Eadie beams proudly and says, "He's pretty now, Mommy." Her blond curls are wild, sticking out every which way, and her princess pajama top is missing. She looks a bit feral.

It takes every ounce of restraint to resist making a scene. I grit my teeth as I slowly approach them. "He certainly is, honey." Gently, I confiscate the sticky bottle and add, "But you're not supposed to do this without help." I hid my scant collection of nail polish for this very reason. I imagine our four-year-old scaling the tower of cabinets that flank my bathroom vanity, and a shudder ripples through me. A fall from that height could have resulted in a trip to the emergency room! How long has Travis been out? "Where is your shirt?" I ask, afraid to know the answer.

"I gots the paint on it," she admits with a frown. A reasonable action to take, considering her bare chest is splattered in what looks to be a Zorro-like signature. Has she attempted to paint on a necklace? I take in the damage with calm, measured breaths even though a voice in my brain is screaming *This is not OK!* Not only has Eadie painted everyone's nails, including Willow's, she's also painted the rug. The couch. The handcrafted, one-of-a-kind end table I'd scored at a flea market. And the wall. Our living room resembles a cave with primitive drawings of stick people holding strange alien shapes I can't decipher. My brain goes into triage mode and filters through a list of possible removal options when Ruby stirs in the baby swing. And that's when I notice her bright-pink fingertips—which she's seconds away from stuffing in her gummy mouth.

"Oh my God!" With lightning-fast reflexes, I whisk Ruby into my arms.

My outburst is loud enough to rouse Travis, and he jolts upright, rubbing the sleep away. "What happened?" His eyes go wide when he registers the neon pink smeared on his toes.

"You weren't watching them," I snap, restraining the baby's hands. "That's what happened." Ruby starts to wail.

His eyes flicker from his toes to Eadie to the bedazzled wall and then to me, and I can see the wheels of his brain slowly turning. He sweeps Eadie up in a frantic movement, and they follow me into the kitchen, where I run water over the baby's hands. "I accidentally fell asleep. Just for a minute," he says, stumbling over the words.

I shoot daggers at him, too annoyed to entertain this line of reasoning. Travis has always operated under the delusion that any mistake can be smoothed over by inserting the word *accidentally*.

"Clearly you were out for longer than a minute," I say, still seething as I work soap over Ruby's tiny hands. But it isn't working and only makes her cry louder. I'll have to dig around for some acetone; I'm not a toxin-free tyrant like Sonia, but the thought of defiling our infant with chemicals sends my head reeling.

"OK, maybe a few minutes," he admits, "but they're fine. Crisis averted." But the color has drained from his face, and I know he's just as terrified as me.

"This time!" I shout, because this is exactly the kind of thoughtless behavior that will steal Willow from me. As the date of her accident draws near, the less patience I seem to have with Travis. "Do you realize how high Eadie had to climb to get it? We're lucky she didn't break her neck. Not to mention, the stuff is poison. She could have ingested it or broken the bottle or—or . . . died!" I admit this part is a tad over the top, but when Travis looks at me the way he is looking at me now, like he can't understand why my face has turned the color of a tomato, I feel it's important to go to extremes. "I mean, what would have happened if Ruby swallowed it? Have you thought of that?"

Travis rolls his eyes, and the action alone flips a dangerous switch somewhere in my psyche. "Come on, Audrey. Nothing happened, OK. You're overreacting."

Few accusations ignite a fire in my belly like *You're overreacting*, and I feel the anger rise in my throat. "And why is that? Could it be that maybe I have to overcompensate?" It's true but harsh. My heart is still hammering in my chest, and the adrenaline has made me reckless with my words.

"Wow." Gaping at me, he shakes his head, resigned. "That's what you really think, huh?"

"It's not what I think, Travis. It's the truth. You get to be the fun one, and I get to be the evil witch who shuts everything down. Do you think I want to be this way?"

"Honestly"—he lifts his chin, challenging me to disagree—"yes. I think you love it when I screw up so you can tell me how I should have done it better. I think you thrive on being right all the time."

"So, you agree. I'm right?"

"No!" he blurts out. "You're a total control freak who doesn't trust me."

"Because I *can't* trust you!" I point out, breathless. "Let's face it. I'm the only reason the kids are alive!" He hangs his head, and there's a heavy pause. Briefly, I worry I've said too much. Speaking to him like this conjures the rice explosion—and the effective pause button on our marriage. In his arms, Eadie darts her eyes between Travis and me, her bottom lip quivering in a way that diffuses my anger. "I'm sowwy," she says, her tiny voice trembling. "I didn't mean to. It was a accident," she adds, stealing a line from Travis.

"It's OK, honey." I rein in my breathing and flash her a reassuring smile. This isn't her fault. It's Travis's fault. None of this would have happened if he had been paying attention. Still, maybe he is right about one thing. Maybe I've let my emotions get the better of me this time. But before I can walk back my verbal assault, he says, "Fine. Maybe I am a mess, but at least I'm not mean. Sometimes, Audrey, you talk to me like I'm . . . like I'm an idiot."

My pulse slows, subduing the rage in my veins. "I don't think you're an idiot. I just . . . I was scared, OK? And maybe I shouldn't have yelled at you," I admit, aware that Eadie is studying my every move. "But it's only because sometimes I feel like I can't depend on you."

The stretch of silence that follows spurs a prickle of guilt.

"I'm sorry," he finally says, his voice lower. "I shouldn't have fallen asleep. I won't let it happen again." There's a flicker of remorse in his expression that makes me almost believe him, but I only nod. Relief trickles through me, and I feel my chest lighten. Even though Travis can be out to lunch, I'm not ready for this marriage to go south. Not yet. Not until I make this epic sale. Besides, the prospect of navigating a break when I'm operating on a few hours of sleep and as the sole source of food for another human makes me dizzy. For better or worse, Travis and I need each other right now.

I take a deep breath, trying to focus on today's silver lining. I got a second "meeting" with the richest person I've ever met in real life. If I'm able to woo Julian, it could launch my career in ways I'd never imagined. Maybe money can't solve everything, but it can solve some things, make me less dependent on a husband who can't be trusted to stay awake while I'm away. At the very least, I could afford a Roomba. More importantly, I'd be in a better position to leave Travis. When the time comes. If the time comes.

As if reading my thoughts, Travis looks at me expectantly. "So," he asks, letting the pause linger, "how did the open house go?"

My sour mood ebbs, and a smile takes over my face. "Amazing." Remembering my morning with Julian, a thrill of excitement colors my cheeks, replacing resentment with hope. "I think I might have a buyer."

He seems impressed. "Wow, that's good news."

"Very good news," I affirm. And then, at the risk of more conflict, I broach tomorrow night. "I'm meeting them tomorrow evening to discuss an offer—maybe even potential business down the road."

"Tomorrow night?" His smile sags. I knew he wouldn't be thrilled about it, but I was hoping he'd understand.

"Yeah. Just for an hour or so. I won't be long." Considering the state of our living room and the fact that I was moments from calling Poison Control, I can't believe I'm asking Travis to solo parent again. But I can't afford to lose this client. Julian had shown real interest in the property and hinted at a possible business partnership. At least that's what I've convinced myself of.

"I can't," Travis says. "We've got a gig tomorrow night at the Crow's Feet."

"That's right," I say, realization dawning. "I forgot." I can't blame him for this one, because when I check my calendar, it is right there in bright green. Every Monday is band night. I'm probably imagining it, but he seems a little disappointed that I haven't remembered. Surely he wasn't expecting me to go see his set. Before Ruby was born, I would sometimes haul Eadie to whatever hole-in-the-wall restaurant hosted amateur nights. The two of us would order french fries and wave and blow kisses from the audience. It was a fun getaway back when I only had to wrangle one toddler, but I can't imagine exposing our newborn to amps and drums, let alone manage both kids.

"Well, then," I say, trying to muster confidence, "we'll just have to find someone who can babysit."

"Right." He snaps his fingers, as if a thought has just popped into his head. "Hey, you know what would have helped in this situation?"

"What?"

"My parents. But someone forced me to uninvite my mother, and I had to listen to her sobbing on the phone for half an hour." There's a smugness in his tone that makes me bristle, but he isn't wrong, so I resist the urge to become defensive.

"Fine," I say. My mind is already busy filtering through potential options. My first inclination is to ask Lexy. One of the benefits of having kids the same age has been calling on each other in situations like this one. But that was before Ruby was born. Now that a newborn is part of the equation, the balance of our friendship is inequitable. "I'll figure something out," I pronounce. I always do.

~

When evening arrives, I put Ruby to bed first; then Travis and I snuggle up on either side of Eadie in her bed. "Do you want me to read you a story?" I ask.

"The bats!" she says.

I skim the bookshelf, then pluck out the book with a shiny black bat on the cover. We've been working our way through it, and Eadie has developed a fascination for them that borders on obsession. I read about how bats are the only mammals that can fly.

"What's a mammal?" she asks.

Travis takes this one. "It just means that bats don't lay eggs like birds. The baby comes out of the mother's tummy, just like you came from Mommy."

"Out her bagina?"

Travis cuts me a *Help!* look, so I take the reins. Since her sister was born—again—Eadie's been asking all sorts of questions about how she got here, and I've been as honest as possible without going into the messy details. "I guess you could say that."

Eadie furrows her brow. "But if the mommy is upside down, how come the baby doesn't fall?"

"I think bat mommies are really good at catching their babies," he says, shooting me a smile. It's the look we exchange when we have no idea what we're talking about and hope Eadie doesn't suspect anything.

"And the babies stay close because they know that the mommy will take care of them until they're ready to fly away," I add.

"Like you and Daddy take care of me."

A lump sprouts at the base of my throat at the mention of Travis and me as a team. He encircles us with an arm, and my heart skips a beat at his touch. "That's right." As I finish reading, I feel his hand migrate to the small of my back, where it rests, warm and solid, an unspoken apology.

CHAPTER 21

After everyone is asleep, I sneak out of the house and slip behind the wheel of my Honda, ignoring the urge to vacuum the Froot Loops littering the back seat. I only have a few precious hours before Ruby's next feeding, and I'm desperate for some Lexy time, especially with the prospect of signing Julian as a client. My best friend has a way of bolstering me when I'm feeling nervous in a way Travis has never been able to do. He needs to be the hero of my story, swooping in and solving my problems with practical and painfully obvious suggestions; Lexy just listens and strokes my ego with soothing affirmations, tricking me into believing that I'm capable of doing anything.

When she opens her front door wearing a soft pink pajama top and matching shorts, I feel a bit dowdy in my sweatpants and milk-stained T-shirt. Even so, I pull her into an almost violent hug, drawing an "Oof" from her chest. She smells just as I remember, like Bath & Body Works wrapped in Sephora. God, I've missed her.

"Everything OK?" she asks, when I finally release my grip. "Your texts sounded urgent. What's wrong?" Her makeup-free face is taut and clear, while mine bears the remnants of the day's mascara pooling around my sunken eyes.

"Everything," I say, blowing past her. Letting the weight of the past few weeks melt my bones, I sink into her plush velvet couch. Being in Lexy's house is a balm to my jet-lagged soul. While a few superficial things have changed over the years, the atrium-like living room with skylight is still brimming with edgy artwork of shapes and plants I can't identify. Whereas my walls are a mosaic of candid family snapshots stuffed into mismatched frames, the Brennan home features only a single professional photograph of baby Payton above the fireplace. In the giant canvas print, she's perched naked on a bed of white faux fur wearing a crown of vines, like some sort of fairy heiress.

Lex darts into her spotless white kitchen and grabs a glass of wine for herself and a ginger ale for me. She parks beside me, tucking her toned bronze legs beneath her bottom. "Here," she says, pushing the can into my hands. "Drink. Then spill."

Obeying her, I pop the can and take a small sip, followed by a cleansing breath. "OK, so you know that guy at my open house today?"

She cuts me a pointed look and lets out a wolf whistle. "You mean the chiseled god wearing Saint Laurent? How could I forget?" Then lowering her voice, she adds, "Don't tell Sterling this, but I may have daydreamed about him a little on my way home. I almost ran a stop sign."

Her approval fuels my enthusiasm, and the words spill out of me like helium from an overinflated balloon. If anyone will understand the stakes of this deal, it's Lexy. "Well, he's a real estate developer in the market for a home here. And he's open to working with me on future projects. And I can't tell you how I know this, but let's just say I have it on good authority that he's going to infuse this town with a lot of money, and I have the once in a lifetime opportunity to work with him." By the time it's all out, I'm nearly breathless. But maybe I shouldn't have told her. She did get me the job at Harlow, after all, and I don't want her to feel like I'm leapfrogging, especially since, between the two of us, she's the one who probably deserves this break.

But if Lexy is jealous, she doesn't show it for even a second. "Seriously?" She shoots me an incredulous look, her mouth gaping. "That's amazing!" She nudges my shoulder, jostling my drink. With lightning-fast reflexes, I manage to save it from defiling the immaculate white cushions beneath me. "So, what's the problem?" She arches a thin eyebrow. "Why do you say it like it's a bad thing?"

"It's not, it's just . . ." I try to formulate a response that won't make her question my sanity. This version of my best friend has no idea how successful Julian Mitchell really is or just how monumental this deal could be for my future. What's more, she's entirely ignorant of the fact that I'm living a rerun, that Travis and I have been thrust into the hurricane that was our marriage and I'm not sure how to navigate my way through it a second time. Over the years, Lex and I have had hundreds of conversations on this very couch in which I complained about my lopsided relationship. And though I'd like to think I've progressed since then, I feel myself hurtling toward another emotional dump. "It's just a lot, you know. With a new baby and Travis's job. Sometimes, it feels like I'm doing all this in spite of him, instead of with him."

"Don't tell me," she says, setting her drink down on the glass coffee table, "he's making you feel guilty about work again."

"Yes," I say, grateful that Lex has once again managed to pinpoint the problem and validate my feelings with so little to go on.

"Is he still training for *American Idol* with Thing One and Thing Two?" She means Marcus and Dane, who both channel Led Zeppelin vibes with their shaggy hair. Maybe it's an unfair characterization, as my beef isn't with them, but even so, I nod.

"I have a meeting with Julian tomorrow night, and I completely forgot about Travis's set." I blow a chunk of hair from my eyes and train my gaze on the ceiling. "There's no way I can cancel on this client, or he might think I'm not up to the task. For once, I wish Travis could just disappoint everyone else and support me. But anytime the question of childcare comes up, it's me who has to figure it out. And I need this, Lex," I say, burying my head in my hands. Because right now, work is the only thing I seem to have any control over. "I'm desperate for a sitter for tomorrow night." I venture to meet her eyes, too embarrassed to ask her for help. But before I can formulate the words, Lex puts me out of my misery.

"I'll watch them," she says, like it's no inconvenience at all.

A rush of relief floods my system. "Seriously?"

"Of course. Payton will be thrilled to play with Eadie, and Sterling is home tomorrow night, so he can help. Besides, I'm just dying to get my hands on that baby."

My lungs collapse in relief. "Lex, you have no idea how much I appreciate this," I say, overcome with emotion. It shouldn't surprise me that my best friend has once again managed to scrape me off the asphalt and save the day, but I'm struck by how much this woman has done for me over the course of our friendship without asking for anything in return. "I owe you," I say. "Big time. Seriously—anything you need, I'm your woman."

"I'm sure I'll think of something." A smile teases the corners of her mouth. Then she takes another sip of wine and leans in. "Until then, tell me more about Ruby. Is she a good sleeper? How's the nursing going?"

"She's . . . getting there," I say, fudging the truth. The colic is still an evening battle, but singing seems to help, and Travis is great at that part. I forgot how good he was when she was at her worst, how I depended on him to show up at the exact moment I was on the verge of absolutely losing it. Gingerly, he'd scoop her up and cradle her to his broad chest, cupping a sturdy hand to her bottom as they bounced to the rhythm of whatever Aerosmith song he converted into a lullaby. He's a natural when it comes to nurturing them in that way, his hands too busy holding their hearts to pick up dirty socks. Maybe I've never really given him enough credit for that. Maybe I even resented him a little for being able to reach our children in ways I never could. "And she's a great eater," I add. "It's been an adjustment for everyone, but we're starting to settle into our new reality." Or at least I am trying to.

From somewhere upstairs, Payton lets out a shrill whine I recognize. "Mommy, I need you!" As Lex moves to put her drink down, Sterling's voice calls back from above, calm and sure. "I've got her, babe." A door closes, muffling the little girl's pleas, and Lex relaxes again on the sofa.

"How do you guys do it?" I ask, truly curious. As I look around the Brennan home, I'm struck once more by the stark contrast to my own. Where her husband is proactive and reliable and her floors gleam with polish, Travis is disorganized and forgetful, and my home is sticky.

"Do what?"

"Make it look so easy?" From the moment I met Lexy, she radiated efficiency. With a cell phone in one hand and a fully stocked diaper bag in the other, she always seemed to balance motherhood and her career without having to sacrifice her mental health. She makes being a mom look chic. From my vantage point, her marriage to Sterling is the stuff of dreams. He has always been supportive of her career and ambitions in a way I envy, taking sick days when Payton caught a cold, baking treats for career day, offering to drive carpool when Lexy was late. In other words, an equal partner.

"Actually, I never wanted kids," Lexy says with a shrug as she settles against the backrest. "Sterling was an only child, but I was the oldest of six. After parenting my younger siblings all those years, having a baby was the furthest thing from my mind. But Sterling was so persistent." Having the benefit of five years of friendship, I already know all this, but I listen intently, because I'm desperate for a crumb of wisdom. "Finally, I told him that if we were going to do this, it had to be fifty-fifty. I wasn't going to sacrifice my perfect pair of boobs and Friday happy hours just so he can get his white picket fence. He knew from the beginning that I expected him to be fully present. When Payton came along, we had a plan." She pulls another sip from her glass, then casts her gaze upward, where her perfect family is nesting. "And for the most part, Sterling has held up his end of the deal."

I can't help but wonder how my life might have played out if I'd had a clearer vision of what I wanted. Ever the planner, Lexy had mapped out her future ahead of time, accounting for all the potential detours and speed traps, while I had been thrown into parenthood without so much as a seat belt. When Travis and I found out we were pregnant, we were shell shocked at first, then nervously excited at the thought of bringing a baby into the world. But we hadn't been prepared. "I wish we'd laid a little groundwork before having Eadie, but things just happened so fast. Most days, it feels like flying an airplane while building it."

"Except, in your case, the copilot is asleep at the wheel," she says, tipping her drink to me.

"And the passengers are feral," I add.

And just like that, we bowl over laughing, lost in the ridiculousness of it all. For a moment, things almost feel normal, the way they were before I slipped down the stairs and into my past. Two friends commiserating about the demands of motherhood, in all its impossibilities.

CHAPTER 22

The next morning Eadie awakens, dark and early, from a nightmare and bounds into our bed at 4:00 a.m., squeezing herself between Travis and me. My feet are icicles, but Eadie is a furnace in her fleece pajamas and kicks off the covers like a synchronized swimmer. As I cling to my tiny piece of quilt, I'm jealous that Travis is managing to sleep through the mayhem, especially since I've already fed Ruby twice during the night. By the time his alarm finally sounds, I've drifted into a catatonic state, staring at the ceiling fan, wondering what fresh new hell awaits me this morning.

It's Travis's first day back at work, teaching music at Bonnet Hill Middle, and my first day alone with the girls. Sort of. Does it count if I can't remember this part of my life? Considering the sleepless blur the past ten days have been, it's no wonder I've chosen to block most of it out. I'm surprised to realize I'm actually nervous about being alone with the kids. This makes no sense, as they are, of course, *my* kids. Before my fall, I'd grown accustomed to their independence. But a future where I can pee alone now seems like a distant mirage. As angry as I was about the whole nail polish disaster, I've come to depend on Travis to entertain Eadie while I'm nursing. Which is all the time. What's more, Eadie practically worships her father, and the two of them make a pretty adorable team when they sing made-up nursery rhymes or hunt for bugs in the backyard as he regales her with fart jokes. It pains me to admit this, but I'm going to miss him today. And I shouldn't. It won't make things any easier when I wake from this entirely-too-real dream.

Travis grabs his satchel bag and kisses the girls goodbye. Then he wraps an arm around my waist, and his lips press against mine, warm and familiar. I can taste the remnant of his aloe shaving cream, and it sends a flood of tangled emotions to my chest. It's only a peck, and yet whenever Travis kisses me, time seems to slow. It feels dangerous to let myself get lost in this false version of us, the one that won't last, so I pull away first.

From the front porch, Eadie and I wave as we watch his truck round the corner. Irritating as Travis can be, he's been my life preserver in the ocean of parenthood, one that is now drifting farther and farther away, until all that's left is a speck against the cloudless autumn sky. And just like that, I'm alone.

Looking at Ruby in my arms, with her blond fuzz and contented little smirk, I feel a foreboding sense of worry. This was always the hardest part for me, managing to survive the minutiae of each day with two small humans. Just one eternal round of diaper changes and laundry and saying the word *no* over and over ad nauseam. I could never figure out how it was possible to be so bored and so busy at the same time.

I inhale a long fortifying breath, then release it a little at a time. If I'm going to keep my cool, I need to stick to a routine, get everyone on a schedule. First things first. Eadie's hair is a tangled nest that must be brushed, but it's going to take a stealth approach. I invite her to the couch under the guise of reading the bat book. When she's occupied by the pictures, I sneak the brush out of my robe pocket and gently run it through her hair. Despite my light touch, she screams with the shrillness of someone being murdered, and the five minutes it takes me to tame it feel like a hundred.

Next, I head to our bedroom. The laundry situation has become unavoidable, as the hamper has officially begun to smell. Ruby is down to her last clean onesie, while I have resorted to wearing Travis's old band T-shirts. And not the good ones. Today's selection is faded gray and full of pinprick holes, the Smash Mouth logo worn so thin it's all but gone. All this is compounded by the fact that Eadie rotates through about six thousand outfits a day, milk spills and paint spatters dotting our ever-growing pile.

Gently, I place Ruby in the bouncer, then haul three armfuls of dirty clothes to the laundry room, where I come face to face with my arch nemeses—the green monsters. I used to think that if every living thing on the planet were to decompose, the green monsters would still be alive and well. The ancient washing machine and dryer, a vintage 1965 Maytag set in avocado green, were a housewarming gift from Grandma Beatrice, who once claimed they were too precious to sell or give away to "just anyone." Lucky me. Last year, we finally unloaded them onto the curb and bought a shiny new set in bright white. And yet, here they sit, like twin zombies that refuse to die. Not only does the washer operate at the decibel level of a landing zone, but the dryer only remains closed if I wedge a broom between the wall and the door. Cursing also helps. Grandma Beatrice showed me how to perform this task, then lovingly patted it and called it "a little ornery." I prefer to call it a giant piece of crap. I drop an armful of whites into the washer hatch, pour in the soap, then twist the knob and wait for the inevitable shaking to begin.

Next, I scramble up some eggs and butter a slice of toast for Eadie, who is seated, bright eyed, at the breakfast table, then sprinkle a few red grapes onto her sectioned princess plate. On reflection, I ask, "Wait, does Mommy let you eat grapes?"

"Yes," Eadie says, leering at me as if I'm an impostor, "but you always cut them in half."

"Right," I say, shaking the rust from my brain. This is all coming back now. One by one, I pluck up the grapes. It's strange to think I knew this information once, had memorized each tiny milestone by heart. But Eadie has grown so quickly over her short life, I hadn't thought to pay attention, and now I wonder how old she was when I entrusted her with a whole grape. It bothers me I can't remember.

"But I don't want them cut in half anymore," Eadie protests, because now that I've presented an alternative way of consuming fruit, it has become the preferred and thus only acceptable way.

"No, sweetie. You know the rules." Thank God one of us does.

"Don't cut them!" she shouts, reaching for a grape. She steals two before I can stop her and shoves them in her fat cheeks.

"Eadie, spit those out," I command.

With a defiant crinkle of her nose, she levels her gaze at me, daring me to say it again. But in the name of safety, I cannot let my four-year-old have the last word here, so I crouch down and lock eyes with her. "I said, spit those out." Extending a raised palm, I wait for her to comply. Instead, she slowly begins grinding her back molars. I'm not sure how to proceed. The old Audrey, so naive and unprepared, would probably have gone with a threat, leverage Eadie's love of *Paw Patrol* or Barbies. But new Audrey has read a lot of articles about empowering your child through choices, letting them feel like they've made the correct decisions on their own.

I clear my throat politely and try again. "Eadie, would you like to choke on the grapes and go to the emergency room, or would you like to spit them out and get a cookie?" It's a blatant bribe, but in this case, it's a bribe that works. *Damn if Travis wasn't right.* I banish my guilt and determine to stop rewarding bad behavior. After this one last time.

Eadie spits out two masticated chunks of red into my waiting palm and pulls her eyebrows together. "What's a 'mergency room?"

"It's a place where people go so they don't die," I point out, tossing the handful of mush into the garbage disposal.

"Gwapes would make me dead?" Her eyebrows are nearly touching her hairline now.

"No, just . . ." I draw in a cleansing breath. "How about we find something on TV," I say brightly, making my way into the living room.

I locate the remote and find a cartoon on PBS, hoping that Eadie will forget the whole conversation. But I should know better.

Eadie tugs at my robe. "When do I get the cookie?" she asks, staring me down like a mobster who has come to collect.

I head to the pantry and rustle up a box of OREOs, then dispense one to Eadie, who immediately perches herself in front of the television. I'm not sure how long I can depend on public broadcasting to entertain my child, so I whisk Ruby from her bouncer, then sink into the couch for a nursing session. Lulled by the sound of Ruby suckling and the theme song to *Curious George*, I feel my eyelids grow heavy. I will them to stay open, focusing on George, who has somehow acquired a white coat and is pretending to be a doctor. He manages to cure two patients, which has me wondering how stupid a person would have to be to take medical advice from someone who is so clearly a monkey. This animal has committed a serious crime, and he's being celebrated for impersonating a professional. I wish I were a monkey. Life would be so much easier if I knew that I was going to eat bananas for every meal instead of having to come up with some crowd-pleasing spread three times a day. Do monkeys have taste buds, I wonder? By the time George has cured the third patient, I've completely dozed off. My head falls back against the sofa, and my muscles go slack as I loosen my grip on the baby.

When Eadie jumps onto the couch, startling her sister, I jolt awake, wondering how long I was out. For a moment, I feel guilty that I was so hard on Travis yesterday. I'd forgotten how delicious sleep was when I was drowning in diapers, when uninterrupted dreaming felt akin to a luxury vacation. Then another worry creeps in. If I can't even manage our two kids, will they prove too much for Lexy tonight?

"Mommy, I'm bored," Eadie says, bouncing on her haunches.

"Well, what would you like to do?"

She shrugs. "I don't know."

Suddenly nostalgic, I think about the leaf rubbings we used to make with crayons and the Play-Doh villages we carefully crafted with toothpicks. But when I suggest these ideas, she crinkles her nose. "Well, what about your kitchen?" I try, remembering all the tea parties where Eadie would put on her sparkliest dress and feather boa and attempt a British accent. *Would you like another spot of tea, Mommy?* And I would dutifully extend my cup and lift a pinkie as we toasted. It occurs to me that Eadie hasn't played tea party in years, not since Tara Smothers made fun of her at her seventh birthday party and she relinquished her special Mrs. Potts and Chip set to Ruby. My heart contracts at the memory of her in tears, swearing off birthday parties and tea parties and Tara Smothers all in one breath.

"No, not that." A mischievous grin takes shape on her face. "I want to play hide-and-seek."

Oh, God no. I'm perfectly happy to sit here and don a silly hat and pretend to drink whatever invisible mocktail Eadie dreams up, but hide-and-seek is, without a doubt, my least favorite game. It means I will have to leave the warm indentation on the couch and traverse the entire eighteen hundred square feet of our home, hiking up and down the stairs—a task my postpartum body is not prepared to take on. But Eadie is biting her bottom lip with those exquisite baby teeth, looking at me with big doe eyes, and I can't bear to let her down, especially knowing that in five years, she won't ask me to play with her anymore.

"All right," I agree, feeling a smile take over. "But I get to hide first."

Elated, Eadie plops onto the couch face down and pretends to shut her eyes. I can hear her counting to twenty, except she skips from five to sixteen, and a rush of urgency sends me skittering into the kitchen. Still clutching Ruby to my chest, I slip into the open pantry and ease the door closed behind me. In the darkness of my hiding spot, I feel around and locate a bag of what appears to be Goldfish. Good thing it's dark in here, because the tapeworm is back. Nutrition labels be damned. I peel it open and shake a few fish into my palm, then toss them into my mouth.

As I munch quietly, I can hear the scurry of little feet traversing above me as Eadie scales the stairs. "Mommy, where are you?" she shouts, throwing open doors and shower curtains. Finally, the patter of bare feet on linoleum draws closer, and the door swings open, flooding me in light. "I found you!" Eadie squeals. She is beaming, and the warmth of her joyous smile makes my insides melt. *Oh Eadie. I've missed you.* The crackers are suddenly dry in my mouth, and there's a lump in my throat that won't let me swallow. This is the little girl I remember, the one who made me a mother, the one who taught me how to sing and dance and be silly. The one who didn't tiptoe around cracks but dove headfirst into the joyful mayhem like a dolphin in the wake. Somewhere along the way between the grind of school and work, I lost this version of her. I can't be sure, but I think it began to fade as Travis and I started to argue more. Tears pool in the corners of my eyes.

"Mommy, don't cry," she says, touching a sticky hand to my cheek. "You did a good job."

I know she's talking about my hiding skills, but still, I can't help wondering if I really have done my best. Did I do everything I could for this family? Did I try hard enough to salvage things with Travis for the sake of the girls? Clearing my throat, I paste on a smile. "Mommy's OK," I promise.

With pursed lips, Eadie studies my expression until she's convinced I'm telling the truth. Finally, she dashes off in a run and shouts, "My turn!"

Dutifully, I begin counting aloud, but pull my phone from my robe pocket and unlock the screen. There are three unread messages—all from Lexy. My heart sinks as I read them.

Bad news. Payton woke up with a stomach bug.

She's been throwing up everywhere all morning! I'm so sorry but I don't think I can keep your girls tonight.

Please don't hate me!

I know she isn't to blame, but I'm crushed all the same. In spite of my disappointment, I peck out a half-hearted reply.

Oh no! Hope she feels better soon! Don't worry about us. I'm sure I can find someone else!

But it couldn't be further from the truth. My meeting with Julian is in seven and a half hours, and I don't know of any babysitters I'd trust with a newborn and a preschooler. My mind filters through every possible replacement. I ponder Mrs. Murray, as she's retired and always nosing around. Her visits are usually ill timed and almost always include some thinly veiled criticism of my parenting abilities. *Such a shame that Eadie doesn't play outside more. Children these days are so addicted to their devices.* For now, I'm willing to overlook these annoyances because I'm desperate. But the truth is, she's never been comfortable alone with my kids for more than a few minutes. There is another possibility, but I'm not sure if I'm desperate enough to go there yet. Sonia extended an open invitation, and now is as good a time as any to take her up on it. My thumb hovers over her contact information as I toy with the idea. I'm about to text her when Eadie's voice echoes through the kitchen. "You stopped counting!"

Startled, I tighten my hold on Ruby, nearly dropping the phone. "Sorry!" I yell back, stowing it away. "Four, five, six . . ." When I reach twenty, I emerge from the pantry and lower Ruby in the bouncer. Eadie is a predictable hider, but I can't let the game end too soon. Stalling, I throw open the cupboard beneath the sink and find my cleaning supplies. Then I round the wall to the living room, where I peek behind the couch and open the utility closet, but it's empty, as expected. Slowly, I scale the stairs and head for the hallway bathroom, making a big show by announcing, "I wonder where Eadie could be." Quietly, I cross the threshold and reach for the closed shower curtain covered in pink and blue polka dots, and with one sweeping motion, I swish it open. "Gotcha!"

But Eadie isn't here. Disappointed, I peek my head out the door and start for her bedroom down the hall. I've played hide-and-seek a million times with this little girl, and she always hides in one of three places. If she isn't in the shower, then she's slithered beneath her bed. But when I lift the yellow comforter, all I find are a few scattered toys and lost socks. My pulse ticks up a notch, though I'm certain I'll find her in my bedroom. Before her fourth birthday, she stumbled upon all her presents in my closet, and ever since then, she likes to poke around in there, hoping another robotic talking kitten will magically appear. Fighting off a nagging worry, I head downstairs to my bedroom. The sliding closet door is slightly ajar, but when I push it all the way open, Eadie isn't there.

"Eadie," I say loudly, "Mommy gives up. Come out now."

I'm met with an unnerving silence. My skin prickles with goose bumps as I canvass the rest of the house, opening every curtain and tossing back every pillow. "Eadie, it's time to come out now!" I shout. But the only sound I can make out is the blood rushing through my chest in frantic beats. By now, I've searched every inch of the house, every corner, every door, even the refrigerator. But she's gone.

A sinking helplessness grips my gut, squeezing tighter every second Eadie doesn't answer. This is new. This is not the history I recall. I would remember a feeling like this, so primal and raw. Terror grips me with icy hands as the future that is supposed to be mine slips further and further away.

CHAPTER 23

With Willow on my heels, I circle the perimeter of the house for the third time, my bare feet squishing in the dewy grass as I shout Eadie's name to no avail. Tears stream down my face, and I'm seconds from calling the police when Sonia's voice trills from across the street. "Audrey, is everything OK?" she asks, removing an earbud. She's wearing purple yoga pants and a matching sports bra, her shiny black hair tied back in a high ponytail. Pushing a stroller, she jogs over to meet me.

Under normal circumstances, I would smile and reply with a cheery *Fine!* But there's no room in my thoughts for anything but my little girl, the warmth of her sticky cheek against my own, the tinkle of her mischievous laugh. I would give anything to hear that sound right now. In my gut, I don't think Eadie would have gone outside. But in this sideways version of my life, anything seems possible.

"It's Eadie," I say, mopping the tears with my sleeve. A wave of shame colors my cheeks. What kind of mother loses a child in her own home? "We were playing hide-and-seek, and I can't find her anywhere."

"Don't worry," Sonia says, gently placing a hand on my arm. There's a deep line in her forehead that makes me think she really cares, and my heart swells. "We'll find her. Are you sure you've looked everywhere inside the house?" I want to say *Of course I'm sure. Would I be traipsing around barefoot in my robe if I hadn't?* But all I can manage is a frantic nod.

"All right, let's start there. I'll help you look." Gently, she takes Penelope from the stroller and cradles the baby to her chest, then leads me up the stone pathway through the front door. Once inside, Sonia wraps the baby in a blanket and rests her next to Ruby's bouncer. Then she inspects the pantry, moving around boxes and bags while I scour the kitchen yet again. Logic tells me I won't find Eadie here, but my heart is crying out for me to do something, so I fling open every single cupboard door, even the ones on top. My hands are shaking. I worry my body knows something my mind doesn't want to acknowledge, but I refuse to slow down long enough to let the fear settle in.

And that's when I hear something unusual. From the threshold of the laundry room, Willow is whining, her tail wagging as she jerks her head toward the green monsters behind her. I swivel and see the broom resting on the floor instead of its usual spot, jammed against the wall. The mouth to the dryer is hanging wide open, a gaping invitation for visitors. Or in this case, one very small visitor. Willow starts barking, short, frantic bursts of panic. I sail past her and crouch down to peek inside.

Nestled atop a pile of clothing, Eadie lies inside the dryer like a kitten, her chest rising and falling with each shallow breath.

"I found her!" I call out, joy flooding my veins. Breath returns to my lungs, and I let out a sigh of pure relief.

"Oh thank God," Sonia chirps, flying over to meet me.

I reach inside the dryer and wedge my fingers beneath Eadie's sweaty back, careful not to wake her. Willow and Sonia follow behind as I cradle her to my chest and carry her to the sofa. She feels so small in my arms, so malleable. I can't remember the last time I carried Eadie, the "grown-up girl" in my future, all elbows and skinny legs. For a moment, I breathe her in and savor her youth.

"Poor thing tired herself out," Sonia notes with a frown. "I wonder how she managed to find her way in there." Her nose crinkles in a way that makes me self-conscious. I know exactly how Eadie wriggled inside Grandma Beatrice's death trap, but I don't feel like explaining the broom mechanics of our defective appliance. I'm sure Sonia has a top-of-the-line laundry room at her house.

"She's always been determined," I say. And it's the truth. Eadie practically walked out of the womb a curious child, always asking questions, never satisfied with the answers I gave. In the first grade, she begged me to take my nighttime retainer to show-and-tell, an idea I vehemently opposed. The next day, I received a mortifying call from Mrs. Credence, alerting me that I might want to sanitize the object in question as it had been handled by about a dozen six-year-olds before she could confiscate it.

"That's quite the dog you have there. She really saved the day," Sonia notes, bending down to scratch Willow. She's rolled onto her back in prime petting position. She will stay there as long as Sonia keeps scratching.

"She did," I reply, my chest swelling with gratitude. And suddenly, I'm reminded that in three days, Willow is supposed to die. Time keeps stubbornly marching forward. But this time, I'm not going to let it happen. I'm going to repay my best friend with the gift of life. It isn't lost on me what could have happened if Willow hadn't discovered Eadie, but I can't let myself entertain the list of tragedies or my heart will crack. I force a smile.

"What's her name?"

"Willow," I say.

"Willow," Sonia repeats, as if she's trying out the word. "You know, a lot of serums and scrubs use willow bark. It has natural healing properties. The Native Americans chewed it for pain relief."

"I didn't know that," I say, though this fact feels vaguely familiar, like something I stored away in a forgotten pocket of my mind. "I named her for the tree. One of the things I loved most about her were those big brown eyes. They reminded me of a weeping willow. They were so sad."

"Sad but strong," Sonia points out, running her fingers over the dog's belly. "The bark is weak, but it's one of the easiest plants to propagate. Takes a lot to kill the roots. Sorry," she says, a smile touching her lips as she gives Willow a final pat. Rising to her feet, she adds, "Sometimes I go a little overboard on the research part of my job."

"It sounds like a great gig," I note, "getting to work from home and test out free products."

But Sonia doesn't seem as impressed. "Yeah, well . . . it's a job, I guess."

I'm not sure how to respond. I should say something else, but I'm out of suitable topics, and besides motherhood, the two of us have precisely zilch in common. The weight of the silence starts to make me uncomfortable, so I scramble for a new line of conversation. "Can I get you anything to drink? You look . . . sweaty." More like glistening.

"You caught us at the tail end of our morning jog," she says, scooping up Penelope. "But I'm fine. I should go home and get cleaned up."

"Thanks again," I say, following behind as she retraces her steps through the house. We filter onto the porch, and the morning sunlight casts a halo over every yard, with their vibrant blooms and neatly groomed grass. Sadly, Travis and I do not have any horticultural talents, and our yard bears the evidence. The Knock Out roses I planted our first year here were supposed to be invincible, but I managed to kill them after only a couple of seasons. "Your roses are beautiful," I say, catching sight of the cascading pink buds that flank Sonia's navy blue front door.

"Thanks." She shrugs off the compliment. "I'm kind of a wannabe gardener. Mrs. Murray has been giving me tips. Honestly, I think it's more out of pity than a genuine desire to help, but I'll take whatever help I can get."

"Oh, she does that for spite," I say. Mrs. Murray has made a habit of bringing over her extra tulip bulbs and daylilies when she thins them out every spring. At first, I thought she was doing it out of kindness. But when she ended her initial visit by noting, "This neighborhood used to have such curb appeal when Beatrice was still here," I received the message loud and clear.

Sonia laughs. "You're probably right about that." She smiles genuinely, and I am forced to admit that despite the two thousand humblebrag selfies she posts daily, Sonia is a kind person.

As we admire her home across the street, embarrassment rises to my cheeks. "Just so you know, I don't usually lose my kid. I think I'm just a bit overwhelmed right now." While I had planned to be productive today, Eadie's antics have stolen the minutes, and I'm suddenly keenly aware of the laundry piles dotting the floor, the dirty dishes stacked in the sink, and the faint smell of sour milk emanating from my robe. I can only imagine what Sonia must think of me.

"Of course you are," Sonia says in a way that makes me feel seen. "You just had a baby, and you're chasing around a preschooler. You're allowed to feel overwhelmed." Her brown eyes soften as she levels her gaze at me. Suddenly, I'm immensely grateful it was Sonia who found me sobbing on the front lawn instead of Mrs. Murray. She would have offered to help, but not without reminding me how irresponsible I had been. With Sonia, I don't perceive a hint of judgment. "Listen," she says, locking in on my gaze, "my offer still stands. I'm happy to help out and keep the girls for you if you ever need a moment."

"Oh, I couldn't ask you to do that," I say instinctively. But as soon as the words are out, I regret them, because Sonia just might be the only person who can help me right now.

"Audrey." The way she says my name with such authority makes my spine stiffen. It feels like I've just been called out by a teacher in front of the class, and I have a gut feeling that whatever she is about to say will be impossible to refute. "I don't mean to pry, but I do live across the street, and I've noticed that you've barely left this house since Ruby was born, not even for a walk. Wouldn't you like to take a nice hot shower and put on something pretty and go out somewhere fancy with that tall drink of water you're married to?"

I bristle. "Travis has plans tonight," I say, not entirely sure I appreciate the way she's just complimented my husband. I pull the edge of my robe to my nose and discreetly steal a whiff. Sure, I've been hunkered down for a couple of weeks, but I haven't morphed into Oscar the Grouch just yet. I'm not living in filth. Even if Ruby did have a blowout this morning on this very robe.

"Even better." Sonia gives an easy shrug, bouncing her perky ponytail. "Then you'll go somewhere alone," she adds, dragging the last word out, making it sound sexy. And I have to admit, it does sound sexy.

"Actually," I reply, letting the thought take hold. Maybe Sonia is right and my emotions are all over the place because I'm suffocating in this house. Maybe the fact that I nearly dialed 911 during a game of hide-and-seek is just the wake-up call I need to do something for myself. "I do have something kind of important to do later this evening."

And just like that, a solution presents itself. I won't have to cancel my meeting with Julian Mitchell tonight. I'm not going to let this deal slip through my fingers. I never thought I would say this, but somehow, Sonia Gill, of all people, has managed to save me.

CHAPTER 24

It's a quarter past four when Travis's truck finally whirs into the driveway. Before he can hang his bag on the coatrack, Eadie barrels into him. "Daddy!" she squeals.

"There's my girl," he says, bending down to receive her. His khakis are wrinkled, his brown curls slightly mussed, and yet he's still miles ahead of me in the style department. At least he's wearing pants. I'm still sporting my robe and haven't gotten around to brushing my hair, although Eadie has attempted to braid it in an intricate series of knots and bows. "How was your day?"

"I got stuck in the green monster and Mommy gave me whole grapes but we didn't have to go to the 'mergency room." There is a serious crinkle in her brow when she leans in and whispers in his ear, "That's where people die."

"You were in the dryer?" he says, throwing me a look. I can't tell whether he's worried about my appearance or Eadie's revelation. Both are valid concerns.

"Hide-and-seek," I supply. "Maybe it's time we replace the green monsters with something a little less . . . lethal?" Or at least something built within the last fifty years.

"No way," Travis says firmly. "Those things are solid. No reason to fix what isn't broken. They still have another ten years of life, at least." Which is more than I can say for this marriage. I roll my eyes but let it go for now. When it comes to spending money, Travis is unbearably stubborn.

He stands up and stifles a grin. "There's a, um, sock on your butt," he says, twirling a finger.

I crane my neck to see and quickly peel it off. After five loads of laundry, the static from the dryer has made me a human magnet. My hair is basically dandelion fluff. Maybe it's my hair or the sock or the fact that Eadie is wearing her swimsuit in the middle of September, but Travis seems to pick up on my exhaustion. "Everything . . . go OK today?" he asks.

Aside from losing our preschooler and having a panic attack in full view of our perfect neighbor he secretly covets? Not to mention that Ruby seems determined to poop on every shred of clean laundry, including me. And by the way, colic o'clock is in T-minus thirty minutes. The rest of the day involved reading *All About Bats* over and over and accompanying Eadie on about four thousand trips to the bathroom, where I sang back up to the tinkle-and-toot song Travis taught her. "It was great," I lie.

"What did you do today, Daddy?" Eadie wants to know.

"Hmm . . ." Travis squints, and I know he's preparing to play Two Truths and a Lie. "I scraped gum from the inside of a clarinet. I sent a kid to detention for farting in class. And I threw noodles at Principal Phillips in the cafeteria. Started a food fight, we did. The whole place was covered in spaghetti."

"No, you didn't!" Eadie squeals as he tickles her ribs. "That one's the lie!"

"You're right," he confesses. "I made that one up. What did you guys do?"

The question sets my teeth on edge. While I can't point to a single task I actually completed today, I didn't stop moving for a minute. I started to fold the laundry, but Eadie pilfered a bag of CHEETOS and attempted to open them on the sly, resulting in an explosion of orange dust all over the kitchen floor. After I cleaned up the mess, I meant to get back to the folding, but Ruby woke up from her nap and required an extra nursing session. Then Eadie demanded a book and an episode of *Paw Patrol*, during which I managed to actually make a dent in the mountain of clothes. But as soon as I'd achieved a neat little stack of baby onesies, Eadie performed an impromptu cartwheel and scattered them everywhere. I'm exhausted and have nothing to show for it besides our two children. At least they're breathing.

"We went to the car wash!" Eadie says. Her infectious giggle has Travis captivated.

"What a fun idea, Mommy," he says, shooting me a smile.

I don't tell him that Eadie spent most of the day pretending to be a baby too. That apparently, she didn't realize Ruby would be sticking around this long and has made it her sole mission to cry for attention at the exact moment I need to nurse or change a diaper. I don't tell him that she threw an *Exorcist*-level tantrum when I caught her flushing baby wipes down the toilet and how the only way I could calm her down was to pack everyone up and go through the car wash, where Eadie insisted on wearing the swimsuit she outgrew last summer.

"Sounds like a great day to me," he notes approvingly. "So . . . what's for dinner?"

The question feels like a physical assault. Against my instincts, I adopt the sweetest tone I can manage, but my eyes are practically bulging out of their sockets. "Well, Ruby is having breast milk, and Eadie is having frozen nuggets and peas. Take your pick."

Noting my icy tone, or perhaps the way my left eye has begun to twitch, he gives a slow nod, like maybe he's mistaken my fake niceness for the real thing. "Nuggets it is."

"I don't want nuggets. I want buttatoes!" Eadie protests.

I overrule her. "Everything is in the freezer," I say, placing Ruby in her bouncer. "Can you get dinner started while I get ready for that thing I told you about?" If I seem like I'm in a hurry, hopefully he won't ask too many questions. I don't want him to google Julian Mitchell and realize I'm having drinks with a guy whose cheekbones could slice butter.

"Sure," he says. Before I can escape to our bedroom, he asks, "Who did you find to watch the kids?"

There's a beat of loaded silence. "Sonia," I say, without meeting his eyes.

"The same Sonia you said was 'surface level' just a few days ago?"

"That's the one," I reply as nonchalantly as possible.

Travis cups a hand to his ear, like maybe he hasn't heard me correctly. "The same Sonia you called a social climber?"

"Not exactly." It sounds like something Lexy would have said, but I don't recall using that exact phrase.

"The same Sonia you once said dresses like—and I quote—'a wannabe cast member of *The Real Housewives of Nowhere, Texas*'? That Sonia?"

For a person who never listens when I tell him that pizza boxes aren't supposed to go in the recycling bin, Travis has suddenly developed perfect hearing. "Yes, that same Sonia," I concede.

"That's mighty convenient."

"What is that supposed to mean?"

"Nothing," he says, opening the freezer door. "It's just that up until now, you wouldn't give her the time of day. And all of a sudden you're trusting her with our children." He pulls out the bag of frozen nuggets and casually rips it open.

Now I'm seething, especially after the day I've had. Who the hell is Travis to tell me who I'm allowed to stop hating? "Sonia is a mother," I say defiantly. "And if you must know, we had a . . . connection the other day when she stopped by."

He holds up a finger. "Was that before or after you rejected her hug?"

I refuse to dignify the question with a response, so I excuse myself to the bedroom, where I begin rifling through my closet. Loudly. It's been ten days since Ruby was born, a fact that still seems surreal, but it means that I'm unable to squeeze into most of my old things. From the back of the hangers, I pluck out my trusty black cocktail dress with the low back and plunging neckline. There's just enough give in the nylon waist that I can pull it off, at least for a couple of hours—if I feed Ruby right before I leave. I discard my robe and am peeling off my nightgown when Travis throws open the door. I scream, scrambling to hide my body with the dress.

He looks behind him as if maybe there is another reason I've cried out like a banshee. "You know I live here, right?" he deadpans.

"I know," I say, breathless. Although, truthfully, this is a fact that keeps escaping me, especially when I'm naked. Holding the dress in front of me like a shield, I rearrange my expression into something less terror stricken.

"Because you seem on edge lately. Like you're uncomfortable being around me." He's right, for good reason. Maybe it's because my stretchy stomach is not as tight as future Audrey's will be, or maybe it's because he hasn't laid eyes on my bare body in months. He inches closer until we're standing face to face and there's nothing but a thin piece of black nylon between us. The sudden proximity makes my pulse quicken. "Did I do something wrong?" His blue eyes are begging for reassurance, the same blue eyes I will one day ask to leave this house and move into an apartment six miles away. Regret swallows my anxiety. I suppose I can't blame him for something that hasn't happened yet. "No . . . you didn't. I'm sorry," I say, softer now. "You just scared me, that's all."

Satisfied, he gives a nod before registering the scant dress I'm clinging to with white fingers. "Is that what you're wearing tonight?" He raises an eyebrow. "Pretty swanky for a work meeting." A whistle escapes his lips. "Must be an important client. Who are they?"

Sweat tingles in my armpits. "He's a property developer from Atlanta," I say, breezing over the pronoun.

But Travis doesn't let it slide, and his eyebrows shoot up. "He?"

"Yeah, I told you about him." Sort of.

"I'm a thousand percent certain you didn't. Is he young? Old? Attractive?"

Not old, but older than us. Definitely attractive, not to mention fabulously wealthy. And single. But if I mention any of this to Travis, it will only make him worry. And there is nothing to worry about. "He's a client, and this is a business meeting. Period," I say, hoping to end the conversation. "Besides, I just had a baby. I'm not exactly oozing sex appeal right now, if you know what I mean."

But Travis only narrows his eyes at me. The weight of his gaze makes me feel guilty for a crime I haven't even committed—unless wondering whether Julian sleeps in boxers or briefs is a crime. Does that make me an adulterer? "Is it so wrong for a guy to be worried about his wife going out with another man?" He's staring at my dress like he's imagining what's behind it, and the attention makes me squirm. "Especially when she looks as hot as you do."

My stomach does a little flip, but I don't allow the compliment to set in. I barely have enough time to shower and dress as it is. What's more, I don't want to encourage Travis down a path destined for failure. The sooner we realize we aren't meant for one another, the better. I swallow hard. "Please, Travis. I'm going to be late."

He seems disappointed, and it carves a tiny hole in my heart. "Whatever you say."

I hurry past him for the shower, but he catches me in his arms, pulling me into his chest. "I'll miss you," he says in a low voice, his eyes studying my mouth in that familiar way that makes me feel powerless. And before I can register his hands sliding down to my hips, his lips are on mine. His touch ignites a reaction in my body I can't control, but the formula still works. Every sensation hits like clockwork. My chest is heaving, my head is swimming, my knees are barely managing to stay upright. All systems are go except for the little flashing red light in my brain that blinks "Abort! Abort!"

"I have to get ready," I say, pulling away, my fingertips grazing my lips as if they've been stung.

Still holding me, Travis hangs his head. "All right," he finally says. He sighs, then looks at me, defeated. Relieved, I make my escape, but a jolt snaps through my body when he smacks my butt. He flashes me a wink. "Go get 'em, babe."

CHAPTER 25

Sonia was right. There is something about dabbing on a little lipstick and throwing on a clean dress made of something other than terry cloth that makes me practically giddy. Breathing in the fresh evening air, I can feel the waning sunlight infusing me with a new zest. Goodbye, Diaper Genie, and hello, world. I have joined the land of the living. Striding beneath the bright turquoise awning in front of Sunny's, I feel lighter, more like the real me than any time in the past few weeks. When I catch a glimpse of myself in the bar window, somehow future Audrey is staring back, confident and holding her shit together like a boss. Not a stray sock or Froot Loop in sight. Tucking a curl behind my ear, I smack my lips together, then separate a chunk of mascara from my lashes. By the time I've given my spiel about rising property values, Julian Mitchell won't know what hit him. Or at least his bank account.

Inside the bar, I take in the thrum of bodies and clink of glasses over hushed conversation. Mosaic pendant lights adorn each cloistered booth, and a Willie Nelson tune plays faintly in the background. From his seat against the far wall, Julian lifts his glass to me, and I scurry over. He's wearing black slacks and a blue collared shirt, the top button casually open, revealing a sliver of his smooth chest. On another man, it's a look that might scream *sloppy*. But on Julian, it's totally suave. When I realize I'm staring, I divert my eyes and shake off the awkward vibe with a professional smile.

"Sorry, I'm a little late," I say, sliding across from him, remembering how Eadie burst into tears when Sonia arrived. Guilt almost prevented me from leaving at all, but when Sonia produced a package of rainbow nail wraps and Hello Kitty stickers, Eadie was too preoccupied to notice me slip out the door.

"Thanks for coming," he says, his lips curling up at the corners. "I'm glad we could make this happen."

"Me too."

"Hopefully it wasn't too much trouble to come during off hours."

"I'm in real estate. There's no such thing as off hours." I offer a wry smile.

"Can I get you anything to drink?"

"Maybe just a Diet Coke," I say.

"You sure?" He lifts an eyebrow. "Bartender tells me they make a mean mojito."

A tiny wince crosses my face. I didn't leave any milk in the fridge for Ruby, and I'll have to nurse her in a couple of hours. But if I tell Julian I just had a baby, will that make him question my abilities right now? I've always tried to keep my personal and professional lives delineated with clear lines because it never serves me well to share too much about myself with clients. When Travis brings up the kids in conversation with colleagues, it makes him sound charming. When I do it, it makes me seem unfocused. "I'm . . . not really a drinker," I say, hoping that will be enough to stave off any further questions. What does it say about our culture if I'd rather let him believe I'm a recovering alcoholic than a lactating mother?

"Impressive." He cuts me a disbelieving look. Then, steepling his fingers he says, "You know, I did Dry January this year, and it nearly killed me. Hardest thing I ever did."

I agree. And if I'm going to be thrust into my past with nary a heads-up, at the very least I deserve a stiff drink. Or five.

He shifts in his seat. "I hope you don't mind me saying this, but you look amazing."

Blood rushes to my cheeks, and I'm too flustered to make eye contact or manage more than a garbled "Thank you." The compliment hits even harder since I've just given birth. When I risk a glance, I catch him looking at me like he wants more than just a house, making me second-guess my decision to leave family off the table. Maybe I should figure out a way to work Travis into the conversation, let him know I'm strictly off the market, not to mention drowning in diapers. I twist my wedding ring, like maybe the act alone will send a message. But Sonia's words echo in my head, and I can't deny how amazing it feels to be away from my family for just one night, to enjoy a conversation with another adult without being interrupted. For once, I feel interesting and articulate. Maybe even beautiful. It's a bit intoxicating, even better than alcohol. I'm not ready to shatter the illusion yet.

Julian waves over a waiter and orders another gin and tonic for himself and a Diet Coke for me.

He studies me for a beat, making me wonder if I've remembered to wear nursing pads, until finally he clears his throat. "Listen, I've been thinking a lot about the house, and I'd like to move forward." His tone is all business now. "I can pay the asking price, in cash, no contingencies, with a three-week close."

"Are you serious?" I say, before realizing how unprofessional I sounded. Adjusting my tone to something less Valley girl, I say, "Of course. I can make that happen. I'll reach out to the seller ASAP." My brain is reeling, recalculating the commission on a $2.3 million home. I will walk away from this deal $60K richer. And all because I pushed a little harder, forced myself to change my past, like some sort of time-traveling real estate superhero. The truth of Lexy's affirmation burns white hot in my soul. *Network to net worth.* This is my moment.

"One more thing," Julian adds, halting my mental celebration. "Before we move forward, I'd like to take my boys by the house, make sure they'll feel at home there. Think we can make that happen before the end of my trip? I was thinking Thursday. Late morning?"

"No problem," I say, but even as I answer, I'm running through the series of events that will have to happen to make that possible. As always, I'll have the kids that morning, and Travis will be at work. There's no way I can ask Sonia to keep them again after she was so generous about tonight. Besides, I don't want her to think I'm abusing our friendship. Or neighborship. Whatever this is. Maybe Mrs. Murray? The idea of asking her makes my neck go itchy.

"Wonderful," Julian says, pulling his nearly empty glass to his lips. The waiter arrives with our order, and I raise my drink and take a generous gulp. "Now that that's out of the way"—he leans in, steepling his fingers—"let's talk business. What prospects did you have in mind?"

I rest my glass on a cocktail napkin, taking a beat to assemble my thoughts. Between the round-the-clock milk factory I'm running and rescuing preschoolers from dryers, I've barely had time to prepare. But future Audrey has the benefit of five years of lived history. I know exactly which areas of town will appeal to Julian because I've watched his businesses crop up in real time. I've totally got this. I take a deep breath and pull back my shoulders. "Well, there are a couple locations that have untapped potential for nightlife, specifically near Heron Point Lake. A waterfront villa might be a good option, with seafood restaurants and a boardwalk. In a landlocked Texas town, folks are always looking for weekend water getaways—Airbnbs, Jet Ski rentals, that sort of thing."

"Hmm . . ." Julian massages his chin. "That's not a bad idea."

Feeling emboldened, I continue, my voice growing more animated with each suggestion. "Or if you want to go the more urban route, there are plenty of areas downtown ripe for revitalization. Loads of mom-and-pop stores in the town square already draw decent crowds on the weekends from neighboring cities. It's cute, quaint, and totally ready for a trendy restaurant or two, something that lets people feel like they're getting a homey experience in a five-star setting."

"You mean mashed potatoes and gravy with their Prada bag?"

"More like mashed potatoes and gravy with their Vineyard Vines bag," I say, my smile widening. "This is still Bonnet Hill, after all."

"You've done your homework," he says. "And you've certainly given me a lot to think about."

Feeling optimistic, I let myself enjoy the rest of my evening, finishing my Diet Coke and ordering a second with a basket of sweet potato fries. Julian steals a few. The ease of this simple interaction, so ordinary yet intimate, makes me feel a fleeting stab of guilt. I remind myself that in five years, Travis and I won't share a bed anymore. Maybe this is the way things should have happened all along. Maybe I was supposed to share this moment with Julian in a dusky bar, discussing the future that should have been mine all along. If only. After the ice in his glass has long melted, I tell him that I really should be going.

"Why the rush?" He checks his watch. "Thought real estate agents didn't have off hours."

My neck flushes with heat. "Maybe not, but this one is running on about four hours of sleep," I say, throwing him a smile. Not an untrue statement. I rise from my seat. "But I'll see you Thursday for the showing. I'll draft the paperwork tonight, and you can sign the offer there." I pull out my phone and open my calendar, but when my eyes skate over Thursday's date, my blood runs cold. September twentieth—the day I've been hoping I will be able to rewrite history and keep my best friend alive. A reminder blares its bright-yellow highlighter. How could I have been so stupid?

Thursday I will hopefully make the biggest sale of my life.

And Thursday Willow is supposed to die.

~

"So how did it go?" Travis calls out from the bedroom. I'm changing in the bathroom, still too vulnerable to be caught naked around him again, but the door is slightly ajar, just wide enough that I catch a glimpse of his boxers.

"Great," I reply, unsure how much to tell him. I don't want to get my hopes up about potential business opportunities, but the Thornwood Estates sale seems solid enough to share. "He's putting in an offer this week." I lock eyes with Travis in the bathroom mirror, my brain buzzing with anticipation. I still haven't worked out how I'll keep Willow safe. And every time I think about what is supposed to happen, the wind gets knocked out of me. The accident is supposed to occur around 6:15 p.m., and I should be home ages before. Just in case, I plan to crate Willow while I'm out that day.

"Wow, that's good news." He seems impressed, and part of me wonders if he ever truly believed I could have this kind of success, especially so early in my career. "Geez, that's like"—he makes some rudimentary calculations on his fingers before holding up three—"thirty thousand dollars." The number rolls off his tongue in slow motion. He is totally gobsmacked, which makes me stand a little taller.

"More like sixty thousand," I correct him, then spit in the sink and rinse.

"Holy crap." He massages his forehead. "This is huge, babe. We should celebrate this weekend. Let's get a sitter."

By *we*, I assume he means me. But still, the sentiment is nice. I peel back the covers and climb into bed, ensuring that no part of my body is touching his. "Maybe," I say. "First, I have to get through one last showing." I fluff my pillow. "The client wants to bring his kids."

"That's good, right?"

My shoulders sink. "It's fine. It's just . . . I don't have anyone to watch the girls."

His excitement wavers. "You know I'd stay, but I can't miss any more work. I've used up all my sick days as it is."

"I know, I wasn't asking," I say, though admittedly I sort of was. My options are quickly evaporating, as Lexy has caught Payton's stomach bug and I don't feel right asking Sonia again, even though she did report that Eadie and Ruby were absolute angels. They were tucked into bed thirty minutes before I got home. Escaping the chaos of bedtime was an unexpected surprise. Eadie rarely remained in her room after Travis and I put her to bed. I half wondered if Sonia had drugged her with some sort of natural sleep supplement.

"Just take them with you," Travis suggests. Like it's an easy solution he can't believe I haven't considered. Which I have. But since I can barely manage Ruby and Eadie within the confines of our home, it seems imprudent to take this circus on the road.

"Maybe," I concede, because no matter how hard I concentrate, I can't heal Lexy before the showing. "It's just . . . unprofessional, you know. I mean, what does it say about me if I have to bring our kids along to a business meeting?"

He lifts an eyebrow. "Isn't your client bringing his kids?"

"That isn't the point. His kids are older. It isn't exactly the same thing," I point out, annoyed that Travis can't intuit this on his own. "Besides, I'm the one who has everything to lose here. I have to project confidence."

Travis squeezes my arm and trains his eyes on mine. "And you will."

At this point, I'm not sure I have another choice but to bring Ruby and Eadie along. I can do this. I just have to make it through the morning. Then I'll spend the afternoon with Willow in the safety of our home where she won't leave my sight.

Everything is going to be fine.

CHAPTER 26

On Thursday, I wake up before dawn to feed Ruby. As I rock her back to sleep, she grips my finger and studies me with drowsy eyes. Between blinks, she stares so intently that I wonder if perhaps she knows what I'm thinking. When I hold her like this in the quiet, it's impossible not to imagine her dancing around our living room, casting a spell over the rest of us with her silly laugh. Eadie used to say that we favored Ruby, that we spoiled her because she was the baby of the family. As much as I denied it, there was a splinter of truth in the accusation. Of course, I love the girls equally. But when Ruby had come along, all her firsts were a little sweeter because I knew I would never experience them again. With Eadie, I'd been too nervous to slow down, to really pay attention.

As I hold Ruby now, I conjure the smell of her clothes after a long day at school and her phase of eating only yellow things. The way her blond hair will lighten to a snowy white, how she will lisp *s*'s, and how I'll be a little sad when she finally stops. Once she's asleep, I press a kiss to her forehead and tuck her into her bassinet.

With Willow trailing, I slip out the door and make my way downstairs. I clip her leash to her collar, and we silently pad outside into the dark, crisp air. Across the street at Sonia's, there's a dim light glowing through the upstairs window. I wonder if she's up taming her hair into sweeping curls, pureeing homemade organic baby food, or lifting weights. I'm not usually outside this early, and there's something almost reverent about the neighborhood.

Willow forges ahead, stopping every so often to sniff a patch of grass. Maybe she senses something different about today. She's more jittery than usual, pawing at the dirt as we go. She bores quickly of each new spot and tugs on the leash like we're behind schedule. "Don't worry, girl. You don't have to be in such a hurry," I reassure her. "We've got time." So much more time than we had before. Still, an undercurrent of worry pulses through my veins. When we round the block, I don't yet go home but rather follow Willow's lead around one more time, letting her tell me when she's ready.

As we walk, I imagine her splashing in the plastic pool at Ruby's first birthday party, running alongside her when she learns to ride a bike. I can smell the wildflowers and wet earth and sweet grass when we take her camping on warm summer nights. I try to picture what our lives will be like in this new story, the one where she gets to live. Could I forgive Travis for letting her die if it never happens in the first place? Could we make a new life together, a better life, one where the world is in full color? When we reach our driveway for the second time, Willow turns to look at me, as if answering the question, and for the first time in a really long time, I think we just might get everything we ever wanted.

~

By the time we arrive at Thornwood Estates, Eadie has consumed nearly all the snacks I packed for the morning. We'd been out of red grapes and CHEETOS puffs, which caused a minor breakdown. But she seems to have found the Goldfish and applesauce pouches an acceptable substitution. Thank God I hadn't caved to Travis on that one.

"I feel sick, Mommy," Eadie says. It's been precisely seven minutes since I passed a sippy cup of chocolate milk into her eager hands.

"Slow down on your drink, honey. It's not a race."

"I can't. I drunk it already."

I gape at her through the rearview mirror. "You finished it?"

She nods, worry seeping into her penitent eyes. "I have to go to the bathroom," she says softly. Her legs are twisting in what I immediately recognize as the potty dance, which means I have approximately two minutes to get her to a bathroom before disaster ensues. I let out a sigh.

I put the car in park, taking note of Julian's black Mercedes already in the drive, then conjure my most mom-like voice and take a deep breath. "Remember," I say, turning to face her, "I need you to be on your best behavior today. Got it? No running, no screaming, and no crying. I need you to be a big girl."

"I have to go!" she yells, dashing whatever hopes I have of getting through this showing unscathed.

At breakneck speed, I fly out of the car and open the rear door to release her from her booster, then circle around to unlatch Ruby's car seat. I had counted on her being asleep, but the excitement of Eadie's morning tantrum shot all my plans to hell. Now she's wide awake, rooting around for something to suck on, which is not going to be me. I fumble around and locate the pacifier she hates and ease it into her open mouth, but she ejects it almost immediately.

"Mommy, I gotta gooo," Eadie whines, clasping a hand to her pants. From the way she's contorting her body, I'm worried she may already have. With one arm looped through the car seat handle and the other firmly attached to Eadie's hand, I shepherd her up the drive, passing Julian and his two young sons, who look on as if they've stumbled upon a group of traveling street performers. What must he think of me? I hadn't even mentioned having kids, and now I'm casually bringing them along to a meeting? Catching sight of the smaller boy, I recognize Malachi's wide brown eyes, five years younger.

"Hi," I say, flashing them an apologetic smile. "So sorry. I hope you don't mind I brought my kids. My sitter bailed at the last minute," I lie. Maybe if I make it seem like this isn't a big deal, he won't think it's a big deal. I just pray Eadie doesn't pee her pants.

"Of course." Julian matches my steps. "Do you need help with anything?"

"Oh, I'm fine," I say, fumbling with the key. "Just a little bathroom emergency. Not for me," I clarify, throwing a nod toward Eadie.

"I figured as much." He smiles, then gently lifts the car seat from my aching arm.

"Thank you." A swell of emotion crests in my bosom. "Again, I'm so sorry about this."

"Totally understand," he replies warmly, and I think he actually might. Julian has two children of his own, after all, one of them not much older than Eadie. This can't be the first time he's encountered a bathroom emergency or a whiny preschooler. Malachi must be about five years old, and his older brother looks to be a tween or thereabouts.

"Mommy, I'm going to potty in my pants right now!" Eadie groans, snapping me back. With unsteady fingers, I turn the key and hurry Eadie inside, leading her to the closest bathroom. "I'll be right back," I say. I suddenly resent Travis teaching her the tinkle-and-toot song, which she is singing with the fiery passion of Celine Dion. Once she has finished her business and washed her hands, we emerge to find Julian bouncing a fussy Ruby around in her seat.

"She seemed upset," he says, looking bewildered. "But I don't think she likes to be bounced either. Also, I'm pretty sure she threw up . . . something."

My client is shushing my baby. I want to crawl into the earth. "Thanks for trying." Carefully, I unlatch the restraints and lift her out, then press her to my chest, silently praying that the morning excitement is behind us.

"Allow me to introduce you to my boys," he says, gesturing to them. "Josiah is nine, and Malachi is five."

"Nice to meet you both." The older son is lean and tall for his age, the spitting image of his father, with a strong jawline and perfect cheekbones. Looking at him, it's impossible not to think of Eadie. Nine-year-old Eadie, who is gangly and awkward, not a tween but not a little kid either. I suspect Malachi must take after his mother. Wearing a red, white, and blue Braves jersey, he is soft and pudgy, with big brown eyes and a mouth full of baby teeth. "You've already met Ruby here," I say over her fussing, "and this is my oldest, Eadie. I think you two are a grade apart," I say to Malachi, who hides behind his father's leg. I know this because by next fall, I'll start seeing the boys around Bonnet Hill Elementary. Immediately, I regret my words. I'm giving stalker vibes again.

Even so, Julian doesn't seem fazed. "Nice to meet you," he says and reaches out a hand, but Eadie seems unimpressed and folds her arms.

When Ruby finally quiets, Julian peeks at her face, which is red and blotchy with tears. Milk dribbles down her quivering chin. "She's adorable," he says. But the moment she locks eyes with him, an earsplitting scream escapes her chest.

"I think your baby hates me," he notes, and I can't tell if he's kidding or not. Actually, I think he might be right. Anytime he comes close to Ruby, the decibel level of her cry rises to a fever pitch.

"She doesn't hate you. She's just tired," I say, over her wailing. "Probably hungry." Because she's always hungry.

"I'm hungry!" Eadie announces.

"No, you're not."

"I am! We don't have any food at our house *at all*," she proclaims.

Julian looks confused.

"That's not true," I reassure him. "We have plenty of food. She just doesn't remember that she ate all of her snacks in the car already." Hence the potty break.

"I didn't like those ones," she mutters. The little traitor. "I want buttatoes!"

Suddenly, I feel hot and cold and clammy all at the same time. I didn't put on enough deodorant for this kind of sabotage.

Eadie turns to Malachi now and, apropos of nothing, asks, "What's your second favorite animal?"

"Uh . . . I don't know." He shrugs. "Maybe . . . a snake?"

She thinks about this for a moment before conceding with a nod. "That's a pretty good one. Mine is bats 'cause they don't lay eggs. The mommy bat pushes the baby bat outs her bagina and then she has to feed it milk like a people baby. Except bats don't barf. And our baby is always barfing."

Malachi's eyes go wide. There is a mortifying beat of silence that no one seems to know how to fill. Finally, Julian cracks a smile, then stifles it with a fist.

I think I may have stopped breathing somewhere around the *vagina* part. I wrap an arm around her shoulder and pull her into me. "That's enough bat facts for now, honey." I need to initiate damage control immediately, so I rifle through the diaper bag in search of a bribe. "Look, Mommy brought you a sucker," I say, presenting her with a bright-red Tootsie Pop.

Now I just need for everyone to forget the last sixty seconds and move on, which everyone seems amenable to. "Well," I say, gesturing toward the kitchen, "should we begin the tour?"

"Let's do it," Julian says, following my lead.

Eadie unwraps the sucker and plugs her mouth. I pray it will be enough to silence her for the rest of the showing, but her impulse control is in short supply today. As we stride through the kitchen, I recenter myself and shore up my confidence, pointing out the fabulous lighting and floor-to-ceiling windows. Eadie remains close, inspecting each new room with curious eyes.

"It's the perfect space for entertaining," I say when we reach the dining room. "I imagine you guys could throw quite the party here."

"I don't think we'll be hosting parties anytime soon," Julian says, raising an eyebrow. "We just need a place to start fresh, you know? A blank slate to create some new memories together."

It's a sentiment that resonates deeper than he can possibly understand, but I simply nod and smile. Is it ever really possible to start over, or are we destined to keep reliving our failures, no matter the place? New walls. Same heartaches. Even so, I say, "I think this home could be exactly what you and your boys are looking for." And it just might give me a fresh start too.

"You know something, Audrey . . ." He regards me curiously. "I think you might be right. But before we move forward, I do have a couple of questions I'm sure you can resolve."

I muster a confident smile, hoping I can remember all the details. "Fire away."

"Do you know anything about the HVAC or filtration system? Josiah here has a pretty serious case of asthma. If it's not already equipped, I'd like to get an estimate on that. Also, I noticed some cigarette butts near the front porch. Considering his health, we don't want to buy a place where there was heavy smoking."

"Understood," I say with a nod. "I don't have the answer off the top of my head, but I'll find out ASAP and let you know."

Eadie wrinkles her nose. "Who was smoking?"

"No one, honey," I say, glossing over the possibility.

"I smoked one time!" she announces, seeming proud that she can contribute to such an adult conversation.

My face is on fire. I can't feel my toes anymore. "No, you didn't," I correct her, wrapping an arm around her shoulder.

"I did!" she shoots back, defiant.

"She didn't," I say to Julian, in case he didn't hear me the first time. And though he throws me an understanding nod, I'm only 90 percent sure he believes me.

~

Over the past twenty minutes, Josiah and Malachi have been polite and respectful, though they haven't offered much in the way of conversation. Meanwhile, Eadie has treated us to an interpretive dance, approximately 167 bat facts, and a rather extensive repertoire of potty jokes. Thank you, Travis. If she says the word *poop* one more time, I'm going to lose it.

We reach the backyard, where I decide to wait with the girls while Julian and the boys inspect the game room upstairs. I take a seat at the patio table and hope the Zen vibes of this warm September morning will rub off on the crabby infant in my arms. Tiny waterfalls flow in tranquil rivulets, leading into a glittering lagoon that reaches from gate to gate. The trickling sound of water washes over me, calming my nerves and clearing my head. Eadie quickly discovers a giant patch of rocks jutting out over the hot tub and begins scaling them like a mountain goat. It looks steep, possibly dangerous, but after trailing her like a zoo handler all morning, I don't have the energy to stop her. With Ruby tucked in one arm, I pull out my phone and glance at the clock. I've got plenty of time before Willow's accident is supposed to occur, and I'll be home well before this evening. Feeling calmer, I fire off a message to Lexy.

How are you feeling?

Almost instantly, trailing dots appear beneath my text.

A little better. Which is good because Sterling is sick now. What about you? How's the showing?!

My children are conspiring against me. It will be a miracle if he still buys this house after the Perkins family roadshow.

I check on Eadie again, who is now lying on her tummy, peeking over the edge of a giant slab of flagstone. She dips her hand into the waterfall below. "Please be careful," I remind her. "Don't get too close." I'm not worried she'll jump in. She was terrified of swimming pools at this age. My phone dings with a reply.

Good thing your kids are cute. People LOVE babies! So WORK it to your advantage. You've got this, babe. Network to net worth.

Easy for her to say. Her morning isn't being undermined by a tiny motormouth obsessed with bat poop. A sunbeam emerges from behind a puffy cloud, and the warmth on my face provides a tiny dose of joy wrapped in nostalgia. I remember how strange this period of my life was, how utterly impossible it was to explain the competing emotions in my body to Travis. Living almost entirely for these two humans we created was amazing and priceless. It was the best thing I've ever done.

And it was hard.

So hard it's no wonder I can't remember much of anything. The years were short, but the days were endless, stretching into one another like taffy.

Julian appears through the sliding glass doors with Josiah and Malachi following close behind. "Well, what do you think, guys?" I ask, rising to meet them.

"It's nice," Josiah says.

Malachi seems indifferent.

Julian nudges his shoulder with a fist. "He's just mad that there isn't a basketball hoop."

"Or a theater room." Malachi lifts his eyebrows. "Mom has a theater room."

"I thought you said this place had a spa or something," Josiah says, unimpressed.

"Oh, it does." I motion to the hot tub, where Eadie is still puttering around. "And a fully heated infinity pool. And honestly, there's plenty of space in the side yard to add a basketball court if that's something you want to pursue," I suggest brightly.

This seems to satisfy Julian. "Great idea."

I'm about to lead him over to the swath of grass in question when I hear a heavy thud, followed by a piercing scream. My stomach flips when I see Eadie, her body limp, lying at the foot of the rocks. "Oh my God!" With Ruby still in my arms, I run toward Eadie, my thoughts spinning with worst-case scenarios. Julian matches my pace, while the boys hang back, gaping with wide eyes.

In the short distance it takes to reach her, I imagine Eadie's front teeth knocked loose, or her perfect porcelain nose shattered. When I drop to her side, she lifts her chin, which is gushing blood. There's a gash on her lower jaw where her chin hit the pavement.

"Hold the baby," I say, pressing Ruby into Julian's arms, where she promptly erupts into tears. I'm too panicked to care whether this is appropriate.

"Is she all right?" Julian asks over the crying.

My pulse is racing, but as I inspect the damage, it becomes clear that aside from a few scrapes and bruises on her knees, the gash on Eadie's chin is the worst of it. And it's bad. I remind myself that head wounds are supposed to look worse than they are, but the girls have never hurt themselves like this before. Josiah supplies a roll of paper towels from inside the house. I apply pressure to the wound, but it doesn't respond to my efforts. Blood leaks onto the rocks and seeps into the pool. Tiny streams of crimson curl and disperse in the water like smoke.

"She's going to be fine," Julian says, touching a hand to my shoulder. "Just needs a few stitches, I'll bet. Don't worry, Audrey. This kind of thing happens."

For some reason, this simple act of kindness makes me want to cry. Oh my God, I *am* crying. What is even happening right now? Quickly, I wipe away the tears and scoop Eadie into my arms, grateful for her whining because it means she is OK. Everything is going to be OK.

CHAPTER 27

It's 3:45 p.m. when I finally exit the urgent care center. Four traumatizing hours have passed since we arrived, and I'd been in such a frantic state when we got here that I can't remember where I parked the Honda. We spent 96 percent of that time in the waiting room, watching an injury parade roll through the automatic doors, each case of heart palpitations and labored breathing more pressing than a four-year-old with a laceration.

"Is this the 'mergency room?" Eadie asked. "Am I going to die?" Feeling guilty about our earlier conversation, I calmly explained that we were in the emergency room, but that she was definitely not going to die. Eadie then watched with wide eyes as a man in an orange vest limped up to the nurses' desk and removed a bloody foot bandage to reveal a nail poking through the center. I tried to shield her eyes, but she wiggled around my blockade, entranced. "I hope you don't die!" she shouted after him. I know what we'll be discussing on the ride home because she's already asked four thousand questions about the likelihood of stepping on a nail. I can't figure out if she is horrified or intrigued by the idea.

My limbs are heavy and sore from carrying the girls. I've never been more eager to get home. Willow has been in her crate all day. And while I'm relieved that I had the foresight to lock her up, the idea of her being confined for so long has been eating at me. I need to let her out in the backyard. No walks for her today; I don't trust her anywhere near the street. My white dress shirt is smeared with blood and baby vomit, and my mascara and eyeliner have pooled in macabre semicircles beneath my eyes. With my pale complexion, I could pass for an extra on a horror movie set. Or a KISS member. Or a corpse. I feel like the latter. *Just take them with you.* Travis's words grate at my already shot nerves. In the excruciating thirty-six minutes we'd spent at my listing, our children had somehow managed to evacuate every possible bodily fluid.

By the time we leave, I'm too sapped to analyze the potential fallout of this morning's events, which may very well have cost me a life-changing sale. For now, I'm grateful that no one is bleeding or crying or telling knock-knock jokes, which Eadie regaled me with the entire time we waited for a first-year med student to glue her chin back together. If I'd known that was all she needed, I might have just superglued it myself.

Eadie passes out the minute we merge onto the main road, so I tug out my phone, planning to leave Travis a thorough message about the day's happenings. But he picks up after the first ring, which surprises me. He never answers during the school day, and he doesn't get home for another hour. Thursdays are green for after-school jazz club.

"Why aren't you teaching?" I ask in lieu of a greeting.

"Well, hello to you too."

"Sorry, I just meant . . . I didn't think you'd be home for a while."

"Half the sixth grade is out with a virus, so jazz club was canceled. I just got home." I can hear the pop of a can opening, followed by a long guzzle.

My breath stalls. My fingers go numb around the phone. "Don't let Willow out!" I shout. "I'll do it when I get there." The light ahead of me changes from green to yellow, but slowing down is not an option. I press my foot hard on the gas and barrel through the intersection.

"Geez, I think I'm capable enough to take care of our dog. I just let her out."

A coldness seeps through my veins, prickling my skin with goose bumps. "No no no no no no no. You idiot!"

"What the hell, Audrey?"

"Front yard or back?"

"What does it matter? She always comes—"

"Front yard or back?!"

There's a heavy pause, punctuated by my sharp inhale. Whatever he says has the potential to stop my heart. I cannot watch Willow die again. But maybe I never had a choice? Maybe, in spite of everything I've been doing to revise the past, the same events were always destined to occur.

"Front," he finally answers. And as I press my eyelids closed, I think I can actually hear the sound of my heart breaking.

~

There are moments of my life that live in Technicolor and others that fade into the recesses of my mind, fragmented and thin. So much of my childhood is transparent to me, and while I know I must have lived it, the specific details of any given day are intangible. I push down the memory of my mother arguing with a strange man as I cower beneath my comforter. I can never recall his features, not because I've blocked them out, but because no man ever stuck around long enough to make much of an impression. Life with Iris was always an adventure, but not the kind that included vacations and theme parks and surprise road trips to the beach. It was more of an exercise in blind hope. Hope that the electric bill would be paid on time, hope that dinner would be more than Cup Noodles or cereal, hope that whatever derelict place we were struggling to afford would shelter us for a few more months, at least until the next temp job or new boyfriend came along. There are swaths of my life that seem to have evaporated, years for which I cannot account. But interspersed in the forgotten tomb of memory are vivid flashes that will never dull. The evening I lost Willow will live among these moments.

Eadie wanted pancakes for dinner. We were out of eggs, so I slipped out for a quick run to the grocery store. Travis stayed home with the girls, and I left the four of them watching cartoons in the living room. Willow was tucked between Eadie and Travis, who scrolled his phone, completely disengaged. I'd asked him twice if he could walk the dog, as I was completely exhausted from a full day of entertaining the kids. And yet there he sat.

If I'm being entirely honest, I didn't only go for Eadie. I went for me. Being home with the girls, reliving the same day over and over again in my pajamas, left me drained. I was desperate to escape for a few moments, put on clean clothes and peruse the real world. To feel human again. Usually, when I made a grocery run, I stuck to the edges, grabbing only what I needed. But on this day, I took my time, moving like molasses through the bowels of the store. I even spent an extra five minutes sniffing candles in the household-goods aisle, debating whether to buy Lavendar Breeze or Summer Rain. In the end, I bought neither, realizing that Travis would only see it as, quite literally, burning money.

When I pulled onto our street, I was refreshed and ready to meet dinner head on. As I rounded the corner, our house came into view, and that was when I noticed the lifeless black lump in the middle of the asphalt. My mouth went dry. At first, I convinced myself it was a garbage bag. But as I neared, there was no mistaking the light stripe running down her back. I slammed on the brakes and threw the car into park, abandoning it in the middle of the street. In the distance, the faint echo of a nursery song disappeared on the breeze.

I ran to her, losing my flip-flops in the chaos and stubbing my toe. But I didn't feel it, because my body was numb. I knelt and stroked her hot fur, whispered that everything would be OK, even though I knew in my heart that things would never be the same again. A river of blood trickled from her ear and pooled near her head. Her breath was shallow and faint, but her body was warm, so I convinced myself that there was still time if someone could help me move her. Where the hell was Travis?

As if hearing my silent plea, Travis emerged from the house, disheveled and confused. When he caught sight of me huddled over

Willow's body, saw the deserted car with the door hanging open, his face drained of color, and he flew barefoot across the yard. Without speaking, he helped me load her into the back seat and watched, guilt stricken, from the porch as we drove to Dr. Chang's office. It was a tender mercy that we arrived ten minutes before her practice closed for the day. The vet technician met us in the parking lot and helped carry her into the building. She felt so heavy in my arms, so much bigger than the puppy I'd once plucked from the back of a van.

"I'm afraid there's simply too much damage to her organs. I've administered some pain relief, and she's comfortable for now." Dr. Chang locked in on my eyes in a way that made my stomach congeal. "But Audrey, the best thing you can do for Willow is give her a pain-free death." The words landed with a thud at the bottom of my heart. For some reason, all I could seem to think about were those damned candles, how I'd wasted five whole minutes while Willow lay dying in the street. Would five minutes have been long enough to prevent the accident in the first place? If only I could go back and do it all over, reset the clock and make everything right.

"She won't feel anything," Dr. Chang went on, her voice calm and warm, like freshly baked bread. As she went about the ritual of ending Willow's life, she narrated the process of each step, as if this would somehow make it easier for me to accept what was happening. I heard her voice, but the words were incoherent. All I could focus on was Willow. Even now, I can remember every second of our last moments, a frame-by-frame reel of Willow blinking up at me. One, two, three times, slowing down with the effort, as if it took everything she had. And on the fourth, when her eyes should have opened again to meet mine, they didn't.

"I'm so sorry for your loss," Dr. Chang said softly. "I'll leave you alone with her for a moment. I believe your husband just arrived. I'll send him back."

Tears clouded my eyes, heavy and hot. How could Willow be gone when she was still right here? How was I supposed to return to a house where Willow didn't greet me at the door and shadow my steps for every minor task? Somehow, all those insignificant snippets now felt precious. I should have memorized them. Behind me, the door opened and closed. And though he didn't speak right away, I could feel Travis in the room.

"I'm sorry," he said softly. "I just let her out for a second," he pleaded. "She was supposed to come back. She always comes back." I could sense his tears as he spoke, but they didn't soften the edge in my tone when I finally worked up the resolve to say something.

"You were supposed to be watching them," I muttered without turning around.

"I was."

"You never loved her like I did," I shot back. "She was always an inconvenience for you."

"That's not true, Audrey! I loved Willow as much as you did. It was an accident!"

"No, this was not an accident, Travis. It was careless and stupid and lazy, but it wasn't an accident." My voice was shaking. "It never should have happened. It wouldn't have happened if I had been there!" Hearing my words aloud induced a fresh current of pain that ripped through my chest. If I hadn't been selfish, if I hadn't needed that brief escape, if I had just been where I was supposed to be, Willow would still be breathing.

Even so, I couldn't stop myself from saying the one thing I knew would break him. "You did this," I said softly, my tone cold. Tears burned the corners of my eyes and slipped freely down my cheeks. "This is on you, Travis. I will never forgive you for this." It hurt too much to admit that maybe I was just as much to blame.

CHAPTER 28

My heartbeat is in a race to outpace the Honda when I swerve onto our street and floor the gas. Sweat beads sprout along my hairline, and it's all I can do to keep from crying. All those years when I lay awake at night, wishing for one last chance to hold Willow—and against all the laws of nature, it actually happened. But I squandered the universe's gift. I was selfish and bored and prideful, and I lost sight of the most important thing.

Our house emerges as a pinprick in my windshield, steadily enlarging as I speed toward it. Frantic, I scan the horizon and breathe a sigh of relief when I realize that Willow is nowhere in sight. Hope rises in my chest. Maybe she came back. It's early, after all. Maybe there's still time.

I park in the drive, not bothering to unlatch the girls, who are both asleep. Puttering around in her flower beds, Mrs. Murray jabs a trowel at me as if I've just committed a crime. I suppose I have. "Have you lost your mind? You're liable to kill a person, driving like that! What in the Sam Hill do you think you're doing? Do you hear me?" But I'm too frantic to apologize. A faint melody echoes through the neighborhood as an ice cream truck drifts farther away, and my vision goes blurry. Chest heaving, I fly up the front steps and burst through the door, where I find Sonia and Travis in the kitchen. She's wearing a black sports bra and the tiniest pair of shorts I've ever seen, glistening with the fresh glow of a workout. "Audrey," she says, like I've caught them off guard. I'm too flustered to analyze her presence, but I hope it has something to do with Willow.

"Where's Willow?" I ask, breathless.

Sonia seems concerned. "You're white as a sheet."

"Where is my dog?" It isn't so much a question as a demand.

"She's right here," Travis says, looking at me like I've grown a third eyeball. "Sonia brought her back."

Wagging her tail, Willow emerges from the living room, her limbs perfect and full of life. It feels like someone has just yanked a knife from my heart, and my entire body seems to fold in on itself when I kneel to her. She pounces into my arms and licks the tears on my cheeks, a soft whine of elation punctuating her fervent kisses. I check her from head to toe, peeling back her fur in search of blood or scrapes, but there isn't a flaw. She's perfect. When my pulse finally slows, I ask Travis to bring in the girls, then rise to my feet, turning to Sonia. "Thank you for bringing her home."

"Found her on my run," she says, practically beaming at the scene.

"I can't thank you enough." And I mean it. I will never be able to repay this woman. I don't even care if she's in love with my husband or if Travis thinks she's hot. She brought my best friend back, and for that, I owe her everything.

"Of course. I recognized her right away. I remember you saying how skittish she could be off leash."

"Right. I did say that." As I speak the words, something novel occurs to me, something that has the potential to change everything in this new reality. Five years ago, Sonia came to my house one morning, and I didn't answer the door, choosing sleep over awkward conversation with my new neighbor. But a couple of weeks ago, when presented with the same choice, I chose the latter. And that seemingly insignificant, entirely uneventful exchange means that Sonia knows Willow. And thus, Willow's life has been spared. I changed something, and the future was altered. I have no idea what this means. Will fate require me to sacrifice something else I love in return? The thought makes me uneasy, but I shake off the worry. For now, Willow is here with me, licking my hand, nuzzling her head against my leg, and I am overwhelmed with gratitude.

"Well, I'd better get going," Sonia says. "I left Penelope at home with Amir, and he'll be wondering where I am." Her brown eyes meet mine, warm and full of empathy. "I'm really glad she's OK."

"Me too," I manage. "And I'm so grateful to you." Sonia cannot possibly understand just how much.

"Hey, what are friends for?" She flashes a brilliant smile and heads for the door, her sleek ponytail swinging behind her. Before she reaches it, she swivels, snapping her fingers like she's forgotten something.

"Oh, I meant to tell you. I'm having a barbecue in a few weeks. You'll come, won't you?" I can see hope in the creaseless planes of her face when she presses her palms together. "And bring Willow!"

After what Sonia has just done for me, there is only one answer. A genuine smile takes shape on my lips. "Of course. We'll be there."

~

The next day, I stay home with the girls and Willow, too afraid to let her out of my sight. I worry that death may be lurking just around the corner, patiently waiting to pounce when I finally let my guard down. I spend the morning making Play-Doh villages with Eadie, and then we read *Stellaluna* on the couch, followed by the bat book. I recite all sorts of information Eadie already knows by heart, how the bats help farmers by eating pesky insects and how they are the only flying mammal, how the oldest bat is over forty years old. "There are thousands of baby bats in the cave, but the mother bat can always find her baby," I read. Eadie looks up from the crook of my arm, her eyes full of questions. "But how does the mommy find her baby if there's so many and they all look the same?"

"I don't know," I admit. "Maybe the baby has a special smell the mommy recognizes." I narrow my eyes at her. "How do you think I would find you in a crowded room?"

"Because I look like you?"

"That's right." I smile.

"But what if there are too many people? What if it was so many kids you couldn't ever find me and I stayed lost forever?"

I wrap my arms around her compact shoulders and shift her into my lap, then fit my chin beside hers. "Eadie, it doesn't matter where you are or how many people are around. I will always find you." I give her a squeeze, and she giggles, wiggling out of my grasp. Her feet patter up the stairs. I'm 99 percent certain she is going to change into her third outfit of the day before we've even had lunch.

I scoop Ruby from her bouncer and nestle onto the couch for our second nursing session. She's finally beginning to settle into a routine instead of demanding food at random hours. Her evening colic never arrived last night, and I'm finding that our time together today as been almost . . . peaceful. I'm beginning to think that I could stay here, that I'll be totally fine if things never go back to the way they were before my fall.

I could do this.

I could relive this part of my life with my babies and my dog and . . . maybe even Travis. I'm still not sure what this means for us, whether I should trust him again, whether I should work to make this marriage last instead of preparing for its demise. If I never have to resent him for the loss of Willow, maybe we could make it after all. Last night, we had the most honest conversation we've had in ages. I told him how upset I was that he never listens when I share important information. I told him that Willow was my dog first and, as such, I pull rank where she is concerned. Under no circumstance is she allowed off leash unless it's in the backyard. He seemed penitent and understanding, even vowing to walk her more after work. But no matter how intrigued I am by the idea of a perfect family, I can't seem to forget his words the night he left. He called me an ice queen and stormed out, never fought for us. He even started dating someone else. Clearly, I wasn't enough the first time around, or he wouldn't be with Jamie.

When the girls go down for their naps, I tug out my phone and check my messages. I texted Julian early this morning to apologize and check on the status of his offer. But he hasn't responded, and I'm starting to worry that we scared him away. I wouldn't blame him. I've made my peace with losing the deal. I am so lucky that Eadie and Willow are safe. No one gets everything at the same time, so maybe I'll have to wait a little while for my career to take off. And that's OK. All I want is the decency of a response.

I decide to call Lexy, hoping to catch her on a lunch break. She picks up after the third ring, her voice upbeat. I can tell she's chewing, and I imagine her shoveling a forkful of salad into her mouth. "Hey, babe. How did it go yesterday?"

"Terrible," I admit because there really isn't any other way to spin the facts. "I had to take Eadie to the emergency room for a cut. I haven't heard from Julian since, and I'm pretty sure he's avoiding me."

"Oh my God, how is she?"

"She's fine," I reassure her. "But it was an absolute disaster. I'm pretty sure blood in the pool is not a great selling point."

"Well, at least it was memorable."

"What am I doing here, Lex?" I groan. "Am I crazy thinking that I could work this deal? Was it stupid to take on so much right after having Ruby?"

"No, of course not." She takes a long sip of something and clears her throat. "Listen, if he doesn't text back, just let him go. There are bigger fish in the sea, and this guy is not worth the headache. Just enjoy your time with the girls, let me help you with the rest of your showings—and for God's sake, get some sleep! You shouldn't be chasing Eadie around giant houses. You should be resting, enjoying your time off. Hell, it's what I would do."

"Maybe you're right," I concede, thinking about how nice this morning has been.

"Of course I am. No more worrying about this listing. No more thinking about work at all. I've got you."

"All right," I sigh. "Thanks, Lex."

There's truth in my friend's words. I know I should listen to her advice even if part of me wants to keep calling Julian until he picks up. But she's right. With my family intact and my dog still alive, maybe I've already achieved the big break I was hoping for. And for now, it's enough.

CHAPTER 29

When the weekend arrives, Travis reminds me that his band scored a coveted spot at the Bonnet Hill Septemberfest, a huge honor for their trio; the headliners are all washed-up groups I've actually heard of. I'm 90 percent certain he mentioned it before, but I was only half listening, too worried about my precarious deal with Julian. When I try to recall the event, my brain comes up empty. Five years ago, I didn't attend. Back then, Willow had just passed away, and I'd been nursing a broken heart as well as an infant.

Since Ruby's birth, my attendance at Travis's performances steadily declined until, eventually, I stopped going altogether. It was easy to justify. It wasn't my fault that we didn't have the money for a babysitter. And the usual venues were too smoky for children, not to mention crawling with illness. Back then, it made good sense to put the kids to bed early and revel in a few blissful hours of work emails. But this time around, with Willow miraculously alive and a new forecast for the future, I'm actually looking forward to getting out of the house. Hopefully, it will take my mind off the fact that Julian hasn't returned any of my texts. Besides, the festival is a family event, outdoors, and loaded with kid-friendly activities, like a dino dig and a miniature grocery store. Eadie will adore it.

When we arrive, Travis wrangles the double stroller out of the trunk, along with his guitar, and the four of us meander through the crowd of sun-kissed bodies clutching iced teas and craft beers. The late-September air is thick with the doughy scent of corn dogs and funnel cakes. While Travis searches for Marcus and Dane, I commandeer the stroller and decide to peruse the various booths selling personalized cutting boards, bohemian jewelry, and artisan jams.

When we come upon the dino dig, Eadie's eyes light up. From the shaded edges of the sandbox, Ruby and I watch as she unearths chunks of fool's gold and quartz and tiny plastic dinosaurs. As a soft breeze whips through her curls, my gaze drifts to my sleeping baby, and I'm overcome by a nostalgia that draws tears to my eyes. There is so much about this stage I let slip away, so many ordinary afternoons like this one that I should have pasted in my internal scrapbook before they were eclipsed by a thousand others. Before long, Eadie enlists the help of a little boy about her age. And by the looks on their faces, they are completely intent on tunneling to China. I'm not sure I'll ever be able to tear her away.

When she's collected a tidy little pile of treasures, I check my watch. Travis's set is coming up. Miraculously, I manage to lure Eadie back into the stroller with the promise of a frozen lemonade. We make our way to a crowded concession stand, where we endure a sweltering wait that tests everyone's patience, including that of the strangers around us. And just like that, my nostalgia evaporates along with my good mood. By the time we make it to the front, I'm desperate for a bathroom. Eadie is whining about the heat, and Ruby is wailing to be picked up, but there's no way I'm relinquishing my place in line to address any of these problems, because just being here feels like I've mastered a level on *Survivor*. Above their screams, I relay my order. Eadie announces that she is starving, so at the last minute, I throw in a corn dog and fries, even though the price is borderline criminal. Much to everyone's relief, we move out of the growing line where I scoop Ruby into my sweaty arms and wait for our number to be called.

"Audrey," someone calls out, a voice I immediately recognize. With wild eyes, I whip around to find Marcus jogging toward us, raising a hand in greeting.

"Hey!" I plaster on a smile. It's been months since I've seen him. Months in my old life, at least. His chestnut hair is shiny and longer than I remember, brushing the tops of his shoulders. It definitely looks better than mine, which has been zapped by the humidity and the stress of corralling two tiny humans.

"Thought that was you." Slipping a tattooed arm around my waist, he leans in and plants a friendly kiss on my cheek. "Oh wow!" he says, putting a palm to Ruby's back. "Is this baby Ruby?"

I nod, shielding her head from the sun with a hand. Her papery skin is dappled in red blotches, and I worry that maybe I've let her get too hot. "This is her," I say proudly. "Though I'm afraid you caught us at a bad time. She's a little grumpy." As am I.

"She's adorable," he says. "Hey, Speedy Eadie!" He holds out a closed fist and waits until Eadie meets it with a coy smile and a tiny graze of her knuckles. The girls have always loved Travis's bandmates; it doesn't hurt that they often bring candy.

Digging his hands into his jean pockets, Marcus shifts his weight and redirects his attention to me. "So, how've you been since the baby? We've been meaning to check on you, but Travis said you weren't up for company yet."

God bless my husband for listening to me at least some of the time. "I'm great," I lie. "It's just been a little stressful at home with so much . . . change." I swallow hard. *Change* isn't really the right word. I'm not sure what term could accurately sum up the last few weeks, but *batshit crazy* comes to mind.

"Totally understand." Marcus nods empathetically, though he can't possibly know the extent of my problems. He doesn't have kids, and he's never been married. "Which is why I told Travis not to feel bad about the whole Nashville thing," he adds. "Of course, Dane and I were disappointed, but we totally get it."

This tidbit of information throws me for a loop. "What do you mean?" I say, scouring my memory in case Travis had mentioned another gig. With everything that's happened lately, it's entirely possible I missed something.

"He didn't tell you?" Marcus blows out a long breath, then sucks in his lower lip, like maybe he wasn't supposed to let this part slip. "Figures." He rakes a hand through his hair. "We finally found a decent drummer, Dane's cousin, who used to sub in for some pretty big names in the industry. He landed us a gig opening for Salvage Sound last month, but Travis said it wasn't a good time."

My brain stumbles over the name. Salvage Sound is Travis's favorite band. They are the entire reason he started making music in the first place and even inspired his career. And Travis turned them down. This fact ricochets around inside my skull, leaving me dumbfounded. I think of the concert tickets I purchased for his birthday. Was that why he took Marcus to the concert instead of me? Was he trying to make it up to his friend for thwarting their dreams? "I had no idea," I finally say, feeling ashamed. "Travis didn't tell me." I wonder why. I'd like to think that if he had, I would have told him to go for it. But the truth is, the timing would have been terrible. Besides, he barely managed the time off work as it was. Travis saved me from having to be the villain by doing the responsible thing. So why do I feel so guilty?

"It's all right," Marcus says, as if it's no big deal. But I know it totally is. Travis owns every Salvage Sound album on vinyl. As a teenager, he once sold plasma just to buy a ticket to one of their concerts. "We knew you needed him more than we did. Hell, you and the girls are all he talks about," he adds with a chuckle. "But I have to admit that family looks good on him. Maybe one of these days, I'll take a page from his book and finally settle down."

The pieces of information slide into place, triangulating on my pride. Maybe I wasn't the only person in this marriage who had made sacrifices for the greater good. Maybe Travis had collected regrets that were no less valid than mine.

Later, I scope out a grassy patch overlooking the stage, then spread out a quilt where the girls and I can listen to Travis's band perform a few covers. We're far enough from the action that the amps aren't overpowering, and the late-afternoon breeze is almost refreshing. They end with a song Travis wrote when we were dating, and I feel my heart contract.

You ask me for the time, and I tell you I don't know.
The world spins so much slower every time I hold you close.

It's about us. Before the kids, before the mortgage, before the jam-packed calendar and empty bank account. When we used to take his old Jeep out to the woods and sleep under the stars with nothing but a tarp and a couple of sleeping bags. *You ever think about how short life is compared to space?* he asked me, our backs flush with the cold ground, one arm cradling me against his chest. "I mean, one day on Venus is like over two hundred days on Earth. Time is sort of meaningless, if you think about it."

"Maybe not meaningless," I said, burying my chin in the warm crook of his neck. "More like relative. Just depends on where you're standing in the universe."

He pulled back to study my face, a faint beam of light emanating from the lantern casting a flickering glow around us. "Then I guess I'm in the right place," he said, tilting my chin toward his. And we kissed, long and slow.

I try to picture Travis saying goodbye to his dream, and something breaks inside me. He cups the microphone with both hands and leans in, delivering the last line with a tenderness I've seen over and over when he sings to the girls. The richness of his tenor voice blankets the crowd, but this time, it feels like he's singing just for me.

CHAPTER 30

It's a little after 5:00 a.m., and the sun has yet to appear. If my hazy memory is to be trusted, I fed Ruby around midnight. Judging by the tender ache in my breasts, it's past time to nurse her again. Worry ricochets in my sternum as my fingers fumble around for the baby monitor on the nightstand. Since Ruby moved to the nursery last week, we've both been sleeping for longer stretches, but I can never shake the fear that maybe I didn't hear her cry out for me during the night. I check the monitor, and a note of panic rises in my chest. The little green light is off. It makes no sense. I test the volume religiously every evening before melting into bed. Was I so tired after the festival last night that I forgot? What if she stopped breathing? Ever since Willow cheated death, I'm acutely aware that there are no guarantees that everything will turn out as it had before. The future has never felt more fragile.

My heart vibrating, I race up the stairs and throw the nursery door open, expecting to find my baby in a puddle of tears. Instead, Travis greets me with a finger to his lips, shushing me before I can make sense of the scene. He's perched in the rocking chair, cradling Ruby like a football against his chest with a bottle, Willow cuddled at his feet. Instinctively, I want to ask if he's filled it with formula or the breast milk I left in the freezer, but I can't bring myself to interrupt this moment. It feels too sacred. The sight of the three of them cuddling in the quiet morning tugs at my emotions. Willow doesn't usually tether herself to Travis the way she does to me, but maybe she's warming to him.

Or maybe she wanted to be sure he was tending to Ruby correctly. I'd always assumed she was following me around when I trailed the kids, but it occurs to me now that she might be just as attached to them. The thought makes my eyes sting with fresh tears. Willow's devotion to the people I love somehow means more than her devotion to me. "I didn't hear her wake," I whisper, moving slowly across the room. Willow's ears perk up at my presence, and she rises to greet me.

"We were hoping you wouldn't," Travis replies softly. Tired circles are etched around his eyes, but he looks content. I think about what Marcus told me and feel a rush of warmth. I picture Travis quietly slipping from bed, planting a soft kiss on my forehead, and turning off the monitor. I remember this now, Travis taking on feedings as nursing became more predictable. In the beginning, it was hard to let him. I worried he wouldn't know how to comfort Ruby the way I could. But truth be told, maybe what I truly feared was that he would be better at it than me, rendering me obsolete. "Now, go back to sleep. I've got her." With that, he leans back against the rocker, lulled by the gentle sound of Ruby's suckling. The picture of the two of them, so serene and snug, makes me wonder. If our marriage is a tapestry, maybe this was the part right before the threads began to tangle? Knowing what I do now, could I prevent the knots and avoid all the heartache down the line?

The first time I laid eyes on Travis was in the middle of the H&M I managed. I was repricing a rack of belts when he emerged from the dressing room stuffed in a putrid orange sweater, so tight on his broad frame I got secondhand embarrassment. I pretended not to notice, but he caught my eye and waved me over. "Excuse me, ma'am. Can I get your opinion on something?" He gestured to his unflattering top and did a little spin. "Do you think I have the complexion to pull this off?" A smolder took shape on his face as he flexed his biceps in the mirror. At the time, I thought he was serious, but I soon learned it was just typical Travis.

I pressed my lips together, struggling to find a polite way to tell him the truth. "No. But for what it's worth, no one has the complexion to pull off that sweater. You look like a squash."

He considered my observation, crinkling his nose. "Not exactly what I expected you to say. Don't they pay you to sell this stuff?"

"They pay me to make sure the store doesn't burn down," I said. "But I would definitely burn that shirt. It's not doing you any favors." Feeling altruistic, I plucked a baby blue gingham button-up off a rack. "Here," I said, pushing the hanger toward him. "Try this one."

"Are you sure?" Unconvinced, he inspected it at arm's length. "It's just that . . . I'm taking a woman out tonight."

"Mm-hmm," I said, not sure why he was telling me this, the price gun growing heavy in my hand.

"Her profile said she's a Longhorns fan, hence the orange," he explained. "And she's a premed student, which means she's way smarter than me. So I need to look like the kind of guy that's responsible but not boring. You know what I mean?"

I actually did.

"Ooooh, maybe I should add glasses," he said, noticing the rack of eyewear behind me.

Defenses lowered, I stifled a smile. It was sort of adorable how much effort he was putting into a first date. The last guy who took me out showed up in wrinkled cargo shorts and spent an entire hour ranking the cinematography of Nicolas Cage movies. "In that case, just trust me," I said, confiscating the sweater. "Definitely not this one."

A few days later, I'd nearly forgotten about his chin dimple and those deep-set blue eyes when he materialized at my cash register. "I need to return this," he said, sliding over the shirt I'd sold him.

"I take it the date didn't go well?" I flashed him a quick glance as I searched for a tag to scan.

"That depends." He leaned in and made a face that confirmed my suspicion. "What does it mean if you tell a girl you had a really great time and you'd like to take her out again and she responds with the phrase 'No, thank you'?"

I did my best to keep from wincing. "I think it means she's very polite. She could have just said no."

He pursed his lips, considering it. "Or"—he held up a finger—"she didn't like the shirt."

"Unfortunately," I said, pushing the item toward him, "I can't refund this because, A, you've just admitted to wearing it while eating, and, B, there's no tag."

"But I didn't get anything on it," he said, disappointed. "It's one of the many things I'm good at. Eating without spilling anything on myself."

"Truly, you're a catch. I can't imagine why things didn't work out with her."

"What can I say? I'm a graceful diner." He puffed up his chest. "Come on, I'll prove it to you. Let me take you for a pretzel or something."

His directness flustered me. He wasn't the first guy to flirt with me in the store, but he was definitely the first to make me blush. And he was cute. Nevertheless, no girl in her right mind said yes on the first ask from a stranger. "I have to work," I said, trying to look busy.

"Don't they have to give you breaks?" he pushed. "Isn't that, like, federal law or something?"

I shook my head. "That's not a thing here."

"Come on, fifteen minutes," he insisted. "That's all I ask. I have to repay you for your help."

"The fact that you're here trying to return this means I didn't help you."

"Maybe you did, though." The weight of his gaze made my palms sweaty, but I couldn't seem to look anywhere except those endless blue eyes and that playful grin. Even with a five-o'clock shadow, he was ridiculously kissable. He leaned forward, planting his brawny hands atop the counter. "Maybe finding out that girl was the wrong person for me brought me one step closer to finding the right one." A subtle smile teased the corners of his mouth, just enough to make me reconsider.

I chewed my lip, letting the invitation marinate. There was something about the way he'd flexed his muscles in that ridiculous sweater that made me curious. I threw a discreet glance at my watch, then checked behind me to be sure someone could cover my absence.

Just fifteen minutes. Just one pretzel with the first man who had made me smile in months. Just the first day of the rest of my life.

CHAPTER 31

I decide against going back to bed. I'm too wired to sleep, and Eadie will be bouncing off the walls in less than an hour, so I pull on a pair of running shorts and a T-shirt, then wrestle my feet into a pair of tennis shoes. Willow tilts her head as if to ask where we're going, and I run a hand over her sleek fur. Stolen moments with Willow like this are few and far between. Since her brush with death, I've been trying to make the most of our time together, because it all still feels too good to be true. I clip her leash, fluff out her yellow bandanna, and we head into the crisp morning air, our footsteps pounding out a gentle rhythm.

With Willow leading, we round the block, then venture into an adjacent enclave with tidy townhomes all lined up on electric-green lawns. This part of the neighborhood is a recent addition, expanded to accommodate the flocks of people moving to Texas for its lower cost of living. It's dotted with glittering community pools, pristine playgrounds, and a newly minted fitness center. But even with the flair of sleek roofs and freshly paved streets, something is missing. Grandma Beatrice's house may not be glamorous, but it does have a certain charm. The pavement, slowly worn by decades of children's bicycles, is ensconced by a tunnel of elderly oaks. The uneven sidewalks sprouting weeds are rife with character and memory, and that's not something that even a real estate agent like me can easily put into words.

When I reach our street again, it occurs to me that even if we could afford something newer, I wouldn't want to leave. I love our home. We moved in a few months after Eadie was born, with the intention of renovating. But with both of us working and raising two kids, we only got around to making a few cosmetic updates—like the laminate floors in the living room. We relied on a DIY YouTuber who'd forgotten to mention safety goggles. Travis nearly lost an eye sawing the quarter round. I built the floating shelves in the bathroom myself, smoothing every bump and divot with sandpaper, because the ones at Wayfair were overpriced.

The sun peeks out from behind our roof, casting a warm neon glow over Sonia's place. Her roses meander along the trellises flanking her front door, and her mailbox planter is dotted with fresh zinnias. Our house doesn't get morning sun, and any time I plant something, it dies on arrival. As I admire Sonia's raised beds overflowing with marigolds, something in the periphery pulls my attention. Smoke is trickling from the Gills' side yard, just beyond the wooden fence. A bonfire, maybe? It hasn't rained in weeks, and the county is under a burn ban. It's way too early for grilling—or a bonfire, for that matter. I consider knocking on the front door, but they might still be sleeping. Instead, I creep to the side of the house and press my ear to the fence. But I'm met with silence. Willow whines, as if she, too, senses something is off, and it only fuels my worry.

I'm not the sort of person to trespass on my neighbor's lawn, but the smoke seems to be worsening, and I'd hate myself if something terrible happened to the Gills when I could have prevented it. My stomach in knots, I decide to locate the source before yelling *fire* and waking the entire house. Sonia called me a friend after all, even saved my dog. And isn't that what a friend would do? When I've finally worked up the courage, I draw in a steadying breath and press my weight against the gate door. It groans open, eliciting a gasp from the other side.

A burst of coughing fills the air as Sonia jumps up from a lawn chair rather ungracefully. With one hand, she attempts to clear the smoke away while the other holds a vape pen. Her hair is piled atop her head in a messy bun. I've never seen her like this. She's in oversize gingham pajama pants paired with a tank top that is supposed to be white. It's covered in splotches of unidentifiable yellow that I suspect are the work of Penelope.

"I'm so sorry!" I say, backpedaling. "I saw the smoke and . . . I didn't mean to just walk into your yard. I was worried." *Stupid Audrey!* Why did I jump straight to an emergency? What kind of person just walks into someone's backyard with so little to go on?

"It's OK." This is the first time I've seen Sonia without makeup, and I can't discern whether she's upset or just tired. There are shadows beneath her eyes, not unlike the ones I've earned over the last few weeks.

"There was smoke," I explain. "I thought something was burning."

Sonia chuckles. "Guess I can't blame you. This isn't exactly on brand for me." She takes another drag from the pen. In all the years I've crossed paths with Sonia, she has been gracious and polite, sometimes annoyingly so. But never sarcastic.

The vapor is cloying, so a quick escape feels like the best option. "I'll just . . . let you get back to . . . you know." But as I move to leave, Sonia calls after me.

"It's not the same as smoking, you know." She seems nervous, as if she knows the narrative I'm already spinning about her. But she's wrong. All I can think about is getting back to my own derelict yard and neglected plants. Hopefully Willow has enjoyed our walk, because it's going to be our last for the foreseeable future. "It's chamomile and lavender," she points out, even though I didn't ask. "I'm basically breathing in a meadow." This may very well be a fib she's concocted to allay her guilt. But since I've just consumed cake for breakfast, I'm hardly one to call her out.

"And I don't do it all the time," she adds, setting herself down in the chair once more. She gestures to the one beside her. "Only when I'm contemplating running away to somewhere warm and tropical." Though she says this with a smile, there's a hint of truth beneath her crumbling veneer.

I inch my way toward the chair. I've never been great at making friends, but even I can sense that she needs someone to talk to.

"My parents are visiting again . . . unexpectedly," she explains, before taking another drag.

This sounds like a surprise enemy invasion. I wonder how long her parents plan to stay, but I'm not dumb enough to ask. "I totally understand," I say. And it's the truth. When Iris comes to town, always unannounced and never with a plan, I tend to revert to fight-or-flight mode. For a woman who didn't care whether I ate lunch or not, she sure has a lot of opinions about Eadie's limited palate. While she reorganizes my pantry, claiming that my methods are feral, I invent any number of excuses to run unessential errands, leaving Travis to deal with her. It isn't fair to him, I know, but my mother has a way of bringing out the worst in me. For the first time, it occurs to me that I've been keeping Travis at arm's length, not unlike the way Iris handled me.

Sonia turns her head away and emits another stream of smoke. "It's just that . . . they pushed me to get married, then begged for a grandchild. And now that I've finally given them one, nothing is ever good enough. They practically move into my house with enough luggage to start a commune, all so they can hover over my parenting and insult my career."

It's hard to believe that the Sonia I know could disappoint anyone, and she definitely doesn't vape. But considering she saved Willow, I owe her a sympathetic ear at the very least. "Could be worse," I say with a shrug. "At least they want to be involved."

She bristles. "Well, excuse me if I prefer their involvement from eight thousand miles away, when we're separated by a decent-sized ocean. What's wrong with video chat and Skype? Are all of these technological advancements for nothing?"

"It's not you," I say. Maybe she was right about the chamomile and lavender, because I'm starting to feel more at ease. "They get closer to the end and start to realize how badly they parented the first time around. They see your kid as the do-over. The second chance. Never mind the time they left you at a sleepover for two nights to go clubbing in Fort Worth. Suddenly, they've become experts on screen-time studies." As soon as the admission is out, I wonder if I've said too much. Sonia and I aren't the sort of friends who share personal details about our lives, let alone our childhood traumas.

Sonia shakes her head. "No, it has more to do with me than Penelope. They're here to right the ship."

"How so?"

A beat of awkward silence ensues. "They sent me to college in America to be a doctor or a politician or a biological engineer." She cuts me a pointed look. "Not an influencer."

"But surely they must be proud."

She scoffs. "They're proud of Amir for bringing in a noble paycheck. They're proud of Penelope for carrying on the family cheekbones. But no . . . they are most certainly not proud of me." She lets out a sigh. "Let's just say social media isn't the sort of career they want to bring up at dinner parties."

"Why not?" I ask. "Thousands of people value your opinion. If you wear a Birkin bag to the beach, they wear their Birkin bags to the beach. Politicians only wish they had that kind of sway."

This earns a tiny smile. She shoots me a side-eye. "I would never wear my Birkin to the beach."

"Listen . . . all I'm saying is, don't listen to the haters, even if they happen to be related to you." It sounds like something Lexy would say, and I'm proud to be the one to dispense advice for a change. "You can't please everyone, and life is short. Your parents already had their chance at a career. Now it's your turn. The only thing you owe them is to live a good life. One that makes *you* happy."

She considers this as she reaches a lithe hand to stroke Willow's fur. Willow nuzzles her and rolls onto her back, exposing her soft undercoat. "Any tips on how to do that?"

"Do what?"

"Live a life that makes you happy?"

"Aren't you happy?" I ask, genuinely surprised. It only made sense to assume as much when phrases like *#happy* and *#zenvibes* and *#thesimplelife* punctuate her morning posts.

"I think so," she concedes. But she seems uncertain as she mindlessly strokes Willow's belly. "After I had Penelope, I struggled to . . . acclimate. We'd just moved here, and I didn't know anyone. I had my online following, sure. But living, breathing people?" She shakes her head. "Not so many."

A trickle of shame seeps through me. Penelope is a few months older than Ruby. If I'd known how alone Sonia felt, I could have been there for her, just as she's been for me after having Ruby. Why hadn't I? How many times have I seen her outside, coming and going, never once moving past a superficial greeting? There have been so many opportunities to introduce myself, invite her over for drinks, walk over a casserole. I don't excel in the art of casserole making, but that is what neighbors are supposed to do, right? An apology feels like a weak gesture. Still, all I can say is "I'm sorry I didn't come over sooner."

"Only took a fire to get you here," she jokes. "I totally understand." She waves away my guilt. "You and Travis have your hands full over there. Honestly, I don't know how you do it."

"Do what?"

"Manage two kids between jobs. I can barely keep my head above water with Penelope." This, coming from the woman who snaps a selfie every morning with a new look of the day. It strikes me as borderline hilarious. My look has evolved into the look of the year as it is always the same look that can pretty much be summed up by a "before" photo in one of those TV mommy makeovers. Lexy was right. I suffer from basic-white-girl syndrome. And possibly a vitamin deficiency, as evidenced by all the hair I seem to be losing in the shower.

I shoot Sonia a dubious glance. "If it makes you feel any better, I don't think we're really managing." More like surviving a daily battle. Admittedly, things have been better lately between Travis and me, but it's easy to be happier with Willow still in the picture. It doesn't change the fact that I'll always shoulder most of the childcare, make most of the concessions in my career, quietly resent him every time he's late or forgets to pick up a kid or doesn't check the shared calendar I've so carefully curated. "Sometimes . . ." I hesitate, worried that maybe I'm sharing too much with the woman who supposedly spread lice rumors about my family. But when I look up at Sonia, her brow is furrowed, like she's really listening. I don't know why, but I feel certain I can trust her. "Sometimes, I don't think we'll make it out of these early years unscathed, you know?"

She pulls her eyebrows together, considering this. Then her face relaxes into a smug grin. "Nah. Never gonna happen. You and Travis are the real deal."

I cut her a sharp look. "What makes you say that?"

She draws her supermodel legs beneath her, then lets out a weighty sigh. "OK, don't think any less of me. I promise, I'm completely sane. But ever since I was little, I've had this uncanny ability to predict whether a couple will stay together. It's like . . ." She purses her lips. "Like I can tell the future, but only about certain things. Like relationships," she points out. "And also, Nordstrom shoe sales."

I arch an eyebrow, but I'm totally invested in whatever she's about to say.

She leans forward conspiratorially. "OK, the first time it happened, it was my aunt and uncle. I mean, people in my family do not get divorced. But even at nine years old, I just knew they weren't going to make it. They did all the same things as my parents—family vacations, two kids, same cultural background, Sunday dinners at my grandparents' house. Never even a whisper of a fight. But every time I was around them, the air just felt . . . stale. They stayed together twenty-three years, raised four kids, but they never could fake their way to happy. No chemistry. Then I became a fortune teller on every major celebrity split." She counts them on her fingers. "Brad and Gwyneth, Brad and Jennifer, Brad and Angelina—"

"Pretty low-hanging fruit, don't you think?"

"That's fair," she concedes. "But Selena Gomez and Justin Bieber. I totally called that one."

I shoot her a playful smile. "Got any examples that are a little . . . poorer?"

She seems to mull over the question. "Me and my first husband," she says more seriously, casting her eyes to the ground. "I think I knew from the beginning we weren't right for each other, but I couldn't stand the idea of failing at something that was supposed to be easy, you know?"

"I'm sorry." I feel guilty for ever calling this woman surface level when clearly I know so little about her.

Sonia shrugs. "It was a long time ago. All I'm saying is, I've seen the way he talks about you when you're not around, the way he's anxious to get back to you and the kids whenever I catch him alone. I've watched him open your car door and reach for your hand and swing Eadie around in the yard. It's obvious he's happy." She almost winces. "I realize that sort of makes me seem like a stalker, but in my defense, Penelope doesn't do much yet and the days are long," she reasons. "Sometimes I get bored."

Her honesty surprises me, but it's refreshing. I can't help but smile.

"Trust me, I don't get breakup vibes from you and Travis. It's just not in the cards."

Maybe Sonia thinks she can predict the future, but I've actually been there. I know what's waiting on the other side, and it doesn't look much better than the view here. Worse, in fact. I know that only a few months after our separation, Travis will start dating a woman named Jamie, and I can't scrub this knowledge from my brain. Had he been waiting for this marriage to fall apart so he could be free of me, live his life without constant nagging? Still, a part of me hopes that maybe she's right. Lately, I'm terrified that my time here is over, that I'll be zapped back to my regular life without getting to say goodbye.

"Thanks," I say, grateful for her vote of confidence, even if I'm not entirely convinced. I lean forward in my seat. "I should have said this sooner, but if you ever want to hang out or just talk, I'm free. I mean, in between Eadie's tantrums and Ruby's colic, I'm one hundred percent down to hang out."

She smiles, diverting her gaze.

Willow whines softly, reminding me that she hasn't eaten breakfast yet, and the sun is rising higher above my roof. "We should probably get going," I say, pushing myself up by my palms.

"Audrey," Sonia calls out, and I turn to meet her gaze. "Thank you for making sure I wasn't on fire."

"Of course," I say, letting a smile form on my lips. And I'm not lying. "Anytime."

CHAPTER 32

Two weeks have gone by with no word from Julian. While I've all but given up on the possibility of a sale, I can't shake the feeling that something is off. I can't blame him for bailing after the bloody debacle with Eadie, but aside from that, he'd been enamored by the house. "I just don't understand why he won't respond to my messages?" I throw myself onto the bed and stare at the ceiling, my body entirely limp, like a fainting Victorian woman. "I mean, it's common courtesy to inform a person if you no longer require their services."

"He's probably just busy," Travis says through his toothpaste.

"*Or* maybe he thinks I'm a terrible mother who lets her four-year-old light up cancer sticks. I swear, there were moments when I think Eadie was actually trying to throw me under the bus."

"I don't understand why you can't just call him," Travis says.

"Because I sent him three texts already," I explain for the hundredth time. "At this point, calling him reeks of desperation! And Lexy says it's beneath me."

"Lexy says a lot of things, doesn't she?" he mumbles loud enough for me to hear.

"What is that supposed to mean?"

"Nothing . . . it's just—" He shrugs. "Sometimes you value her opinion over mine."

I sit up, my back ramrod straight against the headboard. Over the past couple of weeks, I've been pleasantly surprised by the synchronicity in our home. Things have been better between us than I remember, which is likely due to the fact that Willow is alive and healthy. His accusation catches me off guard. "I do not."

"Forget it." Travis rinses his mouth out and spits, then circles around the bed and peels back the covers.

"No, I don't want to forget it." Glossing over our arguments was exactly what led us to separation, a short hop, skip, and jump away from divorce. "I want to know why you feel that way."

He plops into bed, then emits a heavy sigh. "OK." He turns to face me. "You remember that crime docuseries I suggested, the one about the hotel where that girl died and everyone thought it was haunted?"

I comb through my mental drawers, fairly certain when I land on a vague memory of the show in question. "I think so."

"You said, and I quote, *That's not really my speed.* But then a few weeks later you came home raving about the same show. You said Lexy suggested it and it was supposed to be *totally binge worthy.*"

"OK," I admit, letting the memory seep through me. "But that was one time. It's not like I make a habit of it."

"What about when I bought the wrong kind of diapers? You were fine with them until Lexy told you they weren't the right ones."

I admit he has a point. "You're right," I concede. "I'm sorry I've made you feel that way, Travis. I didn't know it bothered you."

"You never asked."

I let the comment wash over me and feel a twinge of guilt. I strive to emulate everything in Lexy's life in my own—the immaculate house, the successful career, the seamless work-life balance. And because I so desperately want those things, I do value Lexy's opinion, sometimes more than Travis's. Sometimes more than my own. But in the absence of a doting mother to show me the ropes, who else was I supposed to shadow? Still, Travis isn't wrong. "Maybe you're right, and I'm overthinking this." I grab my phone from the nightstand. Then drawing in a full breath, I bite my lower lip and dial. When Julian answers, I'm caught off guard.

"Uh . . . hi," I manage. "It's me. I mean its Audrey. Perkins."

"Audrey." He says my name like he's greeting a friend he hasn't seen in years. "I was just thinking about you."

"You were?"

"I was wondering how your little girl was faring after that nasty tumble."

The invisible fist clenching my chest releases its hold. "Oh, she's fine," I say. "A little bit of glue and she's back to her old self again."

"That's good to hear."

He doesn't say anything else, and heat flushes my neck. Finally, I clear my throat.

"Listen, I was calling to touch base about the property in Thornwood Estates. I know it's been a while since we've spoken. Are you still interested in moving forward?"

I hold my breath, and the silence hangs until he finally says, "About that . . ."

And that's all it takes to knock the wind out of my sails. He explains that his boys weren't totally sold on the house, how maybe he didn't think things through all the way before committing to such a big place, that perhaps an apartment or a condo would be better for a migratory bird like him.

For one brief moment, hope swells in my heart, because I'm not totally out of the equation. Not yet. "I'd be happy to show you some properties more suited to your needs. There are loads of places here perfect for someone like you, places where you wouldn't have to worry about keeping a yard."

"Thank you, Audrey," he says, in a way that tanks my spirits. "But I've actually decided to go with a different agent."

It feels like a stone has hit me in the gut. I expected him to pass on the house, but dumping me for someone else hits harder. It's not like he signed a contract or anything, so I shouldn't make it into a bigger deal than it is. To him, it's just business, but it feels cruel.

"It's not personal," he goes on, as if inferring my thoughts. "You just really seemed to have your hands full, and someone reached out with a listing I couldn't refuse. It's perfect, like it was built for me. Hopefully you understand."

And though I mumble something resembling a yes, I can't make sense of it.

I am incredulous. "Of course," I say. "Best of luck to you." I wonder who the lucky agent is. It certainly wouldn't surprise me if Douche Bag Tag struck, just as he had in that other version of my life. Poaching clients is totally his MO. "Just one more thing," I manage before he ends the call, afraid to let the opportunity slip away. Maybe it's better not to know, but something tells me I'll regret not asking. "Who's the agent?"

There's a beat of silence, and I can tell he's trying to remember the name. A man like Julian Mitchell must meet with loads of people. It can't be easy to recall them all.

"Alexis," he finally says. "Alexis Brennan."

~

"I can't believe she would do this to me," I say, pacing the length of our room.

Travis scrunches up his face. "I don't get it." He's sitting on the bed, his eyes following my footsteps. "I mean, how did she even know who your client was, much less get his phone number?"

"I don't know." I'm nearly apoplectic. "I mean, he's a pretty wealthy guy, has built up a solid reputation around Atlanta, so it's possible she might have known who he was when I dropped his name."

"Right, but it doesn't explain how she got his contact information." Travis rubs his forehead. He's been stuck on this one point for the past hour and a half, working through the layers of my story. If I weren't so blindsided by Lexy's betrayal, I might find his loyalty endearing. It feels like he's on my team again, like in the early days of our marriage, vowing not only to love me forever but to hate whoever I hate.

And then a detail so negligible comes to me. I never gave it a second thought. "Oh my God. I gave it to her," I realize. "I got locked out of my listing one morning and had to use Julian's phone to call for help. I called Lexy. His number is in her call history." The implications sink in slowly, painting a clear picture of how my best friend screwed me over right under my nose. Over the past few weeks, I'd willingly fed her details about Julian's needs. Had she been storing them away to use against me?

Travis gasps. "That bitch!"

"Right?" I say, grateful for his validation. I climb onto the bed beside him, tucking my feet beneath my gown. "I mean, what kind of person would cheer me on, tell me to go for my dream—all the while undermining me like a psychopath?"

"What are we gonna do?" Travis says. There's a storm brewing behind his eyes, and I sense that he is fully on board with whatever crazy thing I'm going to say next.

I flirt with the idea of calling Lexy or driving to her house, confronting her in front of Sterling so he can know exactly the sort of person he married. But I'm still relatively new at Harlow Realty. What's more, I wouldn't have been hired if Lexy hadn't pushed me to get my license and put in a good word. Going after her, even if it's justified, feels wrong. Besides, I don't want to sink to her level.

"Nothing," I finally say, feeling the knot in my chest loosen. "I don't want to talk to her. I don't want to look at her. It's too humiliating."

He cuts me a look of disbelief. "Seriously? She's the one who should be humiliated. She lied to your face and poached your client."

"She also got me the job in the first place," I point out. "And maybe it *was* too big of a deal for me to work on my own."

"Who cares? She's a shitty friend. I say we drive over there right now, bust in a couple of taillights, let her know she messed with the wrong woman." Travis pummels a fist into his open palm. He's kidding, but there's an undercurrent of anger that endears him to me.

"It's not going to change anything, Travis. I know who she is now. And that's all I can ask for." It's been over three weeks since I've slipped into the past, and the one thing I've learned is that time is truly the best teacher. It shows you who people really are. But more importantly, it's shown me who I am. And I don't think I'm the sort of woman who wants to go all scorched-earth on a person who pulled the wool over my eyes. If anything, maybe I'm the one who deserves punishment for not reading the signs sooner. I thought Lexy was my friend, and not like the other catty moms who I knew talked behind my back when I didn't volunteer at the fall carnival or forgot to send money for whatever fundraiser the PTA was hosting. I level my gaze at Travis, needing him to hear me. "Promise me you won't do anything, OK?"

He scowls like a child. "Fine," he grumbles, then leans in to kiss me. "Your wish is my command." The warmth of his lips pressed against mine echoes through every part of me. But it's his loyalty, the way he's sticking up for me, that pulls at my heartstrings.

~

When the lights are out and the stillness of the night envelops us, I can hear Travis breathing, slow and deep. His hand fumbles in the darkness. When he lands on my fingers, he squeezes tight. His voice is soft, so low it's barely a murmur, but I hear the words clearly. They hit me in the center of my soul, and I know he means them. "Love you, Audrey."

The sound of his voice so close to my body settles me, making me feel like I am finally home. But I'm not sure I'm ready to say it back. I miss when saying those three little words didn't take all my courage. The truth is, I can't remember the last time I told him I loved him, and what kind of wife does that make me? All these years I've believed something was wrong with Travis, but maybe it's the other way around. Maybe something is wrong with me. My voice catches as I whisper, "I love you too."

It's the truth. I just wonder if it will be enough.

CHAPTER 33

The next few weeks come and go in a blur. I've made it a point to try to get out of the house at least once a day with the girls. We've met Sonia and Penelope a couple of times at the park. Even though the babies are too young to play, there is something encouraging about hanging out with other people, especially since Lexy and I are on the outs. Confused by my sudden silence, she's called or texted at least once every day, but I've yet to respond. She isn't worth the energy. I'd much rather spend my time with the girls. And Travis, who is turning out to be more helpful than I remember. Ever since Lexy's betrayal sent me spiraling into a mini depression, he's been picking up the slack around the house, taking the girls and Willow on long walks, and rustling up frozen dinners. He's even planned a family outing this weekend and did all the prep work, including making lunches.

On Saturday, we arrive early at the Dallas Zoo. Travis has strapped Ruby in the baby carrier, her purple bucket hat neatly tied around her chin. We flank Eadie as she skips on the meandering path that loops the crocodile enclosure toward the Okapi Forest. Eadie's been itching to see an okapi since spotting them in an episode of *Wild Kratts*, dubbing them "zebra butts." As we trail behind, Travis reaches out and grabs my hand. My face flushes, and I wonder if he notices the effect his touch has on me. For the first time in months—years, really—the tiny vibrations connecting us are somehow tuned to the same wavelength.

A little farther ahead, I catch sight of a young couple—maybe in their twenties—on a stone bench. Not that it matters. They could be anywhere right now and wouldn't care where. They are only dialed into one another. The man leans forward to brush a wisp of hair from the woman's eyes, and his hand lingers on her dewy skin. As we approach them I notice the way his eyes catch fire when she laughs, the way he can't stop staring at her lips, and I envy them a little. In another life, they could have been Travis and me. When the man drops to one knee, there is a collective gasp from onlookers as he pulls a small velvet box from his coat pocket. His words are inaudible, but whatever he's saying has made the woman cry fat tears of joy. She cups a trembling hand over her mouth and nods vigorously.

"Bold move," Travis says, pulling me out of the moment. Tears blur my vision, and I blink them away. "Proposing in public like that. What if she'd said no?"

"Look at them," I said, unable to tear my gaze from the scene. Spontaneous applause has broken out as the woman pulls her fiancé to his feet and wraps her arms around his neck. They are beaming. "He knew he had it in the bag."

"Wish I'd had that kind of confidence," he admits.

"What?" I whip around to face him, confused. "Of course you did. You knew I wanted to marry you. By the time you asked me, we'd already started picking out a venue."

"Yeah but . . . it's a different feeling when you're actually in the moment. It felt a bit like skydiving, not knowing if I had a parachute. I mean, I was fresh out of college. It's not like I had much to offer you. I was afraid you might have changed your mind." He looks from the couple to me, uncertainty clouding his gaze. "Sometimes I wonder . . . Why *did* you say yes?"

I consider the question, remembering how we'd just learned we were pregnant. Thinking of how afraid I was to have this baby on my own, not wanting to write the sequel to my mother's life. But that wasn't the reason I married Travis. A gentle wind rustles my hair, and with it comes the answer, so simple and undeniable. I thought he already knew, but maybe I've never told him. "Do you remember when that huge storm rolled through, and my power went out? I was trapped at my place with no food or electricity. There was a tornado warning, and my apartment was on the fourth floor. I think maybe fifteen minutes after I called you, terrified, you showed up at my door in a giant yellow raincoat and galoshes with a flashlight. At first, I thought you were emergency personnel. But then you held up a gallon of water and a huge box of those little Hostess Sno Balls cakes I love." I smile at the memory. "And you hate coconut."

"So, you married me because I brought you shitty junk food?" Travis raises an eyebrow, but there's a grin beneath his question.

"No," I say, my lips curling up at the corners. "I married you because you braved a tornado for me." I think of all the times I'd been home alone during a storm, when Iris was working late, not knowing when she'd come back. Not knowing if the roof would cave in, if a bolt of lightning would spark a fire, if I'd die alone. "No one had ever done that for me."

A look of remembrance passes between us, and he smiles. "Well, whatever the reason," he says, his gaze traveling to Eadie, who is steadily outpacing us, "I'm glad you said yes."

He cradles Ruby's back with a cupped palm, then squints at me. "Sometimes I still can't believe we have the two of them, you know? Five years ago, Eadie wasn't even a blip on our radar. You ever worry we're doing it all wrong?"

"Only all the time."

"No, you're great with them," he says. "It's harder when you're the dad."

"You can't be serious," I say, throwing him a quizzical look. As the person going through nursing pads like toilet paper, I'm not sure he understands just how insulting his comment is.

"That's not what I meant. It's just that, none of this comes naturally to me, you know. My dad wasn't really around for my childhood. I don't think he changed a single diaper or read me a story. That was all my mom's territory."

"Travis, you're a great father. Eadie adores you, and so will Ruby." I don't even have to project about this part, because I know that over the next five years, he will win over our second-born just as he has our first. He'll be the fun one, the parent they ask to tuck them in at night and make up silly songs. "You're going to be their everything. Their whole world."

He thinks for a moment, then shakes his head. "Well, if I'm their world, then you're the sun, the moon, and stars. Their whole little lives are wrapped up in you, Audrey. I mean, you're feeding Ruby with your body. I'll never have that kind of connection. How am I supposed to compete?"

I laugh. "It's not a competition, Travis. It's a partnership. And it's not like any of this comes naturally to me either." Even when I was a kid, I sensed that Iris was counting the days until she was free of me. What's more, she still hadn't nailed down a time to visit the baby, and I knew we wouldn't see her until Christmas.

"Which makes it all the more amazing that you're the best mother our kids could have asked for."

A swell of emotion lodges in my throat. "Really?"

"Babe." He stops walking and examines my face like he's looking for cracks. "There's no us without you." He pulls me into him. We inch forward with Ruby dozing against his chest and Eadie skipping up ahead. I wonder if future Travis still feels this way. I wonder which reality is the truer version of us. Because this feels so right. Maybe this is the way things should have been all along. Maybe losing Willow was the glimpse, my ultimate what-if, and this is reality. Because nothing has ever felt more real to me than this moment.

I study the adoration in my husband's eyes as he looks at Eadie. Sunlight pours over the three of them, bathing everyone I love in tones of sepia. The picture nearly steals my breath. In real time, the aperture of my lens widens, blurring the background, and everything important comes into sharp focus. This is the center of my life, stripped to the bones, the very heart of everything that matters.

I hope I get to keep them forever.

~

Travis makes mac and cheese for dinner, and I gratefully devour a bowl. Afterward, I nurse and bathe Ruby, then rock her to sleep. Later, we read to Eadie the book about bats, and she reiterates her disappointment in the lack of them at the zoo today. Travis promises her that he will make up for it tomorrow, and for now it's enough to satisfy her curiosity. We plant kisses on her cheeks, tuck in fingers and toes, and as we slip out the door, her eyelids grow heavy.

When we're finally in our bedroom, I take careful note of the door latching as Travis shuts it behind him. Heart fluttering, I rifle through my drawers, trying to look busy. The idea of sleep has never seemed less appealing. Ever since he kissed me this afternoon, it's all I can do not to throw myself at him. But I *did* just have a baby, and my body is not the same as before pregnancy. I miss future Audrey's workout sessions and her tightened abdominals. Maybe he isn't interested anyway?

Chewing my bottom lip, I mull over what to wear. I've already decided against my pineapple muumuu, but I don't own anything remotely sexy. Sweatpants say *Closed for business*, but a T-shirt and shorts could be a subtle invitation he could read either way. I'm debating wearing one of *his* shirts when I feel his arms slide around my waist and his cheek brush against mine. The bristles of his five-o'clock shadow graze my skin as he gently lifts the hair from my neck and plants a trail of kisses. Each one is like a tiny firework. I close my eyes and bask in the smell of his heady scent, sweat and cedar.

I remember this feeling, when everything inside me burned to be close to him, when the best medicine after a long day was the feel of his skin pressed against mine. There's an ache radiating from the center of me that I know will only be cured when I'm in his arms, in our bed, completely wrapped up in him, body and soul. I've never wanted to be held by him more than I do right now.

Slowly, I swivel around and meet his gaze, hungry and heavy with the weight of a question, and my mouth goes dry. Part of me is still afraid we'll mess this up again, but the other part wonders if this could be a clean slate. I think my heart has left a dim light flickering for him all these months. Just in case. But now I'm certain—if given the chance to go back to the beginning, to share a greasy pretzel with him in that food court instead of heading home to my empty apartment, I would choose Travis again and again, every single time.

His clear-blue eyes move over my body, taking me in completely. The hopeful smile on his lips unlocks a reservoir of memory, bringing to the surface a thousand nights when we lay fingers and limbs intertwined, entirely complete. It's all too much to keep at bay, and whatever walls I've been struggling to hold up come crashing down like sand. On tiptoes, I crane my neck to reach him, and our lips collide. He threads his fingers through my hair, and we move together in a seamless dance—familiar, and yet it feels like the first time.

When I finally pull away, my lips still tingling with the taste of him, I can't remember why I ever stopped kissing him like this. So, I kiss him again, long and deep, until we are both breathless. My clothes fall to the floor. He leads me to our bed. When I collapse into him, time becomes foreign, so trivial that I no longer have the slightest interest in untangling the past from the present. Our life together is a beautiful blur of messy moments, and we are the sum of them all.

"I love you," Travis whispers, stroking my cheek as he draws me against him. And the world finally spins as it should.

CHAPTER 34

A sliver of sunlight slips through the curtains, casting an amber hue on Travis's bare chest, where my head has safely nestled all night. When I begin to stir, he tightens his grasp around my shoulders. It feels good to be desired by him, to know that he wants to keep me here as long as possible. I can feel his nose in my hair as he plants a kiss, then lets out a contented sigh. Peace filters through me. The future I was desperate to return to is now a distant memory I want to store away. So, I've decided that two things can be true at once. I can miss the life I had and also be terrified of going back to it. It turns out I much prefer this season-three twist.

Morning arrives in full force when Eadie bangs on our door with something like a blunt-force instrument. It turns out to be a maraca. "I want pancakes," she says, not the least bit tired. Still in her *Frozen* pajamas, she is sporting gloriously matted bedhead, like something straight from a Dr. Seuss book. I smile and rustle her hair, then head upstairs to Ruby's room.

Trailing a finger down her sticky cheek, I coo a greeting, and I'm 99 percent certain she smiles at me. I don't remember her doing that this early, and it feels like another tiny miracle in this near-perfect weekend. Minus my backstabbing ex–best friend. I still haven't responded to Lexy. My phone harbors no fewer than twenty unanswered texts, all dripping with confusion. As far as I know, she has no idea that I've figured out her game. The extent of her duplicity has left me feeling raw and exposed. The only thing softening the blow is Travis and the girls.

I feed Ruby while Travis pours batter onto the griddle. Eadie is mopping her pancakes with syrup while Willow licks up the bacon crumbs that have fallen. When the baby is happy and full, I set her in the bouncer and dry the dishes while Travis washes. There's a palpable current of electricity between us. Last night was the match that relit our marriage. It finally feels like we're a team again, doing chores side by side on a lazy Sunday. Somehow, the humdrum rhythm of our daily life feels almost fulfilling. So much so that when it's time to toss the laundry in the dryer and jam the broom against the wall, I don't even curse.

Later, Travis rustles up a couple of planks of wood and saws them into shapes that he nails together in the form of a box with even interior slats and a slanted top. When it's finished, Eadie paints four bats on the exterior, one to represent each member of our family. Ruby's bat appears to be crying large blue drops, while mine is inexplicably three times the size of the others. Eadie explains that it's because I'm full of milk, which feels accurate, honestly. After it dries, Travis attaches our new bat house to a long wooden post, and we secure it in the backyard, high above the fence.

"How will the bats know how to find their house?" Eadie asks. "They can't see in the dark."

"I don't think they have to see it to know it's there," I explain. "They feel it." I study her, remembering Eadie as she grows, yelling at Ruby for stealing her special scented markers, crying in my arms when her project about water conservation doesn't win the science fair, catching fireflies in our backyard. I see every variation of her future self, and I can't wait to meet each one.

~

When we arrive at Sonia's place, we meander through the wrought iron gate that leads to her backyard. I'm floored by the measures she's taken for a simple barbecue. Her entire lawn has been transformed into a tropical paradise, with pastel hibiscus garlands crisscrossing the giant gazebo and colorful paper fans dangling from its ceiling. There's a drink table trimmed in grass fringe, featuring piña coladas in frosty mugs with slivers of pineapple perched on the rims. As we approach, I take in her hula skirt and plunging pink halter top. Suddenly, I feel entirely out of place in my jeans and blue T-shirt.

"You came!" she says, drawing me in for a hug. My shoulders stiffen, and I don't allow myself to relax, but she doesn't seem to notice. "Honey, this is Audrey, the woman I've been telling you about," she says to Amir. I want to ask whether he knows about the whole Eadie-getting-lost-in-the-dryer thing. I feel like I deserve the right to defend myself. Or maybe she's just told him I'm the sad woman across the street who can't seem to get out of her robe all day. But something tells me she hasn't said anything bad behind my back. Just like I never told Travis about finding Sonia in a cloud of smoke. It feels like there's an unspoken trust that I have no interest in breaking.

"So nice to meet you," Amir says, shaking my hand.

"Thanks for having us," I reply, gesturing to Travis, who is carrying Ruby against his chest, and Eadie tucked between us.

"And you brought Willow!" Sonia squeals, reaching for her. Willow paws at the air, and I can tell she's itching to say hello. I loosen the slack in her leash and let her bury her nose in Sonia's skirt. "I'm so glad she turned up the other day," she says, more to Willow than to me. She scratches behind her ears, using a voice meant for babies and adorable animals.

"This looks amazing," Travis says, scanning the yard.

"Cliché, I know." She scrunches up her nose. "I mean, luaus are overdone, but the party store was out of carnival decor, so it was either this or pirate patches."

"It looks like Moana's village," Eadie notes with wonder.

Sonia smiles and plants her hands on her knees. "Thank you very much. I'll take that as a compliment. I love your hair." She gestures to the pigtails that took me a solid twenty minutes to secure atop Eadie's head.

"Mommy pulled my hair, and I was screaming."

"I *brushed* your hair," I clarify, placing a hand atop her shoulder. "She's extremely tender headed," I add, for Sonia's benefit.

"Oh, I have the best moisturizing serum. Works wonders on tangles," she says to me, her almond eyes lighting up. "Remind me to get it for you before you leave."

"That would be great," I say, and I'm not even lying. Brushing Eadie's hair is still a DEFCON 1 situation. She screamed so loud this morning I think we're both still a little on edge.

"Well, make yourselves at home," Sonia says. "And don't forget to take a family picture at the photo booth."

With that we move about the yard, greeting neighbors we've never met. An empty nester couple on the other side of Mrs. Murray invites Eadie to swim in their pool. A widower, Stan, shows me photos of his late wife and tells me how much she would have loved Willow because they once had a black Lab named Jax who was afraid of water. There's another youngish couple who has just moved in a few houses down with twin three-year-old boys, and we schedule a playdate for next week. I'm already looking forward to it. There are so many faces I've seen in passing, while driving to work or taking Willow on walks. But I've never taken the time to get to know any of them. Guilt seeps through me with each introduction, remembering how I'd declined Sonia's invitations over the years. I'd taken her for a social climber, starved for attention, when it seems she'd just been trying to bring the neighborhood together.

"So," Travis says when we're seated on our blanket, nibbling at potato salad and chicken sliders. "Does this mean you like Sonia now?"

"I didn't *not* like her. I just . . . didn't know her," I admit. "And now that I do, she seems like a nice enough person. And she comes with free drinks." I raise my piña colada and wink. It's the first drop of alcohol

I've had in six weeks. But I've decided that after all I've been through, I deserve it. I'll pump and dump when we get home.

"You let her hug you," he says, a smile tugging at the corners of his mouth. He stretches onto his side, propping his head up with an elbow.

"Well, what was I supposed to do? Push her into the tiki bar?"

"You shoved my aunt Denise into our new KitchenAid for less. She had to have her hip replaced."

"She didn't fall! And she was already scheduled for that surgery. You always exaggerate that story." I flash him a flirtatious eye and take a sip of my drink. "Besides, doesn't it make you feel special, being one of the few people I want to hug?"

"True." He squints at me, shielding his eyes against the fading sun. "Maybe there's still hope for you. Maybe you're not an ice queen after all." He nudges my shoulder playfully, and goose bumps sprout along my arms. Slowly, I rub them away. The phrase needles me, conjuring the memory of the night things fell apart, the hurt in Travis's eyes and the brokenness in our daughters' faces. I can't shake the feeling that it means something, but I don't want to ruin this idyllic afternoon with needless anxiety.

Travis must not register the shift in my mood, because he pulls out a bottle of bubbles and starts blowing, to Eadie's delight. She pops up and leapfrogs about the blanket, catching them between her palms, while Willow yips, caught up in the excitement. Ruby is entirely enamored by them, as am I. Golden hour has arrived in all its glory, illuminating my family in a halo of orange sunlight. It's all I can do to keep the tears out of my eyes. My whole world fits on this blanket.

The air carries notes of freshly cut grass and sweet meat and a hint of magnolia. In the distance, a melody emerges, so soft at first that I can't make out its source. But as it draws near, my blood runs cold. Frantic, I reach for the leash, but it's too late. Willow has darted off, whizzing past guests and tables of food, heading for the open gate. My heart is in my throat as I sprint after her at breakneck speed. But she's too fast. By the time I make it past the gate, Willow is in the street, her eyes fixed on the ice cream truck sailing down the blacktop. I scream her name, and she stalls for just a moment to look back at me.

And that's when it happens.

Like a thunderbolt, a blue car comes careening down the road. There's a shrill whine, followed by complete silence, and the car is gone as fast as it appeared. Like a ghost. Or a dream. It doesn't even stop. I let out a scream as I fly to her, then collapse onto the hot asphalt. Her eyes are closed, but I can feel her rib cage moving up and down with shallow breaths. I'm losing her. I am losing her all over again, and this time it is entirely my fault. "I'm so sorry," I whisper, my voice laced with tears. I can feel myself coming undone, like a thread has just been tugged, and my muscles go slack. I bury my face in Willow's fur, praying for a miracle.

A siren blares, getting louder as it approaches, and I'm flooded with relief that maybe medical help is on the way. Maybe it isn't too late for Willow, maybe I can still fix her. But there's something strange about the sound piercing the silence, so persistent it almost annoys me. It isn't a siren.

It's a horn.

I whip around just in time to see the grill of a truck as it barrels toward us, but my feet are heavy as stones. I can't seem to move them. I won't leave Willow alone. Not when she needs me most. Out of the corner of my eye, I catch a glimpse of Travis running after me, and we lock eyes long enough for him to read the apology on my face. *I'm so sorry.*

Like a bullet, the truck crashes into my body, hurling me against the pavement.

CHAPTER 35

My right arm throbs, seeming to pulse in time to a rhythmic beeping. I don't know where I am, but I don't think I'm dead. Surely, dead wouldn't hurt this much. My back feels like it's on fire, and my head is swimming with a sharp, persistent pain. The kind of pain that makes me wish I were dead. Somehow, I've survived the crash. But what about Willow? Where are the girls and Travis? When I finally manage to pry my eyes open, my vision is blurry. With each fuzzy blink, shadows separate from the light a little more, until finally I can see that the shadows aren't shadows at all. They're people. My people.

"Dad! She's awake!" Eadie says, tugging at Travis's elbow. Her lisp is gone. Her face is longer, her perfect freckles intact. She is so grown up, so beautiful, just as she was always meant to be. And yet, I can still envision the soft, rounded line of her jaw, and the ghost of her baby voice beneath this older version in full bloom.

"Mommy!" Ruby squeals. "You're not dead!" She climbs into the bed and nestles herself in the crook of my good arm. The other one still throbs and seems to be mired in concrete. When I try to lift it, a blistering pang wrenches through me.

"Don't try to move it!" Travis yells, lunging toward me. Then he presses the offending limb to my chest again. "Ruby, be careful. Don't crowd her." But Ruby can't be restrained. She rests her head on my shoulder, and I breathe in Froot Loops and crayons. Heaven.

Ruby cups a hand to my ear and whispers, "I didn't want to tell you this, but you're a mummy."

My body hurts too much to press her on this. But judging from the stiffness I feel in every limb, I concur with her assessment. "What happened?" I groan, still unable to make sense of my surroundings.

"You fell down the stairs." Travis's once-full cheeks are hollowed out, and his hair is receding. There's a weariness about his expression that alarms me. He's a total wreck. "You broke your arm and got a pretty decent bump on the head."

"Daddy found you!" Ruby adds proudly.

"For a while there, we weren't sure if you were going to wake up." His voice cracks, and there are fresh tears on his cheeks. "You were out for two whole days." Groggy as I am, I can't make the math work. I was gone six weeks. Six weeks of round-the-clock nursing, and diaper changing, and never-ending laundry. Six impossible weeks with Willow. And just like that, I hear the blare of the horn, see the grill of the car as it barrels toward us, and a gaping hole rips open inside my chest.

"Where's Willow?" I ask.

Travis seems concerned. There's a crease above his brow, and he's looking at me like I might have broken more than just my arm. "Girls, let's give Mommy some space. Run down to the nurse's station and get someone." Discreetly, he swipes away tears.

Ruby plants a kiss on my cheek before crawling out of the bed. Then Eadie steps forward and looks me over. Tears spring to her eyes, and she throws herself onto my chest, her sinewy arms curling around my neck. "I'm glad you're OK, Mom. I missed you," she says into my hair.

I missed you too. I inhale her scent, catching notes of the little girl who used to play hide-and-seek and once painted my living room in bright-pink nail polish. Or maybe not. I have no idea what's real or imagined anymore, which history is correct. When Eadie pulls away, I study her face, trailing my finger beneath her chin, but there is no scar there.

When the girls are out of sight, I repeat the question that has made Travis so uncomfortable because I am desperate to know the answer. "Just tell me what happened to Willow."

Travis lowers himself to a seat and rakes a hand through what's left of his hair. Worry is etched into his eyes, and I can tell he's exhausted. Has he been by my side this whole time, wondering how to tell the girls their mother might never wake up? "Audrey, Willow died five years ago."

I hear him, but when I open my mouth to respond, nothing comes out. There's a pressure gathering in my chest that seems like it might cause me to explode. I don't know how to feel about this news. Losing Willow once was hard enough, but losing her twice is shattering. She was right at my fingertips. I felt the warmth of her breath on my skin, heard the sound of her bark, saw the unwavering trust in her big, sad eyes. And now she's gone. Whatever atoms that composed my best friend are scattered to the four winds, floating somewhere out there on the edges of the universe, existing without me. How am I supposed to return to a world without her in it? What's worse, how do I go on knowing I've let her down—again?

"I'm sorry. It was my fault," Travis says. His eyes are watery and full of heartache. "I should have listened to you."

A sob escapes my chest, and I start shaking. I try to breathe in slowly, but my body convulses with each inhale. Tears stream down my cheeks, and my eyes sting. Before all this, I would have given anything just to hold Willow one more time. And now that I have, I realize it isn't enough. It will never be enough. I don't want to fall apart like this in front of Travis. He must think I've gone insane. Or have brain damage. But when I cover my face in my hands, he just wraps an arm around me. I want to melt into him, bury my nose in his neck and get lost in his scent. "Don't worry," he says softly. "It's going to be OK."

After everything that's happened, I have no reason to believe that this is true. But his voice is so familiar, the vibrations melding into my body like a healing serum. My breathing slows, and the tears begin to ebb until, finally, I can fill my lungs again. "I'm OK," I whisper. Travis nods and pulls away, still studying me like he isn't sure whether I'm telling the truth.

I draw a hand to my head and note the strands of hair sticking out every which way like an unkempt nest. "Oh God," I say, suddenly remembering the whole reason I fell down the stairs in the first place. Smoothing it down, I cringe, thinking there are still tiny eggs incubating and hatching there. It's the cherry on top of what is turning out to be the most humiliating weekend of my life. "I still have lice," I admit, letting my head plop back against the pillow.

"Don't worry about it." He waves away my concern. "We'll deal with it later."

It doesn't escape me that he's included himself in that sentence, and an uncertain look passes between us. I'm not sure how to file away this information. Are we going to be one of those divorced couples? The amicable and friendly type? Or does he want to give us another shot? We never got to meet up and discuss where we stand.

Travis stares at me a beat too long, and I wonder what he's thinking. I wonder if he has regrets about our life together, if he misses anything about our time as a family. I wonder if he's thought of me as much as I've thought of him these past three months. Or maybe he's filled in all the gaps with Jamie. Finally, he pulls away and clears his throat. In Travis fashion, he cracks a smile to lighten the mood. "Looks like you're going to have to rest up as long as you're in that getup." He gestures to my fractured arm.

He has a point. My cast is bulky and stiff and smells faintly of cheese. It seems the mere act of looking at it has brought on the intense need to claw my trapped skin. "I *am* a mummy," I say, deflated. I attempt to wiggle my outstretched thumb and wonder how I'll manage to hold a cell phone or drive a car or pack lunches for the kids. I think of the six thousand emails I need to sift through for work and the girls' school—teacher newsletters, band newsletters, counselor newsletters. Why the hell are there so many newsletters? Not to mention the extracurriculars. *Stupid Audrey.* It was terribly irresponsible to fall down the stairs. The universe should have just finished me off. At least then I wouldn't have to make dinner. Every. Single. Day. How the hell am I going to get anything done like this?

"I . . . I have to call the kids' school, I need to tell morning carpool I can't drive this week, I've got to check in with a client about the house I showed them. Oh God, they probably think I just ghosted them. Eadie has snacks this week for softball, and Ruby has to make a clay sculpture for show-and-tell and—"

"All taken care of," Travis says.

I open my mouth to respond, but nothing comes out. I narrow my eyes, trying to make sense of the words.

"I called the school and told them to contact me going forward," he continues. "And I've cleared my week to take the girls to dance and softball. Oh, and I called Harlow, and he contacted your clients. They were super sympathetic. Sent flowers and everything," he says, gesturing to the collection of colorful plants in the window. "The whole office is pulling for you."

What is happening right now? This is not Travis. This is not the man who didn't know where to go when Eadie got that terrifying ear infection last year. Pediatricians and dentists and ophthalmologists. Those were all my domain. "What about all the bedding," I point out. "There are still loads of laundry and—"

"Done," he says with an air of finality. "Determined little jerks, aren't they?" he notes. "I mean, millions of years of evolution manage to knock out all the cool animals, and still these suckers are going strong. Seems unfair, if you ask me." Throwing up his palms, he leans back in his seat. "All I'm saying is I'd much prefer if Eadie brought home a saber-toothed tiger." He drops his gaze to his lap, and when he looks up again, his face is stricken. "Listen, Audrey. I'm sorry I let you take on so much. Since you've been out, I feel like I got a glimpse of what you do for us. You did things so well, so seamlessly . . . I didn't understand.

I mean, your phone goes off every two seconds. I don't know how you manage to do it all."

I wasn't managing. I was surviving. But I don't tell him this, because bless his heart, he is here, and he is trying. Instead, I swallow and manage a nod.

"I'm here. And I'm going to be here for everything from now on. Anything you and the girls need."

For one delirious moment, I think maybe he is going to tell me that we made a mistake, that he never should have agreed to the separation. I think maybe he is going to fight for me. But then he drops his head, unable to meet my eyes, which are filling with tears. I bat them away before he notices.

"Audrey, I don't want to be one of those couples that splits up and ends up hating each other. We don't have to be enemies, you know." There is an air of defeat in his tone that breaks my heart. I am so not ready to throw in the towel. "I guess what I'm asking is . . ." He looks up at me, his blue eyes pleading. "Can we be friends again? For the sake of the kids?"

My voice is paper thin, barely audible. "Of course," I mumble, because what else is there to say? I can't tell him that I've fallen through a wormhole and changed my mind. Especially when he seems to have moved on with someone else.

The prospect of leaving this hospital and going back to our home alone makes my chest hurt. It feels wrong. I want to trail a hand down his cheek, to tell him that maybe I was shortsighted and stubborn and resentful. But before my brain can decide if this is a good idea or not, he plants his hands atop his knees and pushes himself up with a groan. As he walks away, I think about stopping him, but I'm not sure I can trust my heart. After all that's happened, I have no idea what's real anymore, and the last thing I want to do is confuse him. It wouldn't be fair. When he reaches the threshold, he turns back and snaps his fingers as if he's just remembered something important. Hope blossoms in the pit of my stomach. "One more thing. I ran into Sterling this morning, and he mentioned that Payton and Lexy had lice last week. So that's probably where you guys got it."

"Oh," I say, letting the information slide into place. And even though my head is still a confusing maze of events, I clearly remember my phone call with Lexy right before my slip. She didn't mention anything about having it too.

She knew.

And she didn't think to warn me. A fresh current of resentment swells up, followed by an immediate stab of guilt. I've been so wrong about so many things, including the man standing in front of me, the man who has painstakingly cared for me while I was in la-la land for two whole days. Tears spring to my eyes, but I force a grateful smile. "Thanks, Travis," I manage to say. "For everything." He can't possibly know how much I mean those words.

"My pleasure," he says in a way that makes me believe him. And then my best friend in the whole world turns and walks out the door.

CHAPTER 36

My hand quivers as I bring a spoonful of bran flakes to my mouth. Before it reaches my lips, milk dribbles down my chin, spilling onto my chest. I still haven't mastered the mechanics of basic daily routines while trapped in this cast. Every time I attempt to perform the smallest task, I'm immediately reminded that my right arm is out of commission.

Yesterday, Travis drove me home from the hospital and left a few precooked meals in the freezer. In our time apart, he's learned to make ravioli and a pretty decent meat loaf. It seems the single life has agreed with him. Or maybe Jamie taught him his way around the kitchen. I'm still too raw to ask about her. What's more, this morning he made breakfast and lunch for the girls and drove them to school, even leaving chicken-and-dumpling soup from my favorite restaurant in the fridge. I tried to protest, but he was firm that I'd just have to accept his help.

For all intents and purposes, we are still functioning as a married couple, albeit one who doesn't live together, which feels strange, considering that only a few days ago I shared my bed with him. It's hard to accept that the feel of his skin pressed against mine was a mirage, all in my head. If I close my eyes long enough, I can still feel him holding me. I miss the person I was when I was with him.

When the girls are at school, I'm not sure how to spend my time without work, so I sink into the couch and flick on the television. A baby cries a shrill, high-pitched whine, sending a tingling to my chest. I look around for Ruby. But of course, she isn't here, and she isn't a baby anymore. It seems my body didn't get the memo that I'm no longer responsible for feeding on demand. I lift my shirt and press my fingers into my stomach, no longer fleshy and loose. Thanks to a rigorous FlexCore routine, it's firm and defined, which should make me happy. But it doesn't. Instead, it feels like something vital has been sucked out of me, and I can't reconcile the person I am with the person I just was or the person I want to be.

A knock at the door pulls me from my trance, and slowly I emerge from the sofa to answer it. When Sonia appears on the other side, dressed to the nines in an adorable strapless sage jumpsuit, I offer a tepid smile.

Despite her flawless look, she seems nervous. "Sorry for just dropping in, but Travis mentioned you were home, and I couldn't help myself. We've been so worried."

The sight of her calms my nerves. "Thanks. I'm good," I reply, though this couldn't be further from the truth.

"That's great to hear." She seems relieved, her doe eyes awash with empathy.

I open my mouth to say something, but it occurs to me that this Sonia doesn't know anything about me or the revisionist history in which we are friends that I've concocted in my brain. The silence is deafening, so awkward that I feel my face flush hot. Still, this could be a chance to finally get to know her. "Do you want to come in?" I hear myself ask, opening the door a smidge.

The shock is evident in her face. Her eyes go wide, and a small smile touches her painted cherry lips. "Love to."

When we are seated at the kitchen table clutching hot mugs of coffee, I thank her for the birthday present and dinner the other night and ask her for the recipe. She says it was nothing, that she was happy to help, and once again reiterates how horrible she feels about my accident.

"I just can't imagine if Travis hadn't found you," she says, then takes a tiny sip of her drink.

"Me too." I know I could have suffered so much more than a broken arm and a concussion if Travis hadn't arrived minutes after my accident. Fortunately, he returned for Noodle. And when I failed to answer the door, he let himself in with the hidden key.

"He's such a great guy," Sonia says, then blows on her coffee. "And he obviously adores you."

Her observation catches me off guard, and my skin prickles with curiosity. It wasn't like Travis and I spent time with her. Maybe she was spying from across the street, in which case she must have noticed his truck missing in the drive. Had she seen something between us that I hadn't? "Actually . . . we're separated." I clear my throat. "It's been a rocky few months. And before that, a rocky few years," I admit.

"I'm so sorry. God, I had no idea." Gently, she puts down her mug.

"It's OK." I wave away her concern. "We've been drifting apart for a while now. All those little things that used to only mildly annoy me didn't seem so little anymore. It was like . . . like I couldn't forgive him for the small stuff because I was holding on to this huge ocean of resentment." As I think of Willow, a swell of emotion lodges in my chest and tears spring to my eyes. "The thing is, I'm not really sure anymore if separating is the right thing." Embarrassed, I wipe my cheeks, but I don't think I've managed to hide anything from Sonia. "Not that it matters. I think it might be too late."

She leans forward and places a warm hand on my arm. "You know, I was here when the ambulance arrived. I watched the medics carry you out and load you into the back. Travis stayed with you the whole time. He asked me to keep the girls so he could ride with you, couldn't bear for you to be alone when you woke up in a strange place. He was frantic, Audrey. And the whole time I stood there watching him, I thought to myself, *God, I hope she pulls through, because if she doesn't, this poor guy is going to crumble.*"

My heart aches at the idea of Travis in that kind of pain. I imagine how I would have felt if something like this had happened to him. It would have been agony. "It's just that . . . sometimes I wonder if he would have chosen me if I hadn't gotten pregnant with Eadie. She was the glue that welded us together in the beginning, and I'm not sure if he would have made the same decision if things had been different." Desperate, I search Sonia's face for answers I know she can't possibly provide. Still, I ask the question that's been weighing on my heart for months. "How do you know if you're staying for the right reasons when kids are involved?"

Sonia seems to consider this for a moment, then levels her gaze at me. "Look, I don't know anything about your marital struggles, and I'm not trying to tell you what to do. All I can say is that the man I saw that day did not want to leave his wife. And it didn't have anything to do with kids. I saw the face of a man hopelessly in love."

I want to believe her, but all I can picture is Travis walking away the night of our argument. Travis playing guitar with some woman named Jamie. Travis at the hospital asking to remain friends. He had the chance to fight for me, and he didn't take it. "It's just hard, is all."

"You know, I don't tell many people this"—she glances at the ring on her finger—"but I was married before Amir." She hesitates before adding, "He left me."

My skin prickles. This information should come as a shock, but it doesn't. Still, I can't imagine any man leaving Sonia. "I'm sorry," I say, because I'm not sure how to respond.

"It's fine. It was a long time ago. No kids. We were young, didn't really know ourselves that well, much less each other. I'd just gotten into vlogging and spent all my time in front of my laptop. He worked a lot, too, and when he came home, he wanted me to put the camera away and just be real with him. But it was impossible. It was like . . . I needed that fix. I needed the validation. Then one day, I shared a video in which I laid our worst arguments bare for the whole world. And he rightfully called me out on it. After that, it was just a matter of time."

"And he left you?"

She shrugs. "I don't blame him. It was pretty much the most difficult year of my life. I'd like to think I learned from that experience, things that have helped me be a better partner to Amir. I guess what I'm trying to say is that marriage is hard. But so is divorce. All that really matters is whether you love each other enough to make it work."

Somewhere deep inside the walls of my heart, I know she's right, but even so, I can't make Travis take me back. I can't erase the horrible things we've said to each other over the years.

It's kind of Sonia to try to make me feel better, even if she has no idea how complicated my marriage has been. Guilt trickles through me.

"Sonia, I think I owe you an apology."

"Why?"

"I made some assumptions about you that . . . might have been influenced by some inaccurate information," I say, reflecting on Lexy's toxic gossip.

She purses her lips. "Let me guess. I'm an ego-driven attention seeker with no real friends?"

"No, of course not," I say, though she isn't entirely wrong. "Just the first part . . . maybe. I mean, obviously you have loads of friends." One hundred and twenty-two thousand of them, to be exact.

"It was the Brazilian wax, wasn't it?"

I let out a subtle groan and pinch my thumb and forefinger together. "I mean, it was a tad over the top."

She winces. "Had a feeling I should have sat on that idea a little longer. But once it's out there, there isn't much you can do. The internet doesn't forget." She lets out a small sigh. "Just so you know, what you see on my page isn't who I am. Not really. I'm way better at curating an image for my online persona than I am at making actual friends." I think of Sonia in her stained pajamas, hands trembling as she takes a pull from her vape pen, and my heart softens. She shakes her head. "I don't know. Maybe that's why I bother you all the time, try and get the girls together. It's why I stalk Travis when he gets the mail or takes out the trash. I guess . . . I guess I thought maybe we could be friends." Cupping a palm to her forehead, she lets out a groan. "God, that sounds so stupid. I'm a grown woman."

"I'd like that," I say, thinking of our playdates at the park, playdates she can't possibly remember.

"Really?"

"Yeah. I mean, obviously I need a friend who can help me in the fashion department, and you seem so put together all the time." I gesture to the glossy waves cascading over her shoulders. "You could help me with my . . . image. Though, I have to warn you, you'll be getting the short end of this arrangement."

"I doubt that." She flashes me a genuine smile, one that makes me feel like I've known her forever. "So does this mean you're coming to my annual barbecue from now on?"

I take another sip of my drink, then throw her a smirk. "That depends. How do you feel about lice removal?"

~

"How was school?" I ask the girls.

"Great!" Ruby shouts. "We were supposed to do capital letters, except someone burned a bag of popcorn in the microwave and we had to have a fire drill." She throws open the refrigerator and helps herself to a snack.

"Sounds like a fun day," I say from my sofa perch, where I've nested most of the afternoon. After Sonia helped me de-lice my hair, carefully inspecting every strand, I finally feel clean. She'd reassured me it was no big deal. But as someone who has performed this task more times than I care to admit, I know it totally is.

"What about you?" Eadie asks, cuddling up next to my good arm. "What did you do today?" It's the first time in months she's asked me a question without any snark or bite, and I'm not sure what to make of it.

"Not much. Hard to do a lot when you're a mummy." I tuck a strand of blond behind her ear, noting the subtle changes in her profile. It still amazes me how much she's changed over the years and yet how much has remained the same. While Ruby could pass as my clone,

Eadie has always been a true blend of me and her father. Travis's eyes stare back at me, piercing my soul. "I'm sorry, honey, but I don't think I'm going to be much fun until this cast comes off in a few weeks."

"It's OK." She shrugs. "We don't have to do anything."

"You sure?" I study her face for signs of disappointment. "Maybe we can have a playdate, invite Payton over to hang out," I suggest brightly, though I'm not sure if I'm ready to see Lexy yet. Of course, I'm fully aware that my mental break has no bearing on reality, and I can't blame my friend for crimes she committed in my imagination. Nor can I keep Eadie from seeing her best friend just because I have reservations about Payton's mother. Still, I can't seem to shake the feeling that things are going to be different between Lexy and me going forward. Real or imagined, I don't think I can trust her judgment anymore, least of all where it concerns Sonia.

"Mom, I didn't want to tell you"—she pulls in a shaky breath—"but I don't want to go to Payton's house anymore."

I sit up a little straighter. "Did something happen?" I knew the girls had been hanging out less in the weeks leading up to my fall, but I'd chalked it up to getting older and diverging interests. Eadie was getting more into dance, while Payton had chosen to focus on soccer. It was only natural for their friendship to evolve and mature over time.

Eadie hesitates, chewing her bottom lip. "It's Mrs. Lexy," she finally admits softly. "I overheard her tell Payton's dad that you weren't good at your job and that she was never going to hire you."

And just like that, I realize my psyche was onto something I'd been too distracted or too gullible to acknowledge. This revelation should disorient me, but for some reason I can't say I'm surprised. I pull Eadie into my chest, her wiry frame trembling, and feel her sniffle into my shoulder. "Oh, honey, you don't have to worry about that. Trust me, it's OK if not everyone likes me. It's just the way life goes sometimes. But I'm glad you told me." I plant a kiss in her hair.

"It's not that," she says, looking up at me. Her eyes are red and puffy. "I was really worried when you were gone. I didn't even give you a hug when I left to go to Dad's." She swipes at her tears with a sleeve. "And when you stayed asleep so long, I kept whispering in your ear, telling you to come home, but you didn't wake up. You couldn't hear me."

My heart turns to lava. "Oh sweetie," I say, raking my hand through her hair. "I think . . . I think maybe I did hear you. I did wake up, after all." I pull her chin forward to be sure she hears the next part, wondering if she will remember all those nights I read to her while she was tucked into my side. "I will always find my way back to you."

CHAPTER 37

Lexy shows up the following morning in oversize sunglasses and a denim romper, bearing a bouquet of pastel daisies. Before I can greet her, she pulls me into a violent hug. "Don't do that to me again! I've been worried sick about you for days." Slipping past me, she lets herself inside, then removes her glasses, her gaze sweeping over my house like she's looking for dust. "How are you feeling?"

"Great," I say, accepting the flowers. It is a surprisingly true statement, as my head feels almost normal. I dart into the kitchen to put the flowers in water and return, my face placid. Lexy plops onto the sofa, drawing her feet beneath her. I don't bother sitting; this won't take long.

"When Travis called, I was totally frantic," she says, gesticulating with her hands to drive home the point. "I mean, you could have died!"

"I suppose that's true." I fold my arms.

"Was it that loose tread on the top step?" She shakes a finger at me. "Didn't you ask Travis to fix that months ago?"

"It wasn't the step," I say, doing my best to remain neutral. "Actually, it's not Travis's fault at all. If anything, he saved me." Every time I remember this, I feel a rush of affection for him that makes my throat grow thick.

Lexy seems unimpressed. She blows a chunk of platinum from her eye. "Well, in any case, I'm glad you're OK. Do you have anything bubbly?" She massages her throat. "I'm parched."

"No, we're all out," I say, skirting the request. "Actually, it's kind of your fault." No point in beating around the bush.

"Excuse me?" She touches a hand lightly to her chest. "Audrey, what's this about?"

"Lice," I say flatly.

Her eyes dart to the side, confirming my accusation, but clearly she isn't ready to show her hand. "What is that supposed to mean?"

"It means that you and Payton had lice last week. Sterling mentioned it to Travis." I let the words sink in. "And you didn't tell me. Never gave me a heads-up or an *I'm sorry*, since you guys likely passed it along. You couldn't even be bothered to help when I was drowning over here in laundry. I was trying to carry all the bedding down the stairs when I almost fell to my death."

A trace of regret creeps into her eyes, and she wrings her hands. "I'm sorry, OK," she says, her shoulders deflating. "God, I feel terrible. And you're right. I should have said something. I was just . . . embarrassed, you know." There's an unusual undercurrent of nerves in her demeanor. "Can you forgive me?"

"Yes," I say, waiting a few seconds before adding the next part. "I can forgive you for the lice, but not for the dagger in my back."

There's a beat of loaded silence before Lexy speaks again, her tone indignant. Standing up, she scrunches her face like she's misheard me. "What are you talking about? Look, I'm sorry I neglected to mention the lice thing, but I could never have imagined it would lead to you falling down the stairs. I love Eadie as if she's my own. I helped you get the job at Harlow." She jabs a thumb to her chest. "I'm a good friend to you, Audrey."

"Would a good friend have poached my client?" At first, I'd written off Lexy's betrayal as the creative musings of my injured brain. But Eadie's revelation sparked a question that has been nagging at me all day, so I did a little research. If Julian showed up at my open house in my dream, there's a good chance he'd shown up before. When Lexy had "helped" with my listing.

She bristles, then collects herself, straightening her spine. "I don't know what you mean." But the look on her face means she absolutely does.

"Julian Mitchell," I clarify. Lexy goes rigid, the disdain slipping from her face. When she doesn't say anything, I forge ahead. "Let me spell it out for you. While I was on maternity leave with Ruby, you offered to show my listing, the one in Thornwood Estates. And just when you thought the open house was finished, in walked Julian, with his expensive watch and designer shoes. And when you found out who he was, you steered him away from my listing and directed him to one of yours. Let me guess. You showed him that pretentious condo on Eighth Street downtown, didn't you?"

I can tell the accusation has struck a nerve, because she stumbles over her next words. "It . . . it wasn't like that," Lexy finally says. "We had a vibe. Besides, a big house like that wasn't right for him. I merely . . . suggested another option."

"Which happened to be an option that directly benefited you. I don't know why I didn't put two and two together sooner. Tell me the truth. Is he the reason you secured enough business to open your own agency?"

"The conversation was organic, OK. It just happened once we got to talking," she reasons. "It's just business, Audrey." She delivers this line matter of factly, like I'm just another coworker rather than the friend who babysat her child and brought her Mexican takeout when she rolled her ankle in a tennis match last year. "And if you want to make it in this business, you can't get your feelings hurt every time someone takes an opportunity. You would have done the same. It's like we always say, network to net worth."

This part of her defense offends me most. I never want to be mistaken for the kind of person who would take advantage of a friend without a hint of remorse. "That's the difference between you and me, Lex. I wouldn't have done that to you."

Lexy throws up her hands like I'm the one being unreasonable. "Look, I can't help it if you weren't up to the task."

"I had a baby! I wasn't incompetent," I point out, my voice escalating.

"Exactly! You'd just had a baby," she says. "You had your hands full. You wouldn't have had the time to work this deal anyway. Can't you see I was doing you a favor?"

"By stealing my client?"

"He wasn't your client yet."

"But he could have been."

Closing her eyes for a beat, she draws in a deep breath. "Look. The only reason you got this job in the first place is because I put in a good word for you. And you hadn't been at the company long enough to work a deal that big. You didn't . . . you hadn't earned it."

A coolness settles into my bones. Lexy's motives have become perfectly clear. "Oh, I see. I didn't have you pegged for the jealous type, but I shouldn't be surprised, the way you always harp on Sonia all the time. Who, by the way, happens to be a decent person."

"Are you serious?" Her mouth is agape, her eyes wide. "You're hanging out with the social climber now. Who *are* you?"

By now, I think I have a pretty good idea how to answer that question. Even so, I don't feel the need to tell her, of all people. So instead I say, "The only social climber around here is you."

She blinks a few times, like my words have stung her. "Fine," she says, putting on her sunglasses. "Looks like you've already made up your mind. Best of luck to you at Harlow's." She reaches for her handbag and strides purposefully toward the door, then turns to throw one last barb my way. "He's getting old, you know. If I were you, I'd be careful about making enemies with the wrong person. This is your career we're talking about."

"Oh, I'm not worried about my career. I'm getting my broker's license too." I feel a twinge of victory when her cheeks sag ever so slightly. "I've already got a stellar social media team, and we're gonna blow you out of the water." This is a bit of a stretch, as I haven't yet asked Sonia if she'll help. But from what I know of her so far, I can't imagine she'd be opposed to the idea. I'll bet she loves a makeover project. "This is just a courtesy, to let you know. You're not the only agent in this town with connections, Lex." She's staring at me with an open mouth, and I can't blame her. I'm a little taken aback by my own moxie. I shrug. "Network to net worth, babe."

CHAPTER 38

When I enter the pub, it feels as if I've stepped into a dimly lit cave. A wooden bar is tucked against the far wall, and directly to my right, a sorry excuse for a stage is squished between two booths. I spot Travis illuminated in faint blue light, his diminishing hairline reflecting a slight glare. Looking thinner than I remember, he's leaning into the microphone, wearing baggy jeans and a white T-shirt with an open flannel. I've never heard this song before. I wonder if it's new. Marcus and Dane accompany him with a steady backbeat. The song is slower, more stripped down than the garage band titles they usually perform. From what I can tell, it's a love song, and I can't help but hope it's about me.

Sneaking to a two-top near the back, I prop my cast on the table and strain to catch the next line.

You always keep me guessing, and I'm guessing you don't mind,
that when I left with just myself, we left the best behind.

His tenor voice is smooth and clear, so familiar that it propels a rush of memories. In my mind's eye, I see him flexing his muscles in that hideous orange sweater. In a giant yellow raincoat on my doorstep during a storm. In stained Christmas pajamas, rocking our baby in the still of the morning. I conjure every side of my remarkable husband who, despite his flaws, has always been my home.

I check my watch, wondering if the girls are still awake. Sonia was kind enough to keep them tonight so I could catch Travis's set. Just being in a bar on a weeknight brings me right back to when we were dating when he pulled me on stage in a room full of strangers. To date, it was the most terrifying moment of my life. But once he started singing next to me, encouraging me with a wink, we managed to muddle our way through the first verse of "Livin' on a Prayer." I felt so safe with him. Like I could tackle anything because he looked at me like I was the only person in the world.

When the waiter catches sight of me, she scurries over. I'm ordering a cranberry vodka when the song fades out and I hear Travis say, "Do we have any volunteers?" Only about five or six other tables are occupied, and when none of them respond, Travis tries again. "Come on, who's up for some impromptu karaoke, folks?" Again, silence.

Peering into the audience, he shields his eyes from the spotlight. "How about you, miss, back there?" He's pointing a finger at me, but I look around anyway, because there is no way I'm ungluing myself from this chair. "The mummy woman has her hand up."

A few laughs trickle through the room. Mortified, I realize that my elbow is propped against the table, my thumb stubbornly extended. "Nope. Wasn't raising my hand," I say, pulling it toward me.

"Come on up here," he insists, waving me forward. "Don't be afraid."

"No can do," I shout back.

"I have it on good authority you've got a crap singing voice, ma'am, so there's no pressure to do well. We can't all be Whitney Houston." He flashes me a wry smile and adds, "Don't worry. I'll pick something easy."

I'm grateful for the darkness because I'm certain my face is flaming red. The idea of singing in public makes my stomach churn, but the fact that Travis is asking me to join him is hard to ignore. Maybe this is his way of making amends. And if that's the case, I don't want to push him away. With the speed of a sea cucumber, I slide off my stool and meander across the empty dance floor. The audience claps dutifully, and a few whistles echo throughout the room, giving me a boost of courage. When I reach the stage, I thank them with a slight curtsy, but their enthusiasm will not be enough to work a miracle. This is going to be epically bad.

"You ready for this?" Travis asks, narrowing his eyes, like he's sizing me up.

"No." I stare daggers at him, but a tiny smile tugs at one corner of my mouth, because out of everyone in this bar, he's chosen me. Again. "Just don't pick anything with more than three notes, OK?"

He covers the microphone with a palm. "I got you," he says, flashing me a wink, and I can't help but swoon a little at the gesture. With that, he turns to the guys and says something I can't make out.

When the music begins, I smile at the selection because it's "500 Miles" by the Proclaimers. He knows me too well. This song is impossible to screw up. Travis handles the verses and points to me for the chorus, which I deliver with unparallelled gusto. My *da-da-da*s are respectably loud and only a little off key. Even better, I'm singing alongside him, and for a few perfect moments, it feels like we can do anything together.

~

After Marcus and Dane have packed up their amps and left, a soft rock tune plays gently over the speakers, filtering over the sparse crowd. Travis and I sit across from one another in a booth. The pleather seat sticks to my thighs, and I almost regret borrowing Sonia's flutter-sleeve baby doll dress. It barely covers my bottom, but she insisted. Despite my misgivings, I have to admit that it does make me feel like someone different, someone braver, and I need all the help I can get for this conversation.

"I'm glad you came," he says. In this lighting, he looks so much like Eadie it makes my heart twist.

"Me too." Feeling on display, I stir the ice in my glass. "You guys sounded amazing. Better than I remember. Was that a new song?"

"Yeah. Just something I've been messing around with. Still needs a lot of work." He takes another swig of his beer, runs a hand through his thinning hair.

"Well, I thought it was great."

"How's the arm?" He gestures to my cast.

Inspecting my very obvious injury, I release a heavy sigh. "Only a few more weeks in this thing, and then I get to go back to my old life." *My old life.* As soon as the words escape my lips, I realize I'm not sure which version I'm referencing. I miss them both.

He seems to contemplate this for a minute, and I can't decide if he's happy or disappointed. Finally, he nods and says, "That will be nice. Guess that means I'll be out of your hair for good. You won't need me at all anymore."

He's wrong, because I do need him. More than ever. But my thoughts are all tangled. Since my fall, I've had the impression that he didn't mind taking care of me, that maybe he even enjoyed picking up the slack at home. I want to tell him that of course I still need him, that I can't imagine the second half of my life without him. I want to tell him that he is my safe place to land. But the words are still lodged in my throat, too raw to speak aloud.

Travis's eyes flicker toward the empty dance floor. "You want to dance?"

"Seriously?" I peer around, noting the dim chatter of the few other patrons nursing their drinks.

"Don't I look serious?"

With a wry smile, he leads me to the middle of the bar. His hands encircle my waist, and I wrap my good arm around his neck, careful not to hold him too tight. Rocking back and forth, we inch our way around the floor, our faces so close they are nearly touching. I am keenly aware of his breath on my neck, and it's impossible to ignore the goose bumps that have sprouted along my arm. I gather my courage. "Travis,

I . . . I came here tonight because I needed to tell you something." I fight my way through the rest of the words. "I think I might have . . . made a mistake. That night, when I told you I wanted to take a break. I wish I hadn't said what I said. I didn't mean it." I venture to meet his gaze, but when we lock eyes, his expression is impossible to read. I can't decipher how he feels, and I've had to squelch every ounce of my pride to admit this.

"You seemed pretty sure about it that night."

"I know. But I wasn't finished with *us*. I just . . . didn't have anything left. I was so tired of doing everything, of holding all the things for everyone—all the time."

He seems annoyed. "Why didn't you just tell me that?"

"I don't know. I guess I just . . . needed you to see that I was struggling and fill in the gaps."

"I'm not a mind reader, Audrey."

"I know. And I realize now it wasn't fair of me to ask that of you."

"It's hard for me, too, you know. When I don't know what you're thinking and you ice me out. You tell Lexy all our problems instead of me, and then it's like I'm the odd man out in this marriage. You don't even let me touch you anymore." He pauses for a beat, looking hurt. "I don't want to beg you to want me."

"I do want you," I say, my voice pleading. It's the truth. "It's just hard to be close to you when you have no idea what's going on inside my head."

"Then tell me." His eyes are desperate, and I know I owe him an overdue explanation. Time to lay it all on the table.

Deep breath. Moment of truth. "I love you, Travis. But you suck at helping out around the house and keeping up with all the girls' activities. I'm the one who runs the bath and brushes tangles and helps them with their homework. I'm the one who signs all the permission slips and books the doctors' appointments and chaperones field trips and smears sunscreen on faces. I'm the one who makes Christmas magic and birthday magic and tooth fairy magic. I make my own gold-dusted coins, for God's sake! I'm the one who painstakingly color-codes the calendar. I know you think it's over the top. But I have to do it, because when you underprepare, I have to overprepare. You think I knew how to French braid or check for lice? I didn't. No one ever did those things for me when I was small. I had to YouTube it all, because I didn't want the girls to be like me when I was their age—the one whose mother can't get her shit together. And I'm just one person. I have a job too. But for some reason, it's like I'm the default parent, the person everyone goes to for every single minor issue. And I can't do it alone anymore. Not when you promised to be there every step of the way." By the time I finish, I'm breathless, completely emptied out.

For his part, Travis takes it all in stride, chewing on the feedback I've just doled out. "Point taken." He nods guiltily, clears his throat. "Many points taken."

"There's something else." Something that's been festering in the darkest parts of me. Something I'm still too ashamed to admit aloud, but at this point, I can't afford to hold anything back. "I blamed you. For Willow," I say softly.

There is a crack in his features that makes me regret my honesty. "I know." He swallows hard, and the silence that follows feels charged. Finally, he says, "You know I loved her, too, right? But not for the reasons you did. I loved her because you loved her. The worst thing that could have happened occurred on my watch. Do you know what that did to me? No matter what I did after, I could never make up for the fact that I was the reason your best friend died."

"I know that now." And though I'll never be able to prove this to him, I feel the truth of it in my bones. "It could have just as easily happened on my watch. I think it was just . . . her time. And I want you to know . . . I forgive you."

I wait for him to say something, but he only nods, not meeting my gaze. The song is nearly over now. I can feel the eyes of the other patrons on us, but I don't care, because this is exactly where I belong. I want this dance to last forever. We are swaying cheek to cheek, and yet I have no idea what's going on inside his head. And then, I feel him inhale, long and slow. He's smelling my hair. Something inside me breaks loose, and I feel my bones melt. I am weightless in his arms.

"I miss you, Audrey. I miss holding you like this. I miss watching shitty television with you. I miss sending you stupid Reels. God, I even miss the smell of your bougie shampoo. I miss everything about you."

"I miss you too," I say, letting myself move closer to him. In this dim bar, it feels like we are a perfect couple experiencing the best part of the movie. As long as we are holding each other as a sweeping eighties love song envelops us in a cloud of new love, we are safe. No worrying about who is going to make dinner or drive carpool or miss a meeting to take the kids to the dentist. For now, we are sheltered from all responsibility, lost in the idea of what we could be.

He pulls away to look at me, his eyes leveling a challenge. "Two truths and a lie?"

I squint up at him, wondering what he's holding back. "Sure. Hit me with it."

"The past three months have been the loneliest of my entire life. I stopped buying those little TV dinners that look nothing like the picture on the box. They taste like rubber." He takes a breath, making me wait for the last one. "And I bought those little drawer organizers you're always talking about," he finally says, instantly lightening the mood.

"You didn't," I say, confident I've snuffed out the lie.

But the look on his face tells me I'm wrong. "And a label maker," he adds.

I tilt my head. My feet are rooted to the floor now, and he follows my lead, stilling his steps. "You did not."

"I did," he affirms. "The girls have so many toys, and they all come with about a million parts. It's the only way I can keep everything from getting lost."

I cut him a disbelieving look. "Who are you, and what have you done with Travis?"

He shrugs. "Told you. I've changed. Well, maybe not entirely. I still eat the TV dinners when I'm desperate. But only when they're on sale."

I can't help but give a little chuckle. Of course only when they're on sale.

I've changed too. Every inch of me wants to believe we can rewrite our story. Still, I have to be sure he understands what I need for this marriage to work. "Does that mean you won't be a cheapskate anymore? Or that you won't wait for me to tell you when something needs to be done? Does it mean you'll actually be on time? Are you going to remember the birthday parties and ballet performances and bake sales and newsletters?" Oh God, the newsletters! "It's not just the things you see me do, Travis. It's everything that just magically happens, not because I'm any more capable than you but because I care."

"I care too. And you're right about a lot. But not everything. Look, I admit, I don't help enough with chores, but that's because when I load the dishwasher, you're just going to redo it anyway. When I screw up the laundry, you get upset. When I make corn dogs for dinner, you make snide comments. I save food past the expiration date because I worry all the time about money. I didn't exactly choose a career with a lot of upward mobility. And I know it sounds stupid, but when you started earning more than me, I felt like I was failing you. Like I couldn't take care of you."

Guilt washes over me. Of all the excuses, I didn't expect that. "Travis, I don't need anyone to take care of me. I need a partner. I'm sorry if I ever made you feel . . . irrelevant. I was grieving Willow and angry, and I gave you the worst pieces of me." The next part is harder to say, but if we're going to give this marriage another shot, he deserves credit for all I failed to notice the first time around. "I know you gave up your big break for us."

"What are you talking about?"

"After Ruby was born, you were supposed to open for Salvage Sound. In Nashville. But you turned it down."

He blinks a few times. Confusion ripples across his face. "Did Marcus say something?"

I shrug, not sure how to answer that question. In this timeline, I haven't seen Marcus in months before tonight. "The point is, I know you've made sacrifices too. I'm sorry for never acknowledging them."

He manages a sad smile that pricks my heart. "Don't you know, Audrey." His voice is tender now. He brushes a strand of hair from my cheek, and the warmth of his finger sends tingles down my spine. "It wasn't a sacrifice."

"Of course it was."

Travis's eyes lock on mine. I can tell he appreciates the acknowledgment, but there's a fleeting trace of stoniness there when he says, "Just don't tell me you want to fix things if you don't mean it. I can't lose you twice. It almost killed me."

I'm surprised by the admission, and I'm certain he must see it in the way I blink. "But you seemed so . . . fine. Better than fine, actually. You started working out, losing weight. I figured you were dating again. Or at least thinking about it." I'm too embarrassed to make eye contact for this part. "The girls told me about Jamie."

"Who?" He pulls back, looking confused. Then the whites of his eyes grow twofold. "You mean the babysitter?" Glancing around, he lowers his voice. "Holy shit, Audrey. I may not be dad of the year, but I'm sure as hell not a pedophile."

"Jamie's the sitter?"

"And she happens to be fourteen. Sometimes, when I'm with the girls, I can't get anything done. Jamie lives a couple apartments down, and her parents couldn't afford guitar lessons." He shrugs. "We made a trade for babysitting. I should have told you, but I didn't want you to think I couldn't handle things on my own."

As the truth settles in, I'm overcome by equal parts relief and remorse. What else had I assumed?

"And as for the weight loss," he continues. "Well, I guess it's easy to lose weight when you stop eating. I haven't exactly been taking care of myself."

A false memory tugs at my mind. "So . . . no cheesecake in bed?"

"I wish. It's not any fun getting fat without you."

The idea of Travis wasting away claws at my heart. I'd been angry, but I never stopped loving him.

"Any other burning questions?" His eyes sparkle with that familiar brand of humor meant just for me, and I break into a smile I can't stifle any longer.

"As a matter of fact, I do have one." My good arm still resting around his neck, I narrow my eyes and look up at him. "There's something that's been bothering me for a while now, and quite frankly, I don't know how to ask this without sounding petty, so I'm just gonna come out with it." I take a deep breath. "Travis Beauregard Perkins, did you steal our jointly earned Paulo's Pizza points?"

"Wow, you went there, huh?" He shakes his head. "Using my middle name to shame me into admission? How dare you?" he says a little too ardently. But his face tells a different story. Finally, he deflates like a cheap pool toy. "All right, maybe I did. But in all fairness, you had just asked me to move out and my better angels were on vacation. It was a weak moment," he admits.

I know he's trying to lighten the mood, but the reminder of separation night steals my smile.

"Travis . . . that night, when I told you I wanted to separate, I thought . . . well, I kind of thought you'd fight me on it. I thought we'd argue like we always do, and you'd tell me I was overreacting and we'd go to bed angry, like usual. I didn't think you'd actually leave."

He looks genuinely surprised. "I thought it's what you wanted. I may not be great at listening, but I heard you loud and clear. And I'd do anything for you, Audrey."

Hot tears prick my eyes, because I believe him. But somewhere along the way, I stopped telling him what I needed. "After Willow died, I would have given anything to hold her one more time. I'm never going to have that chance again, because she's gone." My voice is wobbly, full of emotion. "But if I learned anything, it's that I was so lucky to have her in my life. She saw me at my most vulnerable moments, and she asked for so little in return. I'd never had that before from anyone. Not Iris or any other relationship. And I couldn't save her."

He cups my chin in his palm, steadying me. "Listen to me, Audrey. It wasn't your fault. It was mine." It occurs to me that we aren't moving anymore, and the song finished long ago. The bartender is wiping down the counters, and a few more patrons trickle out the door.

"I wasn't finished," I say, breaking away because I need him to hear me. "It doesn't matter whose fault it was. The point is, I couldn't save Willow, but I can save us." A hint of doubt still nicks at the back of my mind. "Tell me the truth, Travis. If you could go back to the beginning—before the kids, before the career, if I hadn't gotten pregnant—would you have chosen me? Would you have given up your dream?"

"That's easy." He smiles. "It didn't even feel like a choice. Everything in my life was better because of you. Eadie was just like this amazing bonus. I mean, sure, I probably wasn't ready to be a father, but I was stoked to do it alongside you." His hand creeps a little lower down my back, and he draws me in until his lips nearly meet my ear. "What about you? What would you choose?"

If I'm being honest, the answer has been clear since he drove me and newborn Eadie home from the hospital. He'd been so worried about our safety, so careful to see that we made it home together as a family.

"I'd choose us again. Every single time."

Travis lets out a subtle sigh. "OK. Here's what I propose," he says, sandwiching my good hand between both of his. "A do-over."

"We can't change the past," I say. Even though, somehow, I've managed to relive my hardest days, in the end, everything happened the way it was meant to. All that changed was me.

"Just hear me out," he pushes back. "When the girls are old enough to fall in love, I want them to choose someone who will pull their weight. Someone who won't expect them to carry all the things. So, I have to show them what that kind of person looks like." He pulls in a long breath. "We made vows to love each other through the good and the bad, but we had no idea what that meant because we were too blinded by love. But I can see it all clearly now, and I know what I'm committing to." His fingers tighten around mine, and he drops to one knee. I hear gasps from the few remaining patrons at the bar. "Audrey, from this day forward, I promise to always share my pizza points with you and to split the last slice of cheesecake. To buy the expensive applesauce, even when it's not on sale. I promise to actually read the teacher emails instead of just assuming you'll do it, and I promise to back you up when you tell the kids no, even if I already said yes. I promise to restock the toilet paper without being asked. I promise to make dinners and learn to braid and to fix the tread on the top stair. I promise to be on time." He pauses a beat before adding, "OK, I promise to try to be on time. To make you laugh when you get that serious crinkle in your brow, and to hold you when you cry. I want to be there for all of it, Audrey, because I want to do it alongside you. The dull stuff and the hard stuff and the magical stuff. Because . . . without you, none of it matters."

My eyes film over with tears, and when I'm finally able to speak, my throat is thick. "Me too," I say stupidly, because there's no way I can top that. "I love you, Travis." A tide of hope crests in my heart as the last five years collide with the next five and the next and the next, until all I can see is a lifetime of unexceptional moments, glittering and exquisite in all their normalcy. I want it all.

"I love you too." He rises to his feet, then pulls me close and presses his nose against my cheek. His warm lips come down atop mine, and we move in a familiar rhythm that banishes every stray thought that would normally upend a moment like this. Every tab in my brain closes, my hard drive crashes, and the world around us melts away into a sea of white noise. I'm vaguely aware of a few lone workers clapping, but I'm too wrapped up in Travis's musky-oak scent to acknowledge them. When we finally come up for air, he tucks a blond wisp behind my ear, then grazes a hand down my cheek. "What do you say? Do you think we can make this work?"

And for the second time in my life, I say, "I do."

EPILOGUE

November

The first whisperings of fall rustle the oaks and send a shiver through my limbs as I meander about Sonia's dimly lit backyard. Rubbing my elbows, I find her refilling the half-empty punch dispenser on the patio wreathed in twinkling lights. She's wearing a stunning two-piece halter dress in candy apple red, and her matching lips pop against the black curls cascading over her exposed shoulders. "Can I please put on a sweater now?" I ask, knowing what the answer will be.

She puts down a bottle of sparkling cider and cuts me a disappointed look. "Don't you dare. You didn't get to wear the gown you wanted at your first wedding, and this time, everything has to be perfect," she says, gesturing to my expertly curated ensemble. "You will not defile this look with synthetic wool."

"This is *not* a wedding," I remind her for what feels like the thousandth time. But I have to admit, she isn't wrong about the dress. Since Sonia offered to host "Audrey and Travis's Celebration of Love" (her branding, not mine), I've wrestled with the idea of accepting her help. But the guilt quickly dissipates as I run my fingers over the champagne-colored mermaid dress she scored from one of her sponsors. It's way more expensive than anything I could have purchased, and there's a sexy slit that ends mid-thigh, a detail I never would have gotten away with when I was pregnant with Eadie.

Per the concessions Travis and I have made, Sonia will post a few pictures of the evening, showcasing candids of the ceremony beneath the floral arbor of silk roses and baby's breath that she and I cobbled together. It turns out I'm completely fine with posing as a prop for her Insta feed if it means I get to wear these designer slingback shoes. They're dusted in a glittering gold, and the impractical heel has tested my ankle twice already. But these shoes actually make me feel like a different person. And maybe I am.

Over the past few months, so much of me has changed. Now, when I look in the mirror, I see only fragments of the woman I used to be—so small, so mired in fear and worry, so afraid of tragedy that she spent every inch of mental space planning for catastrophes. But after everything that's happened—the sweet, the bitter, the maddening, the impossible—it occurs to me that you never know when you're in the best moments of your life until they are swallowed by the next moment and the next, until all you have left is the devastating knowledge that, when all is said and done, you actually had everything you ever wanted.

Tonight, every tiny detail is a precious, glittering gem that I'll tuck away in my mental curio cabinet—the subtle wink Travis gave me before we exchanged vows, the warmth of his breath in my hair, Ruby and Eadie's silliness as we danced the robot during the chorus of "Somebody to Love."

A sly smile plays on Sonia's lips. "Come with me. I know just the thing to warm you up." She threads a lithe arm through mine and leads me through the waning crowd. We hadn't wanted a sprawling guest list, and the fifty or so family and friends have dwindled to a few clusters scattered across the teakwood dance floor—Lillian and Bill, a few of Travis's teaching buddies, Marcus and Dane, Mrs. Murray, and a handful of neighbors. I'm still a bit surprised to see them all here, but Sonia promised a night of dancing and fruity drinks and trendy appetizers I can't pronounce. Hard to refuse. Lexy is notably absent, but it doesn't bother me like I thought it would. Maybe some friendships aren't meant to last, and some people come into our lives for a season to show us the worst of ourselves. Others materialize in the unlikeliest of ways and show us the best. Sonia pulls me through the maze of people until a path clears, and I can see moonlight illuminating the overgrown trellises at the far edge of the yard.

And that's where I see him.

Even with his back turned, I can tell from the way his shoulders hunch that he's holding something with care, and I presume it's a ukulele. With a sly grin, Sonia gestures her head in his direction, and I happily oblige, wondering if he's planned to serenade me with another spontaneous rendition of Aerosmith's "I Don't Want to Miss a Thing."

Pinching the sides of my dress, I lift the hem and tread over to my husband, who somehow looks even better in a tux than he did nine years ago. His shoulders are broad and defined, the soft curves he had in college now chiseled down to the body of an older man. "You're not feeling sick, are you?" I call out as I pick my way across the grass. "I had one too many of those spinach galette things, and I don't think it agreed with—"

My breath hitches. Travis swivels to face me, and there is no mistaking the tiny bundle in his arms. Even in the dark, I can make out the honey-colored fur pressed against his tux. "Is . . . that what I think it is?" I manage.

"Do you want it to be?" Travis asks, his tone a mix of hope and uncertainty.

The question hangs, and for a moment, I just stare, unsure I'll be able to make my feet move any closer. Willow's face floats into my mind, her chocolate eyes so like the ones that belong to this adorable creature staring back at me. Right into my soul. It feels like a betrayal to want to hold this puppy, and yet there is a tiny glimmer of joy threatening to burst through the heartache clouding my eyes.

"Are you sure about this?" I ask, but we both know the question isn't meant for him.

Travis only shrugs. "The shelter was at capacity," he says, as if this might help me make a decision. "It's a boy," he adds. "Thought it was only fair to have another guy around, considering I'm outnumbered three to one."

My cheeks are wet, but I can't figure out if they are tears of joy or sadness. For the past five years there's been a hole in our family, and maybe this dog is just the right size to fill it. I think about what Sonia said: how Willow came into my life with a purpose, how her very name suggested she was medicine for my soul, how the tree can sprout new life even when it's cut down to the trunk, the roots still full of promise. In that way, I think Willow will always hold my past. But maybe this dog could hold my future. If we're lucky, maybe he will be there to watch our children grow up, to witness the awkward first dates and teenage heartaches and high school graduations. I will always love Willow, but maybe there's room in my heart and on my mantel for that love to keep growing.

"What do you say, Audrey?" Travis has adopted a Scooby voice and is waving at me with the puppy's paw. "Think you have it in you to fall in love again?" And even though he's nuzzling the puppy's ear, I know he isn't just talking about the dog.

I clear my throat and slowly close the distance between us. "I think so," I say, scooping the puppy into my arms. He's warm and velvety and teeming with life. "As long as we agree that he isn't *my* dog. He's ours. Which means that we all have to take care of him," I add sternly. The puppy licks my face, as if to agree, and his breath takes me right back to holding Willow for the first time. It's the smell of teething on shoes and accidents on the carpet and dirty tennis balls in the yard. But I'm ready for it. Actually, I can't wait.

A broad smile takes over Travis's face, and he waves the girls over. They're wearing flouncy white chiffon dresses trimmed in gold petals that Sonia picked out. "She said yes!" he shouts, cupping his hands around his mouth. Before I can comment on the fact that I've been the victim of a shameless conspiracy, Ruby and Eadie descend on us and dissolve into delirious screams. By now, the puppy is going wild with excitement and wriggling to get free, so I release him on the grass, and the girls tear off after him.

As I watch them wrestle in the yard, my heel gets stuck in the dirt, so I slip off my shoes and dangle them from my fingers. "Not fair," I say, only half serious.

"It's a wedding gift," he reasons.

"Which we agreed we weren't doing since this is not a real wedding."

"Come on. You know I can't be restrained by gift-giving rules. And you have to admit, he's pretty adorable. I guarantee this will be the second-best decision you ever make in your life."

But he's wrong. Because nothing in life is guaranteed, not even this marriage I have defied the laws of time and space to redeem. But it's truer now. Stronger. Strong enough to sustain us when everything else seems uncertain and we can't see the years ahead and we're tired. So very tired. Travis reaches for my free hand, and his touch sends a shiver through me. "Can I take you home now?" he asks, his blue eyes pleading. "You know I never last long at these kinds of things."

I cut him a playful look. "Not even your own vow renewal?"

"Hey, you know who you married."

He's right about that. The man I married is messy and stubborn and perpetually late. He is as much those things as he is loyal and bighearted and forgiving and funny, the kind of funny that makes my side cramp and my cheeks hurt from laughing. It's the best kind of hurt, and I hadn't realized how much I missed it until I nearly lost him.

"Besides," he says, inching closer, "I'd like to be alone with my wife." With sure hands, he pulls me in, and my body melts against him, just as it always has. My shoes slip from my fingers and fall to the ground. And I kiss him. His lips are soft and sure and perfect, and I know deep in my bones that this moment is, and has always been, our destiny. Audrey and Travis. Travis and Audrey. His hands slide down to my waist and rest there. When I finally pull back, he nuzzles my neck, and as the warmth of his breath grazes my earlobe, I'm reminded of a few key truths I somehow allowed to slip away: that control is not connection, that success is not measured in dollars and cents but in laughter and tears, and that being able to count on the people I love most is not a weakness. It's a gift.

"I suppose I could make time for that," I whisper, because time is really the only thing we have to give each other. My heart beats to the rhythm of this perfectly imperfect little family of ours, and I hope I will always be lost in the music of us. I don't know what the future has in store, but I know it's big enough to hold my sticky life. I think I'm finally brave enough to trust this love that reached into the past and saved me. I want to return the favor again and again and again.

ACKNOWLEDGMENTS

This book would not exist without the help of a village. I'm forever indebted to my agent, Ann Leslie Tuttle, for taking a chance on that first story I wrote and for sticking with me. Having a supportive teammate in my corner has made all the difference! Thank you to Chantelle Aimée Osman for kindly taking on this manuscript after an unexpected transition and to Laura Chasen for helping me sharpen and expand the story. Your feedback was invaluable! I think you just might be the other half of my brain. Alicia Clancy, I greatly appreciate your initial notes as they guided me throughout the process. You are missed! To Carmen Johnson—thank you for another seamless transition and for guiding this book through the publishing process. Additionally, I'm immensely grateful for eagle-eyed copyeditors like Jenna Justice, Jen Bentham, Alicia Lea, and the entire Lake Union team.

To my amazing beta readers—Mandy Burton, Nancy Fagan, Kyla Najjar, and Molly Ballistic—you were so kind to donate your time and expertise. Truly, your comments and suggestions were a gold mine. Any remaining mistakes or inconsistencies are my own. To my friends who keep me sane with dinner dates and tennis matches, thank you for providing a safe space to discuss the topics I write about and for consistently showing up for me to support each new project.

As far as families go, I'm incredibly lucky to be surrounded by so much love and support. To my mom and sisters, I don't know how I would survive without our daily Marco Polos and the free therapy you provide. Additionally, I'm beyond thankful for my daughters, who collectively inspired the characters of Eadie and Ruby. For Annabeth, who taught me about head wounds in the middle of Barnes & Noble; for Scarlett, who sometimes still mispronounces *potatoes*; and for Camilla, who has definitely never smoked! Being your mother has been the most exciting adventure of my life. Lastly, thanks to Brent for shoving a laptop in front of me when I didn't think I could do this. If I could go back to the beginning of it all, I'd choose us again, every single time.

ABOUT THE AUTHOR

Photo © 2024 David McClellan

Laura Barrow, the author of *Call the Canaries Home* and *If We Ever Get There*, is a former teacher and a lover of books. She received her bachelor's degree in music education from Centenary College in northwest Louisiana, where she grew up. She now resides in northeast Texas, just outside Dallas, with her husband, three daughters, and one energetic labradoodle.